Up in
SMOKE

Other Police Chief Susan Wren Mysteries

Winter Widow

Consider the Crows

Family Practice

Murder Take Two

A Cold Christmas

Up in
SMOKE

Charlene Weir

Thomas Dunne Books
St. Martin's Minotaur
New York

THOMAS DUNNE BOOKS.
An imprint of St. Martin's Press.

www.minotaurbooks.com

Library of Congress Cataloging-in-Publication Data

Weir, Charlene.
    Up in smoke / Charlene Weir.—1st ed.
        p. cm.
    ISBN 0-312-31020-X
    1. Wren, Susan (Fictitious character)—Fiction.   2. Political campaigns—Fiction.   3. Police—Kansas—Fiction.   4. Police chiefs—Fiction.
5. Policewomen—Fiction.   6. Governors—Fiction.   7. Kansas—Fiction.
I. Title.

PS3573.E39744U6   2003
813'.54—dc22

2003047296

First Edition: November 2003

10   9   8   7   6   5   4   3   2   1

FOR MY SIBLINGS, MEL, VERN, BERNEAL, AND CAROL. AND IN
LOVING MEMORY OF ELLEN AND NORM. ALL THE BROTHERS
ARE VALIANT AND ALL THE SISTERS VIRTUOUS.

FOR MY SON AND DAUGHTER, CHRISTOPHER AND LESLIE,
WITH MUCH LOVE AND THANKFULNESS FOR MY GREAT GOOD
FORTUNE IN HAVING THEM.

ᴀCKNOWLEDGMENTS

I owe endless gratitude and thanks to my editor, Ruth Cavin. If there is any grace and cohesiveness in my books, it is due to her diligent and ever sharp editorial pencil. She is a joy to work with.

Boundless thanks to my agent, Meg Ruley, who took on an unknown long ago and has stuck with me even though I'm still an unknown. Thanks also to her assistant, Annelise Robey.

Grateful appreciation goes to Avis, Pat, Barbara, Elise, and LaRae for all the help, encouragement, and "there, there" pats on the back.

And once again Suzanne Schwartz, R.N., F.N.P., came through for me when I needed medical information. Not only were my questions answered, but a generous invitation was given to call upon her with future questions. Much thanks.

O lost, and by the wind grieved . . . come back again!

THOMAS WOLFE

Look Homeward, Angel

Up in
SMOKE

1

—

*T*hin clouds floated across the night sky and the air smelled of coming rain. Fireflies blinked on and off, crickets chirped, and cicadas buzzed in mad frenzy, singing away the last heat of summer.

She was heavy, awkward to carry, and the blanket wrapped around her kept slipping. The garage was dark but enough light slanted in from the front porch to make the Mustang visible. When swinging her around, her feet struck a stack of rakes and shovels leaning in the corner. They clattered to the cement floor.

Damn it!

Inside the house, the dog barked furiously, throwing itself at the connecting door.

Trunk won't open! Oh God, come on! Stuck! Come on, come on!

There. Okay. The car dipped as her weight landed heavily inside. The trunk lid slammed shut with a solid thunk.

A shattering crash of window glass came from the back of the house.

The dog raced into the garage. Hackles raised, it lowered its head, threatening, growling with menace.

Just as it attacked, a swipe with a shovel and a kick dropped it in its tracks.

2

Casilda had been on the road too long. Mind-numbing fatigue painted hallucinatory images, turning ordinary trees, rocks, and mailboxes on posts into animals about to leap in front of her. The windshield wipers swished and thunked through hypnotic arcs. The Honda's headlights flashed on a square of wood, a spray-painted sign. *Baptized with Fire!*

She jerked alert with an unwarranted sense of impending doom. The high beams plowed through the dark, striking silver reflections from slanting rain, the only color in the entire universe. This was black-and-white Kansas before the tornado hit and Technicolor blossomed.

Piteous howls came from within the cat carrier buckled in the passenger seat. Lightning forked across the black sky. Cass hunched over the wheel and counted *one two three four* to find out how far it was. She thought the formula was one mile for each count.

Thunder rumbled.

Montgomery Cadwallader the cat shrieked.

"We couldn't be lost. We're almost there. I promise. Couldn't you ease up?"

His answer was a blood-curdling scream. With everything she owned in the trunk, she'd driven nonstop from Las Vegas, eighteen hours so far, that being easier than trying to deal with the cat at a motel.

Three and a half weeks was long enough in the city that never slept, neon lights, slot machines, blackjack, and people hoarding eternal hope. Of its own volition, her hand left the steering wheel, wrapped itself around the opposite wrist and her thumb felt the crisscrossed scars on the soft vincible skin on the inside. Deliberately, she changed hands and rubbed similar scars on the opposite wrist. Old scars, no longer sharp and angry looking, only pale and ineffectual. She could still recall the astonishing rich red well of blood. After long months fighting the Black Dog of Depression with prescriptions and hours of therapy, she'd felt an overwhelming sense of relief and the sweet feeling of peace as pain seeped away with her blood.

At forty-six, after three careers, she was going home. When she left twenty years ago, she'd had Aunt Jean, then she'd added a husband, and—after so many years of thinking it'd never happen—a baby girl. Now she was alone, except for a cat, and a gun in the bottom of the suitcase.

Her eyes burned and her head throbbed more savagely with each passing hour. She tried rolling down the window for fresh air but got soaked when rain blew in. She wanted to pull over and yowl, too. *Count your blessings*, she told herself. *It's near the end of October, this could be snow.*

Black Dog!

She stood on the brakes. The Honda fishtailed and whipped a fast 360. As though on ice, it hydroplaned sideways and came to a stop with the passenger-side wheels in the mud.

The Black Dog crouched on the road with rain pounding down on sodden fur.

For a moment, Cass thought she'd slipped back over the edge into mental illness, that the depression had returned with ironic cruelty. Been down this road and ended up road kill.

She let her head fall to the seatback and waited for madness to take her. Slowly, the sounds of pounding heart, drumming rain, shushing wind, and unhappy cat assaulted her with wicked taunting reality.

3

She blinked scratchy eyes and peered through the water sluicing down the windshield. The dog crouched on the asphalt looked so much like her imagined Black Dog of Depression that she started to shake.

"Pull it together, Cass!"

Leaning past the carrier to reach the glove box, she fumbled for the flashlight and grabbed a scarf to tie around her head.

Sloshing through inch-deep water standing on the road, she moved the flash beam over the animal. It snarled. Wind tugged at her scarf and tore it away, rain poured over her head, lashed her face and soaked her sweatshirt.

Looked like a wolf. No wolves in Kansas. Except prairie wolves, local name for coyotes. Must be a coyote. Badly injured or it would run. Rabid? Coyotes get rabies? Dogs did, foxes did, skunks did. Probably coyotes did.

Now what? She couldn't just leave it here. It raised its head and stared at her, eyes glassy in the flashlight beam. A crack of lightning lit up the dark. Dog, not coyote. Can't just leave it to get hit by another car.

She edged closer. The dog, probably a relative of Cujo, watched with demonic eyes. She stopped. It struggled to its feet and stood on three legs, one hind leg curled up against its belly, lips pulled tight in a snarl.

"It's me or nothing, pal."

The dog growled.

"I'm the Good Samaritan and you're going to bite the hell out of me, aren't you?" Calling herself all kinds of a fool, she inched closer, hand held out. The dog stayed firm, teeth bared, growling low in its throat. Getting wetter and wetter, she just waited, talking softly.

After what seemed forever and was maybe two minutes, the dog gave a slow tail wag and limped up to her. She ran a hand over its head. It yelped. "And I thought I was having a bad day." Carefully and gently, she palpated the shivering dog, neck, back, abdomen, and finally legs.

Too dumb from lack of sleep to figure a solution, she peered straight ahead hoping to see headlights of another car. All she could see was rain. If she left the dog here, a vehicle could zip along and squash it flat. An eerie chill of being watched ran through her. She looked around, then shook it off. She was in the middle of nowhere, standing in a thunderstorm. Who could be watching? And what did it matter anyway? The dog whimpered with canine misery and swished a dripping tail.

"I'm beginning to feel sorry for you."

It scooted close and leaned against her leg, looking as dejected and pathetic as a dog could get.

"Come on," she said with resignation.

Hopping on three legs to the car, the dog managed with a little boost of its rear end to scrabble onto the back seat. Just as Cass slid under the wheel, the dog shook itself and water flew everywhere. She sighed.

"You want to hear the good news?" she said to her hitchhiker. After hour upon hour of piercing shrieks, the cat was silent. The arrival of a strange dog had stopped Monty's complaining. Groping around the carrier, her hands found a towel and she blotted her face, too late realizing it smelled of something that should be inside a cat.

"Oh, shit." Her whole body ached, she was sopping wet, probably lost, had a mad cat, a rabid dog, and she'd just wiped her face with cat puke. It didn't get any better than this.

She drove on.

The road unrolled in a steady black ribbon of asphalt. Without Monty to keep her awake, the drum of rain and the swish of tires were soporific.

Three miles slipped past.

Lights, made mystical from rain rippling down the windshield, appeared on the low hills. Like Brigadoon, Hampstead rose up from the gloom.

Falcon Road ran along an embankment that led down to the Kaw River. At the far end of the road, she pulled in the driveway and cut the ignition. She slumped back, muscle spasms tingling up her legs.

Frogs carried on a joyous chorus with basses and baritones and the occasional deep croak, like a drumbeat accent.

She wanted a shower and a bed, or maybe a chair to sit in and weep. She looked at the dog, it looked back with serious eyes. She sighed. Livestock first.

After her aunt's funeral five weeks ago, Casilda had cleaned out all perishables, arranged for mail to be forwarded, closed up the house, taken Monty, and fled to Las Vegas. Opening the door was like walking back into a previous life. Everything was as it had been when Jean was alive. Victorian sofa covered in flowered brocade, afghan folded across the back, two high-backed chairs upholstered in blue velvet—just the thing for cat hairs—old upright piano with pictures of Cass and her husband and daughter on the top, silver candlesticks on the mantle, framed picture of a prairie scene on the wall above. Logs in the fireplace waiting for a match, bookmark in the novel on the armchair, *Hampstead Herald* on the coffee table. All that her aunt possessed was still where Jean had left it.

The cleaning company Cass had called had taken care of dust and polished the hardwood floors, but unused air hung heavy throughout the house. She pulled off her wet shoes and went around opening all windows that could be opened without rain blowing in.

She hauled the carrier inside and set Monty up with food, water, and a litter box in the guest bathroom, then went back for the dog who wagged its tail in appreciation of her not abandoning it. Favoring its right rear leg, it hobbled through the rain to the porch where it shook itself vigorously. Cass coaxed it into the kitchen and filled a bowl with cat food and another with water. The dog scarfed down the food in about fifteen seconds. Cass found a blanket in the hallway linen closet and spread it out on the floor next to the refrigerator. The dog looked at the blanket, looked at her, stepped onto the blanket, looked at her again, and lay down with a heavy sigh.

"Good dog."

When she walked away, the dog struggled up and followed. It watched from the shelter of the porch as she trotted through the rain to the car for the bags of groceries she'd picked up earlier. She plopped them on the kitchen table.

"You don't live here, you understand," she told the dog. "You're just visiting."

Hauling her suitcase into the guest bedroom, she dropped it in the corner under the window, then stripped the bed and made it up with clean sheets. From the doorway, the dog watched.

"Did somebody dump you out there on the road?"

The injured leg would have to wait until morning. It didn't seem that serious and she couldn't deal with any more tonight. Anyway, it was way after nine. No vet would be open and she had no idea where to find veterinary emergency service.

The answering machine, on the lamp table by the bed, was frantically blinking with five messages. Her throat tightened and tears sprang to her eyes. Messages for the dead. She pressed a button.

Three hang-ups and then, "This is Gayle Egelhoff. I really need to talk with you. Please call. No matter what time." She rattled off a number. Gayle Egelhoff? Did Cass know the woman?

Beep.

"Cassie, it's Eva. I'm so thrilled you're back. Call as soon as you get in. Love ya."

Beep.

Cass looked at her watch, after ten. She tried the number Gayle Egelhoff had left and got no answer. Tomorrow would be soon enough for Eva. They'd known each other since a hotly competitive spelling contest in sixth grade. Always friends, but never close. Eva was a saint, saints had a way of snagging the fabric of those less exalted.

Without Monty's yowling, the house suffered from lonesome quiet. Cass clicked on the television set in the living room for the sound of human voices, plodded back to the bedroom to dig out pajamas and maybe a robe to put on after a hot shower.

Lost in memories being back in the house evoked, she wasn't really paying attention to the news. ". . . woman called 911 from the trunk of a car—"

A commercial for toothpaste had Cass mentally adding that item to the list of things she needed.

". . . speculation about whether Governor Garrett, in town for a rest, will win his bid for the nomination."

Casilda stumbled around the dog to reach the television set and up the volume.

"How is the campaign going, Governor?" A reporter aimed a microphone at the governor's face as he came down the flight steps of a private plane.

"Jackson Garrett," Cass said. "The hero himself." She hadn't seen him since graduation twenty years ago. Where was Wakely? Ever since the tragedy, she'd heard he was Jack's shadow, a silent hulk in a wheelchair.

Fatigue and self-inflicted nonsense sent nerves crawling along her neck. Nobody ever talked much about that whole awful tragedy.

3

When Mary finally got to Hampstead, she almost wept with relief. She didn't much like driving anyway and driving through this thunderstorm had frightened her until she wondered if she'd make it. Rain came down so hard at times she couldn't see, cars zoomed past splattering muddy water over her windshield. She stopped in front of the first motel she came to that looked decent.

"What a terrible night," the elderly woman behind the counter said in response to her request for a room with a kitchen.

"It certainly is." She signed her name M. L. Shoals. Never Mary anymore, that was her other life. Now she was only M and if people heard Em when she told them her name, then so be it. She pulled her car around and parked at the door with the room number on the key, and retrieved her suitcase from the trunk. The room had a slight musty smell, but no matter. All she wanted to do was take a bath and fall into bed, but first things first. She examined the bathroom and was relieved to discover that the tub looked clean. The kitchen consisted of a tiny refrigerator, a two-burner stove with a tiny oven, and a shelf with a handful of mismatched dishes.

She was quite satisfied. It would do, it was cheap, and, she hoped, she wouldn't have to be here long. She slung the suitcase on the bed, opened it and took out the framed picture of her daughter taken at her twenty-third birthday, and set it on the bedside table. So beautiful. Blond hair, bluish-green eyes. "We're here, darling. We've taken the first step. It's going to be hard, but for you I'll do anything."

Unpacking could wait until tomorrow. Em stripped off her wrinkled clothes, routed out her nightgown, and went to take a bath.

4

$\mathcal{R}$ain lashed the windows, the lights flickered, thunder crashed. Susan slid another log in the fireplace. Maybe the fire would jolly up her mood a little. When the leaves began to turn red and gold, a melancholy had settled on her shoulders that she'd been unable to shake. It irritated her. There was no reason for the blues. Rain wouldn't last forever. The sun would come up in the morning and the morning after that and the morning after that.

Another clap of thunder rattled the windowpanes. She felt like a child who didn't get a promised treat and was still sulking. So she didn't get home at Christmas as she'd planned. That was last December. It's October now. Get over it. Plans don't always work out. So her old boss had not held the temporary position he'd offered her. It didn't mean she'd never get back, that she'd be here forever, for God's sake.

In Kansas. On the prairie. Neat farms, empty roads, an endless sky that stretched from horizon to horizon over vast open spaces, days framed by sunrises and sunsets that fired the spirit, awe-inspiring thunderstorms, and rainbows that brought tears of joy. The very wind and soil formed a race of people who were conservative, hardworking, and didn't trust anyone who didn't fit snugly into life as they knew it.

Arrogantly, they worshipped a God created in their own image.

She pushed a CD of Mozart concertos into the player. Nothing like Mozart to brighten your mood. An old joke flashed into mind. Cheer up, things could get worse. So she cheered up and sure 'nuff, they got worse.

When the phone rang, she turned down the music, trotted to the kitchen, and picked up the receiver. "Chief Wren."

"We have a problem," Parkhurst said.

"What?" she said, more waspishly than she intended.

"A 911 call from a cell phone. Female said she was in the trunk of a car. Didn't know what make of car or where it was."

"The trunk of a car? Was it a kid trying to be funny?" With Halloween so near, that kind of thing happened.

"Hazel didn't think so. Said the woman sounded in pain and groggy."

Hazel, the dispatcher to beat all dispatchers, had been with the Hampstead police department longer than Susan and Parkhurst combined and could run the whole thing herself if pushed to the wall. When Hazel said they had a problem, Susan paid attention.

"You tried a trace?"

"Cell phone people want a number and a warrant."

"I'll talk to them," Susan said.

Of the three companies servicing the area, two gave her no grief and checked into the matter, but told her they had no 911 calls. Since it was coming on toward ten on a Saturday night, the one person she knew well at the third wireless company wasn't at work. She wrangled several rounds with assistant manager Thelma Paxley and lost all of them. Tracing a call required a number and a warrant, no matter who was in trouble or how she got that way.

"Right," Susan said, holding on to her temper. "Will you do one thing for me? Will you zing in on the cell phone call to 911 and ask the caller if she needs assistance? You don't have to give me any information. Just find out if the person is in trouble."

There was silence from Thelma.

"If you don't do this and the woman dies, you will have her death on your conscience."

After a twenty-second pause, Thelma agreed to do that much. Susan hung up and listened to the rain hitting the window. It sounded like gunfire. The lights dimmed, then brightened. She wondered where she'd put the candles and pulled open a cabinet drawer where she thought they might be. To her surprise, there they were, just where they belonged, and snuggled up against them were the matches. She took out two candles and stuck them in holders, just in case.

The phone rang and she snatched it. Thelma informed her there was no call currently in to 911. Either the caller had hung up or had gone out of range. There was nothing further Thelma could do.

Damn.

She tracked down her trench coat, launched herself out the back door into the storm, and staggered on toward the garage. Despite the short distance, she got soaked. She fired up the pickup and headed for the shop. Zero visibility, flooded streets, power lines down. There'd be a slew of minor traffic accidents tonight.

"Heard anything more?" she asked Hazel when she got in.

"Nothing."

"Where's Parkhurst?"

"Out on patrol."

Susan gave a nod, not that he'd get anywhere. With nothing to go on, there was nowhere to look. She gave instructions for patrols to stop all motorists and ask to see inside the trunk. Parked cars—track down the owners and get a look at the trunks. "Anybody who refuses gets cited for DUI and brought in."

She paced up and down once in front of Hazel's desk. "If the woman calls again—"

Hazel looked at her. "Yes?"

Susan didn't go on. Teaching your grandmother to suck eggs, whatever the hell that meant. She went into her office and tackled some of the work on her desk while she waited. Two fender benders on Main Street, streetlights out on Walnut, tree down on Filbert. Collision on Fourth, teenage driver taken to hospital.

Two and a half hours later when there was still nothing further from the woman in the trunk, Susan got in the pickup and battled her way toward home. She had a bad feeling about this.

After rolling into the garage, she cut the lights and motor, gathered her trench coat around her and kept her head down as she trotted to the house. When she got inside, she went to the bathroom, hung the wet coat over the shower rod, and blotted her face and hair with a towel, then went to the kitchen to put on some water for tea. Lightning sizzled, lighting up the sky outside the window.

The lights flickered, came back, flickered again, then went out.

5

   —

*S*ean Donovan jogged through the pouring rain to the press bus rumbling at the curb, clambered aboard, and folded himself into a seat by the window. Pam dashed in, flopped down beside him and gave him a smile. Young, blond, pretty. A new face. The press corps tended toward young, and the turnover was fast—half the faces here were new since he'd last done this stuff. Shaking umbrellas and snatching off hats, they rushed in and stashed tote bags and briefcases under the seats. Rain hammering on the roof flattened the buzz of conversation.

Through the window, he watched highway-patrol cops hover in a shield around Governor Jackson Garrett and his wife as they went with them to the limo. The doors slammed, the troopers got in a cop car, and the long black car pulled away. Aides and political hacks and campaign workers piled into a second limo that followed.

The bus was just revving up to get in line when Sean realized something. "Stop!" He muttered an apology to Pam as he brushed past her knees.

"Where you going?"

"Need to take care of something." At the door, he said to the driver, "I have to get off."

Irritated grimace from the driver—what could he expect from

press people—and the door opened with a hydraulic hiss.

"You'll miss the speech," Pam called.

"Take notes for me."

He'd heard it, or variations thereof, a dozen times, he wouldn't miss a thing. Just as the governor's limo had started to pull out, Sean had realized that Wakely Fromm wasn't in it. Wakely went where the governor went. The story handed out was that they'd been friends since the cradle and the governor had taken care of Wakely since the accident that put him in the wheelchair. Gossip on the bus was that Wakely had a wee problem with alcohol and was often just a little on the wrong side of sober. He owned a house on the edge of town and sometimes the powers of the campaign committee—read Todd Haviland, campaign manager—stashed Wakely there. Since Wakely hadn't gotten in the limo, he'd be at the governor's farm or his own house. Sean wanted to know more about the relationship between Garrett and Wakely, why Garrett took Wakely with him everywhere and why he took care of the man. There was a story there, maybe important, maybe soft human-interest fluff, whatever—it made Sean curious.

He trotted to the hotel garage, up a flight of concrete stairs, and got his rental car. Wakely had a minder who was usually by his side, but even so, with all the politicos gone, Sean might be able to have a little conversation with the man. On the way, he stopped and picked up a bottle of bourbon. Give Wakely a drink or two, maybe interesting words would come forth.

Sean, highballing down the road, wipers working overtime to keep up with the rain pouring over the windshield, topped a rise and sped down the other side only to plow into a flooded spot. Water fountained up on both sides of the car and, as he slowed to a more appropriate speed, he hoped to hell he didn't drown out the car.

Lightning split the black sky in a spectacular forked display of dazzling light. He glimpsed outbuildings and a tractor shelter with huge round hay bales stacked out of the weather. Thunder rumbled. He wondered what it would be like to be a farmer. Owning land you had a responsibility toward, tilling, planting, tending, watching crops grow. Backbreaking, never-ending work, a high rate of serious or fatal accidents. Watching the weather. Is it changing, will it rain, will it stop raining? Investing your soul in acres of dirt. It was a bad time for farming. Farms were going under, people were leaving rural areas in droves. The number living below poverty level was 30 percent higher in rural areas than urban ones. Just as it happened with the decay of cities, crime was on the rise in rural areas, the heartland of this great nation, where children could grow and God and country were respected. Farmers were barely scraping by, most making less than ten thousand a year. They got second and third jobs and their wives and sometimes their children worked. Government money went to large corporate farms and the small farmer got left out.

At the barred gate, one guard dressed in rain gear came out of the hut while another stayed dry. Sean showed his credentials and said he had an appointment with Wakely Fromm. Since Sean had been out here several times, they let him through.

With a sedate speed, he drove the long mile to the house, a large two-story farm house, tan with white trim, a steep roof, lots of mul-tipaned windows across the front, a front porch running the length of the house, a screened-in side porch on one end, large black walnut trees all around, bank of flood lights lighting up the place.

Coat over his head, Sean dashed to the porch, shook the coat, and pressed a thumb against the doorbell.

No response.

Somebody had to be here. There was a housekeeper, a cook, and one or two other people hired to look after the place, plus all the campaign staff. He knocked. Still no answer. Oh hell, Wakely must be at his own house and Sean had no idea where that was. Garrett's people kept that a secret.

Sean knocked again. "Wakely?"

". . . the fuck?"

Ah, the man was in. "Open the door."

A crash, glass shattering, and dead silence.

"Wakely?" Sean banged on the door. "Wakely!"

"The fuck you want?"

"Open the door, Wakely."

17

More clatter, some fumbling at the knob and the door opened. "Crow! Go 'way!"

"It's Sean Donovan. Talk with you a minute?"

"The fuck for?"

Sean squeezed in past the wheelchair and closed the door behind him.

"Crow," Wakely mumbled. "Talk to an old drunk? Put my life story inna paper? Fuck it. Where'sa bourbon?" Wakely pulled at the front of a red plaid bathrobe like a bottle might be hidden inside. His hair was mussed, his jaw unshaven, beard stubble mottled with gray. "How come you're not with the rest of the crows? Carrion crows always picking at his bones." Wakely glared. "Love him! Like a brother! Death fires! Goddamn hero! Put that in your paper!"

Sean slipped out of his dripping coat, hung it on the doorknob, and moved from the entryway to the living room. Braided rug on the hardwood floor, enticing fire in the fireplace, television set tuned to a football game, dark gold-colored couch with brown pillows, bronze easy chairs.

Wakely rolled himself into the kitchen where the wheelchair crunched over shards of a dropped and shattered glass. A bottle lay on its side with the booze spilled around it.

"Fuckin' crows. Snooping snooping." Wakely's face contorted with some inner pain and he took a swing at Sean that nearly threw him from the wheelchair. Sean stepped aside.

Wakely reached down to grab at the bottle and flopped on the floor like a sick elephant seal. He howled and pounded his head on the tile, his scrabbling fingers clutched at glass slivers and fumbled them to his mouth.

"Damn it, Wakely! Stop that!" Sean grabbed his hand and shook out the glass pieces. Small cuts on the man's palms, fortunately none on his face. "Let's get you off your nose and back on your ass."

Holding him under the armpits, Sean hoisted him back in the chair. He was heavier than Sean expected, his upper body was barrel-shaped and muscular. The robe flapped open and his useless legs were exposed, fish-belly white, all bone and atrophied muscle.

"Oh hell, oh hell. S'too late." Tears and snot leaked down Wakely's face. He smeared it around with a fist.

"S'never too late." Sean grunted as he pulled Wakely straighter into the chair and arranged his bare bony feet on the footrest.

"Get it! 'Fore it spills!" Wakely jabbed a finger at the bottle.

It was pretty much too late for that, only about a half inch of bourbon hadn't run out when the bottle hit the floor.

"Damn crows, always pecking. Peck peck peck. Trying to find shit. Give it to me!" Sean handed him the empty bottle and he tipped the last drops into his mouth. "Make him look bad. Nothing to find." He gave Sean a crafty look. "I know."

"Know what?"

"Oh Christ, I've pissed myself."

Not exactly true. Wakely had plastic tubing that drained into a plastic bag, but somehow in all the rolling around something had come loose. "Where is everybody?"

"Gone. Here all alone." More tears.

"Where's the housekeeper and the guy who takes care of you?"

"Sent him out. Needed things. Bourbon. Ice. Don't think I need stuff, like everybody else?" Belligerence edged into Wakely's voice and Sean realized he might as well give it up. He was too late for conversation, Wakely had already consumed too much bourbon.

Playing nursemaid wasn't in his job description but Sean felt he couldn't leave the man this way. He refastened the plastic tubing as best he could and hoped somebody who knew what he was doing would be here soon. With a damp cloth from the bathroom, he cleaned the blood off Wakely's hands and examined the palms. Only scratches. He found a clean robe in what he assumed was Wakely's room because of the apparatus over the bed to assist getting in and out, wrestled Wakely into it, and got him in bed.

"Sorry," Wakely muttered. "Sorry."

"Nothing to be sorry about." Sean dropped the soiled robe in the bathroom.

"Shows what you know. Talk, talk, talk. Tired of it. Thinks she knows."

"Who?"

"Who the fuck you think? Gayle. At me, talk talk talk."

"What did she talk about?" With a clean washcloth, Sean wiped Fromm's face.

Wakely slapped at his hands. "Horse's teeth. Fuckin' horse's teeth. Death fires."

"What?"

The response was a gargled snore.

Sean shook him. "Wakely, what about horse's teeth?"

Wakely mumbled something Sean couldn't understand.

"What?"

"Bourbon. Other one broke." Wakely slipped down into steady snoring.

So much for information. Sean was putting on his coat when the door opened and a muscular young man came in sheltering a bag of groceries under his raincoat. Murray, Wakely's minder. Sean told him Wakely had cut his hands and it might be a good idea to take a look at them.

6

When the doorbell rang, Susan was fumbling for candles, got one lit, and on her way to the living room stumbled over the cat who retaliated by digging claws into her ankle. She opened the door and stared in astonishment at the dark figure dripping water all over her porch. Wind blew the candle flame in a fast zig-zag dance that cast sinister shadows across his face.

"Sure and it's a terrible night, not fit for man nor beast. What kind of place is it you have here that throws God's great thunderbolts down on poor innocent travelers?"

"*Sean?*"

With a whoop, he threw his arms around her, lifted her, and whirled her in circles. He managed to squeeze her breath away, make her dizzy, and get her soaked before he set her down. She staggered as she found her balance.

"Is it the House of Usher we have then?" Her cousin Sean Patrick Donovan pulled off his wet shoes, dropped them by the door, and padded inside in his stocking feet.

"You can stop with the music hall Irishman bit."

"Sure and it seems so fit. Jesus, it's blacker than a coal miner's lungs out there. And periodically a great sulfurous forked tail of light-

21

ning blazes through the night, such that even leprechauns take fright and scuttle back into the shadows."

He cupped his cold wet hands around her head and looked deeply into her eyes. "And so, me darlin', tell me how you really are then."

The tender concern threatened to bring tears. She kissed him. "What are you doing here?"

"Aren't you glad to see me?"

"Yes." He was the cousin, out of all of them, that was closest, a surrogate brother. They'd been inseparable growing up, getting into trouble, exchanging secrets, squabbling and giving each other advice. She was so glad to see him, she could almost believe she'd conjured him up, except for the water he was shedding on her living room carpet.

"I'm with the Garrett campaign." He shrugged off his trench coat and handed it to her.

"Ah." Sean was a political writer for *NewsWorld*.

She draped his coat over the shower door in the bathroom and when she returned, she said, "Without power, I can't even offer you a cup of coffee or some soup."

"That is bad news." He sat cross-legged, in front of the fireplace. In the semidark with the dancing flames fluttering light across his face, she could see that he looked drawn and tired, older. Ha, she probably looked older to him, too. It had been more than a year since they'd last seen each other.

"What's wrong?" she asked.

He looked at her, a long quiet look. "A couple of things," he said finally. "I didn't like the way you sounded the last time we talked."

Crossing her legs at the ankles, she lowered herself to the floor so she sat facing him. "What's the other?"

"She left me."

Susan did a double take. "Lynn? What happened?" His marriage to Lynn had been a stormy one, but they'd always managed to stick together. She didn't like Lynn all that much and hadn't wanted Sean to marry her. Susan wasn't sure Lynn really loved Sean, not the way he deserved to be loved, and not the way he loved Lynn.

22

"She met somebody who stole her heart away," Sean said.

"Who?"

"You don't happen to have any scotch, do you?"

"No, sorry. I do have some wine."

"That'll do."

In the kitchen, she poured a glass of white wine, hacked up some cheese, which she put on a plate with some crackers. She carried the wineglass and bottle in first, then went back for the plate of crackers and cheese. While she was gone, Sean had added wood to the fire and it blazed up, throwing off bright sparks.

She put the plate on the hearth and sat down beside him. "What happened with Lynn?"

He picked up the wineglass. "You're not drinking?"

"Problem at work. I need to stay clear thinking. Where's Hannah?"

"With Mom. A six-year-old didn't fit in with Lynn's plans."

"Where'd she go?"

"That I'm not sure of. She went off with her karate instructor. I'll probably be hearing from her when the joy grows cold."

She took both his hands and pressed them together between hers. "I'm so sorry, Sean. How are you?"

"To tell the truth, it's a bit of a relief. It's been a long time coming. I feel like I've been holding my breath all this time and now I can finally breathe again." He raised her hands to his mouth, kissed the back of one, then the other. "I don't know how she ever came to marry me in the first place."

"It must have been your face." Susan put her hands on his cheeks. "She hadn't known you long enough to be struck by your scintillating personality. She was dazzled by the look of you. Without question, you have a strong and handsome face."

"Are you listenin' to the girl, then? Sayin' it only as the two of us are alike as two roses on a stem."

"This is true," she said.

"Aye, but we can't help bein' beautiful, now can we darlin'? 'Tis ours to bear the terrible weight of it." After topping off his glass, he set the bottle back on the hearth and leaned close to look into her face. Without the exaggerated accent and barely above a whisper, he said, "What's with *you*, kiddo?"

"I'm fine."

"No, you're not, and you're worrying the hell out of me, so cough it up."

A log settled in the fireplace and the momentary flare brightened his face and threw a shadow that made his blue eyes seem black.

"Nothing really. I've been a little down. No reason. Leaves are all turning colors, getting ready to fall." She shrugged. "I feel—a little distant. Like I'm a step or two away from everything and—work"

"You, my darlin' girl, need—"

"A priest?"

He grinned. "So my mother would say. Since I'm not my mother and didn't go into the priesthood like she had her heart set on and slipped evermore from being her favorite son, I was going to say a good shrink."

"Want to go together? We could save money. Each pay half."

Thunder, loud as the boom of a cannon, startled them both.

"If that's the signal for the end of the world, I need another drink." He refilled his glass.

"Relax. Just a little storm." She liked them, pitch-black sky coming alive with jagged streaks of light, smell of ozone in the air, thunder rolling off to the ends of the earth. Almost never did such natural pyrotechnics happen in San Francisco. Rain, yes, but tepid in comparison. At least, she liked them when it wasn't tornado season, and she didn't have a woman out there in serious trouble with no way to get help to her.

Sean raised his glass. "To us, me darlin', may we survive the night and the doldrums."

Before she could respond the phone rang.

7

—

$\mathcal{B}$ernie Quaid dashed through the pelting rain into Nevins Hall, a large stone building on the Emerson campus. Just inside the door, Todd Haviland, the governor's campaign manager, was giving Governor Garrett the schedule, stressing times in an attempt, probably futile, to keep the governor from straying and putting them too far behind. Jackson Garrett had a tendency to talk with the people whose hands he was shaking, ask about their lives and get into a one on one.

Todd looked at Molly, the governor's wife.

"I know my part," she said. "Gaze with stupefied adoration." Two highway-patrol officers, Philip Baker and Arthur van Dever, flanked Jack as they walked down the hallway. They were tense, focused, surveying the area, ready for anything that might be thrown at them. Whenever they were with the governor they were intensely on, aware, looking for danger, evaluating spots as potential hiding places for lurking assassins, locating means of escape. Somewhere out there was a nut with a gun and when he came they were ready. Bernie thought all that heightened vigilance must have them limp with exhaustion when they came off duty. They escorted Jack to the auditorium and waited in the wings as he walked alone to the podium.

The room was packed with college students, local Democrats, Garrett supporters, a few curious, and probably a few just looking for something to do on a rainy Friday night. Local dignitaries sat on the platform, another highway-patrol officer stood between the press pool and the television cameras. The crowd erupted with applause and began to chant. "Garr-ett, Garr-ett."

"Can Kansas put on a storm, or what?"

Cheers rang through the room and echoed off the high ceiling. Bernie had never known a politician who let the energy of a crowd cut through his fatigue like Jackson Garrett. The audience seemed a source of strength that fed into some inner elation. As always, he focused on a face in the crowd and spoke to that person, focused on another face, spoke to him and then went to another. By the time he finished, every person in the room would feel Governor Jackson Garrett had touched him or her personally. He sensed his audience and reached a crowd like nobody else Bernie'd ever seen.

"How many of you think people should make money from sick babies?"

Health care. Students didn't have much interest in it, but the older people did.

"This country has the best resources in the world for health care. Our physicians are the best trained and we have the best equipment for dealing with disease, the newest tests and the latest medicines. Who gets the benefit of all this? It's not only the rich who should get the best in health care. Every person in this country should have it."

He went on to talk about the cost of medicines and what must be done to reduce it so sick people could buy what they needed. When the Governor paused, Bernie froze. *No, Jack, don't do it. No. Not right here in God's country.*

To Bernie, God's country was any small town. Its people always knew for a fact that God took a dim view of bright lights, dark bars, expensive restaurants, foreigners, Darwin, new scientific facts, and minorities. God, they were certain, was partial to the big sky, the sanctity of the land, and all that tumbleweed shit. God was also very big on an eye for an eye. If God didn't see to it, well then, they also knew that

God takes care of those who take care of themselves and they'd snap up their rifles and their handguns and go after that offending eye.

Leaning over the podium, Garrett was talking as he would to friends. ". . . when each one of you who has lost a son or daughter, a mother or father, a friend to a cretin with a gun . . ."

To Bernie's surprise there was some applause mixed in with the boos. Minutes later, Garrett finished as he always did. "With your help and your vote, we'll make this great country an even greater one."

Troopers tensed to leap into action and, sure as shootin', the governor trotted down the steps from the platform and plunged into the crowd filling the aisle between the rows of seats. Harried officers fought to stay with him. Governor Garrett was the worst kind of nightmare for security people. Without warning, he jumped into crowds, was apt to change his schedule on impulse, and refused to wear a Kevlar vest despite pleading from Phil Baker. Jack took each offered hand, looked at each face, and murmured a comment to each person. He got caught up in it, all the excitement, the ambitions, the dreams, but Bernie thought there was more to it. Almost as if Jack had to prove something to himself. That he wasn't afraid? Making up nonsense, Bernie told himself. The governor just needed to meet people up close to keep himself real. Or maybe punish himself. All the handshaking led to a swollen and painful right hand, so swollen and so painful that he had to bury it in a bowl of ice.

"Governor." A television correspondent pushed a microphone in Jack's face. "Will your position on gun control hurt you in D.C.?"

Jack reached beyond the reporter for another outstretched hand.

"Governor," the newscaster insisted.

A thin guy in a gray jacket slid in between him and the governor. "He's got a knife!"

Bernie wasn't sure what happened next, but all of a sudden, the crowd seemed to shift closer, bumping the thin guy into the governor or maybe the guy lurched toward him. Somehow the governor was shoved back toward the steps of the stage and stumbled.

Oh no. Oh God, no. Bernie eeled his way through the crowd that babbled with confusion.

"I didn't hear a shot."

"Did you hear a shot?"

"Somebody saw a knife."

"He was stabbed."

Art van Dever and Phil Baker threw themselves over Governor Garrett. By the time Bernie had elbowed his way through the milling people, the Governor was on his feet.

"What happened?" Bernie asked.

The thin guy in the gray jacket was being taken away by local cops assigned for just such an eventuality.

"Don't move, sir, paramedics are on the way," Art said.

"I don't need paramedics," Jack said. "I'm fine. Just let me finish talking with these good people."

Two young males in navy blue jumpsuits appeared, asking where he was hurt. They came from the ambulance waiting outside, just in case.

"Damn it, I'm not hurt. I'm fine."

"Can you walk, sir?"

"Of course, I can walk. Somebody bumped into me and I stumbled over some idiot behind."

"You don't seem to be putting your weight on your right foot."

"Yeah." Jack took a breath. "Maybe my ankle is a little tender."

"We'll get you to the hospital right away."

"Oh, for God's sake, I don't need a hospital. Stop at a pharmacy and buy an Ace bandage."

"You know we can't do that, sir."

He refused the gurney, but did let Art van Dever lend an arm and joked with the crowd as he limped to the door. Despite his insistence that he was all right, Art insisted on getting him in the ambulance.

Bernie got in the limo that followed. At the emergency room, he found the governor in a cubicle with troopers blocking the entryway.

A stocky man with black curly hair, stethoscope around his neck, was looking at an X-ray. "No break. Bad sprain though. Stay off it." He looked at the governor. "Going to do that?"

Jack nodded.

"Sure you are." The doctor sighed. "At least, keep ice on it to-night."

"That I can do."

Two birds with one stone. Ice on the ankle, ice on the swollen right hand.

A trooper brought in a classy-looking woman with black hair and a man with hard, flat eyes. Local law, Bernie thought.

Art van Dever introduced them. The female of the duo was Hampstead's chief of police, Susan Wren. Bernie looked at her more closely. Police chief? She had a haughty look about her like you see on models in expensive magazines. The man with her was a guy named Parkhurst. You wouldn't mistake him for anything but what he was. Cop.

"It's a pleasure to meet you, sir," she said.

The governor shook her hand and held on to it as he glanced up at her. "Wren? Relation to Dan?"

"Not exactly," she said. "He was my husband."

"Ah," the governor said. "I knew him."

"Tell me what happened tonight," she said.

Jack told her the same thing he'd told Art. Somebody bumped into him, he stumbled and fell.

"You think it was deliberate?"

"I doubt it. There was a crowd and somebody got too close to somebody."

"Did you see anyone you know?"

The governor gave her a dry smile. "My family has a farm out west of town. I went to school here. There were people who came just to see what I looked like after all these years."

He sounded tired, Bernie thought. Todd apparently thought so, too, because he clenched his jaw the way he did when he wanted to move things along.

"If you write a list of everybody you remember seeing, it would be helpful," she said.

"It's a month from the primary," Bernie said. "He has a few things on his mind."

"I understand," she said and gave the governor a look of her own.
He nodded tiredly. "I'll give it a try."

The police chief said what an honor it was to meet him, how sorry she was that this happened and promised to do everything in her power to make sure nothing else untoward happened while he was here.

Jack gave a hearty wave to all the people crowded around as he limped out and asked everybody to remember him on election day. He got in the limousine and Bernie slid in beside him.

"What happened back there?"

"I'm not really sure, Bernie. But I got to tell you that big surge of adrenaline rushed right through me. The one I'm always waiting for. I thought, this is it, I'm dead, just because some asshole doesn't like what I think."

"Who is the guy Art scooped up?"

"Pencil for the local paper. He just had a question and somebody behind pushed a little too close. Probably an accident, but he gets to spend the night being questioned by the highway patrol. And probably Hampstead's chief of police and her trusty sidekick."

"Who pushed him?"

"How could I know? It was just a crowd."

"Right," Bernie said, and wondered if the governor was lying.

Rain poured down in sheets, lightning forked through the black sky. Susan pulled into the parking lot, dashed to the building and in through the door Parkhurst held open. She stopped to take off her raincoat.

"He's in the interrogation room," Parkhurst said. "State guys had a go at him."

"What'd they get?"

"Nothing."

She followed Parkhurst down the hallway and into the interview room. Ty Baldini, reporter for the *Hampstead Herald*, sat on the edge of the long table, feet in tattered jogging shoes, dangling. Late twenties, would have brown hair if it hadn't been shaved so short you couldn't tell what color it was, small silver earring, thin intelligent face, jeans, Emerson sweatshirt with the snarling wildcat on the front. He slid off the table when he saw her.

"What did you do with the knife?" she asked.

"There wasn't any knife!" Ty hauled enough air in though his nose to inflate a dinghy. "How many times do I have to say it? I didn't have a knife. I never saw a knife. There never was a knife."

"A witness saw you with one," Parkhurst said.

Ty rubbed a hand across his shaved scalp. "He's lying."

Parkhurst waited, skeptical.

"Or mistaken," Ty added in a flash. "Look, I can understand the spooks crawling up my ass but you guys know me. What reason would I have to hurt the governor?"

You could be a secret Republican," Susan said.

A corner of his mouth twitched. As pissed as he was, getting even that close to a smile surprised her. "I was trying to get a quote for the paper. For the paper," he insisted, then took a breath and continued with less volume. "I started to ask a question and *boom* somebody bar-reled into me. I went crashing into him. Next thing I know, twenty-five guns are pointed at my face and they're hauling me off to beat a confession out of me."

Susan leaned forward and put her palms flat on the table. "Who bumped into you?"

Ty took in a deep breath as though pulling in a big dose of pa-tience. "I don't know. I told them that about ninety times. No matter how much I say it, *I don't know*. A million people were in that audi-torium and the governor was working through the crowd shaking hands and—" He shrugged. "You don't think I did anything, do you? I mean, you guys *know* me. You have to know I wouldn't hurt the governor."

"Who was near you?"

"You're kidding, right? A million people. All milling around and trying to get their hands shaken—" He broke off, looking puzzled. "Shook—?"

"You were there for the governor's speech?"

31

Ty nodded.

"Was there anybody in the crowd who stood out in any way? Anyone you noticed for any reason?"

"No. I don't know. I wasn't looking. I was focusing on the governor. He's some speaker, you know? It was just a crowd. A bunch of faces jammed together. Most of them damp because it was pissing rain. All excited about seeing the governor and—"

"What?" Susan said.

"These people had to pay money to get in—"

"Ty," Susan said with little patience, "would you just tell us what it is you're seeing in your stare and get it over with?"

"They had to pay, right? Because this was a fund raiser and so mostly whoever came would be for the governor, maybe some came to boo, but not many, because who would pay money just to—"

"Ty!"

"Oh, yeah, right. There was one person who was just watching. No reaction. Didn't cheer, didn't boo. Just watching. Like he was waiting, you know?"

"Male?"

"Dunno."

"What did this person look like?"

"Like anybody."

Susan held on to her temper. "Dark? Fair? Thin? Fat?"

Ty decided he was a man of average weight with an average face, neither dark nor fair.

"Wearing?"

"Baseball cap and sweatshirt, that's why I don't know if it was a man or woman. Sort of unisex clothes."

"Anything on the sweatshirt?"

Ty shook his head. "Plain black."

"Thanks, Ty. That's a great help."

"Look, I wasn't paying attention to anybody but the governor. That's who I was supposed to be looking at. I'm not with the cops. I didn't spend time lasering the crowd to see who was pulling out a gun. I didn't—"

"Did anyone pull out a gun?"

"No!" Ty blurted with exasperation. "I'm just trying to say I didn't pay attention. I was sent there by the paper and I was trying to do my job."

"Okay," Susan said.

"Can I go now?"

She looked at Parkhurst to see if he had anything to ask. He gave a slight shake of his head.

"Sure," Susan said. "If you remember anything else, let me know."

"You got it."

Ty took a step toward the door, then stopped. "Breasts," he said.

"Excuse me?"

His face flushed a delicate pink. "The guy who bumped into me. He had breasts."

Susan raised an eyebrow.

"I mean, it had to be a girl—woman," he added quickly.

"Come back here," Susan said. "Let's go over this again."

"I was trying to think how the shove felt and it popped into my head. I remember feeling—"

She looked over at Parkhurst. He was standing with his back to the wall, arms crossed.

"You had your hands on some woman's breasts?"

"Not my hands," Ty said with exasperation. "My arm. Upper arm where she bumped into me.

8

$\mathcal{S}$ean jumped at a loud crack of thunder. Jesus, there was enough *sturm und drang* to signal the end of the world. He slid another log on the fire and pushed it with the poker. Nearly two o'clock and Susan not back yet. He'd thought of following her just to see what was going on, but didn't think he could get away with it. Stretching prone on the floor, hands under his chin, he stared at the fire and thought about his daughter. Poor kid, abandoned by both parents. Mother ran off, dad sent away on a job. How was he going to make this up to her?

He reached for the wineglass on the hearth and took a sip. What was he doing with his life? Why was he missing out on Hannah's childhood? He'd been with the Garrett campaign since May. In the last six months, he'd been on the road constantly and been home to California twice. All politicians running for nomination were frenetically active, but Jackson Garrett left them in the dust.

No time for anything. Sean needed a haircut and clean underwear. The thing about popping in on relatives, they were obligated to let you use their laundry facilities while you killed time waiting for them to come home. If he'd thought to bring his laundry, he could take advantage of the washing machine and he'd have something to do besides twiddle his thumbs and play Susan's poor excuse for a piano.

Other things he needed: a warmer coat and a new pair of gloves. He'd lost one of the pair he'd thrown in his bag before he left home.

At least he had stamina. Good thing. His peers were all energetic, mostly female and mostly ten years younger. Maybe this should be his last campaign. He was thirty-six years old and getting tired—tired of the travel, tired of anonymous hotel rooms, tired of eternally having to search for late night open Laundromats to have clean socks and underwear for the next day, tired of the politicians who all seemed to blend together so he couldn't distinguish one from another, all trying to manipulate an apathetic public into going to the polls to keep them in office. It was all getting depressing. Thought pieces were dropped to make room for the latest personal scandal and that just diminished them all, reporters and politicians alike, reduced them to small men with puny ideas locked away in puny ambitions.

Except maybe Garrett. He seemed to actually say what he thought. He was certainly the most interesting politician scrambling around to get the nomination. Though Sean felt like a naïve jerk for even considering it, maybe his colleague Pam was right when she said Garrett not only cared for the issues, he cared for your soul.

Sean rolled on his back, put an arm under his head and stared at the ceiling. Maybe there was a book in Jackson Garrett, win or lose. Like the rest of his colleagues, Sean looked at Garrett with a mixture of professional detachment and personal views. Sean liked him. In Garrett's dealings with the press, he'd always been honest, available, humorous and, Sean thought, he was sincere in his beliefs.

Difficult man to figure out. Maybe his campaign manager, Todd Haviland, knew him. He'd been with the man the longest. Or Bernie Quaid. Hell, nobody really knew anybody, but still. Garrett had an air of complexity that set him apart. And he refused to make use of contrived revelations of personal tragedies. In fact, the best way to get on his bad side was to ask about Wakely Fromm, friend, constant companion and confidante. A broken man in a wheelchair who was drunk more often than not. That whole situation might be a puzzle worth solving.

He heard a muffled ring. Tired as he was, it took him a second to remember what had happened to his jacket. Thrown over the back of the couch. He found his cell phone in the pocket. His boss at *NewsWorld*.

"The hot news is that Jack Garrett was injured by a crowd of vicious Jayhawkers this evening," Kat Macklyn said. "This I learn from the opposition and I hear nothing from my man on the spot?"

9

—

Casilda dreamed in black and white, dark dreams. She dreamed of a weeping figure moving through trees, branches heavy with snow and elongated black shadows cast by the moon. She dreamed of a man and a little girl dancing in slow silence, floating lightly even in death. Her pain was brittle and white like old bones. Voices stretched across a fog-laden meadow, calling, pleading, gauzy fingers beckoned, urging her to follow and slip past the edges of the night silvered with moonlight.

She snapped awake to find green eyes glaring at her. They were Monty's. He was crouched on the pillow. On the other side of the bed with its head resting on the mattress, the Black Dog gave a whimper of greeting.

For several seconds her mind shriveled and leapt searching a familiar landing before she remembered. Hampstead, Aunt Jean's house, picked up stray dog. One of the animals had apparently figured out how to work a doorknob during the night and, whatever had happened, they hadn't killed each other. They were pretending détente was the only way to go.

From the strength of the sun behind the closed curtains, she thought it must be close to noon. Stiff from hours of driving yesterday, she hunched her shoulders forward to stretch her spine, then straightened her legs under the sheet and pointed her toes until her ankles cracked.

Pulling in a deep breath for motivation, she shuffled into the kitchen and let the dog out into a sad, storm-battered garden. Sunflowers were flattened and exhausted. Rose petals had been snatched from blooms and scattered in the mud. Maple leaves lay in sodden little heaps of red and gold. She wondered if the fence had an escape hole in it anywhere and stepped out on the back porch. The dog took care of its needs, then limped back to her.

She filled the cat bowl with dry nuggets and Monty flowed up to the counter and dug in. The second bowl she put on the floor. The dog inhaled every chunk in seconds flat and looked hopefully at the cat's dish. Monty growled. Cass headed for the shower and gallons of hot water. Wrapped in a towel, she dug jeans and a long-sleeved knit shirt from her suitcase. While she was getting dressed, the dog padded in and collapsed in a corner. Cass flipped back the bedspread to smooth the sheets and saw splotches of blood. She looked at the dog. Alerted by her expression, it backed away.

Last night in the dark and the rain, with all that black hair, she hadn't noticed, but now she could see a nasty wound on top the dog's head. A flap of fur hung loose, edges crusted with dried blood, wet blood oozing in the center. Why hadn't she seen this last night? Past exhaustion to the point where she'd stumbled when she walked, she hadn't paid attention. The poor dog.

She tracked down the phone book, found her shoes, grabbed a rope from the garage and loaded the dog in the Mustang. At the vet's office, she coaxed and tugged it inside where she explained the dog's appearance in her life and left it to have its head X-rayed, cleaned and stitched. On the way home, she stopped at a bakery and bought two apple fritters. At the next stop she staggered out under a load of flattened cardboard boxes. Monty met her at the door with loud complaints of abuse. Fur all standing on end, he sniffed at every place the dog had been, in case she didn't get the picture. She found the coffee maker and got it going.

Just as she was pouring the first cup, the phone rang, startling her so she sloshed hot coffee over her wrist. The answering machine clicked on with the second ring. Aunt Jean's voice recited the number and politely invited the caller to leave a message.

"Cassie? It's Eva. Are you there? Pick up." A second of silence. "Come on, Cass, pick up!"

She answered the phone.

"Hi, Eva. How'd you know I was here?"

"Everybody knows you're here."

"I didn't get in till nearly ten last night."

Eva giggled. "You have an unknown vehicle. You were clocked in when you turned onto Falcon road and followed all the way to your aunt's house, at which time, the neighbor following you figured out who you were and went home to spread the word. How are you, Cassie?"

"I'm not sure. I haven't had coffee yet."

"I can't wait to see you. Eight o'clock at my house."

"What?"

"I'm having a party. Everybody you haven't seen in years and can't wait to talk with. I'm so glad you're back. It'll be just like old times. We have so much to catch up on. Bye now—"

"Eva, wait! I don't think . . . I mean, I can't—"

"Sure you can. And don't worry about what to wear, just throw on any old thing. See ya."

"Eva, I can't really face people right now. I—"

"Cass, I haven't seen you for years and years and years and years. You have to see people some time. This way you can get it all over at once and it'll be such fun you'll—"

Trying to resist Eva was like trying to stop a waterfall.

"I can't wait. Bye now."

Cass hung up, wondering why Eva had put that funny emphasis on *everybody*. She got out a plate for the apple fritters, sat down and opened the *Herald*. Tearing off a bit of the fritter, she popped it in her mouth and chewed, reading about storm damage. Trees uprooted, basements flooded, power outage, three-year-old killed by falling chimney bricks.

Without warning, the black side of her brain oozed terror. Words

39

swam together, cold tickled the back of her neck. *What the hell am I doing? I can't make a life. They should have kept me locked up. There's nothing I—*

Stop it! Of course, it'll be hard. Don't give up before you start. No gain without pain. Forget that. I hate that stupid phrase.

Focus, Casilda. Move forward. Keep moving. Never stop. Eye on the ball. First day of the rest of your life. Ha! Who said so? It could be the first day of the end of her life.

Her thoughts kept running faster and more mixed up, more non-sensical. She clenched her jaw and her fists.

Watch it, you're working up to a panic attack. And nothing to fight it with.

Right before she'd left Las Vegas she'd made a ceremony of dumping all her drugs, one pill at a time, into the toilet. She sang, a hundred and twenty-two pills in my hand, a hundred and twenty-two pills, if one of those pills should happen to fall—*plop*—a hundred and twenty-one pills in my hand, a hundred and twenty-one pills—. When her hand was empty, she'd flushed.

Stop! Deep breath. Again. Again. Better now? One step at a time. Things to do. Make a list—Forget that. A list wasn't important, speed wasn't important, efficiency wasn't important. Breathing was important, getting out of bed was important, moving was important, never forgetting Laura's face was important.

The chair screeched across the polished wood floor when she abruptly shoved it back and ran to the bedroom for the small zippered bag, plastic-lined and meant for cosmetics.

Three large maple trees grew in the backyard, the tallest in the corner, flanked by a slightly smaller one on either side. They still had leaves on the branches, though the storm had whipped many away. Kneeling on the wet ground, she made two small holes with the tip of the trowel and stuck a candle in each. She struck a match and held it against the wick of the first one until the candle burned, then lit the other. She dug another hole, bigger, rounder. A cardinal, flashing scarlet in the bright sunlight, swooped onto a branch and observed her, tilting its head from side to side, hopped to a lower branch and observed her from that vantage point.

She unzipped the bag and emptied all but a small amount of Ted and Laura's mingled ashes in the hole. Most lay scattered beneath the pine trees in the forest above Chester, California. Sitting back on her heels, she struggled, twisted and pulled to work off her wedding band. She kissed it and placed it on top of the ashes, added a lock of hair from Laura's first haircut and filled in the hole with a scoop of mud, then patted it smooth with the back of the trowel. She scraped together a small mound of fallen rose petals and picked them up. Giants' tears, Laura had called them. Softly to herself, she sang "When You Walk Through a Storm Keep Your Head Up High" as she let the petals slip through her fingers onto the site.

"Welcome," she whispered. "Whatever is to come, you're now part of it." The last small spoonful of ashes she trickled into a tiny suede pouch, took it to the bedroom and put it on the bedside table. When she went anywhere, she'd carry the little pouch in her pocket or purse, so they'd always be close.

Access to the attic was in the hallway. Cass carried in the ladder and climbed up. Steep pitch to the ceiling and bare wood floor thick with dust, the attic was filled with remnants of her childhood and castoffs her aunt couldn't bear to part with. Twin-sized bed leaned against a wall, desk under the window. Shelves piled with board games, jigsaw puzzles, and books. Piggy bank, dress form, old birdcage. She'd forgotten about her aunt's canary. Buddy? Billy? The poor thing led a perilous life, the neighbor's cat always skulked around scheming ways to grab it.

Cass picked up the piggy bank and shook it. It rattled richly. Why had she never smashed it and taken the coins? Shaking the dust off the suitcases, she dropped them one by one to the hallway below and firmly closed the door on the rest of life's leftovers. Weepy hours went by, broken now and then by a teary smile, as memories unfolded while she packed her aunt's clothing. At five thirty, drained and exhausted, she realized she had to pick up the dog before the vet closed at six.

"Where did you say you got this dog?" Dr. Newcomer asked.

"On the old highway into Hampstead. Is it—What's the matter with it?"

The black dog gazed at Casilda with eyes that said what the hell did you get me into? This wasn't in our discussion.

"*It* is a she," he said. "The limp is nothing much. She's got a bruise, probably from a kick. The head wound is more serious."

Inside a shaved strip along the dog's head, ran a row of neat little stitches.

"My guess is she was hit with something that has an edge but isn't necessarily sharp. The wound is more a gouge than a cut. Something came down hard on her head and scraped away a section of skin and hair."

Cass put three hundred dollars on her credit card, stuck the vial of antibiotics in her pocket, filled out a card for a found dog, tacked it on a corkboard with half a dozen others and took the dog out to the car.

At a pet store, she bought dog food, bowls, collar, and leash. The Black Dog in the passenger seat looked on with anxious eyes as she loaded items in the trunk and kissed her when she got back in the car. "It's only temporary," she said.

10

*E*m, sitting on the bed in her motel room, watched the television, transfixed.

Garrett was in a hall, standing behind a table, talking to a roomful of people. "I feel quite strongly that anyone who takes a life should pay for that action. But taking another human life doesn't begin to make amends. Only God has the right to take a human life—"

Somebody has to pay. God's law, an eye for an eye. A tooth for a tooth. Retribution for those who ignore God's law. A death for a death.

The scene on the television set changed to another hall, this one with a stage. Garrett stood, passionate as Hamlet, words hard as sharp stones.

". . . the Bill of Rights. Does any one of you feel that James Madison had bigots in mind when he wrote it? The right of madmen and psychopaths to use assault weapons and handguns to slaughter innocent men, women, and children? I think not, ladies and gentleman, I think he'd feel this country had let itself become a land of potential victims by letting a small group be in charge."

Nausea tickled her throat. She ran to the bathroom and bent over the toilet, heaving in spasms a vile mess of brown hate and fear.

Shaky, she straightened and flushed. Her throat burned and her mouth tasted awful. She washed her face, brushed her teeth, and swished around some mouthwash. The knife felt heavy in her purse. She snapped off the television. It was time.

Damn, Bernie thought. In his room at the Garrett farm, he was watching the opposition on the little handheld television. In politics, any outrageous lie repeated often enough takes on the glimmer of truth and sooner or later is believed.

Someone—and Todd suspected the Halderbreck's campaign manager, it takes one to know one—planted speculation about Jack's marriage with focus on Molly Garrett. She didn't always accompany the governor when he traveled, but Wakely Fromm did. He lived with the Garretts. Had lived with Jack before he married and continued to live with them after he married. Fromm seemed to be with Jack far more than his wife.

Given this golden opportunity, Senator Halderbreck said several times on several different occasions that "there was no proof that Governor Garrett and Wakely Fromm were anything but friends and I deplore this innuendo that anything more could be made of it." And he said it again now.

Reporter: "It's a well-known fact, Senator, that they lived together for years, even before the governor got married."

Senator: "And so what if it is? Does this have anything to do with Governor Garrett's ability to lead?"

Damn. Give it a little time and the information floating on the air would bring the bigots out in droves. Jack spent more time with Wakely than with his wife. What did that imply? Well, any idiot could see, it clearly indicated Garrett was gay. A queer, a fairy, a pervert. Before long there'd be articles and political discussion about a person of this sexual identity in the White House. Would you trust this man to run the country?

Fate had given the opposition a magic wand and they were waving it around like a flag.

He turned off the television and slipped it in his jacket pocket.

Garrett was giving an outdoor speech on the campus that was aimed at women. Day care, shelters for battered women, education to prevent child abuse, better ways of dealing with men who beat up wives, harsher punishment for crimes against women. It was scheduled for noon, the idea being that clerical workers and other nonstudents could listen if they were so inclined.

"Isn't that my jacket?" Todd said when Bernie walked into the living room. "When you going to give it back?"

They waited for Leon and Hadley and then drove to Emerson.

The sky was a soft, clean blue. Wind blew against Bernie's face with just enough bite to let him know that winter was on the way as they hiked to the plaza where Garrett would speak, a little hollow surrounded by a grassy area and stone buildings. Highway-patrol cops, waiting in a knot, were tight-lipped and tense. When Bernie ambled up, officers Art van Dever and Phil Baker were giving instructions and telling everybody to be on their toes.

"This is the kind of scary-ass thing the governor does," Art muttered.

Todd started patting pockets. "Lost my sunglasses," he complained.

"What are you putting on your nose?" Phil slipped on his own sunglasses.

"Picked 'em up at the drugstore. They don't fit right."

Art and Phil left to get Jack. They'd be with him when he came into the plaza and they'd stand in front of the platform watching the crowd while he spoke. Like the Secret Service who protected the president, these cops wore sunglasses in this detail. John Hinckley would be in the history books for shooting Reagan, but a footnote would say that Secret Service agents wore sunglasses because of Hinckley. After the attempt on Reagan, agents picked out Hinckley drifting through the crowds in films of a Jimmy Carter speech. When Hinckley was picked up, he admitted he'd been there to shoot Carter, but an agent was wearing sunglasses and Hinckley couldn't tell who he was looking at. Hinckley was afraid the agent was watching him.

"Probably was," Art had told Bernie. "The guy had the face."

"What face?"

Art shrugged. "*Different.* You look at those old films sometime and you can just see he looks different. You can spot him without even knowing who he is." He gave Bernie a tight-lipped smile. "Somebody's going to do it. Take a shot at him."

"Aren't people screened for guns?"

"Situation like this? Where people just wander in? And it doesn't have to be a gun. Knife, skewer, bomb. Hell, anthrax. Some fucking nutball is going to try. I just pray it isn't on my watch."

A few people had already gathered in front of the platform and Bernie, standing with Todd, studied them. Students, office workers, some faculty maybe, professorial-looking types anyway. Not having Art's kind of experience, Bernie didn't think he could spot *the face* even if it sat next to him.

Only about ten people were milling round the plaza. She was too early, Em realized, there weren't enough people here yet. Somebody might remember her.

The sun was shining, but the wind felt cold as it nuzzled her face and she turned her back to it. Hitching up the strap of her shoulder bag, she couldn't help running her hand across the smooth leather. The knife was inside. She'd have to get close. She was afraid.

Stupid to let doubts get in the way. How long would it take, to slide the knife from her bag, run toward Governor Garrett and plunge it in his heart? All she had to do was get close.

She clamped her teeth. What if she couldn't reach him? She imagined a bullet entering her brain a moment after the knife penetrated his chest—because that's all she'd have, a moment—and she'd fall dead at his feet. Would he look at her as she was dying? Would his face be the picture she'd carry into eternity? She was afraid, afraid of the look on his face, afraid of dying too soon.

"Are you all right?"

Panicky, she turned. A girl, one of the group waiting. Oh God, now she'd been noticed.

"Fine," Em blurted. "Fine," she repeated. "Didn't eat breakfast." She turned her back. Walk, don't run. Walk. She strolled to the other end of the plaza.

More people arrived and they wandered around on the grass. Lots of students, men and women from town. And police. She wondered how fast they were with their guns.

A black limousine with tinted windows pulled up to the curb. A police car glided in behind it. Doors opened on the second car and police piled out. One opened the door of the limousine and when the governor got out police flowed around him. The crowd applauded and cheered. Governor Garrett waved to them.

She could do it, Em thought. She could push the knife in him and create a huge hole in his chest before the police shot her.

The governor said something and the crowd laughed. He started talking about a woman's rights.

Em felt sick again. She shoved through the people pressing in on her, nausea clawing at her throat. Just as suddenly, panic hooked onto her lungs. She couldn't breathe. Gasping and trembling, she stopped and put her arms around her chest. Air air air.

Finally, the vise loosened and air whooshed in. She panted and pulled in another chestful. Tears of shame and humiliation nearly choked her.

Coward, she accused herself. She'd been afraid to take the chance, afraid the police would kill her before she could accomplish her mission. Afraid.

Sean Donovan saw her when he got off the press bus. A middle-aged woman, slightly dowdy, running flat out. At first he thought someone was after her, but she made a sudden stop and clutched her chest with a panic-stricken look on her face. Maybe she was having a heart attack and he should call an ambulance.

Then she straightened and the panicked look was replaced by one of anguish. She had demons, poor lady, they were loose and they were vicious. He wondered what they were. She stared wildly at him and started walking rapidly away.

He turned to look after her. He'd seen her somewhere before, but for the life of him he couldn't remember where. Probably somebody who'd sold him toothpaste or cleaned his hotel room.

Em stumbled to a bench on the grass between the library and the political science building. Just to catch her breath, she told herself. And anyway, if she kept running around in a blind fit, people were going to notice and they'd, for sure, remember her. If that happened she'd never reach her goal. She needed to think. Maybe go about this a different way.

Damp wind blew against her face. She looked at the section of wooden bench beside her. Wet. And her jacket was wet. When had it started to rain? Only drizzle really, but her hair was soaked. It was four o'clock on a Saturday afternoon. She felt disoriented. In her mind, she saw the knife strike the governor's chest and the blossom of red blood erupt. She saw it so clearly, she almost began to believe, then she had to remind herself she hadn't yet accomplished it.

The young woman who'd asked her if she was all right, blond hair and clear blue eyes, had looked so much like Alice Ann that pain squeezed Em's heart. Would the young woman remember her? She had to be more careful. Otherwise she'd be picked up before she could even get to the governor.

She needed an excuse, a reason for hanging around. The street was slick with rain. As she started across, she saw a police car. Her heart banged. Wildly, she looked around. Where to run? Then she forced a breath. Stop sign, he'd only stopped for a stop sign. He wasn't even looking at her, he was looking straight ahead. With the knife feeling heavy in her shoulder bag, she turned right and walked briskly. Cold drizzle fell on her face. The moisture felt cooling and good, washed away the hot sick feeling.

In the next block, she came to it. The answer. A large dingy building with GARRETT FOR AMERICA signs plastered all over the windows. The building at one time was apparently a grocery store, marks were still visible where check stands used to be.

A young woman at a long table, the kind with legs that folded up, watched her come in. Partitions gave the illusion of a reception area. The murmur of voices came from the other side.

"May I help you?" she called when Em hovered in the doorway.

Was this the right thing to do? If people saw her every day, they would be able to describe her to the police. Maybe she should—?

Time to stop dithering. What did it matter if they could describe her afterward. She never expected to survive anyway. "I'm here to volunteer."

"Hey, that's great. We can use the help. Garrett's really the best, you know?" The woman whipped out a form to fill in.

Em accepted it, moved a ways along the table, and sat down. Awkwardly, as though she couldn't remember the spelling, she wrote in the name Em Shoals and the address of the motel, then put check marks more or less randomly beside any task that would keep her at the headquarters.

A young man with springy ginger curls and a pleasant face came from the other side of the partitions. Jeans and a white T-shirt, bulging arm muscles. "Stewart Gallagher." He grabbed her hand and shook it. "This is really great. We're glad to have you." He took a moment to look at the form she handed him. "Come with me," he said. "We'll put you right to work."

The area behind the partitions was one large room filled with long tables of the fold-up kind with volunteers sitting in front of telephones making call after call and reading from a script in front of them.

"With the primaries starting in about ten weeks, we need to identify which voters will vote for Governor Garrett and make sure they're going to the polls. That's what we need you for."

"But I thought the primary wasn't until next year."

"Yep. D.C. in January, ours in February." He grinned. "Voters need to be nudged along, you know."

The volunteers were all young, most probably students at Emerson. She felt odd, different, like she didn't belong. "You have so many already, maybe—"

"Right," Stewart said. "The second shift comes in at night. For the people who have jobs."

"Well, maybe—"

He gave her a big smile. "It's easy," he assured her. "You get a list of voters with information on what party they belong to, the precinct, where they live, and ethnic background. That way precinct captains get a list of Jack Garrett voters to get to the polls." Another big smile. "This is really important. If you do your job, if every volunteer does his or her job, Governor Garrett could get the nomination."

Getting caught up in the fever of his excitement, she smiled back.

"You'll be fine," he said. "All you have to do is follow the script." He introduced her to another young man named Skip who led her to a chair at one of the tables. Skip pointed out the computer list of names she was to call and explained the form that was to be filled out. "Just note whether you talked with the name or not and who the name is voting for. Garrett or Halderbreck. At the end of the day, total up the number who are for Garrett and the number who are for Halderbreck. Okay? If you have any problems, give a holler and I'll come running."

He gave her an encouraging pat on the shoulder and galloped off. She read the script.

> *Hello. This is (your name) and I'm calling for Governor Garrett.*
> *Is (voter's name) there?*
> *If no, May I leave a message?*
> *If yes, Great. I'm calling to see if you'll be supporting Governor Garrett in the primary.*

With some reluctance, Em picked up the phone and poked in the number.

"Hello?" The voice sounded like an elderly woman.

"Hello, this is Em Shoals. I'm calling to see if you support Governor Garrett."

"Oh, absolutely. He's so wonderful. He reminds me of that actor. Oh, you know the one, that was so brave in the movie—"

When she hung up, Em thought how really odd the world was. She'd just gotten a vote for a man who would be dead before the primary.

11

———

When Cass got home, she went back to it, filled boxes of life's left-overs from the attic and stacked them in the dining room. Monty hissed and growled from the top of the refrigerator and the Black Dog stretched out in front of the cold fireplace and moaned in her sleep. At eight-thirty, drooping from fatigue and the satisfaction of accomplishment, she dropped into her aunt's easy chair and clicked the remote for the television. After twenty minutes of watching whatever appeared, she fell asleep.

Blood-curdling barks pierced her dreams. She shot up from drowning, choking on imagined water and her own pounding heart. The doorbell rang.

Sniffling at the crack between door and frame, the dog growled deep in its throat, fur stood up on its neck. Cass put a hand on the collar. "Who is it?"

"Eva sent me to pick you up."

"What?"

"The party. She told me to come get you."

Cass had completely forgotten. "Oh, I'm sorry, I can't go. Tell Eva I'll call her tomorrow."

"She told me you might say that and not to leave without you."

"Tell her I'll call," Cass repeated.

"I'll wait till you're ready."

"I'm going to bed."

"How do you like your eggs?"

"What?"

"For breakfast in the morning. I'm not going anywhere without you. I'll stay all night if I have to."

"This is ridiculous. Go away."

"Sorry, can't do that without you."

Cass yanked open the door. The dog snarled, saliva dripped from very impressive teeth.

"Bernie Quaid," he said. Tall, lanky, curly brown hair, smile, dark blazer, pale blue shirt, and dark tie. "Part-time chauffeur and other end of the spectrum from rapist and murderer. You might want to grab some shoes."

She looked down at her bare feet and the threadbare corduroys with her knee poking through a rip in one leg. "Do I look dressed for a party?" she said.

"You look great. We don't have to stay long."

"No." She had trouble hanging on to the dog who kept lunging at Bernie Quaid as though she wanted to rip him apart.

"Please," Bernie said. "Just make an appearance. Step in, look around, say hi to Eva. I'll bring you right back."

"No."

"Look, I know I'm bugging you. That's the last thing I want, but I'll probably get fired, if you don't come."

She let disbelief leak into her impatience.

He raised his right hand. "God's honest truth."

"I'm sorry about the loss of your job, but I've spent all day with past lives and I'm wiped. Go away." She started to close the door.

"Food," he called through the crack.

Her resolve weakened.

"Great food. And anything you want to drink and my undying gratitude and—"

The second mention of food roused an awareness of hunger she didn't know she had. "I'm going to let you in. If the dog doesn't eat you while I'm trying to find something to wear, I'll go."

"Deal," he said. "Dogs love me." He started in and the dog leaped for his throat. Dragging it back, toenails scraping on the wooden floor, she let Bernie in, settled the dog by the fireplace and told Bernie she'd only be a minute.

She took a quick shower, put on a long black wool skirt and a long-sleeved gold top with a scoop neck. In the living room, Bernie sat frozen in a wing chair, the dog at his elbow growling softly, waiting for an excuse to grab his throat.

"We can go now," she said when he didn't stir.

"Your dog won't let me move." To illustrate, he started to lean forward, the dog's upper lip curled and the growl got more intense.

Cass grabbed its collar and told Bernie to go outside, she'd follow. He rose slowly. The dog hadn't wanted to let him in and she didn't want to see him go. She kept suspicious eyes on him as he opened the door and went out.

In the car, Cass asked Bernie how he knew Eva.

"Just met her two hours ago." And that was all the explanation she got. He mentioned the vastness of the sky, how bright the stars looked, how close the sliver of moon seemed and how different the landscape was than he'd expected, totally flat, not these small hills.

Parking anywhere near Eva's house was impossible. Every feasible niche and some that weren't had a vehicle in it.

"How many people did she invite?" Cass asked.

Bernie drove slowly past the house.

"Reporters?" What the hell? She counted at least five reporters in front, a couple with technicians armed with minicams. Grouped on the sidewalk, they talked among themselves and sipped from steaming paper cups.

Bernie made a U-turn and pulled into Eva's driveway. The reporters surged toward the car. When she stepped out, they drifted back, obviously realizing she was nobody. Arm on her back, as though afraid she might make a run for it, Bernie walked her to the door.

"You're finally here!" Eva gave Cass a fat smacking kiss on the

54

cheek. "I was beginning to think you'd copped out on me. Or fell head over heels and decided on a night of romance with Bernie." Eva had to shout to be heard above the din. Brown hair sleeked back, eyes bright, looking very festive in a long filmy salmon dress, she squeezed Cass in a hug. "It's so great you're back!"

"Eva?" someone shouted from the kitchen.

"Be right there!" she yelled and turned back to Cass. "There's so much I have to tell you that—"

"Eva!"

She took in a long breath of air. "I've really got to see what this problem is. Everything's in the dining room. Help yourself."

Cass had to flatten herself against the wall to squeeze past the closely packed bodies. At first glance, Cass didn't see anyone she recognized. Where were all those old friends Eva had promised? Putting on a party smile, Cass squeezed through the people grazing at a dining room table piled with slices of ham and roast beef, fried chicken, cheeses, breads, crackers, salads, sliced fruit, and fancy cakes. Bottles of wine, designer water, and hard liquor sat on a sideboard.

Bernie materialized at her side and leaned closer to make himself heard. "Gin and tonic? I make a mean gin and tonic."

"Scotch and water. Heavy on the water."

Music throbbed a witless atonal noise that made her temples ache. Bernie returned and handed her a squat heavy glass. She took a sip and choked. He'd reversed the proportions. Smiling and murmuring inane replies to inane questions, she was buffeted through the crowd and funneled into the living room.

"Best fuckin' smoke jumper ever was," a drunken voice muttered. "Anybody doesn't agree can tell it to me! Just try! Try! I'd give my life for him! My life!"

Wakely? His voice startled her. What was he doing here? She'd thought he was pretty much a recluse and seldom left Jackson Garrett's side. Cass squirmed through groups of people and sat in the chair next to his wheelchair. She was shocked by his appearance. He used to be a huge, robust man with boundless energy and a shy sense of humor, now he seemed just a shell, fragile and hollow. "Hi, Wakely."

He jerked back and regarded her with bloodshot eyes. Homely, like an old Irish water spaniel, he had a long friendly face, bristly reddish hair flecked with gray and soft brown eyes. "Well, if it isn't my old pal Cassie! How you doin', Cassie? My God, how many years has it been? Must be fifty." He took a hefty gulp from his glass.

He was maybe three more swallows from passing out. "Twenty," she said. The same number since his spine had been crushed and he'd ended up forever in that chair.

"Twenty!" he shouted as though the answer had just popped into his mind. "Seen the governor?"

Trickles of apprehension crawled along her neck. "He's here?"

"Has to be. I'm here, aren't I?" he demanded belligerently. "Go everywhere together. Everywhere. Together. Everywhere together. Best pal. Hero! Fucking hero!" Wakely listed in her direction. "Don't you say different. Saved my life!" He slammed a fist on the chair arm. "Nothing but a crispy critter wasn't for Jack Garrett." Tears filled his bleary eyes and ran unchecked down his face.

"I know, Wakely."

His right hand shot out and grabbed her wrist. His legs, flaccid in the chair were wasted and useless, but his upper body was thick and muscled and his hand clamped her wrist like a vise. "Wanted to talk."

No one can talk with a drunk.

"Death fires."

She tried to pull her arm away, but he held her anchored in place. "Excuse me, Wakely, Bernie is waiting—"

"Killed her." He leaned so far toward her she was afraid he'd fall out of the wheelchair.

"Who?" She drew back from his stale alcohol-smelling breath.

"Dead. Gone."

"Time to go, pal?" A blond young man, muscles brimming with fine-toned health, like an expensive trainer from an upscale gym, grabbed the chair and pushed Wakely through the crowd, which parted like the Red Sea.

Cass followed in his wake, looking for Eva and finally finding her in the family room, refilling bowls of chips. "Have you seen Bernie?"

Cass asked. "I'm really beat. I need to get home before I collapse."

Eva looked around vaguely. "He's here somewhere. Are you okay? You don't hate me, do you?"

"What are you talking about?"

"Jack. Isn't that why you're leaving? I know I should have told you but I was afraid you wouldn't come if you knew."

Silence slammed into Cass's mind.

Eva nodded. "In the kitchen, I think. I—"

Into the stillness, whispers floated like tattered wisps of fog, with the faintest crystalline echoes. At first they were on the far side of hearing. Gradually, they thickened and shaped as she still strained to hear. *Never came back. Never came back.*

"Cassie, you okay?"

"Fine." Why was she so surprised? Wakely had told her Jack was here. Her mind had simply refused to take it in.

Governor Jackson Garrett, sleeves rolled up, stood at the kitchen sink washing dishes. Head down, he was listening intently to a young woman in a short black skirt and white blouse, one of the caterers. Funny thing, you always forgot how big he was until you saw him again and it jumped out at you. His dark hair was now liberally sprinkled with gray.

He could listen better than anyone. Like you were the most important, most interesting person alive, like he had all the time in the world and he wanted to hear what you had to say. Even Ted never made her feel that way.

Something long dead stirred, opened one eye and flicked its scaly tail.

He handed the caterer a dripping glass. She snatched it and rubbed vigorously, held it up to the light to check for spots and gave it another brisk polish.

"I mean, I'm holding down two jobs now," she said. "I don't see what more I can do."

"It's a cryin' shame," Jack said. "You need some help. It's people like you, baby with special needs and a mother who's takin' medicines that cost more than she can pay." He shook his head. "We've got to do something about this. You and me and every other person in this country. We've got to take care of those who need it. Babies can't be allowed to die because it costs money to save them."

"Governor?" murmured a dark-haired man with glasses, wearing a blue suit. "Rotary Club. We're late."

"Todd keeps me on schedule." Jack took the dishtowel from the caterer, wiped his hands and gave it back to her. Engulfing one of her hands in both of his, he said, "I'm glad you told me about your son. You're a brave young woman."

Tears came to her eyes.

Todd, keeper of the schedule, held a coat and Jack shrugged into it. Just before he ducked out the kitchen door, he spotted her. "Cassie. Oh my God, Cassie."

"Governor—?" Todd said.

"Right. I'm coming. Cassie. Lord, Cassie, this—. Listen, I've got to go, but we're out at the farm. Meet us there at twelve-thirty."

He stared at her a second, nodded, picked up a cane, and limped out.

12

*C*ass found Bernie, told him she wanted to go home, and went in search of her hostess who was on the patio dancing to the noise that passed itself off as music. When an arm shimmied by, she grabbed it and extracted Eva from the man either dancing with her, or just in the vicinity and having a very expressive moment of his own.

"Eva," she shouted. "I'm dead on my feet. I have to go. It's been a lovely party."

"You won't hate me forever because I didn't tell you Jack would be here?"

"Don't be silly. That was all a long time ago." Another lifetime, another set of people.

"Did you talk with Gayle?"

"Who?"

"Gayle Egelhoff. She called asking how to get hold of you. I told her you'd be here and invited her to come."

Oh, Cass thought, the woman who'd left the message on her machine.

"She said if she couldn't reach you she'd come, but since she didn't show, I figured she must have talked to you."

"What does she want?"

Eva shrugged. She'd had a bit to drink and her eyes didn't quite track. "Her husband is Vince Egelhoff. You know, one of the smoke jumpers with Jack that awful time. When all those people died and—" Her dance partner grabbed her and whirled her away.

In the car, Cass asked Bernie, "What is this twelve-thirty at the farm all about?" She cracked the window, cool night air brushed her face. A crisp feel of fall was in the air, crickets chirred, somewhere a coyote yipped.

"Politicians work late at night. Weekends, holidays. All those times when real people have real lives."

"Why was I asked to come?" It had shaken her, when Jack said come to the farm. For a split second, she'd thought he wanted to explore apologies and explanations, but that had all been said and done long ago.

"The governor told me to hire you."

She stared at him. The green glow of the dash lights gave him a ghoulish look. He gave her a quick weighing glance, then returned his attention to the road.

Yeah, right. "To do what?" she asked.

"Full-time campaign staff member."

That knocked her socks off. "Why?"

Bernie shrugged. "Probably because he knows you'll do a good job. He's smart that way."

"Just take me home, please."

"Sure."

"I'm not a politician."

"If we go out there, you can ask him why."

"I don't want to go out there."

"Because—?"

"Because I'm tired. And I don't want to—I just—My feet hurt. I want to go home."

"Okay."

After a moment or so, she said, "You're going the wrong way."

"I know." He kept on going.

"Damn it, you said you'd take me back whenever I wanted."

"Right. Can you hang on just a little longer?"

"No."

"Give the governor five minutes." Bernie glanced at her and quickly threw out, "Two minutes."

Could she do that? Did she want to? No. What did it matter?

"If you don't," Bernie said, "you'll never know what the governor has in mind."

She didn't care.

"Two minutes," Bernie urged. "Then we're outta there."

So she went, mostly because Bernie wouldn't stop and she didn't want to throw herself from a moving automobile. And maybe she did care. A little.

The barred gate was new since she'd last been here, and the man in a dark suit wearing an earring who came out of the hut was also new. He stooped to look at Bernie, and then at her. She was sure she looked half dead, skinny with grayish skin and dark circles under her eyes.

"Casilda Storm," Bernie said. "He wants to see her."

On the long drive to the house, she uneasily regretted not being more insistent about going home. She'd been out here many times when she and Jack were tight, some visceral memory was stirring deep inside.

Floodlights lit up the front of the house. Two troopers stood by the door. In the living room, plates of sandwiches and platters of cheese and fruit sat on tables along with coffee cups and cans of soft drinks. Jack wasn't around, but Todd, the campaign manager, who was with Jack at Eva's party, gave her a smile and a hello.

A man came up and clapped Bernie on the shoulder. "It's about time. Where you been?"

Bernie turned. "Cass, this is Leon Massy. Media consultant."

"The best in the business." Leon was tall with an aw-shucks smile, an abundance of cornstalk yellow hair, and a hint of down south in his voice; from the waist down he was a shocking billow of fat.

"Leon thinks he's hot shit right now," Bernie said, " 'cause he just won a special election in Georgia with a pro-choice ad."

"Yes indeed." Leon nodded with a pleased smile. "Had the founding fathers concerned they'd taken a Yankee viper to their righteous bosoms, until it brought an overwhelming herd of citizens stampeding to the voting booths to demand their right to a D and C. Then they let their clouds of doubt drift away on the sweet odor of success."

He grabbed for her hand, yanked her close, and crushed her in a full body hug, forcing the air from her chest. "Welcome aboard!"

"Uh—"

"He says you're gonna be great, just great. We're gonna win this thing. Right, Bernie? Tell her what we're doin' here. You're goin' to love us."

"I'm not even sure who else is running."

"Honey chile, I'll give you your first lesson in politics," Leon said. "Nobody's runnin'." He wiggled bushy eyebrows. "Yet," he added with a braying laugh. "We're all out there feelin' around and dippin' our toes in the water to see how hot it is."

"Cass." Jack, buttoning his shirt, walked into the living room from the hallway behind her. "Thank you for coming," he said, awkwardly formal. He smiled, a little wary, a little unsure of how she'd respond.

"Hey, not every political candidate seeking the nomination asks me out to his farm."

"Cass—" He looked around, then took her arm. "Let's get out of here."

With a hand on her elbow, he steered her into the kitchen. Two officers followed. "Going somewhere, Governor?"

Jack shook his head. "Just out back."

Floodlights had been set up in the back also. Using a cane and limping slightly, Jack walked across the patio and along a gravel path toward a small grove of trees.

"Not a good idea, Governor," an officer said. "This area isn't secure."

"It'd have to be a great big coincidence if some whack job wanting to kill me just happens to be out there in the dark and I just happen to come out here and he just happens to have a gun."

Cass could tell the officer wanted to say something like, Fuck,

62

yeah, it could happen, but he clamped his mouth and kept his eyes on the tall trees they were heading toward.

"We won't be long. It's too cold, for one thing. I want to talk with Cass. You can stay over there."

With stiff reluctance, the officers moved out of earshot and stood facing them, legs wide apart, hands clasped in front. Jack turned her around so she was facing him and looked directly into her eyes. His scrutiny embarrassed her and a dizzying surreal feeling came over her. Twenty years since she'd seen him. What did he want with her? Stray fingers of wind stirred the hair around her face and she brushed it back.

The silence grew thick and when it started to choke her, she said, "It's late and I'm sure you had a long day and—"

"Would you like something? A drink? Coffee?"

She shook her head and pulled her coat tight.

A trace of a smile. "Hot tea?" He crossed his arms. "I didn't realize it was so cold." He shifted his weight from one leg to the other, easing his injured ankle, and looked up at the night sky. "It's a night of a new moon."

She looked up and saw nothing but stars, cold and glittery, reaching forever across the endless sky.

"I want you to join the campaign," he said in a different voice, softer, full of loss and longing and regret and maybe even a little pleading.

Bernie had told her as much, so that came as no big surprise. "Why, Jack?"

"Foreign policy advisor."

"What? You're crazy."

"The resolution of this war on terrorism and the political consequences are the key issues in this election. You know that area."

She put her hands in her pockets, somehow to keep herself steady. It didn't take a genius to figure out that an old girlfriend wasn't tracked down simply to talk over old times. It only made sense if the old girlfriend in question could contribute something important to the cause. "I know nothing," she said.

63

"Lives are at stake. People are at risk and they aren't confident their government can protect them. Most politicians think it's naïve to tell the truth. I think that's really what people want."

In the silvery moonlight, the lines in his face were smoothed away and the gray in his hair didn't show. His voice had the same passionate intensity she remembered. It could have been twenty years ago, the two of them together, talking way into the night, discussing, arguing, solving unsolvable problems, clinging to each other with sweaty promises. He had gone off to fight a fire and never returned to her. She never knew why.

"Tell the truth," he said. "Create a policy that's sound and build a platform with the best interests of the people at heart, promise to do the best we can and then—" He shrugged and his voice went from oration to embarrassed. "Sorry. Did I sound like I was giving a speech? There's a lot of that going around."

"I can't help you," she said.

"You've been there, Cass. For nine months you were in the Middle East. Lived with them, talked with them."

"Taught them." When she'd been released from the loony bin, she'd fled to the most dangerous place she could think of, the granite mountains on the front lines of the war against terrorism, a place of severe poverty, where most people were illiterate and babies died before they reached their second birthday.

"I know."

"I went there because—" *Because a drunk driver wiped out Ted and Laura and I should have died, too, because I wanted to die and thought I might as well do something with my miserable life until it happened. I thought someone would kill me and save me the trouble.*

"Girls," she said, "Women. They had nothing and—" *And so with no training and no credentials, I taught. And waited to die. They had no schools and no teachers, no books and no supplies. Nothing.* With Ted's insurance money, she'd built a school. Sixty-three girls came to her to learn to read and write. Little Amoli, the first girl in her village to learn to read, wanted to be a teacher just like Cass. Cass had given her the money for training. It all came to an end when Aunt Jean's stroke landed her in the hospital and Cass had to come home.

"They talked to you, these girls, these women. They told you what the thinking was and who the players were and what was happening. I need you, Cass. You can speak out about the harsh realities of the situation and bring a little sanity into campaign rhetoric."

The wind was cold. It swept across her face and reached inside to tickle her lungs. She shivered and clamped her teeth to keep them from chattering. Work for Jack? She didn't love him, that had died years ago. And she had no anger—that, too, had faded into the shadowy mists of the past. She did have some pitiful sad lingering strains of long ago love, but, in truth, she'd lived through far more disfiguring, destructive scars than any Jackson Garrett had inflicted.

He reached down and took her hands from her pockets, held them in his. "Will you jump on this—it's more a hay wagon than a bandwagon—and join Garrett For America?"

"I don't think so." *I won't be around long enough to do you any good.* She pulled her hands away and dredged up a smile. "Hey." She tried for a light tone so he wouldn't think she was just petulant. "What's in it for me?"

He grinned, same old grin. "Anything you want. Secretary of State?"

Her return smile was involuntary. She took a step back, standing this close made her nervous. It was like standing beside a generator and feeling the hum of energy.

"Let's get inside," he said. "It's freezing."

The troopers followed at a discreet distance.

"Wife, Governor." Leon handed him a phone.

"Hang on, Cass, let me just—" He took the phone. "Hello, Molly."

Even from where she stood, she could hear the angry snap on the other end. "Oh no," Jack said. "Oh hell—well this thing just went on— no, no—I'm sorry—I got stuck—You know how it is—Tonight?" He put a hand over the mouthpiece. "Todd, were we supposed to meet with a Kansas City supporter tonight?"

A low murmur of affirmative replied.

"Well, God dammit, Todd, why didn't you—Listen, Molly, here's what—No—we'll be right there—I know it's late. Stay right where you are and—No, no. We'll be there—I know that but—Molly?" He slammed down the phone. "Let's go. Where's the plane?"

"Topeka."

"We're there. Let's get Molly and go on to Oklahoma City for that early morning meeting."

Papers got shoved in briefcases, jackets got pulled on. Jack picked out a sandwich and said to Cass, "We'll talk more later. Todd! Where the hell is Todd?"

"One step behind you, Governor."

"Yeah." Leon had another phone to his ear. "Yep, yep, but Washington—they don't want to commit themselves till they see what you can do. Don't you worry. We're doin' great. They're going to be poundin' down our door."

"Let's go, Leon," Jack said. "Bernie!"

"Right here, Governor."

"See that Cass gets taken care of."

"Yes, sir."

13

—

$\mathcal{D}$rugs, Cass thought, as she dragged herself into the house after Bernie brought her back from Jack's farm. Wellbutrin. A handful. Bottle, make that a bottle of Wellbutrin. As she stuck the key in the lock, she heard the dog make its sing-songy whimpers of greeting and when she opened the door, the dog rushed to greet her. Monty the cat yelled abuse from the mantel.

Right, life goes on. Kneeling, she hugged the dog who wriggled herself in a circle and slathered kisses on Cass's face. Maybe Cass had been foolhardy to throw out all her chemical aids before she left Las Vegas. With dog and cat trailing, she went to the bathroom and checked the medicine cabinet, even though she knew it had nothing more lethal than a bottle of aspirin, and who could guess how old that was.

The animals stared up at her. "Pretend, pretend, pretend," she said. "Pretend everything's all right." A sob caught in her throat and she put her hands over her face. Drugs and relaxation exercises and talk talk talk. She'd grown sick to the bone of therapy talk, the visualizing, the journal writing. The talk of Survivor's Guilt and every other emotion with Capital Letters. She was through with it. Denial was a perfectly good coping mechanism. Hundreds of people used it all the time. To hell with the Psychiatric Wisdom, *you can't run away from yourself.*

Who cares! Mind-numbing drugs, her entire being urged. It's late, yes, but hospitals have emergency rooms. They have physicians who can write prescriptions. Antidepressants to relax. Sleeping pills to sleep. To let you lie down and close your eyes and . . .

Stop it!

Keep busy.

Doing what? Her mind whimpered.

The animals sat side by side in the doorway watching her. Feed the animals. Yes, right. She could feed Monty and the dog.

Tail bristling with importance, Monty led the way to the kitchen. She opened the drawer to get the can opener and her eyes focused on the knife next to it. Ordinary, small paring knife. Black handle, bright blade. She held it up, turning it back and forth and the ceiling light glinted on the shiny surface. With a thumb, she tested the pointed end. Sharp. She could prick the vein pulsing in her wrist. Laying it flat across the old scars on her wrist, she pressed gently. It felt cool against her warm wrist. If she tilted it, the sharp end would be ready to cut. If she pushed down and drew it back and forth—

The dog put its head against her hip and looked up at her, eyes worried.

She threw the knife back and shoved the drawer shut, spooned out pet food and put the bowls in the expected places.

The anniversary of the end of the world was coming. Five more days. October 31. Halloween. *Trick or treat.*

That was some trick fate played on her. She was happy that day. It was a Friday. She'd been proud of herself. She'd just prosecuted a murder case and gotten a guilty verdict. Ted was home from Los Angeles where his firm had sent him to help with a high profile case of fraud. Laura was dancing with excitement because she was getting to wear her Tinker Bell costume. The three of them were on their way to see friends. Moms and kids were going out trick or treating, dads were staying home watching a football game. Laura never got any treats that Halloween, only a viciously cruel trick.

A clown driving from a costume party, flying high on all the alcohol in his blood. Ted was killed instantly. Cass had no awareness of his last breath. Laura died in the hospital twelve hours later. The same hospital where Cass had been admitted for a crushed pelvis, broken left arm, concussion, and broken left collarbone.

Laura'd been terrified. She cried out *Mommy!* Or at least, Cass thought she had. She must have because she heard the echo of that cry in her tortured dreams, beneath the rain just when it started to patter, beneath the call of a bird, faint and far away, and under the sound of violins. And she hadn't answered.

All those hours in intensive care. Had Laura been conscious any of that time? The physician said not, but Cass wasn't sure she believed him. Images plagued her of a terrified Laura in the alien world of the hospital and in pain, waking and calling Mommy and getting no answer. What had Laura thought when Cass never answered?

The doctors and nurses tended to Cass's injuries, monitored her concussion, checked the progress of mending bones, and changed bandages on scrapes and cuts, but they didn't notice the Black Dog of Depression crawling in.

When Cass was released, the house mocked her. Everywhere she looked there'd be a reminder. One of Laura's sneakers with the blinking flash on the side. So tiny. She was so little. So sweet. A towel of Ted's flung over the shower stall the morning before he'd left. A tie pulled loose and flung over the back of a chair in the bedroom. She sat in one chair in the living room, a swivel chair she could turn to the wall, so she saw nothing but a white-painted surface. There she sat for hours at a time, unwashed, wearing an old stained robe, stringy hair unbrushed.

A ghost self broke away and looked down on her with helpless dismay. It wrung its hands when friends came to pick her up for the double memorial service that should have occurred weeks earlier but was postponed until she was out of the hospital. Her ghost self noted the looks of horror on the friends' faces, heard only as low-pitched twitter their murmurs of what to do, can't go out like this. She felt nothing as she was manipulated like a store dummy into clothes. The memorial service was a blur. Brought home, helped into the house, cheery words masking looks of apprehension, and she was alone again.

Silence. Time.

Christmas came. Her ghost self pointed out the knives in the kitchen drawer, the bottles of drugs, of cleaning supplies, gauged the length of electrical cord and the drop off her deck, the gas connection of her clothes dryer.

January came. Her ghost self started slipping its fingertips down her cheeks, clapping its hands, touching her shoulder. Like little fanged ants trying to rouse her.

To get away from them, she left the house. She walked. Pulling on any odd garment that came to hand, she would go out. In the rain, getting soaked, her ghost self had to tell her she was cold. At the BART station, she stood on the platform and looked down at the tracks. Third rail, the lethal one. She watched the trains come in. Which one would she throw herself in front of? Sometimes she would just sit there all day.

She had no feeling of hunger, but sometimes she ate. When his bowl had been empty for too long, Monty the cat yowled at her and she had just enough sense to dump in dry food. Her ghost self was appalled at her bedraggled appearance, unbathed and usually dressed in Ted's old sweats. She took to carrying around his old backpack and like a bag lady picked up odd things that caught her eye, tabs from soft drink cans, small stones, or leaves. And newspapers. She stuffed them in the backpack and took them home to read, but when she got there, she simply stacked them up along the walls.

Friends came. Her ghost self saw how they looked at her and the appalling condition of the house and then at each other. They wanted to take her to the supermarket, make an appointment with her doctor, clean up her house. When one of them offered to take Monty to the animal shelter, she stopped answering the door or the phone. Laura had loved Monty.

If Cass slept at all, she slept in the doorway of Laura's room, prepared to fight with fury anyone who might try to cross the threshold. The quiet house filled her with a dreadful anxiety. She would pace until she couldn't breathe and then she'd race out the door. Once outside, she slowed to an apathetic shuffle, not caring where she went as long as she was moving. In her travels—and travel, she did, she must have walked twenty miles a day—she might stop at a convenience store and buy a carton of milk. She'd stick it in her backpack and find it days later, clotted and smelling.

She barely noticed the weather and made no attempt to provide herself with a coat when it was cold or a hat when rain was soaking into her hair and staining her clothing. Her ghost self watched in helpless alarm. She stepped in front of a car. Brakes squealed and the driver cursed at her.

Continuing to live without Ted and Laura was unthinkable. It was her neighbor who put an end to the down spiral. Concerned because he hadn't seen her that day, he went in and found her bleeding her life away from deep cuts in her wrists.

Major depression. In some weird way, the diagnosis brought relief. A chemical imbalance in the brain. Triggered, perhaps, by the unbearable hand that Fate had dealt her. It didn't mean she would always be a gibbering mass of smelly rags. It meant a crack had appeared in her brain, like a fault line with little branches running deep into her nervous system, from pressure so unbearable that madness was preferred.

This time, in the hospital, she was in the psych ward. No sharp objects, no shoestrings, no buttons. She was aware of being watched, nurses always around, always careful never to leave a potential weapon. Meal trays came with plastic utensils and those were always made note of before the trays were taken away. Despite all the drugs—and she knew them only by color, a pink pill, a white one, a blue and white capsule—she had enough wits for another suicide try, a serious try. The same neighbor who had phoned 911 would continue taking care of Monty. She wanted to be dead.

The only things she had to work with were what she had on. Hospital-issue short cotton gown and cotton pajama bottoms. She climbed up on the bed, tied one leg of the pajama bottoms to the grille over the window, tied the other leg around her neck, and stepped off the bed. She twisted in the air, first one way, then the other, slowly strangling.

A nurse making rounds found her. Though she wasn't aware of it, they did the whole emergency bit, CPR, crash cart, stat this and stat that. She was more interesting than television for a time. That was the end of it. After her third failed attempt at suicide, she gave up. Someone contacted Aunt Jean who came on the wind.

Cass fell into the routines of the hospital, a routine of mindless, soothing sameness. She had no decisions to make. Swamped by drugs, she went where she was told, did what she was told, ate what was put in front of her. After a time, she found that in spite of herself, the pressure of bleak hopelessness in her mind lessened a tiny bit. She began to notice things other than her own miserableness, became aware of the other people on the ward and the nurses.

Then one day the lunch tray included a cup of custard. She picked up the plastic spoon, dipped it in the smooth surface and tasted what was on the spoon. She hated custard. She put the spoon down and let the tray go back, custard uneaten.

She had made a decision of her very own.

On the day Aunt Jean left for home, she brought Cass a card. On the front was a gnarled and bent little creature with a tiny lantern. Under it read: *The good news is, there is a light at the end of the tunnel.* Inside the card said: *The bad news is, this is it.* When Cass smiled, Aunt Jean hugged her and said, "I'm glad you're back."

Cass wasn't back, of course. She'd never be back, not in the sense of being the same as she was before Ted and Laura were killed, but it was a small start and she began to break through the gray and let in a little color now and then. When she was released, she had gone home and collected Monty from the neighbor.

The dog pressed against her leg. She gave it an absent pat and went into the living room to Aunt Jean's desk. Opening the drawer made the bullets clink together. The old revolver had belonged to

Ted's father. Cass had hated it and several times told Ted to get rid of it. He always said he would; she was thankful now he never had.

She swung out the cylinder and pushed in a bullet, hesitated, then pushed in a second.

14

Sunday was one of those freaky warm days that happen sometimes just when everybody's all set for Fall. After the buckets of rain, the air was thick and wet, kinda' like slimy bologna. Tony rubbed his face with the crook of his arm, shrugged off his fleece jacket and tied it around his waist. "Hey, Max, wait up!"

He pushed his Razor scooter hard to catch up with his friend. "Why do we have to go way out to the county road?"

"Because it's the highest hill around."

"There's plenty of closer hills."

"Scared?" Max spurted ahead, weaving his Razor in and out of parked cars along Main Street.

Tony planted a foot on the sidewalk, gave a hefty push and rode the narrow scooter until it started to slow, then gave another push. At the intersection, he bounced off the curb and zipped into the street.

Brakes squealed. "Hey, kid, you wanna' live to grow up!"

Max had them going straight through downtown, store windows all full of Halloween stuff. Once they got past all the stores and stuff, there was hardly any traffic. Max spun tight turns, deliberately slid on wet leaves in the gutters, and zigged and zagged back and forth across the street. Tony just kept slogging, wondering if it was worth it. They kept going, they crossed the bridge and kept going, hung a left on Garden Street and kept going, all the way out to the county road. What a mushbrain Max was. The road was pocked with potholes and every one filled with rain water.

Noggin's Hill was halfway to nowhere. Nobody ever said why it was called Noggin's Hill. Tony thought he ought to ask his uncle Osey. Osey knew lots of weird things like that.

"See?" Max said. "Isn't this great?"

"Yeah. Great." Tony rode up beside Max and looked down. He never realized how really high Noggin's Hill was.

Max farted around trying to find the exact middle of the road, eyeing the downhill slope and scooting his Razor an inch this way, an inch that way.

"You gonna ride or spend the rest of your life measurin'?"

Max took off, yelling, "Geronimo!" The Razor flew, straight as an arrow downhill, through the hollow at the bottom and started up the other side.

Max pulled his scooter off the road and shot his fist in the air. "Yeah! The Champ and Best There Is!" Shielding his eyes with one hand, he looked up at Tony. "Beat that!"

Tony wheeled his Razor to the middle of the road and looked down the hill. Uh-huh. He realized what Max had been doing before. Stalling. Tony followed his example, moved a little to the right, a little to the left.

"Come on!" Max yelled. "We don't have all day."

Tony shoved off, put both feet on the four-inch wide scooter deck and sailed down the road. Yes! He'd get higher up the other side. Doing great! Oh no! Rock! He tried to swerve. The scooter took a right turn leap off the road, juddered over mud, rocks, and rotten green stuff. Momentum shot him over a rise and sent him crashing down the other side. He smashed into a blue Mustang, fell off and the Razor kept right on going and then toppled over in dead leaves.

"Tony!"

Max came skidding down the slope sideways on wet leaves and muddy gunk. "Wow, man! You all right?"

75

Tony retrieved his scooter and examined it for damage.

"Trying to kill yourself?" Max stepped back and looked at the car. He walked his Razor around it. "Hey, how come this car's sitting here like this?"

Tony swiped a sleeve across his nose and rubbed his elbow. "I think I broke my arm."

"Can you bend it?"

Tony tried. "Yeah, but it hurts."

"If you can bend it, it's fine. Don't be such a baby. Boy, look what you did to this car." Max rubbed a scratch on the shiny blue paint.

"You retard. That was already there."

"Yeah? Well, maybe you better get out of here before the owner comes back and wrings your neck." Max looked around. "Where is the owner anyway?"

Good question. There weren't any houses around the guy could be at. Nothing here but weeds and a few trees. "Probably taking a leak."

Cupping his hands around his eyes, Max peered in the driver's side window. "Tony? The keys are in it." He tried the handle and the door opened.

"You think somebody dumped it?"

"No."

"Why not? It's old."

"Not that old and look at it. It's not banged up and the paint's shiny."

"So where's the owner?

"How should I know? Around here somewhere."

"Hey!" Max yelled. "Somebody's stealin' your car!"

A flock of little bitty birds flew away from the trees in a cloud of flutter.

"If anybody was here, he'd come a runnin'." Max folded his scooter, tossed it in the back of the car and hopped into the driver's seat.

"Max! What're you doin'?"

The motor started with a roar.

"Max—"

"Get in! Hurry up!"

"You crazy?"

"Get in! Get in!"

Quickly, Tony popped his Razor in the back with Max's and climbed in the passenger seat. "It's stealing. You don't even know how to drive."

"I've been doing it for years." Max tromped the accelerator. The motor screamed.

"If you know so much, how come you didn't put the gear in drive?" Tony reached between the seats and took care of it.

The car shot backward. Max managed to hit the brakes before the car whipped across the road and down the ditch on the other side.

"Slower, stupid!"

Max crimped the wheel, put his foot on the accelerator and the car leaped ahead. Tony yelled. Max hit the brake. After a few more leaps and stops, Max got better. They drove farther down the county road, past corn stocks and pastureland with cattle grazing.

"Where you goin'?" Tony braced both hands on the dash to keep from being thrown through the windshield. He shouldn't have gotten in the damn car. He should have just let Max go off by himself. But you never knew what the peckerwood might do. Tony needed to make sure Max didn't kill himself.

"You crazy?" Tony repeated.

"It was dumped," Max said. "That means whoever left it doesn't want it, that means no reason we shouldn't go for a ride."

"That means stealing, dumb nuts."

"Goody boy!"

"Don't you think it's kind of a nice car to just be dumped?"

"Then what was it doing there?"

"How should I know? It was just parked that's all. The owner's probably calling the cops right now."

At the next crossroad, Max got the car turned around and headed toward town. Drifting back and forth across the road like he did, he was gonna get them smoked for sure.

"We can outrun the cops," Max said. "This is great!"

"It's dangerous. You don't know the first thing about driving." Tony opened the glove box and pulled out a bunch of papers. He flipped through them, insurance card, clippings about a fire where a bunch of people died, and finally the car registration.

"Think you could do better?"

"Anybody could do better, you dickhead. This car belongs to Vincent Egelhoff."

Max looked at him. "So? You know him?"

"Look out! You're gonna hit that tree." Tony grabbed the wheel and they swerved back onto the road. "That's it. Stop the car. I'm getting out."

"Wimp. Wuss. You're nothin' but a baby. Baby Tony. Baby Tony."

"We stole some guy's car. He's stranded out there somewhere. Turn around and go back."

Like the doofus he was, Max drove right on into town where everybody could see him. Just like it wasn't going to occur to them that Max was twelve and didn't have a license.

He pulled a left on Lyons Street and squealed into Elkhorn Park. Too fast for Tony to sort it out, they spun a half-circle, slid, bounced off the boulder and plowed nose first into the raised concrete base of Horace Greeley. The Mustang's hood rippled like an accordion. The trunk lid popped up. The passenger door flew open. Tony tumbled out, landed on his shoulder, banged his head. He couldn't breathe.

The motor died. Antifreeze started dripping.

Max came running. "You all right?" He knelt and helped Tony sit up. "Say something! You dead or what!"

"What'd you go and do that for?"

"Gimme that stuff." Max grabbed the papers Tony still clutched in his hand and stuffed them back in the glove box.

Tony stood up and rolled his shoulder. It hurt. He felt kinda funny. Dizzy and sorta sick. His head hurt.

"Wow." Max stood peering into the trunk. "Oh man."

"Now what are you doing?"

"There's blood all over. Doesn't smell too good either."

Tony went to check what stupid stunt Max was pulling now.

A woman lay in the trunk. All curved and bent and kinda' crumpled-looking. Bloody hair fanned out over most of her face. The skin was an icky gray color and the back of her head looked kinda squished.

"Hey!" Max shouted.

Tony jumped a mile, then turned and punched Max's shoulder. "What're you doing?"

"Tryin' to wake her up." Max's voice dropped to a whisper. "You think she's dead?"

"No."

"Oh yeah? If you're so sure, whyn't you touch her? Go ahead. I dare you."

Making sure his hand was steady so Max wouldn't know how weirded out he was, Tony reached in and touched her shoulder. Hard, not like a person at all, more like cold inflexible rubber.

Max backed away.

"Where you going?"

"Anywhere, man."

"We have to tell the cops," Tony said.

"You do it. I'm gone."

"Max!" Tony ran after him and grabbed his arm. "We have to get help."

After that it started to get kinda confusing. There was a lot of commotion with people running over to see what happened and pretty soon the cops were there. And not too long after that they were at the cop house and Uncle Osey had his butt on the front edge of his desk and he wasn't looking too friendly.

"Give it to me," Osey said in a cop voice.

"Promise you won't get mad."

"Tony—"

Osey had all the patience in the world, but Tony could see even he was getting a little tight. Tony told it all, except the part where he tried to stop Max taking the car. That made him sound like making up excuses.

Osey looked madlike at him the whole time and that made Tony nervous and he kept forgetting stuff and having to go back and put it in and Max kept interrupting to add his two cents and the whole thing just sounded really snarky and by then even Max knew they were in a whole lot of trouble and kept saying actually it was a good thing they'd done it 'cause what would've happened if they hadn't, she might have been totally rotted out before anybody knew and by the time Tony was finally finished with everything a whole lot of time had gone by and he wondered how an ordinary Sunday could turn into such a mess.

15

———

$\mathcal{T}$he discreet tap on the door was a member of the Sunflower Hotel staff returning Sean's clean laundry, neatly plastic-wrapped. *In at 10 P.M., out at 10 A.M.*, and bless all hotels who provided such a needed service. Some places he'd stayed didn't offer much more than beds and those had dirty sheets. He dumped the package on a chair, found the remote and zapped on the television. As he transferred socks and underwear to a drawer and hung up shirts, he watched a reporter stick a microphone in the face of Congresswoman Stendor as she came from one of the House office buildings.

"Tell us what you think of the growing number of presidential candidates?"

"It reaffirms my faith in the American people. That in these most difficult times, there are so many willing to put themselves in the fray and serve."

"Anyone who stands out as a sure winner?"

"Everyone who runs for president has the soul of a winner." She walked swiftly to the car and slid in.

"What about Governor Garrett?" the reporter asked before she could close the door. "You were classmates at Harvard. Does that mean his soul is more likely to win than the others?"

"It means friends don't have to be in the same political party." She closed the car door with a firm slam and her driver put his foot on the accelerator.

Sean folded the plastic his laundry had come in, dropped it in the wastebasket and carried the pile of Sunday newspapers to the easy chair by the window. *Wall Street Journal, New York Times, Washington Post, Chicago Sun-Times, Dallas Morning News, Houston Chronicle, L.A. Times,* and the *Hampstead Herald.* Outside, the sun shone on the soaked and bedraggled hotel grounds. To keep on top of what was happening in the world, he perused the national news—mostly the same in each one—then went to the political news. All the possibles maneuvering for presidential nomination managed to get their names mentioned somehow.

Most didn't have a whisper of a chance. Some were a joke, some weren't seriously running, just wanted to get their names out there in the country's consciousness for future use—always another election coming up—some wanted to keep their names uppermost in the minds of their constituents, and some were nobodies with a single issue that most of the country had little interest in.

The smart money was going with the incumbent for the Republicans, historically always a good bet. All they had to do was keep patting him on the back and stating he was for God and country. With the Democrats it was all up in the air. Senator Roswell from Missouri, Senator Halderbreck from Massachusetts, Representative Barnes from Rhode Island, and Governor Garrett from Kansas, all with pluses and minuses on their records. Originally Halderbreck looked strong, but then Garrett started turning up in the polls.

The *Hampstead Herald* was thick with articles on Garrett, many with pictures, one twenty years old of Garrett all suited up and parachuting in to fight a raging forest fire. Should be good for a vote or two. Sean was a little surprised to see the photo and wondered where it came from. Garrett shied away from using his smoke jumping days in his campaign. Why? Something strange here. He was considered a hero for what happened in the disastrous forest fire that killed—what was it, five, six people?

Sean folded the paper, dropped it on the end of the bed and grabbed his jacket. One thing about small towns, you could walk just about anywhere. He shrugged on the jacket and set off for the *Hampstead Herald*. Even though the sun was still shining, the end of daylight saving time in the wee hours of the morning had shadows waiting in the wings and the wind was fierce. He turned up the collar of his jacket and upped his pace.

The railroad depot was made of local limestone. Quaint, loads of charm. The whole damn town was quaint. How did Susan live with this? Across from the depot was a squat brick building that housed the paper. Practical, ugly. Made him feel better already. The brass plaque on the front read 1866. Inside, he asked for the library and was directed down some rickety wooden stairs to a basement storage room. The walls were dingy white and hadn't seen paint in a long time. Rolling shelves had rack after rack of microfiche, and, farther back, manila folders filled with news clippings. Beyond that was only murky dimness. He told the troll at the gate that he wanted everything they had on Governor Garrett.

In about ten minutes, the troll brought a set of microfiche cassettes. Sean sat at an old-fashioned metal desk, and scrolled through five-year-old articles. Nothing turned up that he didn't already know. Any hint of something interesting required a different microfiche cassette and requisitioning another set. After the fourth request, the troll slid over the clipboard. "Fill it out and help yourself. Holler if you need anything. I'll be in the back." He disappeared into the gloom.

Sean didn't ask in back of where. He read articles about the fire on Pale Horse Mountain in Montana that happened twenty years ago. One headline screamed FIRE OUT OF CONTROL, with a picture of Wakely Fromm in a jumpsuit with two parachutes hanging around his neck.

"The blow-up was just below me," Fromm was quoted as saying. "The only thing I heard on the radio was 'Run!' The top of the hill was probably a hundred and seventy-five feet straight up and the fire got there in maybe thirteen seconds. Everywhere was this wall of fire, three hundred feet high."

The forest had exploded around them, intense heat turning oak and pine and piñon into fodder for spontaneous combustion. Temperatures reached two thousand degrees that day, hot enough to fire clay and melt gold. Tools dropped by fleeing firefighters were completely incinerated. "You know it's bad," Fromm said, "when the guys are leaving equipment."

Fromm was one of fifty firefighters caught by the swiftness and fury of a wildfire. Tragically, three hot shots and three smoke jumpers were overrun on a spine of Pale Horse Mountain called Horse's Teeth Ridge. They all died on the steep edge of a mountain in a fire that, initially, was so small crews didn't take it seriously. They died near enough to a highway that the cars going by could be seen. They died within view of camcorders held by people in the valley filming the walls of flame.

When Fromm raced to the top of the ridge, he thought he was the only one left alive on Pale Horse. With flames at his heels, he fled in such panic that he ran into a tree and knocked himself unconscious. He didn't know how long he was out. The next thing he knew, Jack Garrett was dragging him and a tree fell on them. He remembered thinking the fire's roar was more deafening than the rage of a tornado funnel.

When Fromm came to, on the other side of the ridge, Vince Egelhoff, another smoke jumper, was screaming. Ribbons of flesh hung from his burned hands. Garrett was wrapping them with wet T-shirts. When they stumbled down to the highway, Garrett made Egelhoff lie in the shade of a county car and watered him down to lower his body temperature, trying to ward off shock.

The incident commander was yelling names at the radio.

Six did not respond.

Sean leaned back. A stray thought wandered into mind. Friday night at the farm when he'd dumped Fromm in bed, Fromm was mumbling about horse's teeth. A touch of posttraumatic stress here? Horse's Teeth Ridge on Pale Horse Mountain? It certainly had sharp teeth. It had taken the lives of six firefighters. Why wasn't Garrett using this stuff?

"Hey, Dudly! You hear they found her?"

Sean turned around to see who was yelling.

A kid, early twenties, buzz cut, jeans and sweatshirt, clattered down the stairs. "Dud?"

"Back here," a lugubrious voice came from somewhere in the rear.

"Did you hear me? They found her. Deader than yesterday's news." He trotted over to Sean and stuck out his hand. "Ty Baldini. A pleasure to meet you, sir."

Sean shook his hand. "Sean Donovan."

"Yes, sir, I know. I've been following—well, covering the Garrett campaign. Just for, you know, the *Herald*. While he's in town. I work here. Reporter for—"

A loud snort came from the murky gloom. Sean assumed it was Dudly giving his opinion.

"Let me tell you, sir, I'm really blown by meeting you. I've read all your stuff and—well, sir, it's just great—"

"Thanks," Sean said. He could do with a little less of the sirs, they made him feel a hundred years old. Ah youth, so fleeting. "Who was found?"

"Oh that. Local news, sir. Nothing you'd be interested in."

"I'm always interested."

"Yeah? Well, it's the woman who called 911 and said she was in a car trunk and didn't know where the car was. The cops tried to find her, but they didn't even know where to look."

"Who is she?" Sean was thinking Susan wouldn't be happy about this.

"Don't know yet, I'm birddogging out to see."

"Mind if I tag along?"

"No, sir, that'd be great, sir."

"Call me Sean," he said as he got in Ty's Trans Am.

Ty drove most of the way across town before he turned into a small park. There were cop cars, ambulance, uniformed cops, and silent onlookers. Sean followed Ty down a gravel path to a blue Mustang with its nose bashed into a concrete circular base around a statue of Horace Greeley. Go west, young man. Seemed like good advice to him.

The trunk lid was open. A kid was snapping photographs. He didn't see Susan anywhere. Just as well. She wouldn't be happy he was here. He edged up behind Ty and looked in the trunk. A woman was curled up next to the jack, head resting on one arm as though trying to make herself comfortable. The shape of her head wasn't quite right, one side was sort of flattened. Dark hair, tangled and bloody, matted to her cheek, pale skin, bluish in the fading light. She had on jeans and a white sweater. The sweater was hiked up in the back exposing two inches of bluish skin. From the side of her face that he could see, she looked early forties.

A crime scene tech was working around the body. That meant a coroner, or somebody, had already come and declared the victim dead. Unless, of course, things were different here, which they certainly could be.

"Who was she?" he asked Ty.

"Gayle Egelhoff."

"Egelhoff? There was an Egelhoff fighting the fire—"

"Husband," Ty said, scribbling in his notebook.

"Baldini!"

Another kid—he must be getting old, everybody he ran into lately looked eighteen—ambled over. Lanky and thin, he looked a bit like a scarecrow, complete with straw-colored hair.

"What are you doing here, Ty?"

Ty just grinned, introduced Sean, and jerked his head at the scarecrow. "This here's Osey Pickett. He's a detective."

Wow, Sean thought, a detective. So this was what Susan had to work with. No wonder she looked sad. Maybe her old man was right, she needed to be dragged back home by any means.

The detective who seemed all knees and elbows jerked a thumb over his shoulder. "Get lost!"

"Come on, Osey, I need information for the paper."

"Scram!"

Ty scrammed and Sean scrammed along with him. "How did you learn her name?" Sean asked.

"Kids who found the body went through the glove compartment

and looked at the registration." Ty had a short stride and Sean adjusted his to keep pace.

"How did kids find the body?"

Ty told him about the great car caper.

"Does Egelhoff know about his wife?"

"He's dead. Weird skiing accident." Ty shook his head. "Man, that was some unlucky family. First her parents get killed."

"Recently?"

"Naw. More'n a dozen years ago, I guess. Twister went through and touched down in just the wrong place. The three of them, Gayle's mother and father and baby sister—I don't remember where Gayle was. Off visiting a friend somewhere. Parents and baby were sheltering in the bathroom, thinking that was the safest place. Turned out no place was safe. Whole house flattened to rubble. Baby didn't have a scratch. Parents killed."

"Sometimes life doesn't give you a fair shake. What happened to Vince?"

"Liked to go skiing with a cousin lives in Colorado. Big snow fall in September. Vince ended up bashing head first into a tree. Died like that." Ty snapped his fingers. He offered to drop Sean back at the hotel and Sean took him up on it.

The phone was ringing as Sean came into his room. It was his old friend Jerry at the *Wall Street Journal*.

"Hey, buddy, you want to know what's going to be in my column tomorrow?"

A fist pounded on his door; this was not the discreet tap of hotel employee, but the fist of authority.

"Hold on." Sean put the receiver on the bed and opened the door. Susan and her faithful sidekick, Parkhurst.

Sean picked up the phone. "Call you right back." He replaced the receiver and turned to Susan. "What's up?"

"Tell me about Gayle Egelhoff."

He could tell Susan was pissed, but he didn't know why, and he didn't have the vaguest notion why she brought reinforcements in the way of the sidekick. "Gayle Egelhoff, the woman in the car trunk?"

"Yeah, that Gayle Egelhoff," Parkhurst said.

Susan sent him a shut-up glance. "What do you know about her?"

If it had been anybody but Susan asking, Sean would have said go fuck yourself. He wanted to say that to Parkhurst anyway. "Gayle Egelhoff, married to Vince Egelhoff, former smoke jumper, who helped battle the fire on Pale Horse Mountain. Badly injured, eventually recovered, died in a skiing accident."

"When did you meet her?"

They were all three standing in the middle of the room and Sean was beginning to feel his space being encroached on, especially by her enforcer who stood around and looked menacing. "You want to tell me what this is all about?"

"You didn't answer the question." Parkhurst moved to the credenza with the television, looked at the keys, change, wallet and other junk from his pockets spread across the top.

Sean watched him, wanted to throw the asshole out. "What's going on, Susan?"

"Police investigation," Parkhurst said.

"Parkhurst," Susan warned.

"And that concerns me—how?"

"Sean," she said.

"You just got bumped up to suspect, pal."

"Pal?"

Parkhurst folded his arms across his chest, like he wanted to hit the dipshit in front of him who wasn't answering questions and was making sure his fists were trapped.

"Oh, for God's sake, stop the pissing contest!" Susan rubbed her forehead with her fingertips. "Parkhurst, wait in the lobby. Sean, sit down and stop behaving like an ass."

Parkhurst clenched his teeth so tight a muscle rippled in the corner of his jaw and sent Sean a warning glance. Sean glared back. Susan sighed. Parkhurst left.

"Sean, just tell me what you know about Gayle Egelhoff and stop acting like an adolescent."

"I'm not acting like an adolescent, I'm acting like your big brother. I want to know what his intentions are."

"Stop it!"

"Why are you asking me about her?"

Susan slapped a plastic baggie down on the bedside table.

He glanced at it. "My business card?"

"It was found in the trunk with Gayle's body. How did it get there?"

"Susan, you can't think I put her there."

"How did it get in the trunk?"

He sat on the foot of the bed. "I have no idea. It's a business card. You hand them out, they get tossed away, they get picked up. It's a business card."

"Tell me about Gayle."

"I'm starting to get really ticked here, Susan. I didn't know the woman, I don't know anything about her, I don't know how the card got in the trunk. The only thing I know is what Ty Baldini told me and the only thing he told me was her name."

Susan let that hang in the air.

"Susan—"

"You'll have to come down to the police department."

"For God's sake, why? You can't think I stuffed her in the trunk."

"I need your fingerprints."

He raised his eyebrows. "You know, unless you charge me with something, I don't have to go anywhere."

"I have a gun. If you don't get your ass down to the police department, I will shoot you. Don't forget, I'm the law around here."

"Ah, since you put it that way . . ."

16

———

"*P*olice!" Demarco pounded on the door. The house, single-story wood frame, white with dark blue trim, was owned by the deceased Vincent Egelhoff, who also had owned the blue Mustang with the dead woman in the trunk. Tentative ID, Gayle Egelhoff, wife of Vincent. Grass recently trimmed, flowerbeds holding the remnants of summer flowers.

Isolating what appeared to be a door key from the bunch found on the ring in the Mustang's ignition, Demarco unlocked the door and pushed it open. "Police! Warrant to search the premises!"

He stepped inside and stood listening, letting his senses absorb whatever the house might tell him, then pulled on latex gloves, covered his shoes with paper slippers and did a quick walk-through. Living room, red brick fireplace, large window looking out at the street, hallway leading to bedrooms. Master bedroom, bed made, paperback mystery on a bedside table, lamp on, closet door closed. He opened it. Clothes hanging on a rod, shoes lined up beneath. Second bedroom, empty, guestroom. Third bedroom, kid's room, mess, like the kid jumbled everything around periodically. Blue plaid bedspread and curtains, boom box on top the bookcase, pictures of male actors Demarco didn't recognize tacked to the wall.

Retracing his steps, he went back along the hallway and through the family room into the kitchen. Window broken from the inside. Looked like a large object had been thrown through it. Nothing identified the object. Cabinets and counter tops in 1950s style apple green ceramic tile. Thumps at the front door had him backing up against the wall in the family room as he eased his gun from the shoulder holster.

The door slammed open, a clunky black shoe kicked a backpack inside.

"Put your hands over your head!" he said.

"Aaaaahh—!"

"Hands on your head!"

Hands flew up and fingers laced over dark spiked hair colored lime green.

"Keep your hands over your head and turn around slowly!"

She did as told. Kid, dressed like a hooker. Five five, brown and brown. Red leather skirt barely covering her butt, tight white halter thing, bare mid-section. Scuffed black shoes with thick soles. Fingernails painted black, embedded with glittery stones.

"Who're you?" he asked.

"This isn't going to be like one of those rape things, is it?"

"Name?"

"Moonbeam."

"First or last?"

"Melody."

"First or last."

"Moonbeam Melody," she snapped.

"Got any identification?"

She grabbed at the backpack.

"Slowly!"

"Stop yelling at me! You're making me nervous!" She unzipped the backpack, rummaged around inside and brought out a purple wallet. When he held out a hand, she reluctantly dropped it in his palm.

He glanced through the wallet, noted her name was Arlene Harlow, and handed it back.

"What are you doing here?" She jammed the wallet inside the backpack and hugged it to her chest.

"Cop." He showed her his ID.

"You creep! You scared the shit out of me! I got mugged in the library last week! Where were you then!"

He put his ID back in his pocket. "What happened?"

She hesitated and he could see her busy little mind making up a lie. "Now's your chance," he said. "Carpe diem."

"Carpe your own diem. Some sleaze stole my backpack."

"Yeah? And what's that?" He touched the toe of his boot to the backpack on the floor.

"I found it in the parking lot."

"Yeah? If I see him I'll shoot him. What are you doing here?"

"I live here." She flounced to the living room, threw herself in an easy chair and crossed her arms. "Don't you have anything better to do than break into people's houses and scare them the fuck to death?"

"How old are you?" he asked.

"Eighteen," she snapped.

"Try again."

"Why?" She eyed him darkly.

"Bus pass is for a minor."

"Sixteen."

He waited. Two beats went by. "Fourteen," she admitted sullenly.

"Fourteen," he repeated. "Going to a Halloween party?"

"No."

"Then why you dressed like that?"

She rolled onto one hip and tugged on the end of the skimpy skirt. "Don't you know anything? This is fashionable."

"For a hooker, maybe. That what you're trying to look like?"

Her pixie face reddened with anger. "What do you know?"

"Well, Ms. *Moonbeam*, being a cop, not too much, but I figure you're not old enough to own this place, so that must mean you're related somehow to the person who does. What's his name?"

"Vincent Egelhoff."

"You live with him?"

She hesitated. "Yes."

"Where is he?"

"You don't know anything, do you? He's dead."

She was right about that.

"A truck slid across the road and smashed into him," she said. "His car went over the cliff and when they got there he'd bled all over the inside and blood spilled out in rivers when they opened the door."

Demarco wondered if slasher movies were this kid's favorite. The one thing he did know about Vincent Egelhoff was that he'd died in a skiing accident. "You don't seem very upset by his death."

"What do you know?"

Right. Sometimes the pain went too deep for the usual show of grief. Sometimes it buried itself and ate at you from the inside.

"Big dumb cop like you came to the school and told the principal and she called me out of class and led me into her inner office and she told me. Unlike you, she had feelings."

"Who's this Egelhoff to you?"

"He's married to my sister."

Okay, Demarco thought, now we're getting somewhere. "What's her name?"

"Gayle." She looked around. "Where is she?"

He could see apprehension start to stir just under the surface. "You live with your sister."

"So?"

"Where are your parents?"

She shrugged. "Tornado flattened the house when I was two days old. It's just Gayle and me."

Ah Christ, he thought wearily. "Your sister is Gayle Egelhoff."

"I just told you that."

"What other relatives do you have?"

She kicked a heel against the carpet. "Just Gayle and me."

"Were you home Friday night?"

"What's it to you?"

"Where were you?"

"Kansas City."

He sent her a look, wondering if she was lying. "What were you doing there?"

"Music Festival. I'm in the Choral Society. We performed. Got a first place."

"And last night?"

"I just told you," she yelled. "Kansas City."

"When did you get back?"

"Duh? I just walked in the door."

"Sit tight." He went into the kitchen.

She could hear him muttering into his radio. Something really, really bad was going on. Her hands started to shake and she jammed them down between the cushion and the arms of the chair. She felt something and pulled it out. Sunglasses. Gayle was always losing things. She tried to swallow and choked. When he came back, she said, "Something happened to Gayle, didn't it?"

He didn't say anything, just looked at her with cop's eyes.

Oh God, she didn't like this. "What happened?"

"Someone's coming. She'll tell you."

"You tell me! What happened! Is she hurt? Bad? Where is she? In the hospital? Is she dead?"

Nothing went on in the cop's face, but she knew. Something really really bad happened to Gayle and she was—Gayle was—

Roaring started in her ears and rushed over her. The edges of her vision got kind of fuzzy and then—

Next thing she knew, the cop had his hand on the back of her neck and she was folded double. She couldn't get up. Oh God, oh God. He's going to kill me. Oh God, please help me. I promise I'll be good. I promise—

He let go. She straightened, took a breath and screamed.

"Take it easy," he said. "You're all right. You just fainted."

"I did not." She clamped her teeth. Cold, it was really really cold in here. Her teeth had started to chatter. "My sister! What happened!"

"Another officer is on her way. When she gets here—"

"I'm fine. See. I'm calm." She sucked in all the air she could find and blew it out slowly. "Tell me now! She's dead, isn't she? Gayle's dead and you won't tell me. What happened to her? Is she dead?"

His cop's eyes bored into her like X-ray vision to read the inside of her brain.

"Yes," he finally said. "She probably died of a head injury."

"What happened?"

"That's what we're trying to find out."

"Where is she? Should I—?" She jumped up and started for the door.

He caught her around the waist and plopped her right back in the chair. "You need to stay here for a little bit."

"Why? 'Cause something's wrong about how she died? Tell me!"

So he told her and it was like her mind started making all this static and she couldn't hear. One thing was really really clear though. Gayle was dead. Somebody had hit her and shoved her in the trunk of the car.

She had to get away. She didn't know what the cops would do with her, but she knew they wouldn't just go away and let her stay here by herself, even though she was perfectly capable. They'd make her go someplace. Not to jail, she wasn't so dumb she believed that, but someplace that would be the same. They'd make her stay there. She wouldn't be allowed to go anywhere. She couldn't see her friends.

"I need some water." She started to get up.

"Stay. I'll get it."

How was she going to get away from Dipshit in there? Meanest-looking cop she'd ever seen. Face probably made by an ax hacking away at stone. She considered crying and nixed it. Probably wouldn't reach the heart of Dirtbag in there. Probably didn't have one.

"You mind if I let the dog in?" He was at the sink filling a glass with water when she darted past, fumbled the door open and took off running.

17

Fucking son of a bitch! Moonbeam slithered under the wooden fence next door, her scarf caught on a jagged board. It ripped when she yanked it free. She moved, not so fast somebody'd think she was running from something, but fast enough so she'd leave space behind her. Beef-brained cop! No way she'd let herself be jerked around by children's services. Line up foster homes. Shit, make her an unpaid servant or a punching bag for some rapist pervert. She upped the pace.

Holding herself tight on no running, she cut across Birch Street and made a right on California. Row of televisions in Nathan's Electronics all flickering with the same thing. Ducking her head, she walked along by the window, until a picture of Gayle came on. She stepped inside. News program, talking about Gayle. She stood there watching until the sales guy gave her a look and started her way, then she lit out.

Only when she heard the sounds of the river doing its rushing, sloshing roar thing, did she realize how far she'd come. She heard something else. Car? She listened. Coming up behind! She slid off the road into the ditch alongside.

Cop car. Pressing up against the dirt, she kept her head down until it was way past. When she figured she'd be permanently deformed if she didn't move, she poked her head up. Coast clear. She clambered up the embankment, dusted mud and dead leaves and shit off her skirt, wincing as she gently brushed over the scrape on her side where her top had slid up when she dived in the ditch.

The wind had picked up and she was way out here and all without a coat. Still headed toward the river, plodding slowly, she kicked around her brain cells to think where she might flop for the night. It wouldn't get dark for hours yet, but it was getting awfully cold.

Hypothermia would set in if she didn't think of something. Stupid cop. Think. Anybody walking around on a day like this without a coat would be picked up for a loony. She was always good at taking care of herself, why wasn't she getting a flash? Brain freeze.

Library? Nah. They probably searched before they locked up. Ladies room? Not a fab plan, but, at least, something. She trudged along the edge of the road as it curved around and then clambered down the embankment to the river's edge. The water looked dark and cold. Her nose started to drip.

Rubbing it vigorously, she clamped her teeth. She never cried. Okay, so she did when Vince died, but that was last month when she was only thirteen and she had Gayle and Gayle had cried. On October 14, she'd turned fourteen and she still had Gayle. Now it was October 26 and she didn't have Gayle. She didn't have anybody.

"God damn you, Gayle. Why'd you have to go and get dead for? Shit shit shit!" The river kept rushing away to wherever it rushed away to as though she wasn't even there. She found a rock and threw it in. It hardly even made a sound with all the rushing and sloshing.

When she was back on the road, kicking rocks and hiking toward town, she thought of where she could go.

"You ran away from the cops?" Sherry, stomach down on one of the twin beds, bunched the pillow beneath her chest and put her arms around it. "You're a fugitive! Wow! You're going to have to keep running and running, like that guy in that old movie. I'll help!" She tossed the pillow aside and scooted around to sit up, leaning forward eagerly.

"They always need somebody they can call, like in emergencies, or to find out what's going on, or if they have a narrow escape and stuff."

Moonbeam lay flat out on her back on the other twin bed, wrist over her forehead, staring at the ceiling. A long dusty spider web hung down in the left corner. Sherry's mom didn't worry so much about spider webs. She was kind of loose about things and was always so busy she didn't pay attention. That was why Moonbeam thought she could come here.

"Hey, you're bleeding."

Moonbeam twisted around to look at the scrape on her side. "I fell."

"Gosh, you want me to get a bandage or something?"

"Naw. It's okay. I probably ought to go so you don't have to lie."

"I'll never turn you in, Arlene, no matter—"

"Don't call me that!"

"Oh, right, sorry, Moonbeam, but do you think this is a really good idea? I mean, you can stay here and all. Mom has a date tonight and she's okay, like if I told her I had a friend staying over and all, but, you know, it'll probably be on the news, about your sister and they're looking for you and everything."

"Yeah, I know. I just wanted a place to get out of the cold."

Sherry lay back on the bed. "I'm really sorry about your sister. What happened, do you know?"

"Somebody whacked her and stuffed her in the car trunk."

Sherry gasped. "Why?"

"Don't know, but I bet it has something to do with that time, you know, a million years ago in that fire where Vince got hurt and everything."

"Why do you think that?" Sherry wriggled down and dangled her legs off the foot of the bed.

"That Wakely guy, you know, the one that got all crippled and has to be in a wheelchair? He came to the house a bunch of times. They talked, him and Vince, all serious with their heads together and if I came in or anything, they just shut up and didn't say anything until I left."

"You know what they talked about?"

Moonbeam put the crook of her arm across her eyes. "Not exactly, but it had something to do with Governor Garrett. 'Cause I heard his name a couple times. Gayle and Vince were acting weird. They whispered, you know? I hated it when they whispered."

"Oh gosh, I'm really sorry about Gayle. I mean, after your parents died and everything and then Vince and now Gayle."

"I didn't even know my parents really. I was only a baby." But she knew one thing. Gayle had told her their mom called her my little love-a-doll. For some stupid reason that almost made her cry. She cleared her throat. "And Rosie's gone."

"What happened to her?"

"How should I know? That cop probably took her to the dog pound."

"Oh no, they wouldn't do that."

"Where is she then? She wasn't there when I got home."

Sherry kicked her heels against the legs of the bed. "That guy that got all paralyzed and everything? Wakely? You think he could have done that to Gayle? Maybe he can walk around just like everybody and he's only pretending."

Moonbeam squelched her with a look.

Sherry flopped over on her back. "Well, it always happens in books."

Moonbeam squeezed her eyes shut real tight, opened wide, shut them, and rubbed them.

"Arlene—I mean, Moonbeam, you might as well go back. I mean, I know it'll be icky and all that, but what're you going to do? You can't just—"

"Yes, I can," Moonbeam shouted. "Just shut up a minute so I can think."

"There's that house that's for sale. You know, the one where the Hudsons lived before they moved."

"Sherry, that's perfect. Can you lend me some clothes?"

"Sure."

"Just a sweatshirt and jeans, and maybe a jacket, if you can. I didn't have time to get anything and it's cold out."

"Arlene—I mean, Moonbeam, maybe you should think about this. I mean, what are you going to do? You can't stay by yourself—"

"I can take care of myself!"

"I know, but what about food? And clean clothes? And school and stuff? And could you really stay in that empty house? I mean, what if it's haunted or something?"

"Don't be stupid, it's not haunted."

"Well, but—"

"They'll put me in a foster home!"

"Think about it, Ar—Moonbeam. Wouldn't that be better than all by yourself? Come on, really, we could still be friends and—"

"We couldn't be friends if I got shipped off someplace. Like Alaska."

"What are you going to do?" Sherry yanked open a drawer, rummaged around and tugged out a sweatshirt which she tossed.

Moonbeam pulled it on. "There's such a thing as an emancipated teenager."

"Yeah, but that's for somebody who has a job and can pay for everything, like a place to live and food and stuff." Sherry handed her a pair of jeans. "They'll be kinda' big."

"I just need to figure out what to do." Moonbeam put on the jeans and cinched them tight with the belt Sherry gave her.

"You're going to get in trouble," Sherry said. "I know you will. You always do and now Gayle and, you know, everything—" Sherry threw up her hands. "And you need money, you can't—"

"I got Gayle's ATM card." Moonbeam didn't have any such thing, but she figured that would shut Sherry up.

Sherry took a deep breath. "You stole it?"

"I did not steal it. She gave it to me."

Sherry looked at her weird. "Why?"

"In case I needed something when I was in Kansas City."

"Oh gosh, I forgot all about the music festival. How was it? Are you hungry? Let's get something to eat."

"It was great." She was going to legally change her name to Moonbeam Melody and be a famous singer. "If you ever tell anybody where I am, Sherry, I swear I'll never speak to you again."

"Moonbeam Harlow, you swear too much."

18

$\mathcal{M}$onday was another glorious fall day with an endless sky blue enough to incite writing poetry. The crisp air smelled tangy and held a hint of coming winter, of the long cold sleep, a preparing for dying. The heavy sense of melancholy that had dogged Susan was with her as she jogged campus paths drenched in autumn sunlight. This golden light of early afternoon was slanted low and hit her in the eyes. The end of daylight saving time yesterday meant the sun would sink earlier and darkness would creep in. There was an ache in her soul that responded to darkness. She was waiting for it.

Slowing as she came up to Eleventh Street, she took the four blocks to her house in a fast walk. In an hour she was to meet Sean for lunch at the Sunflower. She felt like skipping. Screw it, she wasn't hungry, she couldn't afford the time, she had work to do. After a shower, she got so far as picking up the phone to call him, but put it down before she dialed. He'd simply come and drag her out. God only knew why he felt she was in some emotional crisis and he had to get on his white horse and gallop to the rescue.

To prove him wrong, she made an effort. Blue wool dress the color of her eyes and a little makeup added to cover the dark circles beneath them. What she really wanted to do was put on old jeans, an equally old sweatshirt, and listen to Bach. There was nothing like Bach when you were wading through the megrims.

At the Sunflower, she blinked as she walked into the dimly lighted dining room and ordered a cup of coffee. He was ten minutes late.

He apologized, kissed her cheek and slid in opposite her. He reached across the table and picked up her hand. "I figured you for a call and cancel."

"Would you have let me?"

"Not a chance."

The flickering candle in the glass globe on the table sent shadows across his face and she couldn't read what was in his eyes, but she'd known him forever and she could tell something was scratching at his surface blandness. "Why are you late?"

"Fury of a disappointed woman."

"You have a woman to infuriate?"

"Why should that excuse me from pain?"

"I'm sorry about Lynn."

He shook his head. "You were right. I should never have married her."

"I never said that."

"You didn't have to, dear heart, you were thinking it so loudly, the words were glowing on your forehead. I just talked with Hannah. She's hurting. I'm more angry than heartbroken. I knew it was coming right after Hannah was born. Babies are so squally and messy and time-consuming. It just wasn't Lynn's thing."

When the waiter came, Sean ordered grapefruit juice with ice and asked the waiter to give them a minute. "Could be worse, right? I could be going through life being called Cathal."

"Cathal? Who would name a child that?"

"My father. During the Troubles there was a man—"

"The *Troubles?*"

"Of course, The Troubles. Cathal Brugha, leading honcho in the radical side of the Irish Volunteers. I think his name was originally Charles Burgess, or something. He thought the Irish derivative

103

sounded better, given his line of work. Birthday July eighteen, same as mine. Dad felt it was fitting I have his name."

"Why am I not calling you Cathal?"

"Mom wouldn't allow it. You'd know all this stuff too, if you weren't tainted by pale Nordic blood."

"Dutch," she said. The genes of her pale sweet mother.

When the waiter returned with Sean's juice, he lifted it and touched it to her coffee cup. *"Slainte."*

"Shouldn't you be drinking Irish whiskey?"

He set the glass down, leaned in and picked up her hand again, his was cold from the ice in his glass. "Tell me what's wrong, kiddo?"

"What's wrong." She looked up at the ceiling. "Well, let's see. I have a woman killed and stuffed into a trunk and the governor popping in and out of town so I have to deploy resources needed elsewhere and have manpower available for him and I'm a stranger in a strange land. Is that enough?"

"I'm not talking about that and you know it. Spill it, Susan."

Nostalgia stuck its claws in her throat so deep the sweetness turned to pain. Daniel would say that when he wanted to know what was on her mind. *Okay, Susan, spill it.* "I've been dreaming of Daniel lately."

"Bad dreams?"

"Disturbing." She traced a finger in the circle of wetness left from his glass after he picked it up. "I see him jogging on the beach through the fog, but I can't catch up with him. I call. He doesn't hear, or sometimes he turns and sees me and sprints away. Or he's hidden in fog, the fog thins, and he has no face."

"It doesn't take Jung to figure that. You simply didn't know him long enough to know him well."

"Yeah." She hurt for all it was and all it wasn't in a time that faded more and more every year.

"Widow's fantasy," he said. "The perfect man, the perfect love, the perfect marriage." He lifted her hand and kissed the back of it. "He was a man, Susan, a good man, but a man with virtues and flaws, just like all the rest of us. The thing about Daniel is death came at

104

that wonderful exciting and passionate moment when the world was shiny with perfection."

Memories—fragments like running through a kaleidoscope very fast—struck her so keenly she had to fight to keep from bending over and clutching her abdomen.

"Sometimes in the dreams, he's just ahead of me and I run to catch up, but I never can. He's always ahead and he keeps going."

Sean tipped his glass and swallowed the last of the juice, then rattled the ice cubes. "You know what your problem is?"

"I have a feeling you're going to tell me."

"You're lonely."

"Alone," she pointed out. "Not lonely. There's a difference."

"Ah, Susan, you slid into being alone and after a time it got to be familiar and safe and then, my love, it got to be comforting."

"I can rely on it."

"That's the point, it worked for you. You got used to being alone and you made an acceptable little nest, you settled in and let life go by, but it's time, kiddo. Get a life."

She gave him a sweet smile instead of saying mind your own business. "If you're anyone to go by, getting a life has more thorns than roses."

"Yeah well, you caught me at a bad time."

"Want to trade places?"

"Hell no. You don't have a sex life."

"What if I get one?"

"We'll renegotiate."

Sean stood with the rest of the press pool clustered on the tarmac, waiting for Garrett's motorcade. Boom mikes and minicams, print reporters and television cookies with their own cameramen. Each day the pool rotated alphabetically by news organization, networks, magazines, radio and newspapers. They were all here to gather the coverage for the entire group. They got file film, bits of news, sound bites from the candidate and passed it around. Ever since the assassination of JFK, they were here to record history. Robert Kennedy shot, George Wallace wounded, attempt on Ronald Reagan.

They were keeping up the death watch. Who would be the lucky ones to catch history in the making? Up to chance.

An ambulance waited. Highway patrolman Phil Baker had a choreographed plan all worked out should the governor get shot. One late night in a bar somewhere, Sean had asked him what the drill was. Baker told him the closest cops would shield the Governor's body, everybody else goddamn stayed right where they were in case of a second assassin. Malcolm X died because his bodyguards got snookered away by a distraction. Capture the shooter, alive if possible. Get the governor in the ambulance and to a hospital. Phil made it his business to know where the nearest hospital was and the fastest way to get there. Ten minutes, at the outside. If the wound wasn't fatal, there was every chance the governor would survive. Of course, there was always the mortal wound, the one that hit the vital spot. Phil said he had nightmares about these hospital runs.

A black limo sedately rolled onto the tarmac. Like an amoeba, the press pool surged forward. The governor, surrounded by troopers, headed for the twin engine plane. The cops used the press pool in whatever figuring they did to keep the candidate safe. They recognized faces and moved on. Strange faces stood out. Sean thought, if it became necessary, they wouldn't hesitate to use any one of the press to save the individual they were protecting.

The pool shouted questions. Garrett, flanked by Todd Haviland, his campaign manager, shook hands with local cops and answered a few questions. Hadley Cane, press secretary, was listening sharply, ready to deflect, twist, or redirect. Haviland kept the governor moving. Garrett must be late again, he usually was because of his habit of stopping to talk with people.

With Haviland nudging from the rear, the governor went up the flight of stairs into the little plane. Bernie Quaid was the last to get on before the engines fired, the props whirred and the plane started rolling. It gathered speed and lifted off.

Sean noticed a middle-aged woman in tan trousers and brown sweater watching until the plane disappeared in the deep blue distance. She looked familiar somehow. Where the hell had he seen her before?

19

⸺

*E*m climbed in her car and leaned her head on the seatback to wait until her heart slowed. All the time now, she felt queasy. And so tired. Sometimes she wondered if she'd have the strength to keep going. She'd be glad when it was all over. Antacids were in her purse somewhere. She rummaged in it until she found them and popped two in her mouth. The chalk taste was bitter and she wished she had some water. With a sigh, she turned on the ignition and drove away.

For hours that morning, she'd made phone calls, thirty-five of them. Twenty contacts and twelve Garrett supporters. Working so hard to get votes for a man who wouldn't be alive to benefit from them seemed a twisted irony that somehow stood for the way the world was.

The young woman working next to her, pretty young woman, blond hair pulled back in a ponytail, soft blue eyes fired with enthusiasm, reminded Em of Alice Ann. Tears came to Em's eyes. She had a great needy longing to talk with somebody about her daughter, but there was no one. Not even Father Frank. If he knew what was in her heart, he'd first counsel her, tell her what a sin she was contemplating and try to change her mind. Even the thought of it was a sin. When he couldn't sway her, he'd tell the police.

Em had gone to church, regularly and full of faith, every Sunday, did everything the church told her. It was the priest who had taught that God loved the weak, the young, the innocent.

The unborn baby. She clenched one hand into a fist. Where was God when Kirby Vosse bought a gun? Where was God when Kirby murdered Alice Ann and Alice Ann's baby? Now Em had to put things right. If she went to hell for it, then that's just the way it would be.

"Don't worry, Alice Ann, I'm going to take care of this. I won't let you down a second time."

Em drove and drove without seeing the gun shop. Worry mounting that she might have gotten the address wrong, she pulled over, found the map and spread it out over the steering wheel. Glancing through the windshield, she spotted a street sign for Hollis and found it on her map. At the country club, even though she feared she might have gotten lost, she kept going and just past the golf course she saw Turtle Lake Drive. With a sigh, she followed the road until she thought surely she must have gone too far. No, there it was. Winston's Gun World.

The place was huge and empty except for the small, fit-looking man with sandy-gray hair seated at a desk behind the counter. A desk lamp shone down on the pieces of gray metal he was picking up and wiping lovingly with oil. A gun, she thought, taken apart to be cleaned. The loud clicking of her heels on the tile floor made her self-conscious. Nervously, she peered at the racks of rifles and glass-fronted cases of handguns lining the walls. Black, bluish-gray or silver, each one deadly, if used right.

He put down his oily rag and came to the counter. "May I help you?"

"Yes." Her heart was beating so loud she thought he surely must hear it. "I'd like to buy a handgun." Because that sounded sinister to her ears, she added. "For protection."

"Did you have anything in mind?"

"A nine millimeter?"

"That's a pretty heavy gun. You might want to try a thirty-eight." He bent down and took a small silver gun from a tray and placed it on the counter in front of her.

It didn't look very lethal. It didn't even look real. It looked like a child's toy. It was small with a short barrel. Her grandchild, if she'd been allowed to have a grandchild, might have played with something like this. She didn't even know if Alice Ann's baby had been a boy or a girl.

"I'd like to see a nine millimeter, please."

He walked down the counter and retrieved another gun. He put that one in front of her. *Oh, yes.* This one was black and sleek and looked extremely lethal. She ran her fingertips along its length and was surprised at the warmth. She'd expected it to be cold and then realized the case lights shining down on it would give it warmth. She could feel herself growing stronger just knowing it would be in her pocket, or her purse.

"I'll take this one," she said.

"Do you know how to use it?"

"I plan to take instructions."

He nodded. "I just need your signature and in fifteen days you can pick it up."

"Fifteen days?"

"After that guy with Reagan got shot in the head, they passed this law."

"But what if I need it now?" The pathetic wail in her voice didn't change his mind.

"Sorry," he said. "I'd help you if I could."

She'd better pull herself together or he'd remember her as some desperate crazy woman who tried to buy a gun. "Well," she said. She gave him a smile that hurt her face and told him she'd be back. When she got back in her car, she felt like sobbing. Fifteen days was way too long. Jackson Garrett would be gone off somewhere by then. Who knows where he'd be. How could she get close enough to kill him, if she didn't know where he was?

Guns were available on the streets in any big city. She sighed. Hampstead wasn't a big city. Kansas City was near enough to drive to, but it wasn't all that big either. Kansas City, Missouri, was though and it was just across the river from Kansas City, Kansas. For a moment, she was excited, then she came to her senses. She wouldn't know the right street corner, and she wouldn't know the right person to ask. She couldn't simply drive to the seediest area of town and go up to any sinister-looking character.

That was apt to get her killed. She didn't care if she was killed, but she didn't want it to happen until she'd accomplished her mission. After that, she fully expected a police officer to shoot her. Depressed, she went home. The motel room was damp and chilly. She turned on the machine in the window that supplied both warm and cool air and stretched out on the bed. Just as she was drifting off she had a thought.

Pawn shop. Maybe if she was really meek and pathetic and frightened by a man who was stalking her, somebody there would sell her a gun.

She didn't know if Hampstead even had a pawn shop, but if it didn't, there must be plenty in Kansas City. She called the office and asked if they had a Kansas City, Missouri, phone book. The elderly woman in charge brought it to her and told her to bring it back when she was through. It was the only one they had. Em rifled through pages.

All right. The Pawn and Shooters Palace.

Em drove to Kansas City, crossed the river into Missouri and tried to find the address. It took her a while, but she finally found it on the edge of town near fast food places, used car lots, and small eating places that probably served food poisoning with its meals. The Pawn and Shooters Palace was a narrow shop with a metal folding grate across the door, sandwiched between a tattoo parlor and a boarded-up beautician's shop.

She tried to see inside the pawn shop but the glass part of the door was so smudged and dirty it was difficult to see much of anything. A light was on inside, she could tell that much from the faint glow somewhere in the rear of the shop. A teenaged black kid sloped up behind her. Startled, she looked around at the dark deserted street.

"Yo, lady, you going in or you growing roots?"

She seemed unable to move.

He lifted his upper lip to expose his teeth in a sneering smile and pushed around her to open the door and go in. After hesitating, dithering, she went in also. I hate dithering, she told herself.

Inside, there was so much—she didn't know what to call it, merchandise?—piled everywhere that the two narrow windows were blocked. The teenager had melted away somewhere in all the gloom and the clutter.

"Help you?" The man sitting at a desk behind the counter rose and came toward her. He was short, barely five feet, and had some kind of disability that made it difficult for him to walk. He shuffled and didn't put much weight on one foot.

"I'd like a nine-millimeter handgun," she said like she knew what she was talking about.

"Let's see what I have." He showed her two that were exactly what she wanted. Sleek and deadly. She chose one. Then he went through the same thing about forms and a fifteen-day waiting period. She tried pleading, she tried crying, she tried offering money.

"Can't do it," he said. "It's the law."

"Law." Her voice sounded sharp and disgusted, as though she'd stepped in something unpleasant. "I don't think much of the law."

"I could say the same, but it won't change anything."

Defeated, she left the alien claustrophobic place and walked back toward her car. Clouds scudded across the tiny sliver of moon, and the street light was far down the street. She didn't realize she'd parked so far away. Why hadn't she brought a flashlight?

"Whatcha doin', lady?" The whispered words raised the hairs on the back of her neck.

She whirled, heart fluttering in her throat like a caged bird. The kid, the black teenager—African-American. She didn't even want to think anything that might offend him. He wasn't tall, only about her height, skinny, and dressed in baggy jeans and a black shirt. He seemed to jiggle constantly, like he was dancing to music nobody else heard. She'd been stupid to come here, even stupider to come after dark and wander around by herself. Now she was really frightened. Not of dying. She was going to die soon anyway, but frightened of dying before she accomplished what she needed to do.

"Got somethin' to sell?"

"No, no," she said, backing away.

"You was there to buy sumthin then?"

"Yes, I was. But—but—he didn't have what I wanted, so I guess I'll have to go elsewhere."

"Elsewhere, huh? What was you wantin'?"

She swallowed.

"You can tell me. We're in the same kind of bidness, old Jed back there and me. You tell me, maybe I can help you."

"Oh, I really don't think so, I must—"

"Lady," his tone all of a sudden got clipped and impatient. "I don't have all night. What did you want?"

She took a breath hoping it would help her words come out steady, not quavering like a scared old woman. If he was going to kill her, she couldn't do anything about it. She couldn't beat him up and she couldn't outrun him, so what did it matter if she told him. She shouldn't have come here. So stupid. *I'm sorry, Alice Ann. I can't carry out this mission any better than I could protect my baby.* "A gun," she said, proud of herself when she heard her voice steady.

"Little old bitch like you want a gun?"

"That's what I wanted, yes."

"You got money?"

"No, no, not very much. If you'll excuse me, I really must go now."

"How much you got?"

"Hardly any. Please, excuse me. My—my friend is waiting for me, I mustn't keep him. He gets so impatient."

"How much?" He grabbed her purse, scrabbled around inside and came out with her wallet.

"Take it," she said. "It's yours. Take it."

With a wide grin, he snatched all the bills. "What kinda gun you want?"

"Nine-millimeter." She could hear the defeat in her tone.

He sneered. "Any particular brand?"

"Doesn't matter."

He laughed. The whole time, he was jiggling, leaping and jumping around inside, keeping time to music only he could feel. "What's yo address?"

She rattled off the first thing that came to mind. It happened to be the address of her bank at home. He tossed the purse to her. She bent to pick it up and scuttled away like something that lived under a rock. With every step, she feared she'd feel a knife in her back and she'd drop without a sound. Then who would get justice for Alice Ann?

She slid in her car, managed to get the key in the ignition and drove away. In the rearview mirror, she saw nothing but the dark deserted street. The boy had disappeared. Tears made everything so blurred she couldn't see where she was going and she had to stop and get herself in control.

When she finally got back to the motel, she couldn't find her room key and had to ask the receptionist for another. Plainly irritated, the woman gave her a new key but it came with a lecture about being more careful.

20

---

*C*ass woke up stiff and cold Monday morning. Bad night, worse than she'd had in a long time. All night she'd sat in Aunt Jean's rocker, revolver in her hand, rocking and listening to the creak of the floorboards. She fought the voice that urged her to end it, do it now, put the barrel in her mouth and pull the trigger. When she'd dozed off, her hand relaxed and the revolver had fallen in her lap. This time morning won. She woke with a start to gray light coming through the windows.

All day, she carried the gun, put it on the sink in the bathroom when she took a shower, on the bedside table near the cuff-link box with the pinch of Ted and Laura's ashes when she was dressed. In her pocket when she went out. She walked, up the street, along the storefronts, down to the river, stood and gazed at the water. She could simply step in. When it got dark, she made her way home.

The dog rushed to her, making little glad cries of joy. Monty the cat complained loudly of neglect and hunger. She petted the cat, gave the dog a hug, and went to the desk. As she opened the bottom drawer, the remaining four bullets rolled with a dull metallic clink. She swung out the cylinder and removed the two she'd put in last night. Four more days until Halloween. She could wait. She put the revolver back in the drawer, then one at a time, lined the bullets up along the barrel. The shiny brass jackets caught the light from the lamp.

The dog needed to go out desperately and Cass opened the kitchen door for her. When the dog came back in, she fed both the animals and changed clothes. Sometime today she must have fallen, her wool pants were muddy. She couldn't settle, wandered through the house. Anxiety hovered just around the shadows of her mind, creeping forward, crawling back. And she was afraid. Of what? She didn't know. What in God's name was there to be afraid of? Nothing, except herself. It was late, she was tired. She tried to make herself comfortable in Jean's wingback chair, the one placed for perfect television viewing. The dog flopped at her feet. It would let her know if anyone was outside. A tree branch tapped along a window like a finger trying to get her attention. The curtains were open. The window was black, revealing only her ghostly reflection. The dog hadn't moved. It didn't act like anyone was watching them, waiting outside for the right moment.

"Waiting for what? No one's out there!"

She switched off the lamp so she wouldn't be lit up like a stage. New locks, she'd get new locks on all the doors. Windows, too. Then she'd be safe. And the dog would bark. It might even protect her. She looked down at it. It looked back at her and swished its tail back and forth. Foolish to be worried about what would come at her from outside. It was from inside herself that danger would come.

Getting up so abruptly, she startled the dog, she jerked the curtains closed. Dark. Comforting, safe, no one could see her. She took in deep breaths, right, now *let it out slowly through your mouth, think of an empty beach with soft white sand, the surf whispering low—*

The exercises she'd been taught to slow her heartbeat and ward off a panic attack weren't working. She was here all by herself with no drugs. Someone was outside creeping up to the door, waiting, listening—

"This is stupid."

Opening the curtain, she stared out into the darkness. There was nothing there but a small crescent of moon. She dropped into the chair and determinedly picked up the book. Concentrate. Her heart hammered, her chest grew tight, a light buzz started in her head. Despair built into a sense of terrible disaster so close to doom she felt she would die.

Nonsense. I won't die. I've been through this a million times. I won't die!

"I am forty-six years old," she said aloud to wash out the rising roar in her head. "I had a husband. Long after I gave up hope I had a child. I was in hell and I survived. I can survive this. My heart will not stop. I will not be shredded to a victim by a panic attack. No!"

The buzzing in her mind made her dizzy, her head ached. She stumbled through the kitchen, fumbled with the lock on the door until she thought she would scream, got it open and fled out into the night. A rock tripped her and she nearly went sprawling. When she reached the circle of maple trees, she dropped, scooted her back against one and put her arms around her knees. Head down, she pulled in air, feebly trying to use visualization exercises to neutralize a hurricane.

Finally, finally, the terror reached a peak and began the slow climb down the other side. Finally, sanity began to return, her heart began to slow, the dizziness receded and the buzzing in her mind faded. She didn't die.

Raising her head, she noticed the dog beside her. It licked her icy fingers. Each time you survive one of these attacks, you get stronger. That's what the shrinks said. She wasn't so sure. When one came, it was like an old friend and every fiber of her being urged her to accept the invitation, throw away rational thought and give in to total mindless panic. Run. Blindly. Anywhere. Because it promised the blessed relief of oblivion.

When it was over, she was always tired, lethargic, feeling like she'd recovered from a bout of flu that had left her drained and weak. A breeze stirred the maple leaves. She strained to hear. It sounded almost—if she let her mind float—she could almost hear echoes of Laura's laughter.

After a long time—a minute? an hour? five hours?—she shivered and noticed how damp she was from sitting on the wet ground. She uncoiled herself, went back inside with the dog padding along beside her, peeled off her damp jeans, and pulled on a warm robe.

Roaring with avenging fury, the dog scrambled to the door and a minute later the bell rang. Terror reached out and sent a rigid finger touching Cass's heart. Not two attacks in one night! She shoved the dog out of the way and yanked open the door.

"I hope I didn't wake you."

"Bernie! What are you doing here?"

He stepped inside and the dog nuzzled his hand, making little crooning sounds. "I came to bring you to the meeting."

He patted the dog's sides and swung her head back and forth. "Hey, Carmen. Figured out I'm one of the good guys, have you?" The dog slathered him with exuberant kisses.

"Carmen?" Cass said.

"When she whimpers like that she sounds like she's singing. Everybody deserves a name. I figured I'd give you some help with it."

"She's not mine," Cass said.

"Okay. So until she's somebody else's, you need something to call her."

Cass dropped it, she could see she wasn't going to win. "What meeting? It's bedtime."

"Yeah, it is. Remember, I told you when politicians work? We just got back from Omaha and something's come up." He went through the arched entryway into the dining room and picked up the roll of tape sitting on the stacked boxes ready for donation to the church rummage sale, that long day's work emptying the attic and Aunt Jean's closets still waiting. "Not all unpacked yet?"

"That's stuff I'm getting rid of. Look, Bernie. I've thought it over and I really don't want to get involved in a political campaign. I'm not going to be around long enough to do you any good. I wish you all the best of luck, but I'm not interested. Find someone else."

"I don't find people, I just do what I'm told. I was told to bring you." He tipped his head and studied her face. "What else have you got to do?" he said gently.

I have to hang on, she thought. Because she was losing them. She had grieved for Ted and Laura with a keening ache and echoing emptiness, a pain as sharp as pulling her arm through a coil of barbed wire. The pain wouldn't go away. The staggering loss continued to hit her with ever-new disbelief and vacant despair. Every day for the last year, the pain of their loss waited in hiding to leap out and grab her by the throat, to choke the life from her. But now, far worse, the times and duration were growing less. Once, she could see them clearly, she had long conversations with Ted. She saw Laura's smile and heard her laugh and heard her singing to Monty. Now there were only brief flashes, unmoving, frozen like old snapshots. She was losing them and she wouldn't be able to live.

"You might want to put some clothes on," Bernie said. "If you go the way you are, the night guards might get the wrong idea. I'll stay here with Carmen."

Despite his coaxing, Carmen the dog followed Cass to the bedroom and watched nervously as she got out a clean pair of jeans.

"We need to talk about abandonment issues," Cass told her wearily. She pulled on the jeans, zipped them up, stuck her head in a sweater and fought her arms into the sleeves, then slipped a jacket from a hanger. How did it happen that she always ended up doing what Bernie wanted?

"I can't weld myself to some political campaign," she told him as she slid into his car. "I have responsibilities. I can't just take off for God knows where at a moment's notice. I can't—"

"Right. What else?"

"Monty—I can't just leave him. My daughter's cat . . ." My sweet child, my darling Laura. "And now I have some stray dog that somebody injured and—"

"I'm just asking you to come to a meeting, not to slaughter your pets."

"I'd have to be away for long periods of time."

"There are kennels just made for that situation."

"Monty in a kennel?" Cass was horrified. "He'd hate it."

"There are people who do this for a living. They come and stay in your house while you're gone, and give cats and dogs the loving care they've come to expect."

"If anything should happen to me, you'd take care of them?"

"Absolutely."

"Promise?"

"I promise," he said solemnly.

Relief left her feeling lighter. One thing that had pulled her through the night was Monty, the dog, too—now she didn't have to worry. Bernie had no idea how soon he'd have to keep that promise. "Why me? I can understand why you're doing this. You need to make a living—" Something she no longer needed to worry about.

Bernie laughed. "You call this living? I could make more money selling shoes."

"Then why do it?"

"I've been a political hack all my life."

"So you must like it."

"Are you kidding? In the good times, it's vicious and dehumanizing. In the bad times, it's painful and brutal and stressful beyond bearing."

"Then why?" she repeated.

"You get committed, swept away. It's like a disease. Like those people who can't quit gambling? It's this huge gamble. If you win, oh man, do you win. You get the biggest prize imaginable."

"If you lose?"

"You lose everything important to you. Privacy, dignity, reputation."

"Sounds risky."

He glanced at her. "I know something devastating happened to you and you've wrapped a thick layer of numbness all tight around you, but underneath you're a romantic. So is Garrett. That's what it takes. To be a real candidate and a good leader." Bernie shot her a glance, probably to see how she was taking this. "It's not enough to want to make a difference, you have to imagine that you can."

"You're the romantic."

Bernie flashed a quick smile. "If I had any sense I'd be working for the president. He's been at it forever, he rarely makes a mistake, and he'd kill his own mother if that would get him a win. And if the polls showed it would fly, he'd pepper TV with ads showing him sobbing buckets at the pain her death caused him. Garrett is honest and passionate and studies the polls to figure out how to get the voters to understand his side, not manipulate them just to get their vote. I've waited fifteen years for a candidate like him."

It was after nine by the time they got out to Jack's farm. A trooper looked at Bernie, looked at Cass, checked the car and waved them through. The living room had the feel of after-party fatigue. Low-wattage lamps were on at either end of the couch where Jack sat with his wife, Molly. Nora, Molly's personal assistant, sat in an easy chair at a right angle to the couch. Platters of drying sandwiches and cheese and leftover fruit sat on end tables and coffee tables. Jack was half-watching a football game on the television set with the sound low. When she and Bernie came in, he looked up and smiled at her. That old smile she knew so well, and despite all the years that had gone by, and all the water under the bridge, she felt a tug of pain, like an old guitar string that could still give a twang if someone strummed it.

Molly must have felt something in the air, she gave Cass a hard stare that said keep your hands off my property. Molly had nothing to worry about. Cass had no intention of putting her hands anywhere near Jack. Just as well, she thought. She got the impression Molly could be dangerous if she felt threatened.

"Who's playing?" Todd asked. The campaign manager, dark hair hanging over his forehead, glasses sliding down his nose, was sitting on the floor with his back to the wall, forearms resting on bent knees. Tie pulled loose, shirt cuffs turned back, he didn't sound like he cared very much.

"Kansas State against Nebraska State."

"Jack will watch any kind of football," Bernie said.

She knew that about Jack. A fistful of nostalgia formed low in her chest. She felt sadness for the two kids they had been, she and Jack, long ago. Full of youth, sure of themselves, happy and eager for each other, for life. When she sat in the gold easy chair, Bernie retrieved a chair from the dining room and placed it beside her.

It occurred to her there was no bent figure in a wheelchair present. "Where's Wakely?" she asked Bernie.

"His place."

Leon Massy, Jack's media consultant, came in and squeezed into an easy chair that wasn't up to containing his bulk. His dark suit was wrinkled and his tie, red with small flags waving all over it, was loosened. He dropped a stack of newspapers on the coffee table with a loud thunk. *The Washington Post* was on top. "We got a problem."

"It's more than a problem," Bernie said. "It's a catastrophe."

"Worse than my being a homo-sex-u-al?" Jack said.

"I got a call from Sean Donovan."

"What'd he want?" Todd wanted to know.

"He works for *NewsWorld*, different deadline. He told me he got a call from Jerry MacEnrow at the *Wall Street Journal*. They know you met with Halderbreck."

"This is a problem?" From the way Jack said it, Cass thought he felt it was a serious problem.

"Governor, Jerry's column tomorrow is going to say you agreed to take the two spot if Halderbreck gets in."

"Whoa." Jack looked stunned. "That's pretty audacious. Insolent, too." He thought a moment. "When's their deadline?"

"I don't know," Bernie said. "An hour, maybe a little more."

Cass wondered why she'd been dragged here and what this had to do with her. She could be at home, being entertained by panic attacks.

"The bastards will probably say we missed it." Jack looked at Todd. "Flat out deny it?"

"I don't think that'll do it," Leon said. "It must've been leaked from Halderbreck."

"Yeah," Jack said. "Can't you just hear it? 'That Governor Garrett, he's a sharp one, all right. Going places. We had us a real friendly discussion and traded ideas and I'm here to tell you there was real respect and real liking going back and forth. It was an easy visit and, you know what? Jack Garrett just mentioned that Halderbreck and Garrett would make a great team, a hard to beat ticket.' "

Jack changed his voice to reporter's interest. " 'And, Senator, would you accept him?' "

" 'Well sir, it certainly is something to think hard about, isn't it?' "

"Would he actually do that?" Bernie asked.

"In a Massachusetts minute. He's squashing me. Stepping on me like I was an ant coming to the kitchen. Anybody who reads the *Wall Street Journal* isn't going to take a chance on some pissant governor from a state half the voters have never heard of and the other half don't care about, who says he's running for president but uses his free time trying to get invited to Halderbreck's picnic."

"Well, boys and girls, anybody got any brilliant ideas?" Leon's honey-dipped southern voice was crystallized with irritation.

"I need to go home," Cass murmured to Bernie.

He squeezed her hand lightly. "Wait for it."

"Get him on the phone, Bernie," Jack said, "and I'll talk to him."

"Jack," Molly said in a warning voice.

Cass wondered if Molly was happy being married to Jack. He wasn't exactly a restful person to be with even back when they'd been together; now he was focused like a predator on the prowl.

Bernie took a cell phone from his jacket pocket and punched in a series of numbers. He talked a few seconds and handed the phone to Jack.

"Hey, Jerry, Jack Garrett here." He listened.

"Uh-huh . . . well now, the Senator may have been mistaken about . . . yeah, we did meet. A little while back we were both in Boston and it was a good opportunity to . . . we did. We talked . . . uh huh, uh-huh . . . about a lot of things. One thing we talked about was how interesting the primaries were going to be this year and the chance the party had of giving the president a hard time . . . especially about the war on terrorism . . . uh-huh, when was the last time you heard him say anything about jobs? People around here want . . . Well, no, that's not exactly . . . no, I said we had to run it out, get a discussion of the issues. . . . Yeah, and then we had to all get behind whoever the nominee was."

Jack's hand was tight on the phone and Molly watched like she was ready to pounce if he said a wrong word, but his voice was calm. "No, Jerry, we didn't have any kind of discussion about that. It's way too soon anyway. First, the senator has to get out there and see if he can beat some of us. . . . Yeah, it happens. Misunderstanding. No problem. . . . Yeah, thanks."

Molly looked relieved when he hung up and handed the phone back to Bernie. "How much can we trust this Donovan guy?" Jack asked Bernie.

Bernie shrugged. "He's a reporter. From all I know, he's honest. But he's a reporter."

"So," Todd said. "Anyone got any ideas how to go with this?"

"Get something against him," Leon said.

Jack looked at the game on television, gently touched his wife's cheek, and smiled again at Cass. He'd always been able to track five things at the same time. Molly liked the smile for Cass even less the second time.

"Why am I here?" Cass said.

"We're getting there," Bernie said.

Jack stood up, jammed his hands in his pockets, and started pacing. "Follow the middle road. If we beat Halderbreck, we're set for the gold. Right, Bernie? Of course, there's always the possibility we may not beat him. But taking the middle road and losing would put us almost certainly in a position where he'd pick us for number two spot. Lord, Lord, then I'd have four years of walking in the shadow of an idiot."

"We need to figure how much," Leon said, "to distinguish you from Halderbreck and how hard you need to push against him. This campaign shows a rift in the party, you're the future, Halderbreck's the past. Take him on. Be anti-Halderbreck and you'll stand out from the crowd."

"Not too anti-Halderbreck," Todd said. "You want the votes. Not just the antis, the whole party."

"I can't let him slice and dice me," Jack said. "First, he makes me a queer, then unpatriotic for saying we face other problems besides the fucking terrorism threat. Now he has me begging for second place in the *Journal*."

"He has to be careful, too," Leon said. "Slicing you makes you look important. Otherwise, why slice, you know?"

"What about the polls?"

"What about them?"

"New Hampshire, where do we stand?"

"Three," Todd said with great satisfaction.

"And Senator Halderbreck?"

"Oh, hell, he's something like nineteen."

Everybody laughed, except Cass. Why had Bernie been so insistent that she come? She was sitting here like a bump on a log and nobody but Molly paid the slightest attention to her.

Todd shoved his glasses up his nose and looked at her, an openly judging look that was far worse than being ignored. It made her very nervous. With the chair groaning in protest, Leon heaved his considerable bulk up and lowered himself onto the floor where he stretched out on his back, put his hands behind his head, and stared at the ceiling. Bernie got up and rattled through the soft drinks on the dining room table. He found a Coke and held it up to question if she wanted one. She shook her head. He popped the tab, sat back down beside her, and patted her hand.

"We have to do something," Leon said. "If we don't come on strong, Halderbreck is going to pull some kind of shit like this again. He does it often enough and voters are going to start believing him."

"Yeah," Todd said. "The point is what do we do?"

They both looked at Cass and she felt like she was being eyed for the position of Thanksgiving turkey.

Todd shifted his gaze. "Jack?"

Jack looked at Bernie.

"The crows aren't going to like it," Bernie said.

"Screw 'em," Todd said. "Since when have they cared about us. All they want is something blood-dripping to throw at the public."

"What's going on here," Cass said. "And why do I feel like I'm being measured for a noose?"

"We need to leak something to the crows," Leon said.

"Crows?" She looked at Bernie.

"Press."

"And you want me to do it? That's why you're all looking at me? Trying to figure out if I'm capable of doing it right?"

"So she's smart," Todd said. "Okay, what'll we say."

"Just a minute," Cass said.

"This is a very bad idea," Nora said.

"The governor said," Leon's soft southern voice took on hard corners, "that Senator Halderbreck is so stupid he needs help shooting himself in the foot."

"Maybe he tried it and missed," Bernie said.

"What the hell does that mean?" Todd said.

Jack grinned. "Perfect. Who do we leak it to? The Donovan guy?"

"No," Todd said. "He's been at this a long time. He knows his prick from a hole in the ground. Anyway he's print. We need one of the cookies."

"Female reporters," Bernie said.

"Television faces," Todd added.

"You want me to tell one of these—these—cookies, that—that—" Cass held a hand out toward Jack, "he called the Senator from Massachusetts stupid?"

"Got it in one," Todd said.

"Leak it," Bernie said.

"Why me? Why don't you do it. Or Todd?"

"I'd never say anything like that." Todd sounded offended. "Neither would Bernie. He's an old hand. They'd never believe him. You're new. You might accidentally let something slip."

"This is a very bad idea," Nora said again.

Cass agreed wholeheartedly.

21

*Th*e kitchen was black as that shrivel-headed cop's heart and Moonbeam didn't dare turn on a light. Her own house and she couldn't turn on a light! She was a fugitive and old Mrs. Hadwent next door was sure to notice a light. She bashed her toe against the table leg. "Ow. Damn it! Oh damn it!" Crumpling to a cross-legged sit, she grabbed the throbbing toe. "Ow, oh ow, oh ow." Tears clogged her throat. Why was everything so awful?

She rocked back and forth. Why did dirtbag cops have to be after her trying to throw her in jail? Why did she have to be here in the dark? Why did Gayle have to go and die? I am not going to cry. I am not going to cry. I don't cry. She rubbed a forefinger back and forth beneath her runny nose.

Well, fuck it. If she didn't have a right to cry, who did? She was an orphan. Her only relative had been bashed over the head and thrown in the car trunk. Cops were looking for her. She was hiding out in her own house, not daring to turn on the light. So far, this was turning out to be the worst day of her life. And where was Rosie anyway? What the fuck happened to Gayle's dog?

Moonbeam had thought it was so brilliant, sneaking back in here. The cops were done searching and wouldn't be back, so it was the best place to hide. She just had to be careful that Mrs. Hadwent didn't notice anything, and stay away from windows and stuff. But there was food here and water. She could even take a shower as long as nobody saw steam coming out a window or something really dumb like that. And clean clothes.

Except she hadn't thought about it getting dark and not being able to turn on a light and it being really creepy and weird noises scaring the shit out of her and sounds like somebody sneaking in and maybe the psycho killer was coming back. Like he dropped something that would really prove who he was and everything and he had to break in and get it. And he wouldn't know she was here. *Oh, shit. Gayle? I really miss you.*

Who would kill Gayle anyway? Of course, she did have her bad side when she came all over the heavy parent and everything and they didn't always get along like catsup and fries, but, hey, who does? At least, they had each other. Now she didn't even have the dumb dog. Just in case the cops really had taken Rosie to the pound or something, she ought to call tomorrow and ask. There couldn't be too many Belgian shepherds turned in.

Moonbeam stopped rubbing her seriously sore toe and moved carefully and slowly through the dining room and into the hallway, clutching a box of crackers. After dark, she was afraid to open the refrigerator door, thinking even that small light might be noticed. Who knows, but what the cops might be driving by at certain times all night.

Her bedroom was really totally dark. Isn't that just perfect? She shuffled a perilous path from the doorway to her bed and climbed in. Why was she shaking so much? It wasn't that cold.

She pulled the blankets up to her chin and lay staring up at the black ceiling. When she'd been little, Gayle had pasted stars up there, because Moonbeam had been scared of the dark. Well, she wasn't little anymore, and she wasn't scared of anything.

Well, maybe some things, maybe a little. Who wouldn't be scared of a psycho killer? Why had he killed Gayle anyway? Maybe Moonbeam should check out some of those dippy mysteries with gutsy female sleuths and get some pointers on how to find the bad guy. Who would want to kill Gayle? She didn't have anything that was worth anything. Well, just look around this house. Was there anything here that was worth a dime? Of course, ugly old antiques were worth thousands sometimes. And the dirtiest and ugliest were worth the most. Her friend Monica's mother found a table in the attic and it turned out to be worth a bunch of thousands of dollars. They remodeled the whole house and put on a second story and bought a humongous television.

But that's ridiculous, there's nothing like that here. Was anything in the attic? Oh, shit, she was sorry she thought of it. Was that footsteps up there? No! No one was in the attic and no way she was going to go up and look.

She wondered if Gayle had known something. Like, well, the *big* secret. Moonbeam snorted and the noise sounded so loud she scared herself.

She rooted around to get more comfortable. Gayle had been dwelling on all that sad stuff about the fire and everything and the big fight she had with Vince right before he took off for Colorado and had that skiing accident.

Then—Moonbeam squinched up her eyes to remember better— last month just before he left to go skiing, Vince was excited about something. Moonbeam squeezed her eyes tighter and rubbed her forehead to stimulate thoughts. The governor. Yeah, that was it. Vince said he had something to say to the governor. Or maybe he said he already said something to the governor. Moonbeam was sorry she hadn't paid more attention, that she was so busy with her own shit and everything that she didn't even listen. If only she'd been home, if only she hadn't gone to the music festival, then maybe the psycho killer wouldn't have bashed Gayle. She'd be still alive and—

Tears, hot and painful, got all started and Moonbeam mashed her face in the pillow to bury the sobs.

Something scraped against a window. Moonbeam held her breath, her heart flapped like a whirligig. Somebody on the porch?

22

――

$\mathscr{A}$fter hours of struggle trying to get to sleep, Em got up, pulled on some clothes, got in her car and drove, just drove, through the black night, the little town of Hampstead, and into the countryside. Two hours later when she returned she was exhausted. Surely the nightmares that tormented her would be lulled, surely God would let her sleep now, but the torturous dreams were back as soon as she closed her eyes.

Tired as she was, she plodded through her work at Garrett For America local headquarters and was thankful when her shift was over. She drove to the motel, turned off the ignition and just sat there, too tired to get out of the car. The wind whistling past the inch-open window frayed on her nerves. She was always tired now, sometimes so much she simply wanted to sleep, but when she went to bed, sleep eluded her. She started to worry she wouldn't have the strength to accomplish her mission. That must not happen. She must be successful. For Alice Ann and all the others like her who couldn't speak for themselves and had no one else to step up for them.

With a deep sigh, she gathered her purse and the two bags of food she'd bought. She fumbled for her room key and had to put the bags down to find it. "Alice Ann? I'm home, honey. Sorry, I'm late. I stopped to pick up some food. Not that I'm hungry, but I guess I need to eat. Keep my strength up, like everybody always says."

She flicked on the light in the entryway, went into the small kitchen area and dropped the bags on the counter.

"Who's Alice Ann?"

She spun around, heart pounding, knees going weak.

Black kid. Teenager.

For the blink of an eye, everything froze. Then it came rushing back, the noise of her heart, the rattle of the room's heater, a car horn honking outside. The boy at the pawnshop. The one who'd scared her so, stolen her money. Sitting in the overstuffed chair by the bed. He held a gun. Passed it slowly back and forth from one hand to the other. Ran the barrel up and down his jaw. Grinned at her, teeth white in his dark face.

"How did you get in here?"

"Wasn't hard. All's you need is put the key in the lock." He dangled the room key for her to see.

She hadn't lost it after all, he'd stolen it when he grabbed her purse. "What do you want?"

"Aren't ya pleased to see me?"

He got up and came toward her. She backed away until she was trapped in the corner of the L-shaped cabinet in the kitchen area. "You took all my money. I don't have any more." That wasn't true, but if she gave him the rest, she might as well just lie down and let him kill her because she wouldn't be able to finish without money. If she couldn't get to the governor here, she'd have to follow him when he left, watching, waiting for her chance. Get airline tickets, rent cars, hotel rooms. If she couldn't kill Jackson Garrett, nothing mattered. "How did you find me?"

He shrugged. "Address on the key." He laid the gun on the cabinet, but kept his hand around it. "Who's Alice Ann?"

"My daughter. She'll be here any minute. So you just better go."

He gave her a cocky smile and shook his head. "Naw, I don't think so. I think you're here all by yourself, 'cause there's only stuff here for one person."

"You went through my things?" She felt all the starch drain out. Had he found her money?

"What's it matter? Got something hidden you don't want me to see?"

He was either going to kill her, or he wasn't. She wasn't afraid to die, but she wanted Governor Garrett to get what he deserved before she did. If God didn't want that to happen, if He wanted her to die right here and now, then that was the way it would be.

"If you went through all my belongings you know what I have and you know I have nothing of value, so you might as well go."

"I could kill you before I go." He aimed the gun at her head.

"Well, make up your mind," she snapped. "Either shoot me or put that thing down. I'm tired and I'm hungry and I'd like to fix something to eat."

"It's your gun." There was amusement along with menace in his voice. He set it on the cabinet like he was daring her to pick it up. "Isn't it what you wanted?"

She studied his face. He was probably around thirteen. In all her years of teaching, she'd learned a lot about kids. This one was a hood, probably a long sheet of burglaries, break-ins, and assaults in his background, maybe even some kiddie jail time and the Lord only knew what else. "What's your name?"

"Tyrell."

"All right, Tyrell, I hope that's a good gun, because it cost me a lot of money."

"Yeah."

"It cost all I had." She eyed him with her teacher's displeased expression.

A grin played around his mouth. "Yeah, it did that, didn't it?"

"You hungry?"

"Why?" he said suspiciously.

"Good." She rummaged through the bag, found an onion and pulled out the cutting board under the counter. She plopped down the onion, opened a drawer for a knife and put the knife beside it. "Slice," she said, wondering if he might just pick up the knife and slice her.

"What?"

"Slice the onion."

"I don't do that stuff."

"Why not?"

"Bitches do that stuff."

"Really? What do you do when *bitches* aren't around?"

He shrugged. "McDonald's."

"Way too much fat and way too much salt. It's bad for you."

He looked at her like she was nuts. And probably she was, she hadn't been really sane since Alice Ann died. Digging for the pack of gum at the bottom of the bag, she opened it and handed him a stick.

"What's this for?" He looked at the gum like it might explode.

"Chew it while you slice and you won't cry so much."

"I don't cry." And no doubt he'd pound anyone who suggested he did.

"You should. It's therapeutic. There's something in the chemical makeup of tears that is healing."

"You cry over Alice Ann?"

She turned on him. "There is one subject you don't dump on and that is it."

"How come you get so twisted about her? She in trouble or something?"

"Maybe I'll tell you sometime. Right now, slice that onion. Cut off both ends and peel it first." She turned her back on him, shoulders tight, feeling like there might be a big red X painted right between the shoulder blades. She peeled the wrapping from a package of cream cheese, put it on a plate and found a bowl for the bagels.

"Okay, I'm done."

She looked over at the large chunks Tyrell had hacked off. And despite his macho claim, there were tears in his eyes. "Right. Now slice these." She handed him two tomatoes.

"My eyes sting. Like tear gas."

She didn't ask him how he knew about tear gas. "Yes. It's very nearly the same. Slice."

133

Handling the knife like a stabbing weapon, he attacked the tomatoes.

"How come you don't just go to McDonald's? Beats all this slicin' and shit."

"This tastes better." She put on water for instant coffee. "You want some orange juice?"

"Got any Coke?"

"No, sorry."

"Yeah, orange juice."

"In the refrigerator. Help yourself."

He grabbed the carton and started drinking.

"Not that way. Get a glass."

"You're some bossy."

"Where do you live, Tyrell?"

"Here and there."

"You have a home?"

"Course, I got a home. Everybody got a home."

Not everybody, Em thought. "What about your mother, will she worry about you?"

"Doubt it. She's in jail."

"Your father?" Em put the bagels in the tiny oven to warm.

"Don't know where he is. He left before I even knew I had a father."

"There are some dishes in the cabinet right there. Not very fancy ones, I'm afraid, but you can take them to that small table by the window."

He grumbled about bitches work as he took out mismatched plates and more or less pitched them at the table. She forked lox on a plate, took the bagels from the oven and got a fork for the salad.

He scooped up a mound of cream cheese and sculpted it onto a bagel. With the look of a food critic, he took a bite and chewed thoughtfully. "Not bad," he said.

"It's delicious," she said. "Eat some salad."

"Don't like salad."

"It's not polite to say so. Eat it anyway, it's good for you."

He picked out two or three pieces of lettuce and put them on his plate. "Why you want the gun?"

"To protect myself."

He studied her while he chewed. "Naw. You're wantin' to kill somebody. Who is it?"

She shook her head and concentrated on gathering up stray crumbs. "Now why would I want to kill somebody?"

"Is it this Alice Ann you was talkin' to?"

She stiffened. "I told you, we won't talk about her."

"Who is she?"

"My daughter."

"You live with her?"

"She died."

"What happened?"

"She was shot."

"I had a sister once," he said. "She was shot, too."

"Who shot her?"

He shrugged. "Accident. Wrong place at the wrong time."

"I'm sorry."

He shrugged again. "Happens."

Not where she ever lived, it didn't. Where she lived a well-brought-up young man beat up his pregnant wife, was arrested, acquitted, went out and bought a gun. Deliberately, he shot and killed his pregnant wife, there was no accident about it.

From the amount of food he consumed, Em wondered when Tyrell last had a meal and didn't eat much so there'd be more for him. When the food was gone, she told him he had to help her wash the dishes.

"What? I never do no dishes."

"Then it's time you did." She filled the tiny sink with hot water and detergent, washed a plate and handed it to him to dry.

"How come you're not yellin' and screamin' and callin' the cops and tryin' to get me out of here?"

"I don't know, Tyrell. Maybe it's because I might like you if I got to know you."

135

He picked up a plate and vigorously rubbed it with the towel. "Somebody like you like somebody like me?"

"Why not? You seem like an intelligent young man."

He didn't have any parents, didn't seem to have a home, probably didn't have any adult who paid attention to him. Because she treated him like an individual and didn't simply dismiss him as a dangerous young criminal, he stayed, helped fix the meal, ate, helped wash the dishes. She didn't know why he'd come. Maybe he didn't know either. To kill her maybe, or steal whatever was valuable, or maybe just for something to do. She was afraid when he decided to leave, he'd take the gun with him. In his life, a gun must resemble power. She wanted it, she needed it. How was she going to convince him to leave it with her? Offer to buy him a car? Ha, if he wanted one, he'd probably steal one.

"What do you like to do?"

"Play basketball. Hey, looka here, you didn't get this one clean." With glee, he pointed out a spot of smeared cream cheese and handed the plate back.

She washed it again. "You any good at basketball?"

"The best!"

She smiled. "Why am I not surprised. You like to travel?"

"You mean like go someplace?"

"That's usually what travel means."

"Don't know. Never did any."

"Would you like to?"

He shrugged. "Never thought about it." He dried the last glass and put it on the shelf.

Buying him an airline ticket to somewhere like Disneyland obviously wasn't going to work either. What did this child want that she could give him in exchange for the gun?

"I get off work around four tomorrow," she said. "I'd like it if you came for supper."

He grinned. "Do I have to chop?"

"Only if you want to."

"I have to go." He tossed the dish towel on the counter. "Have to be somewhere."

She let the dish water drain from the sink, very aware of the gun sitting by Tyrell's elbow. Would he take it with him?

Giving her a sly look, he picked up the gun and shoved it in his pocket. "See you around," he said.

Her heart floated on despair. He was going to walk out with her gun and she'd never see him or it again. "Are you taking the gun?"

"Yeah."

"If you leave it and come back tomorrow, I'll give you two hundred dollars." She didn't know if that represented a large amount of money to him or not.

He looked at her a long moment. "I'll bring it back tomorrow. You can have it for four hundred."

"No," she said and was surprised to hear steady firmness in her voice. "Take it and don't come back or leave it and come back to-morrow. I'll give you the money and fix supper for us." If he took it, she'd have to think of something else. Maybe she'd simply have to legally go through the fifteen-day waiting period and track down Jack-son Garrett wherever he was at that time.

He thought a moment, then pulled the gun from his pocket and put it back on the cabinet. "Three hundred," he said, to let her know he was still in charge.

She nodded.

When he left, her shoulders slumped in relief. She touched the gun with her fingertips. Hard and cold. Gingerly, she picked it up and held it flat in her palm. Heavy.

Hers. All she needed now was to get close enough.

23

$\mathscr{B}$illions of stars sparkled with cold light in a black velvet sky that stretched from horizon to horizon. The moon, a slim crescent, rode low over the shallow hills. Sean asked himself what the hell he thought he was doing wandering away from the safety zones and drifting into the unchartered areas of the natives. Chasing a whim, that's what he was doing. He'd seen the town car with Wakely Fromm and the kid who took care of him driving off somewhere. Sean was guessing Fromm went to the house he owned, the one where the campaign committee stashed him when he'd be a liability if taken out in public. Too drunk, or too belligerent.

Sean couldn't say why he wanted to talk with Fromm—old reporter's deep down feeling that something was lurking under the surface. Long ago, he'd learned to trust those deep down feelings. With his boss pushing for something over and above the rehash of what the TV cookies were doing, now seemed a good time to have that chat with Fromm. If the man could be found, and if he was able to talk. With Fromm, timing was all. Solid sober and he wouldn't open his mouth, too drunk and he was incoherent, so it was crucial to catch him with just the right amount of liquor in his gut.

The governor was supposedly spending a quiet Tuesday evening with his campaign people. More likely making phone calls. Speaking of phone calls, Sean ought to call his parents. Talk to his mother, talk to Hannah, tell her he loved her. What was going through her six-year-old mind, her mother taking off with a karate instructor and her father chasing wild geese out here where the deer and the antelope roam. In the eerie green of the dash lights, he squinted at the directions the kid at the hotel had given him.

South on Main 1 bl. R on Gulch Creek Dr 4.1 mi. R on Wakarusa .8 mi. L on Cimarron Rd to stone pillars. R on dirt road .3 mi to 3-way split. Take leftmost fork .5 mi to stone fencepost on L with 3 names attached. Western. Kettner. Kale. Take R and go .7 mi to Walnut tree with sign that reads Kale. Turn right immediately around birch tree even though path looks too narrow for cars. Go 1.1 mi.

You can't miss it.

Just when he wondered if this was a variation of the old snipe hunt trick natives played on outlanders, his headlights picked out a tree with a sign nailed to it. It was so dark he had to use a flashlight to read names. Western, Kettner, Kale. So far so good. He turned onto the dirt road and the rental car jounced along jiggling his kidneys, tall bushes on both sides scratched at the car like imploring fingers. He kept a close eye on the odometer and after clocking off .7 miles, he began to wonder if he'd made a wrong choice somewhere and would end up in the middle of a Kansas pasture. Probably with a homicidal bull that would fatally gore him and trample his carcass. No way could he turn around here, this cow path was too narrow with thick brush close on both sides. The options were keep going and hope for a wide spot or back all the way out. Just when he'd decided the kid giving directions had deliberately led him by the gullible nose to the middle of nowhere, he spotted a sign on a tree. And the sign said? He shined the flash on it. Kale. Okay.

He made a right turn around the tree, which the directions said was birch—he couldn't tell a pine from an oak—and watched the odometer until it went another 1.1 miles. He nosed the car as far as he could to the edge of the path and got out. Wind attacked him with fury.

Using the flash, he spotted three concrete steps, trotted up them and followed the pathway. An owl hooted in a tree above, nearly sending him into cardiac arrest. Around a curve sat an old wooden farmhouse with a wide front porch, a barn some distance behind, a silo next to it, and a windmill, black against the night sky. He could hear the creaking of the paddles. Lights were on inside the house. Somebody must be here. Sean hoped it was Fromm. The owl hooted again and he spotted it, silhouetted against the sliver of moon. Scary sad sound in the dark.

He went up the porch steps and knocked on the door. No answer. Asleep or out of it from booze and pills or not here. He tried the knob. Oh ho, now look at this, the door was unlocked. Surely, the good Samaritan thing to do, was go in and see that Fromm was all right.

The house was silent. No sound of television or dishes rattling in the kitchen from someone seeking a late night snack. Lamp on in the living room, shabby couch with a decided sag in the center, shabbier overstuffed chair facing the television set. Lamp table by the arm of the chair. Line of pharmaceuticals. Darvocet. Prilosec. Atenolol. Sonata. He picked Sonata and read the instructions: Take one at bedtime as needed. The bottle was empty.

A feather of worry touched the back of his neck. The refill date read October sixteen and the prescription was for thirty tablets. Today was the twenty-eighth. Didn't mean anything. Fromm could have spilled them, deliberately thrown then away, sold them, flushed them down the toilet. Yeah, right.

"Wakely? Hey, Wakely! Where are you? You asleep?"

Silence.

"It's Sean Donovan! Where are you, old buddy?"

He put the prescription bottle back and went across a hallway into the kitchen. The house had a stillness to it he didn't like, a feel of being vacant. Kitchen table had a few dirty dishes, half a ham sandwich, jar of mustard, jar of dill pickles, package of potato chips, package of cookies.

He went along the hall to the first doorway and gently pushed the half-open door with his elbow. It swung silently inward. Nothing. Empty. A regular-sized bed with a faded green chenille bedspread. Bedside table with paperback books. All science fiction and mystery. On the chest against one wall sat a framed photo of two eager young men all suited up for a parachute jump, arms draped across each other's shoulders. Twenty years younger, Jackson Garrett and Wakely Fromm. Fromm was taller and huskier than Garrett.

Hard to imagine the wasted drunk with the useless legs and the virile young man in the photo were one and the same. Where the hell was he? Someone picked him up and took him back to the farm?

"Fromm? It's Donovan!"

He went farther down the hallway and the smell hit him. Faint, but unmistakable. He'd done enough reporting in warring countries in his younger days to recognize it. His heart revved up.

Images played through his mind as, knowing what he was going to find, he reached for the doorknob. Not smart to stand in the line of fire. He twisted the knob, sidestepped and kicked the door open.

Empty room. He blinked, trying to integrate emptiness with the images in his mind. Obviously, Wakely's room. Bed mussed, bottle of bourbon on the nightstand, picture of a pretty young woman beside it, dirty clothes on the floor. Apparatus over the bed, bars, and a dangling metal triangle, to aid Wakely getting in and out of bed.

He edged along the wall to the bathroom, the smell grew stronger. Acrid odor of gunpowder. Blood, feces, urine.

He pulled in a breath and nudged the door with the toe of his boot. "Aw Jesus," he said softly.

Blood, pieces of bone, gray clumps of brain tissue and hair were splattered over the white wall above the tub. Wakely Fromm, former smoke jumper and lately close friend of presidential candidate hopeful Jackson Garrett, listed to one side in his wheelchair. Wearing pajama bottoms, head and shoulders thrown back, arms hanging down, back of his head blown away. A revolver—an old Colt, Sean thought—lay on the floor, dropped as Fromm's hand relaxed when the bullet entered his mouth.

Sean didn't want to touch anything. He was already worried he might have messed up evidence by blundering around and sorry he'd come in the first place. Susan was going to skin him alive. Watching where he put his feet, he went up to Fromm and put two fingers under his jaw. People had been known to survive all sorts of grievous wounds. Skin cool, no elastic give, no pulse.

Sean looked at his watch. Almost nine. What was it that sent Fromm on the final path? Just tired of it all? The half-man he'd become, the dependence, the relying on other people for intimate attentions that whole people take for granted, loneliness, the feeling of sitting in the chair watching life rather than being a participant? Whatever it was, Fromm didn't even wait out the final hours. Usually it was 4 A.M., that bleak hour the soul couldn't get past.

Sean went out and stood on the front porch looking up at the cold face of the moon and the uncaring glittery stars. Times like this he wished he still smoked. Maybe he should pour a glass of Fromm's bourbon and drink a toast to a downed smoke jumper. The wind had an edge to it that sent cold through him. He shivered, enjoying the feel of it. If he could feel cold, he was alive. If there was pain ahead, he'd give it a smile when he saw it coming, acknowledge a formidable enemy and be glad to see it.

Still studying the stars, he reached in his coat pocket for his cell phone and pressed 911. "This is Sean Donovan . . ."

Susan had just gotten home when her phone rang. She listened for a moment, not making sense of what she was hearing. "What? Where! Right. I'm on my way. Tell Parkhurst I'll meet him there." All the reasons why this was very bad went through her mind as she drove out to the Kale house.

When she rolled up she spotted Sean sitting on the top of three cement steps leading up to a pathway.

"Your buddies are all inside." He waved a hand at the house. "Crawling through blood and brains and picking up wee wiggling things with tweezers."

"You all right?"

"Sure."

She sat down beside him. "In that case, what the hell are you doing out here?"

"Pondering the fleetingness of life."

"You ought to be pondering the fleetingness of freedom. Cops look very closely at the individual who finds the body. I ought to throw your ass in jail."

"Another sign of the moral decline of my favorite cop."

"Didn't your mother ever tell you sitting on cold cement will give you hemorrhoids?"

"Your mother told you that? Mine said I'd go blind from beating the meat."

"That's not an image I need to have."

"Wait'll you see what's inside." He hunched forward and rested his elbows on his knees.

"It's freezing. Why you sitting out here?"

"Your buddies threw me out."

Knowing journalists and knowing Sean even better, she would bet he had seen everything there was to see in the house before he called it in. "You working on an angle?"

"Just sitting here breathing fresh air."

She didn't believe that for a minute. Something was spinning around in his reporter's mind and since he wouldn't tell her what it was, it was probably something she wouldn't like. She put her hand on his back. He stared out at the dirt road cluttered with squad cars, ambulance, her pickup, and the pathologist's old station wagon.

He looked up at the black sky. "It's a beautiful night. Clear, crisp, just what fall should be. I wonder what it takes to stick the barrel of a gun in your mouth and pull the trigger."

"It makes a hell of a mess somebody else has to clean up."

He smiled at her. "You always were tougher than me. I watched you, you know, back home—San Francisco—working, putting on layer after layer of armor, getting too hard to feel anything, dealing with all the stresses and ugliness, putting yourself beyond emotions, so you wouldn't feel the pain of the poor bastards you dealt with every day."

"I need to go inside and see what's going on, then I need to ask you some questions. You want to wait in your car?"

"I keep seeing the picture of that son-of-a-bitch's brains splattered all over the wall."

She patted his knee and got up. Inside, Osey was leaning against the wall in the hallway, waiting for Gunny to finish taking pictures. "He doing all right?" she asked. Gunny was a wiz at photography, a student the HPD snagged to take pictures for them when needed. The quality had leaped up 90 percent from their previous method of using any cop who was available, but there'd been a honeymoon period. At first Gunny had turned green and keeled over at the sight of some of the more grisly objects he was expected to take pictures of, but even though he was getting almost blasé about the whole thing, this one would be hard.

She stuck her head around the bathroom door just as a flash went off and was blinded. She blinked rapidly. When she could see again, she started taking notes and making a sketch of the room. The routine calmed her and she could tuck in the back of her mind the fact that her cousin Sean was mixed up in a homicide. Osey and Parkhurst didn't speak as they worked, didn't make any of the black jokes cops sometimes used to dull the edges of grim scenes. The silence was broken only by the whir and click of the camera as Gunny took shot after shot of the carnage.

When she realized the flashes had stopped, she looked up. Parkhurst was standing by the bathroom door, looking at what was left of Wakely Fromm as if he'd just asked the corpse a question and was waiting for the answer.

"What?" she said.

Parkhurst studied the doorway as though judging how wide it was, looked back at the bed, then over at her. His face never gave a hint of what went on in his mind. She waited.

"Why did he go in the bathroom?" Parkhurst said.

"Why not?"

"He was lying in bed, relaxing, reading, maybe watching television—"

"Was the television on?" she asked.

"Not when we got here. I didn't ask Donovan if he turned it off."

"I'll do it."

"Right." Parkhurst stuck his fingertips in his back pockets. "So, Wakely's in bed, settled for the night, and then he's suddenly swept away by the thought to whack himself."

"Maybe he was lying there trying to decide. Maybe he had thought about it, for days. Weeks, months. Maybe he was getting up the nerve."

"Okay. For whatever reason, tonight it all just got too much and he's made up his mind. He's comfortable in bed. Why get up? It isn't like he can just throw his legs over the edge and stand up. He has to position the wheelchair, hoist himself into it, and roll himself in here." Parkhurst gave a nod at the apparatus of bars and triangle that assisted the paralyzed man to get himself from bed to chair.

"Take a piss?"

"He hasn't done that in twenty years. Plastic tubing and a plastic bag take care of it."

"Maybe he went in the bathroom to empty the bag."

"Right before he shoots himself?" Parkhurst rocked back on his heels.

"Leave less mess on the bed?"

"He's going to splatter bone, brains, blood, and hair all the hell over everywhere and he worries about a little urine?"

"Maybe he kept the gun in there."

"Where? The medicine cabinet?"

"Suicides don't always make sense," she said. "Anybody who's worked himself up to the point where he's planning to stick the barrel of a gun in his mouth and blow himself into the world beyond is not necessarily thinking sensibly. Lots of times, they choose the john. Almost like saying sorry, this is the best I can do, make the cleanup easier."

He snorted. "I thought they were giving the finger to the ones left behind, see what you made me do."

"Yeah, that, too, sometimes." The white wall behind Fromm that held what was left of his head looked like a painting by Jackson Pollock. Bone and blood and gray macaroni-like mass had slid down in clumps and puddled on the floor.

"You reckon suicides ever think about somebody stepping on their brains?" Parkhurst edged closer and crouched to look at the gun. "Somebody could have come in and then backed out without stepping on anything."

"What are you saying?" She knew what he was saying and she didn't like it.

"This is a man in a wheelchair whose best friend is about to make a bid for presidential candidate. Why the hell would he roll it in here, park it and off himself?"

"Maybe felt he was a liability. No money, no family. The friend has been supporting him for twenty years. Maybe felt like a burden. Maybe everything has been taken from him and this was the only thing left he had control over. To live or die."

"It's an old gun," Parkhurst said. "Was it his?"

"Undetermined. Did you know him?"

"Only what everybody knows. After the fire twenty years ago, Garrett took him in, took care of him."

"Why?"

Parkhurst shrugged. "They were good buddies. Small town, knew each other forever, went to high school together, went off to fight fires together."

The sound of voices arguing came from the front of the house and Susan went to see what the noise was all about.

A young man with silver blond hair, carrying two grocery bags was trying to get past the uniforms blocking his way. "What's going on? Where's Wakely?"

"Chief Wren." Susan showed him her badge. "Who are you?"

"Murray Winston. I take care of him. What happened? An accident? Did he fall? I've told him and told him to be careful when he's getting in and out of the wheelchair. He doesn't always check that it's locked. He just—"

"I'm very sorry, Murray." In all her years as a cop, she'd found the best way to bring bad news was not leave people hanging on a thread of hope but come right out with it. "Wakely Fromm shot himself."

"What?" His face tightened with shock. "How bad is it? Will he be all right?"

"He's dead."

Murray stared at her for several seconds, as though she'd spoken a foreign language and he was trying to figure out the meaning of her words. "He can't be dead. I just left him two hours ago."

Susan brought him into a cheery kitchen with yellow walls and gray-and-white tile on the countertops. Angrily, he dropped the bags on the counter and, though clearly reluctant, sat down when she told him to.

"When did you last see him?" She sat across the table from him. Parkhurst leaned at the doorway.

"I just told you. Two hours ago. He was in bed watching a football game." Murray kept his eyes on her, as though warily judging the moment when she'd pounce.

This was a young man who moved lightly, looked fit, with the quick reflexes of a fighter. How easily could he be pushed into striking out? "Where did you go?"

"Shopping. We were out of food and paper towels and—stuff."

"Where do you live, Murray?"

"With him. Wherever he is. I told you, I take care of him."

"Are you a relative or—"

"No. I'm paid to take care of him."

"Who pays you?" Parkhurst crossed his arms.

Murray had to turn around to see him. "The governor. Governor Garrett. Does he know about this?" Murray shot up. "I got to tell him. He'll—"

"Sit down." Parkhurst said.

"But—"

"We'll take care of it," Susan said.

147

With obvious frustration—this was a man more comfortable with action—Murray sat back down and scrubbed his hands over his face.

"You always shop this late?"

Murray looked at his watch. "Yeah. I don't have to worry about him if he's watching football. I can take my time and not have to hurry."

"How long have you been at this job?" Parkhurst asked.

Having to turn his head to see Parkhurst behind him was irritating Murray. "Three years. Little more."

"Who took care of him before that?" Susan asked.

"Uh—a nurse, I don't remember his name. Jim something."

"Why did he quit?"

"He wanted to go back to working in a hospital."

"You a nurse?"

"Physical therapist."

"Has Wakely been despondent lately? Depressed?"

"Yeah. He gets in these moods and lately—yeah, I'd say he's been depressed."

"Why?"

Murray looked at her like she was a half-wit. "He couldn't walk, he couldn't jump out of airplanes, he couldn't f—make love to a girl, he couldn't even wipe his own ass."

"Always depressed, or more so lately?"

"Ever since I've known him."

"Did you like him?"

"Sure. I wouldn't stay if I didn't." He propped an ankle on the opposite knee. Getting relaxed, less worried. "Sometimes more than others."

"What about Governor Garrett? How did Wakely feel about him?"

Quick smile. "Depends on how much he'd had to drink."

"Yes?"

"If he was drunk, he loved him one minute, resented him the next."

"Wakely usually stays at Governor Garrett's farm. Why this place?"

148

Murray shrugged. "You'd have to ask the boss that, the governor."

"Take a guess."

"Oh hell, sometimes Wakely gets tired of it all, you know?" Murray turned again to look at Parkhurst, then back at Susan. "The whole campaign thing. TV cameras, reporters always asking questions. He doesn't always want to be on display. I can understand."

"And the governor? Are there times when he doesn't want Wakely on display?"

Murray closed up, like he felt maybe he'd said too much. "You'll have to ask him."

"Did they ever have a fight, an argument, Wakely and the governor?"

"Not really. Wakely ranted and raved sometimes, the governor was always just patient."

"Never lost his temper?" When Murray turned his head to look at him, Parkhurst moved from the doorway over to a cabinet, so that Murray had to turn the other way. He was pissing on tires and getting Murray's back stiff.

"If that ever happened, he just walked out."

"Since you've been in Hampstead, has anything happened?" Susan said.

"Like what?"

"Did he have an argument with anybody, make anybody mad?"

"Maybe. But it wouldn't amount to anything. Sometimes he ran off at the mouth and irritated people, but—"

"What people?"

"Anybody. People on the street, people running the campaign, people at the market."

"People running the campaign?"

"Sure. They're the ones he sees the most."

"Who in particular did he irritate?"

"All of them. Leon Massy, Todd, even Bernie sometimes and he's pretty hard to get steamed. Nora couldn't stand him. She kept working on Molly to get rid of him." Murray looked at her, startled. "I didn't mean—"

She waved that aside. "What else can you tell me?"

"Well, I drove him here two or three times last month."

"To this house?"

"No, to Hampstead."

"Why?"

Murray gave her a slant-eyed look, trying to decide how much he should tell her. "He came to see a guy name Egelhoff, Vince Egelhoff."

Susan's sluggish mind perked up. Vince Egelhoff, husband of Gayle Egelhoff who ended up dead in a car trunk. "Why?"

"I have no idea. This Vince guy died in a car accident or something and Wakely was kind of shook up."

Skiing accident, Susan thought. Vince Egelhoff had gone to visit a cousin in Colorado and died in a skiing accident.

"Really upset him. He's been moody and negative and—yeah, I'd say depressed, damn depressed. He started talking about how he's nothing but a burden, and the governor does everything for him, and everybody'd be better off if he was dead."

That sounded suicidal to her.

"Do all these questions mean there's something fishy about Wakely's death?"

Smart guy. "We're trying to determine what happened."

"He's been drinking a lot lately."

"You were worried about him?"

"Well—yeah. It was getting so he was almost always drunk now."

"When did that start?"

Murray vigorously rubbed the flat of his hand across the top of his head. "Right after he started seeing that Egelhoff guy."

What was it about seeing Vince Egelhoff that had Wakely drinking more than usual?

"You left him alone tonight." Parkhurst made it sound like an accusation and almost had Murray out of the chair and coming for him. Susan could see the intake of breath and the clenched fists.

"He wasn't mentally incompetent, you know, or senile or anything. He was okay by himself. For a while anyway. Sometimes he wanted to be alone and he'd tell me to get lost."

"Since he knew Vince Egelhoff, he also knew Gayle Egelhoff," Susan said.

"Yeah. He went to see her once."

"When?"

Murray thought a moment. "Friday."

"Last Friday?" The day Gayle was killed. "What did they talk about?"

"I never listened to their conversations but since her husband was Wakely's friend, it was probably about him."

Three friends, smoke jumpers, fought a forest fire twenty years ago. Now two of them were dead. "Did Wakely own a gun?"

"I never saw one."

Susan raised an eyebrow. "It's possible he had one that you never saw?"

"Sure it's possible. I'm not a jailer. I take care of him, not pry into everything."

"Do you own a gun?"

"No."

"Who hired you?" Susan asked.

"The governor."

"He came himself and talked with you?"

"Not exactly. Todd Haviland. You know, the campaign manager. Look, I really have to call and let them know what happened."

"We'll take care of it," Susan said.

24

———

$\mathcal{M}$oonbeam slid off the bed to the floor and slithered across to the window. Moving the curtain aside a fraction of an inch, she peered out. Everything was black. By twisting her neck she could see the roof of Mrs. Hadwent's garage and by looking down she could see the path that led along the side of the house. Couldn't see shit beyond that. What did she expect? Bogeymen looking in the window. That thought scared her so much she almost ran screaming from the room. She couldn't tell what was going on in the front of the house.

Her heart was hammering so hard she wouldn't hear a rock band on the porch if there was one. She had to go into the living room where she could see out the front. Oh God.

Wildly, she looked around for some kind of weapon. Her old teddy bear? That'll do it. The guy will fall over laughing. She had an inclination to pick up the bear and hug it close. Oh God, she was really losing it. Sherry would be glad to hear about this. Maybe what she needed was a shrink.

With all the looking around and talking to herself, she hadn't noticed that the noises had stopped. She nearly dropped with relief. Oh God, it had all been her imagination. Okay, should she climb back in bed and pull the covers over her head, or should she go out and make sure there were no murdering psychos in the house?

She was shaking so hard her teeth were chattering. She clamped them together. She wasn't scared. She could take care of herself. Oh boy, what she would give for a gun. Hold that fucker in her hand and nobody would mess with her. Bring on all your psycho killers, see what I do to them. Yeah, man, holding cold steel in her hand—

Gun. Vince had a gun. Oh, Moonbeam, you stupid shit. Why didn't you think of that before. Where the hell was it? She looked around as though it might suddenly pop up, like on the dresser or something.

She only saw it that one time, going through the boxes in the attic looking for an old picture of her mom. Some of her parents' things were still up there because Gayle found it hard to throw stuff away and she couldn't bring herself to just toss out everything that had belonged to Mom and Dad.

All of Vince's stuff was still in the closet in their bedroom. Probably years before Gayle could have started getting rid of it. The gun had been in one of the boxes in the attic. Moonbeam had no idea where it came from. It must have been Dad's, unless it was Vince's. She could just see Gayle having a fit about it and Vince calming her down and saying he'd take care of it.

Was it still there? Would it be loaded? She hoped so, because she didn't see how she'd get any bullets, her being a fugitive and all.

A loud thump came from the kitchen.

Air got trapped in her lungs. Her heart rammed itself in her throat. Oh shit! Somebody in the house!

So scared she could barely breathe, she eased across her bedroom to the door, stuck her head out, looked up and down the hallway. Empty. Flicker of light coming from the kitchen!

Somebody with a flashlight!

Looking for something?

She wondered if he had a gun. Could she race to the garage, find the ladder, run back to the hallway, climb up to the attic, rummage through boxes, find the gun, run back down and dash in to point it at him before he could kill her?

Keeping her eyes on that flickering light, she backed into the living room. Black as night! Ha, joke. She wished now she hadn't gone around and closed every curtain up so tight not even an ant could get in.

What was he looking for?

If this was just an ordinary, everyday burglar who broke in to steal something that would be just too much. Did God have a sense of humor? Maybe he was punishing her for all those bad things she did and for all the bad words she said and—

Well, if that was true then—

Flickering light coming her way! She started to run and banged into something that shouldn't be there. She careened into the coffee table and sent the glass bowl tumbling. Crash!

She whirled and ran.

In her bedroom, she slipped into the closet, clambered up to the top shelf. She nudged a stack of sweatshirts, jeans, and boxes out of the way so she could hide behind them. She wanted to hold her breath so she could hear better, but her lungs forced air in and out with raspy pants. Her heart was so loud, probably the whole world could hear.

She could hear him searching for her. Muttered curses, throwing things out of his way. She heard a muffled thud. Living room. She listened, straining to hear. Slam of closet door in Gayle's bedroom.

Coming down the hallway! Oh God, oh God. She buried her face in the crook of her elbow to stifle any cries that might escape. He was coming!

He was in her bedroom. What was he doing?

Touching her things? Ugh! Gross! She'd throw out everything she owned. Even her brand new, just bought fake diamond toe ring. She'd—

He was moving toward the closet!

Oh God, please let him just leave. Please let him not find me. Please God.

There was sudden silence. Where was he? She listened.

Then she sensed him at the closet door.

Don't move. Don't say anything. Keep quiet.

The door opened with a jerk.

The flashlight beam slid across the hanging clothes, swept across the jumble on the floor and rose. It moved slowly along the shelf.

A grunt. Then he started pulling things from the shelf.

The flashlight shined right in her eyes. Blinded, she froze.

Abruptly, she started yelling and pushing stuff off on him. Clothes, shoes, boots, books, old junk she'd forgotten she had, rained down on him. She rolled off the shelf, fell into him on the way down, and he swiped at her. She screamed as the knife cut across her upper arm.

He grabbed at her and caught her T-shirt. Yelling, she kicked and fought and felt the shirt tear as she pulled away. She ran. He pounded after her.

Front door. Never make it. Swerving, she dodged into the bathroom and whirled to slam the door just as he raised his arm and slashed down, slicing her throat. Falling back, her face hit the sink. Her hand clutched her neck, got all warm and sticky. Dizzy, she fell forward against the door, pinning his arm.

Intake hiss of pain and a muffled curse. Fumbling behind her on the counter, her grasping hands found soap dish, towel, toothbrush, comb, and—. She clutched the hair spray and, aiming it at his eye peering in, depressed the button.

He yelled, yanked his arm free and the door slammed shut. She fumbled for the lock and turned it. All that hair spray in the small space choked her. She couldn't breathe. He kicked the door and threw himself against it. How long would it hold?

She felt weak, her legs were getting rubbery. Blood covered her shirt and was seeping down into her jeans. She groped for the towel, wrapped it around her neck, and pressed it tight against her throat. Everything seemed wobbly and distant. She couldn't stand up any more, she really really couldn't.

Slowly, she sank to the floor and sat with her back against the door. The kicking and pounding stopped. She thought she might sleep a while. Her head tilted back to rest against the door.

Loud bang. Splintering sound.

Ax. Cutting into the door. He must have found it in the garage. He swung the ax again. She ought to get away from the door. She really really ought to. Another swung and the ax might split her back. Okay, she was going to get up now.

Though her muscles tensed, she could not get her feet under her and pull herself upright. She was sleepy. And cold. Towel around her throat was getting squishy with blood.

If she got up, she could turn on the light. Right. She tried to focus on that thought, but it seemed too much effort. Who needed light? She'd just stay here in the dark and take a little nap.

25

$\mathscr{B}$ernie didn't like it. After taking Cass home, he went back out to the farm, feeling uneasy, dull, lightheaded, and jazzy all at the same time. This was totally nuts. Casilda Storm was a nice lady and he liked her, liked her a lot, if you came down to it. She was obviously struggling with monsters, hadn't got over the death of her husband and child. How could he be part of herding her into election insanity? She wasn't one of them. Far as he could tell, she wasn't even political. How could she carry it off? Nora's right, he thought, mistake. The crows would get suspicious. And that was a bad idea. They had means of retaliating. The pencils chose what they put in print, the cookies chose what they used in their standup television spots. All of them could slant a piece any number of ways.

Just as he came in the door, Molly Garrett came into the living room area from the hallway where the bedrooms were. She was the same age as the governor, forty-six, but looked ten years younger. Petite, five three and slender, short brownish hair with reddish tints where the light caught it, due to some hair person who created that sort of thing, even features a little sharp to be pretty, faint laugh lines around her eyes, blue or green depending on—. Bernie didn't know depending on what. Her mood, maybe. She was attractive without being flashy, elegant without appearing snooty, warm enough to seem within touch and more than what she presented to the world. Quiet-spoken, she kept in the background and fit the slot of politician's wife perfectly, but Bernie had overheard snatches of the fights coming from behind closed doors and knew she had a sharp wit that could be cruel.

He was uneasy about her, too. Sometimes, he got a glimpse of a Molly that was more dedicated to winning than even Jack.

"Tea, Bernie?"

"No thanks, Mrs. Garrett. It's late, I should be going to bed."

He wasn't sure how she did it, but gently, by pushing and nudging, she got him in the kitchen. He squinted as she flipped on the overhead light. Knotty pine cabinets and table, oak floor. Wallpaper with gold and white stripes, countertops with white tile and every fourth one or so was gold. It made him want to squint. Molly took two mugs from the cabinet, white with a gold rim.

"Losing faith, Bernie?"

"Excuse me?"

"Thinking you can't take care of him?"

"Who?"

"Jack. Aren't you the one who has to see that all's well with Jack?"

Is that what he had to do? It was as good a job description as any, he supposed.

"We're going to win, you know," she said.

He thought about asking how she knew, what made her so positive, what lengths would she go to make sure? But he was tired, and he figured she probably didn't know the answers anyway, so he just nodded.

She was opening cabinets looking for tea bags and finally found a box of decaf Earl Grey next to a jar of instant coffee.

"You take milk?" She opened the refrigerator packed with cans of Cokes, Diet Cokes, ginger ale, and pop-top fruit juices and snagged a carton of milk.

"Uh—no."

"Why are you working for us, instead of Senator Roswell?"

Bernie accepted the mug of tea she offered. "Been there, done that."

"Why didn't you stay with him?"

Why hadn't he? Vague and convoluted reasons he wasn't sure even he understood entirely. "It wasn't the senator. And I learned a lot there, but after a while it was always the same, over and over again. It got old. I got tired of rounding them up."

"Afraid of losing?"

"No. We always won. But it wasn't *winning*, you know? And then it would come. The deals. The hundred little things we'd have to give away to get this one with us and that one with us. And in the Senate, we'd get gutted. We'd have to settle for a version that nobody wanted, but we'd all have to take it because it was the closest either side could get to what was really important."

"That's the democratic way." She was leaning against a cabinet, mug raised in one hand, other hand supporting her elbow.

"Roswell knows how to cast a spell to catch the voters," Bernie said. "All the good ones can do it. But it got to seem—too much like a game, you know? Their side would bring in something, we'd take it to our side and negotiate the hell out of it, stick in the candy that would look good to our voters and pass the damn thing. Wow. We got ourselves a victory, right? None of it mattered, because, just as we knew he would, the president vetoed it. But we could still claim a victory, a victory for the right side because we had forced a veto."

"Why do you stay with it?"

Bernie shrugged, a little self-consciously. "I get caught up in the process and I wonder what would happen if someone who really cared about—oh hell, you know, the world and the people. Maybe I'm just jealous Kennedy didn't come along in my time. He talked about sacrifice and what you can do for your country. He was fighting a real fight. It mattered. Everything now is just keeping on keeping on. Treading water, sheltering in place, going with the flow. It's stale and it's beginning to putrefy. It doesn't have any feel to it. There's no sense that any of it is real, or that it's making history."

"But you're still here."

"I want to be part of something important, something real—" He took a gulp of tea, embarrassed at his confessional rambling.

"Stick with us," she said. "Jack's going to win." She put her mug on the counter. "You need to convince Jack that he doesn't need this Cass woman. She's a liability." Molly patted Bernie's cheek and left.

He wasn't quite sure what had just happened here, except he'd tossed out words like a newbie, unprofessional, and Molly Garrett wanted him to extract Casilda Storm from the campaign. He felt a headache coming on. It was late, he ought to go to his room and crash.

Leon breezed in, yanked open the refrigerator, selected a Diet Coke and popped the tab. He lowered his head and stared at Bernie. "You don't look so good. She give you TB?"

True Believerism. It separated the tyros from the pros, the sheep from the goats, the wheat from the chaff. You needed to stay clear-eyed and remember the goals. You needed to keep in mind a man was just a man and couldn't leap tall buildings in a single bound. Damn it, Bernie knew all that, but he couldn't help it. He never forgot the first time he'd heard the Governor speak. Hairs rose on his arm. From then on he was true and surely hooked. He had no distance, wasn't sprinkled with clear-seeing perspective. He was one of the sheep with the soul of a political goat.

Leon, with Bernie following, traipsed back into the living room and used the remote to raise the sound on one of the television sets that were always on, always tuned to news with the occasional break for a football game. Leon collapsed into a chair. "Watch out for Lady Macbeth, boy."

"She says he's going to win."

Leon gave a low chuckle. "Damn straight, she does. You ever see the look in her eye? Same fanatic look Todd's got. He'd give his left nut to win and she'd slaughter her firstborn. Two of a kind." He tipped the can and poured about half down his throat. Bernie wasn't even sure he swallowed.

"And that poor Wanderer they dragged in." Leon gulped the rest of the Coke and crushed the can.

"Cass?"

"I got this feeling if it ever gets to freezing and they ain't got no fuel, they're gonna throw her on the fire."

Bernie had something of the same feeling.

"She don't like it," Leon said. "The Missus. She don't like the Wanderer bein' brought in."

"Why doesn't Molly like Cass?"

Leon gave him a pitying look. "Don't you use your eyes, boy? Any fool can see she's jealous."

"Why?"

"Probably 'cause they fucked like mink way back when."

"Why do you call her the Wanderer?"

"Cause that's what she is. Clear as glass she's got demons, boy, and she's visitin' them. Goin' from one to the next and the next and the next. Poor thing. And it'd probably be a good idea to never leave 'em alone together. Lady Macbeth would chew her into little pieces."

Leon didn't like Molly Garrett and Bernie didn't know why. She was a great asset and worked as hard, or harder, than anyone on the staff. Even the crows liked her, and that took something. She was respectful of them. Bernie wasn't sure the governor loved her, but that didn't have squat to do with the campaign and none of his business anyway.

"D'you ever see an owl catch a prey?" Leon slouched farther down in the chair.

Bernie looked at him. "What?"

"They don't make a sound, owls. Big motherfuckers with these huge wings." Leon held out both arms and tilted them up and down. "And they just glide right at some poor son-of-a-bitchin' li'l mouse just going about his business and *snatch!* they have him. *Scream!* Sharp old talons. Struggle all he wants, no way that mouse's gonna get loose."

"You been working too hard, Leon? You're starting to creep me out."

Leon grinned. "I got this premonition, boy, this feeling there's gonna be trouble." He shook his head. "I don't like it."

Leon had a bit of the carnival charlatan, a showman who played

161

up this premonition business and, even though Bernie didn't believe that nonsense, every time Leon started lowering his voice and intoning about premonitions chaos broke out.

Bernie said good-night and went to his room. He brushed his teeth, virtuously flossed, and went to bed where he dreamed of owls on tree branches silhouetted against a full moon. There was music in the background, singing so soft he couldn't understand the words. He strained to hear. "When you hear them hoot owls hollerin', when you hear them hoot owls hollerin', somebody's dyin', lord, somebody's dyin'."

26

$\mathscr{B}$ernie had just gotten to sleep when Todd shook him awake and told him to get his ass in the living room. As he splashed water on his face and pulled on jeans, Bernie wondered if it was too late to ditch politics altogether and the Garrett campaign in particular and do something else with his life. He wandered in to find the whole gang there and Todd, standing in front of the fireplace, going over last-minute changes in the schedule for Illinois. The latest polls showed Jack weak with the minority vote in that state and Todd was juggling stops, putting in visits with leaders in heavily African-American and Hispanic areas. Nobody'd had enough sleep and they were all tired enough to go for each other's throats. Bernie glanced at his watch. Two A.M. In three hours they'd board the plane.

Nora kept interrupting and Todd was ready to strangle her. She was an irritating woman to begin with and being Molly's personal secretary seemed to give her permission to be an even bigger pain in the butt. Bernie rubbed his aching head, poured a mug of coffee from the ever-ready pot and wondered if he had the strength to track down some aspirin. A handful would go really good with the coffee.

Jack, seated on the couch with Molly, argued that nothing should be dropped, he could visit all the scheduled places, plus the added ones.

Molly said, "Jack, just shut up, for once, and let Todd do his job."

Leon came in with a box of pizza and plopped it on an end table. Leave it to Leon to let no opportunity for food go unpassed.

"How long has this been going on?" Bernie said.

"About an hour." Leon dropped to the easy chair which sagged pitifully under his weight and opened the box. Leaning forward, he breathed in the aroma, then peeled out a slice.

"Did I miss anything?" Bernie grabbed a slice, sat in the wingchair by the fireplace and bit off the pointed end.

Carter Mercado, the pollster, was slouched in the second wingchair on the other side of the fireplace. Leon offered him some pizza. Carter waved it away. Todd took off his glasses and rubbed his eyes. Hadley Cane, the press secretary, pulled up a straight-backed chair next to Bernie. She looked tired, too, and Bernie thought they should all just go to bed because, pretty soon, they were going to start sniping at each other and then there'd be a fight that would take days to dissipate. When Leon clicked the remote to show them the latest TV spot, Bernie knew it was going to be a long night.

Todd and Bernie both said it was good. Jack and Molly went off to their rooms but Nora, Bernie was sorry to see, stayed. She was not only a personal assistant to Molly, she was a close friend and that gave her the assumption she was part of the core group. Since the Garretts didn't say otherwise, so she was.

"You need to have Molly in it," Nora said.

Todd hated her. Even without the interruptions, the compulsive talking, the suggestions, he'd have hated her because she was an amateur. Her only claim to a potential fifteen minutes of fame was that she knew Molly Garrett. They'd been friends since college.

She was one of those people who talked all the time and after a while her voice slid under the skin and made you want to strangle her. Repression had them all snarling at each other. Bernie was scared to death of her—because you never knew what she'd do, she was dangerous. She never thought before she spoke. He was afraid she'd sit in on one of their planning sessions and let slip some crucial piece of strategy. She was sulking because she felt she should be the one to leak the Halderbreck-is-stupid bit to the press instead of Cass. In fact, she seemed stupidly jealous of Cass. Actually, stupid was something else she was, and that made her really dangerous.

"Molly could sit on the desk and they could be talking," Nora said.

To keep himself from strangling Nora, Todd started telling Hadley what to feed the press. In other words how to do her job. Hadley got hot and steamed and started yelling that she was the press secretary, she knew what she was doing. If he pushed her just a little more, she'd quit. Bernie had personally witnessed her quitting four times so far. God knows how many more he may have missed. It was their way of releasing tension, but Bernie worried one time it would go too far and neither one could back down.

"I've got no time for this," Hadley said. "I've got to get out to the press and explain to them what we'll be doing tomorrow. They get real anxious when they're not in on the program." Hadley was expert at drifting through the press pool, dropping them bits of information and telling them how to interpret it.

"You have to be careful with that," Todd said.

"Bullshit," she shot back. "*You* have to be careful. I'm their pal. I give them lots of help and spread around cheer and kindness."

"You need to watch what kind of access you give them."

"Hey! We're doing just fine. Periodically, Jack goes through the press section, says hi, answers questions—"

"Yeah," Leon perused the pizza box and, after careful scrutiny, selected another slice. "He's a maverick and the stakes are getting high. It might be a good idea if you'd pull him back a little."

"He wouldn't go for it," she said. "And right now they like him. As much as they can, since they all tell themselves how objective they are. He treats them well and he's been honest with them, but start hiding him in the crapper and see how ravenous they get."

"I'm only saying you need to pick and choose. Things are getting hot, and formal interviews need to go to—"

"How many times do I need to tell you I know my job?"

"Yeah, yeah, right. I'm just telling you, start thinking about the California newspapers. "The *Chronicle*, the *Mercury News*, and the *L.A.*—"

"I know, I know." She made a brushing aside wave as she went out.

"How much we spending on advertising?" Todd asked Leon.

"Well, right now, we got a million and a half, a little more. After we spend that, we're close to the federal cap and we can't spend more until we win the nomination."

"California's a bottomless pit. We could spend it all just to lose."

"We don't spend and we can forget about the nomination."

Bernie went to the kitchen and fished a Coke from the refrigerator. He wasn't tracking with the arguments going on. His mind was on Cass. The Wanderer, as Leon called her. He was worried about her. Popping the tab, he took a sip and went back to the living room.

"What do the polls say?" Todd asked.

Carter, the pollster, waggled a hand back and forth. "Close. Ads will matter, no question."

"How we doing with ads?" Todd asked.

"Well, in Bill Halderbreck's ads he has all the animation of a houseplant and the humility of a cocker spaniel. And, of course, he's right with you in whatever special interest group you represent. Mention one and he'll step right up there, drop his pants and bend over."

"Everybody knows that," Carter said. "Poll on confidence and integrity and Jack runs a little ahead, but you got to remember Halderbreck's a known quantity. Jack's a risk." Carter leaned back, put his hands behind his head and rested an ankle on the opposite knee. "And, let's admit it folks, Jack has intelligence and confidence bordering on arrogance. That makes people feel inadequate and defensive. We got to make him look smart, but not too smart. The idea of having a smart president is too scary for most folks."

"We got to make him look like one of the guys," Leon said, "for the ninety percent of the people who decide their vote from television ads."

"His parents were farmers," Carter said. "What's more folksy than that?"

"Why aren't we hammering on this hero stuff?" Leon said. "Use Wakely, for God's sake. He's always around anyway. Get him early in the morning, before he gets too drunk to sit up straight."

Bernie could hear the frustration in Leon's voice. Jack wanted to remain a private person, but any politician making a grab for the presidency couldn't keep anything private. Anything a candidate wanted to hide, the media was especially determined to root out.

"I think—" Nora said.

Nobody wanted to know what she thought and everybody ignored her.

Demarco happened to be on duty when the 911 call came in. He and Yancy responded to the address given to them by the dispatcher and they were standing in the living room of a plump elderly woman.

"You will check into it, won't you?" Mrs. Cleary pulled her pink fleecy robe tighter around her ample frame and cinched up the belt. "I had went to the kitchen to fix myself some tea and that's when I heard it. Goodness sakes, it sounded like somebody was tearing the house down."

"Yes, ma'am," Demarco said. Vera Cleary lived next door to the Egelhoff house and she'd called the shop to report suspicious noises.

Yancy asked. "When was that?"

"It must have been about fifteen minutes ago now." Hint of reproach that it had taken them so long. "It's stopped by now, of course. But the screams, my Lord, I've never heard such screaming." She rubbed her hands together anxiously. "And there was all this moaning and crying and sort of mewing sounds, kind of like a kitten, you know? Oh, I just know something is terribly wrong. Will you do something?"

"Yes, ma'am," Demarco said. Owner of the house murdered, victim's sister missing? Damn right, he'd do something.

"You won't just dismiss it as the nervous ramblings of an old woman, will you? I had gone to the phone when I saw the light."

Demarco took her story of noises and screams, moans and cries very seriously. She was maybe mid-fifties, a widow, with short gray hair that stuck out in spikes and nervous because of what had happened to her neighbor. Just before midnight, Mrs. Cleary had seen flickering lights inside the house.

"I thought it might be that girl Arlene who calls herself Moonbeam, the silly thing, and didn't think a whole lot about it, but then a little later after that, I heard all this screaming. Like the poor child was being murdered in her bed. And with what happened to Gayle, being killed and put in the car trunk—well, a person just can't be too careful."

"You did the right thing in calling," Demarco said.

"There's not supposed to be anybody there," she said. "With her husband dead and Gayle murdered and the girl missing—now who could be making all that noise and causing flickering lights?"

"Did you notice anything earlier?"

"No," she said. "But I had went to the market, so I wasn't here to notice."

"We'll check into it," Since Demarco was looking for the girl, this story interested him much.

"What do you think?" Yancy said as they tromped next door to the Egelhoff house. "Burglar knowing the place is empty?"

Nothing was flickering inside the house now, it was completely dark. No moans, no screams. "Could be. You check the back, I'll take the front."

"Right."

"And take it easy. The girl's still missing."

"And we don't have the bastard who killed her sister," Yancy said.

A few seconds later, Demarco heard Yancy on the radio saying no signs of forced entry in the back, the board over the broken window still intact. No signs in the front either. Using the key he'd borrowed from the evidence locker, Demarco unlocked the door. Flashlight in his left hand, gun in his right, he went in fast and low. Living room empty. Table knocked aside. Broken glass on the floor. He listened, then moved into the dining room. Empty. He met Yancy in the kitchen and motioned for him to follow. Demarco went along the hallway. He pointed a finger to the room on the left. Yancy went left. Demarco moved farther along the hallway and slipped into the room on the right. Empty room, neat, bed made, no signs of struggle.

"Clear," Yancy called. Then, "You might want to see this."

Demarco went across the hall. Yancy aimed his flashlight at clothes, shoes, books, stuffed animals, scattered on the floor by the closet. Messy kid? Or had something happened here?

"Somebody looking for something?" Yancy said.

"In the kid's bedroom?" Demarco shined his flash around. "What could the kid have?"

Yancy looked through the closet. Demarco went to check the third bedroom and spotted the damaged door at the end of the hallway. Blood was seeping out under it.

"Police! Come out with your hands on your head!"

No response.

"Come out! Hands on your head!"

Still no response.

Demarco backed up, raised one leg and kicked the lock. It gave, but something prevented the door from opening. He threw a shoulder at the door. It moved slightly, but didn't open. Leaning all his weight against it, he peered through the crack.

"Oh, Christ! Yancy, get an ambulance!"

Yancy keyed his mike and relayed the request. "On the way," he said as he clicked off. "What've we got?"

"The girl. She's been hurt, maybe killed. Lot of blood in there. We're gonna have to take this door off."

Yancy nodded and went for the garage.

"Police," Demarco said through the crack, much softer this time. "Where are you hurt?"

No answer.

"Can you move?"

169

Yancy came back with two screwdrivers and they removed the hinges and took the door off. Yancy flipped on the overhead light. "Oh God."

"Put your hands in your pockets and don't step in blood," Demarco said.

Yancy swallowed. "Right."

A towel lay loose around her neck and the dark wound underneath gaped obscenely.

"You're not gonna be sick," Demarco said. It wasn't a question, it was an order.

"No." Yancy shoved his hands in his pockets.

The girl, Arlene—Moonbeam—lay curled on the floor, one arm trapped beneath her body, the other outstretched as though reaching for something. Demarco stepped inside, avoiding blood and touched the fingers of the outflung hand. Cool. God damn it, we're too late.

He tried to find a pulse on the slack wrist and found none. Easing closer, he leaned over in an awkward position and put fingertips against the corner of her jaw. Pulse. Faint. "She's alive! Where the hell is the ambulance!"

Yancy got on the mike and when he keyed off, he said, "Two miles and rolling."

Demarco didn't like the angle of her neck, but didn't move her. From the linen closet in the hallway, he got blankets and laid them over her.

Two paramedics in navy blue jumpsuits rushed in with a gurney. They snapped a cervical collar around her neck, slapped a bandage on her throat, whipped her onto the gurney and had her in the ambulance in minutes.

"We gotta really pound it," one of them told Demarco. "She's lost a lot of blood."

Demarco didn't ask if she would make it. He knew they didn't know.

27

All five people in the room watched with varying degrees of curiosity or surprise as Susan and Parkhurst walked in, except Todd Haviland, the campaign manager, who looked irritated. Other times she'd seen him, he also looked irritated. Maybe irritated was his usual mood. Bernie Quaid, wearing jeans and a black shirt, introduced the other three. Leon Massy, media consultant, sprawled in an easy chair. Oddly shaped man, normal upper body, hugely fat from the waist down, wearing suit pants and a crumpled white shirt with the collar unbuttoned and the sleeves rolled up. Nora Tallace, Molly Garrett's personal assistant, perched on the edge of a wing chair, leaning forward like she didn't want to miss anything. Brown hair, mid-forties, makeup perfect, beige slacks and sweater. Carter Mercado, pollster, small, short sandy hair, slumped on the couch with his hands in his pockets jiggling change. Empty dishes, pizza box, napkins, soft drink cans, crushed and dented, and empty glasses all over. It looked like a late planning session that hadn't gone well.

"What can we do for you?" Todd said, short, annoyed, they'd interrupted a busy man and he wasn't going to waste time with them.

"Wakely Fromm," Susan said.

"What about him?"

"I have some bad news."

Bernie shot her a look, and even though his face was as impassive as a therapist's she saw a flash of alarm in his eyes.

"What?" Todd said.

These were people who could avoid talking to her if they thought it was in their best interests. "Is there some place where I can tell you?"

Todd looked at her. Weighing options, running through responses?

"The governor's office?" Bernie suggested.

Todd waited a beat, then nodded. "Right." He pointed down a hallway.

"Where is the governor?" Susan, without even looking at Parkhurst, followed Todd. Parkhurst would stay where he was to keep a cop's presence in the room, discourage them from talking with each other.

"Asleep." Todd ushered her into a room with a beautiful cherrywood desk, surface bare except for two phones, file cabinets along one wall, two burgundy leather easy chairs, an aerial-view photo of what she assumed was the farm with the house, barn, pond, outbuildings and windmill on another wall, and on another a photo of two people standing side by side, perhaps his parents.

"Please take a seat, Mr. Haviland." She went around the desk and sat in the chair.

He blinked at her, not used to being given orders, and not liking her sitting behind the desk, but he hitched up his pants and lowered his skinny rear to burgundy leather.

"When did you last see Wakely?" She leaned forward and put her elbows on the desktop.

"Last night."

"What time last night?"

"It must have been around seven." He took off his glasses and chewed on an ear piece. "We were just getting ready to go to the fundraiser in Omaha when Wakely decided he didn't want to go."

"Why not?"

172

"Who the hell knows. He does that sometimes. Plans all set and we're ready to leave and he decides he doesn't want to. More plans have to be made to take care of whatever it is he does want." Todd sounded tired of being jerked around at Wakely's whims, fed up with Wakely in general.

"Who do you mean by *we?*"

"The governor, Molly, state troopers, Bernie, Leon," he rattled off, took a breath and tacked on, "Nora Tallace."

"Does she usually go with you?"

"Yes. What's all this about?"

"I'm sorry to tell you Wakely Fromm is dead."

"Dead?"

Was he surprised? Pretending shock? She could see his busy mind run through implications.

"What happened? Heart attack?"

"Did he have a heart problem?"

"Yeah. Was that it?'

"No, Mr. Haviland. It appears he shot himself."

"Shot himself? Oh, fuck." Todd bent forward, resting his forehead in his hands. He started to rise. The chair wasn't as easy to get out of as into.

"A few questions," she said before he could propel himself upright.

"No time. We have to figure out how to handle this. What kind of spin to put on it. That son-of-a-bitch, I knew he was going to be trouble."

"Has he been trouble?"

Todd shook his head. "No, not really. He lived in that chair. Not the easiest thing to travel around with. Poor old Wakely."

"Was something on his mind lately?"

"Oh, yeah." Todd took off his glasses and pinched the bridge of his nose with a thumb and forefinger. "He's been talking about being a burden and Jack should just go on and do this campaign and leave him out of it."

Todd had gotten his thoughts together and gave her what was, no doubt, going to be the party line. Wakely Fromm didn't want to be a

173

burden to his old friend, so he killed himself. "You sound like you think leaving him out was a good idea."

"Murray mostly took care of him. And there was the plus side."

"What was that?"

"Jackson Garrett never forgets an old friend. Saved his life. The friend has special needs? Jack sees to it. He's a caring man. Vote for him, he'll take care of you too. You have special needs? He'll see to them."

Susan asked questions, including where he'd been earlier in the evening. She might as well have saved her energy. Todd's mind was on the campaign and what kind of mileage he could make from the tragic death of his candidate's old friend.

"Why was Wakely with the campaign?"

"Jack wanted him," Todd said.

"And you didn't?"

Todd shook his head. "Only because Jack needs to stay focused. Keep his mind on the goal."

"The campaign, winning the nomination."

"Yeah. And Jack was worried about him."

"You didn't want him wasting energy worrying about his friend?"

Todd took a fast breath and let it out with a grunt. "I didn't mean that, not really. It's late, I'm tired. I say things I shouldn't."

Accustomed as he was to being thrown questions and avoiding answers if he wanted, she couldn't tell if he actually was tired and made a slip, or simply wanted her to think so.

When Todd went back to the living room, she heard him announce to the room that Wakely had shot himself. Why? To give someone a chance to make up an alibi? To plant that thought firmly in everyone's mind?

She talked with Leon Massy next. He moved like his feet hurt and dropped immediately into one of the chairs, which groaned in protest on receiving his bulk.

"Wakely offed himself?" Leon stroked his jaw with thumb and forefinger. "Jesus, poor bastard. Why'd he go and do a thing like that?"

He had a soft compelling voice with a hint of the south, a voice that had you leaning closer to hear better.

"Give me a reason?"

Leon shifted, working out a more comfortable position. "Hell, I hardly knew the man. He was just always there. Poor son of a bitch."

"Did he own a gun?"

"He shot himself?" Leon shook his head vigorously, maybe to dislodge the image of Wakely pulling the trigger. "Jesus."

That, and variations thereof, was about all she could coax from Leon and while he appeared willing to be of help, he didn't actually say anything. These political people were so used to dealing with reporters that their skills for talking but not saying anything were well honed. She asked him where he'd been since seven this evening.

Bernie Quaid seemed saddened by the death, but had nothing to say on the question of why Wakely might kill himself.

"Did you like him, Mr. Quaid?"

Bernie looked startled, then slightly ashamed. "I don't think I ever thought about it. Wakely was just Wakely. The governor's friend. Part of the team."

"Was the rest of the team nice to him?"

Bernie took in a quiet breath. "We mostly just ignored him." He looked at her. "A campaign takes up all your energy." Apology in his voice. "All your time, all your thoughts. You don't have anything left to use on anything else. Was Wakely unhappy? Did we like him? If it didn't affect the campaign, it wasn't of interest." He gave her a thin smile. "That makes us all selfish bastards with an eye firmly fixed on the main chance." He nodded. "It's the nature of the beast. We're not heartless, not really, just doing a job."

"With high stakes."

"Yes, ma'am. The highest. Winning is everything and if we win, we win big."

"Was Wakely a liability?"

Bernie scratched his jaw. "Not really. He told everybody who'd listen what a great guy the governor was and he wouldn't be here today if the governor hadn't saved his life."

Save a life and that person is yours forever. Sooner or later did the saved person turn into a burden? Maybe such a burden, the saver resented ever having saved him in the first place?

"How did Governor Garrett save Wakely's life?"

"It was a long time ago. They were caught in a fire. Wakely was injured and the governor carried him to safety."

Having been a firefighter should be a big plus for him when voters were making selections. She prodded Bernie a little, asked more questions, asked where he'd been during the evening. She couldn't get a hold on whether he was lying or withholding. Like he said, they simply kept firmly focused on their goal, get Jackson Garrett the nomination and even the death of one of their own didn't deflect them.

She rubbed fingertips across her forehead where a dull ache had started some time ago. It was late. Maybe Dr. Fisher would turn up something interesting in the autopsy. By interesting, she meant something that would show, one way or the other, suicide or homicide.

Carter Mercado, the pollster, answered her questions, but didn't give her anything. Wakely was always there. Carter barely knew him.

Nora was miffed at being questioned last. Not because she had anything to say, but because she was a woman who wanted everyone to recognize her importance. Susan wondered vaguely about her background. How had she gotten this sense of her own entitlement? Or was she supremely unimportant in everybody else's world and had to grab whatever opportunity came by to show herself this wasn't true?

"I don't understand it, really," Nora was saying. "I mean, Jack supported him. Gave him money for everything he needed and paid that man—that physical therapist person—that looked after him all the time." She crossed her legs. "We're always talking about money. There's never enough for this, never enough for that. Well, right there's a place we could save." She said this as though she'd said it many times and nobody listened.

Susan didn't think campaign funds could be used to pay a physical therapist. Money spent on Wakely would come from the governor's own accounts.

"How Molly put up with it, I don't know," Nora continued. "I keep telling her she ought to put her foot down."

"She disliked Wakely Fromm?"

Nora opened her mouth to say something, gave Susan a quick glance and then said hurriedly, "Oh, no, of course not. He was Jack's friend. It's just that—" Nora brushed imaginary lint from her pants.

"What about you? Did you like him?"

"Well, I can't say he was my best friend," Nora said with a slight smile. "But I certainly didn't dislike him."

Susan started to ask her the same questions she'd asked the others: Where were you this evening? Suddenly, Susan heard voices in the hallway.

"Why the hell didn't you tell me?"

"It's late. You need—"

Before she could rise to find out what was going on, Governor Garrett slammed in. She shot up.

Todd was right behind him. "Governor, we've got to be in Chicago at nine. There's no—"

"Go away, Todd."

Nora popped up and scuttled off.

"Don't keep him long," Todd said to Susan over the governor's shoulder. "We're in the middle of a campaign and it's important—"

The governor, in gray sweatpants and gray sweatshirt, shut the door in Todd's face and turned a blazing fury on her. Even with his eyes puffy from sleep and pillow creases on his face, Jackson Garrett was a formidable presence in the small room. To her relief, he reached inside for hobbles and got himself under control. At the cabinet under the window, he opened a door and got out a bottle of brandy. He unscrewed the cap and tossed down a gulp. He asked her if she'd like anything. She declined. He replaced the cap, returned the bottle, and sat in one of the burgundy chairs.

"Wakely shot himself?" He waved at her to sit back down.

"Yes, sir, that appears to be the case." Feeling slightly one-upped, Susan sat at his desk. "I'm very sorry."

"Appears," he repeated.

"Yes."

"You wouldn't be asking all these questions of my staff if you didn't feel uncertain."

"Yes, sir, that's true."

"Did you come to ask me if I killed my old friend?"

"Did you?"

"No." He hunched over and rested his forearms on his knees. "I feel like I've lost part of myself." His voice was so soft she had to strain to hear. "We were friends from the time we were boys. No one else shares the memories we have."

If the governor felt Wakely'd been a nuisance or a burden, he was thinking fast and showing her a grieving man. An act? She didn't know.

"Was he depressed?"

"We should have known."

"Known what?"

"That death was coming at us on that mountain." Garrett pushed himself up, went to the window and stood looking out. With his back toward her, he studied whatever he was seeing outside and said, " 'About, about, in reel and rout, the death fires danced at night.' "

"Excuse me?"

Garrett turned, leaned against the window sill. "He's been depressed for years, every since the Pale Horse fire and he ended up in that chair. He hated it, being in that chair, dependent on somebody else for anything."

"More depressed than usual lately?"

"I don't know. Truth is, I haven't paid as much attention lately as I should." He pounded his fist against the wall. "Aw, shit. Wakely, why'd you have to go and do this?"

Susan pushed him a little. Why would Wakely pick this time to kill himself, what did the other staff members think about him, was there anyone who didn't like him, who might want him out of the way? Where was Wakely all evening? Where had the governor been? But she didn't push too hard. He was the governor, after all.

"Right now," he said, "is when I should be saying if only I'd known. If only I'd known what he was thinking, I might have done something, I might have helped, I might have stopped him. With Wakely, it wouldn't have mattered." The governor turned and leaned wearily against the wall. "Whatever he decided to do, he did, there was no way to stop him." The governor's voice was thick and his eyes teary. "He was a good friend. I'll never have another like him."

"Did he own a gun?"

"Yeah. A couple handguns and a rifle."

"Do you know what kind?"

The governor rubbed his eyes. "An old thirty-eight and a Glock. The rifle, I think, is an old Remington."

There was a tap on the door and Molly Garrett came in. "Jack, what's going on?" She'd taken the time to put on a green silk dressing gown and comb her hair.

Husband and wife shot each other a glance. And exchanged some information. Susan didn't have a clue what it was.

"Go back to bed," he said.

"What's happened?" Molly sat in a burgundy chair and smoothed the dressing gown over her knee.

Jack sat in the other chair.

Susan was trying to figure out how to politely ask him to get the hell out, when Molly said, "She wants you to leave, Jack."

His fury rushed back and he clamped his jaw.

Molly patted his knee. "You can go. It's all right."

Reluctantly, he got up. At the door, he sent her another glance and this one held definite warning.

"Jack is devastated," Molly said when he'd shut the door.

"They were friends for a long time."

"Forever." Molly smiled.

"How did you feel about Wakely Fromm?"

Molly sent her a shrewd look. "I didn't resent him, if that's what you're getting at." Her tone was mild, but there was an edge underneath that suggested she was lying.

"He lived with you, was with the two of you throughout your marriage, went with you when you traveled. Anyone would start to resent that after a while."

"Yes," Molly admitted. "There were times . . . but I was fond of him."

"Did you ever wish he weren't living with you?"

"Yes, there were times like that, too, but he had his own quarters, you know, he wasn't always in our laps, or at our dinner table. He wanted to be by himself much of the time."

"Your husband spent a lot of money taking care of Wakely, paying his living expenses, paying the physical therapist. You didn't get a little annoyed at that on occasion?"

"It is Jack's money after all."

"Not campaign funds."

"Certainly not. And it isn't as though Wakely had no money of his own. He had a disability—uh—uh—thing. And his family owned a farm. It came to him when they passed on."

"Now money going out for Wakely's care and expenses can be diverted to other things."

"Oh yes, but if you're saying that's a good thing, this is going to upset Jack so much it will throw him off stride. Maybe too much to continue. If Wakely's death costs Jack the nomination, the savings won't be worth it."

Susan asked questions: When had Mrs. Garrett seen Wakely last, what was his mood, where had she been during the evening.

"Nobody seemed very broken up by the death of one of their own," Susan said to Parkhurst after a patrolman had escorted them to his Bronco. "Except maybe the governor." She told him what Garrett said.

"Wakely wasn't one of them," Parkhurst said. "He was like a pet, sometimes a nuisance, foisted on them by their star."

"True," she said. "Poor man. No wonder he was depressed."

She told Parkhurst what all her questioning had reaped. Nil. "Not

180

a one of them has an alibi. They all said they were together from about five o'clock on, but not solidly. They were all in and out. Any one of them could have slipped away, gone out, snuffed Wakely and slipped back."

"I like to know why things happen," Parkhurst said. "If Wakely killed himself now, there was a reason. I want to know what it was. Did he have a personal life? Any friends besides His High Muckety-muck the governor? What did the poor peckerwood do all the time? What did he think about? If I know all that shit then I can get the whole picture."

"You think it wasn't suicide." No inflection in her voice. She didn't think so either.

"People die all the time and some of it's senseless. Dope dealers kill each other over territory. Addicts kill to get money for dope. Husbands kill wives because dinner is late, wives kill husbands because they're tired of the slobs sacked out in front of the TV all the time. There's always a reason. Even if it's senseless, there's a reason. What was his reason?"

"You don't buy that he could just get tired of the whole thing? Tired of being the governor's friend, tired of being taken care of, tired of being in the wheelchair, tired of being dragged around all over the country with this campaign."

"I like to know the truth. Whatever it is."

"Oh, truth," Susan said. "Have you ever noticed truth is a very slippery thing?" She looked at him. "Especially if we're telling it to ourselves."

"You talking of the Governor's little speech about Wakely doing whatever he decided and nothing could stop him?"

"Yeah. Did that feel like the truth to you?"

"It felt like somebody trying to deal with guilt."

"Yeah, that's what it felt like to me, too," she said. "We lie to ourselves, we lie to each other, we lie about each other." She looked out the window. In the pale silver starlight, the wind rolled across the grasses like the waves of ocean surf. A white-tailed buck, with a swift graceful arc, leaped into the tunnel of their headlights and left an imprint on her retinas. It seemed a thing of rare beauty after the bloody scene at Wakely's house.

Parkhurst slammed on the brakes. She tensed for the impact and then let her shoulders slump in relief when she saw the buck bound across the road, down the ditch, up the other side and sail over the fence.

"You know what struck me?" she said. "No disbelief. From any of these people. No 'He couldn't be dead. I just saw him an hour ago, he was fine. He couldn't possibly be dead, he was just here.' Governor Garrett didn't even ask to see his old buddy's body."

"Yeah."

Most people did. Relatives and loved ones couldn't believe in a sudden death until they saw the body. "He'd know reporters were swarming in even as we breathed."

"Yeah," Parkhurst said. "Like your cousin."

"What's that supposed to mean?"

"I wonder how objective you can be."

"Sean had nothing to do with Fromm's death, suicide or homicide."

"Right."

"Nothing," she repeated through clenched teeth. "I've known him all my life. He had nothing to do with it."

"Ah, all your life. 'He was such a nice quiet boy. I just can't believe it. Why, I've known him all my life.'"

"Oh, shut up."

"If there's one thing you don't ever get over, it's your childhood," Parkhurst said.

She didn't know what he was thinking, but she was thinking she didn't need this. It would get sticky. You don't just poke a stick in the middle of the governor's campaign and stir it around. And in a homicide investigation, you didn't just stir, you roiled that sucker around until it bubbled up in a cauldron like Shakespeare's. Bubble, bubble, toil and trouble.

"I've got a bad feeling about this, Susan."

"It couldn't just be indigestion, could it? What did you eat for supper?"

Wakely's death made headlines in the *Hampstead Herald*. It made the front page in the *New York Times* and the *Washington Post*.

FRIEND OF GARRETT TAKES LIFE

28

$\mathcal{C}$ass didn't like this at all. Even while she showered and pulled on tailored black pants and a beige sweater, she was trying to think how she could get out of it. Bernie was probably on his way to pick her up and she had no way to stop him. If she didn't answer the door, he'd keep pounding until she did. If she told him she was sick, he'd haul her to a doctor. If she ran out the back door, he'd probably call the cops and report her missing. Of course, that would give her—what? Three days before they'd do anything? This is not going to work.

Carmen went into her defending-the-home bark and a few seconds later the doorbell rang. So much for running. She let Bernie in.

"Still haven't gotten rid of them, I see." He nodded at the boxes stacked in the dining room.

"All in good time." She had other things on her mind. Today was Tuesday, Halloween was Friday. The anniversary of Ted and Laura's deaths. Three more days. Now that the decision had been made, she felt calm, relaxed, more unburdened and free than she'd been since she'd come back to Hampstead.

"Need some help?"

"Thanks, I can manage." She slipped on her coat and they went out to the car. "The news last night reported Wakely's death." She'd been shocked and saddened. Friends all those years ago, when they'd been young, she and Jack and Wakely. Sometimes Wakely had a date and the four of them would go out. Sometimes it was just the three of them. A big strong man, fearless when jumping out of airplanes and fighting fires, he was shy around people but he had a quiet sense of humor that surfaced when he felt comfortable. "What happened? He shot himself?"

"Apparently."

"Poor Wakely," she said as she got in the car.

"Fasten your seatbelt." He handed her a newspaper.

She took it, clicked in the seatbelt and read headlines suggestively wondering about the friendship between Jack Garrett and Wakely Fromm.

Cass tossed the paper in the back. "How could anybody think Jack was gay?" She well and truly knew he wasn't, but giving interviews that twenty years ago the two of them made love at every opportunity probably wasn't what the campaign committee wanted in the news.

"I can't believe it would make a difference."

"Where you from, lady?"

"Aren't we stooping to the same level by sneaking in something about Halderbreck?"

"That's how the game is played."

"Well, it's not very honorable."

"Politics isn't about honor," he said. "It's about winning. If the truth has to be sacrificed, so be it. If one reputation has to be rolled in the mud to save another, then okay. It isn't a Queensbury rules let's-all-play-fair sport, it's a give-no-quarter war. Facts get twisted to fit the needs of the person running, rumors get created for the same reason. The needs of the voters get overrun by the more immediate needs of the candidate."

Bernie hunched his shoulders. "Sorry. Didn't mean to get carried away."

"What happened? A few days ago, you were a dedicated player."

He shook his head. "I'm not sure this is a good idea."

"I'm with you there. It's stupid. Nobody's going to pay any attention to anything I say."

He drove out to the Garrett farm and eased through the media crowd clustered at the gate throwing questions and jabbing mikes at the car. It was all rather horrifying.

Nora, Molly's personal assistant, was carrying on a monologue, as usual, and as usual, she was pissing everybody off. Cass could tell Todd was on the point of losing his temper. Everybody but Molly disliked Nora, Todd more than the rest.

Nora sat next to Jack on one side of the dining room table, Todd and Leon sat on the other. Todd made a come-on-over gesture indicating that Cass and Bernie should join them. Nora smiled at Bernie and glared at Cass and went on talking. When she seized a subject she'd go on and on until she set everybody's teeth on edge. The politicals put up with her because of Molly, ignored her as much as possible and made jokes about her behind her back.

"He's going to do something awful," Nora was saying. "I know it."

"Halderbreck," Todd muttered to Bernie. "Nora had a hot flash or something."

Nora shot him a look of pure hatred. Todd produced a smile very close to angelic.

"I've been talking with Willa Hughes," Nora said.

Jack looked blank.

"One of the press," Nora said shortly. "You need to pay attention to them."

"Right." No hint of impatience in Jack's voice and he had a look of close listening, but Cass knew his mind was working on something far away from whatever Nora was talking about. "What about Halderbreck?"

"How well do you know him?" Nora asked.

"We're colleagues, not friends. The media likes to paint him as an oddball eccentric but he's a God and family kind of guy."

"Well, I ran into him the other day in Washington and when I told him you were going to be the party's candidate and become this country's next president, he laughed."

"That's what I'd do if somebody told me Halderbreck would get the nomination and win the election."

"It wasn't a funny laugh, Jack." Nora leaned closer to him. "There was no humor in his eyes. And he started rambling about how you can never tell and things aren't always what they seem and it was a horse race."

Jack nodded agreement. "Halderbreck does tend to ramble."

"When I asked him what he meant, he said the convention would be the telling."

"Nora, that's way in the future. Let's not get ahead of ourselves. We have long miles to go before then. He's probably warning me if I get that far, his people can snag enough delegates to prevent a first ballot nomination."

"What would happen then?"

"We storm the place and hope we can get more votes than they can."

"What if it goes several ballots?"

Jack looked directly in her eyes and spoke clearly. "Nora, we haven't even won a primary yet."

"He kept talking about the day of reckoning, the day of reckoning, and saying he'd be in the winner's circle because he stood up with right and good."

Todd shifted in his chair and looked about to make some squashing comment.

"Does he know anything bad about you?" Nora looked pointedly at Cass.

Cass felt a little prick of irritation. She was the something bad that could be used against Jack? How? Maybe it was the excuse that would be used to get rid of her. Molly didn't like her, and what Molly didn't like, Nora didn't like. Little did they know they didn't need an excuse. She wouldn't be around long anyway.

"You mean besides being a homo-sex-u-al?" Jack said.

"You can laugh, but I'm worried. He's going to toss in a grenade and blow us sky high."

"Nora, come on. Don't worry. I can weather anything he throws at us."

"We gotta roll." Todd stood up and everybody else began to scramble.

"Molly!" Jack yelled. "Let's go!"

Jack and Molly got in the waiting limo. Cass, Bernie, Todd, and Leon piled into the one behind it. They were headed thirty-five miles to a luncheon in Lawrence where Jack would speak to a group of University of Kansas alumni.

"Don't wait," Todd told the driver. "We have a schedule."

The driver put the limo in gear, but before he could pull away, Nora came running up. Todd grimaced and opened the door for her.

". . . Sorry, just had to pick up something at the last minute. I couldn't go off without . . ."

Todd folded his arms and closed his eyes. He didn't suffer fools politely and he made no secret of the fact that he thought Nora a fool.

Thirty-five miles. With Nora talking all the way, it was going to be a long trip.

"Just look at all these empty fields." Nora bustled around settling in her seat. "Why doesn't somebody do something with them?"

Since everybody else ignored her, Cass felt pressured to respond. "It's farm land. Crops will get planted in the spring."

"Well, I know that. What is it they grow here?"

"Wheat, corn, soy beans—"

"That's interesting, thank you, dear. Do people really live in these old houses way out in the middle of nowhere?"

"They're farm houses. People have lived in the same house, many of them, for generations."

"Well, some of them are falling down. Look at that old thing. It's nothing but rotting wood."

"It's The Hanging Barn," Cass said. That even got a rise out of Todd who opened his eyes for a moment, then closed them again.

"People who want to commit suicide come out here and hang themselves."

"Why would anybody want to come out here to hang himself?" Nora said.

Bernie thought, shouldn't the question rather be, why would anybody want to hang himself?

"It's where I'd come," Cass said. *If I didn't have the gun.*

Bernie shot her a look, but only asked mildly, "Why is it called that?"

"Quantrill," Cass said. "In eighteen fifty-six, filled with a fervor of rightness, Quantrill and his Raiders slaughtered an antislavery farmer and his two sons. The farmer's wife, overwhelmed by grief, hanged herself in the barn. Since then, a number of people have hanged themselves there."

For the rest of the trip, Nora talked about the senseless act of suicide and how she, herself, didn't understand it at all. Fortunately, they arrived at Lawrence and Nora got out, or Cass might have found herself yelling at the woman.

The room where the luncheon was held was all very nautical with framed pictures of boats on the wall, ropes dangling here and there, anchors and nets propped in the corners. Pretty funny, Kansas being nowhere near a seafaring spot. Molly and Jack sat at the speaker's table with important looking people about whom Cass hadn't a clue, except they had money. She sat next to Bernie at a banquet table with Nora and Todd seated on the other side and wondered how long this would take and when she might be expected to get home. She had no idea what had happened to Leon. Off somewhere making media consultant decisions probably. Lunch was an unexpected surprise, the baked chicken was actually quite good. When the mousse and coffee came, she excused herself and went to the ladies room.

Just as she slid down her trousers and underwear and was about to sit, her cell phone rang.

A women washing her hands called out, "I think your phone is ringing."

"Oh, thank you." Cass unzipped her bag and fumbled for the phone. "Hello?"

189

"This is your old friend Marsha."

She did have an old friend Marsha, but this wasn't her voice. This was the voice of Todd Haviland, campaign manager, sitting back there in the dining room. "Uh—this isn't really a good time, uh—"

"Call me Marsha. Tell me how you like working for Garrett For President?"

"Well, I don't work for him yet. I'm only thinking about it. I'm not sure I will." Her voice echoed with a tinny edge. "It might be interesting. You know, finding out how our democracy works."

"Stop a minute. Listen . . . listen . . . okay. Call me Marsha."

Irritated at being put in this ridiculous position, Cass threw in a sweet snag. "Marsha, these people are not above putting on a charade."

"Don't ruin this opportunity. We can't try more than once," Todd said sharply.

"Yeah, all the juicy stuff, you know? The stuff that never gets on the news."

"Good. Keep going."

Cass lowered her voice. "Oh, like just yesterday he said Senator Halderbreck was so stupid he needed both hands and a map to find his ass." She felt silly and self-conscious and had no idea if anyone was listening. If no one heard her, the great performance in the ladies room was wasted.

"That's great! Don't forget to flush."

Cass flushed, washed her hands and went back to the table. Todd ignored her. Molly gazed with adoring admiration at Jack as he spoke. After the speech and the handshaking and the back slapping, they all trooped out. Herds of press surged toward her, microphones bristling. Head down, she kept going. Obviously, her little staged bit had been heard.

When they got back to Hampstead they stopped at the Garrett For President local headquarters where Jack shook hands with the volunteers.

* * *

Em hadn't been there when the governor came. She felt both anger at a possibly missed opportunity and relief that she hadn't been forced to use the opportunity. She worked steadily throughout the afternoon, following the script and dialing the numbers on her list. She kept her head bent and didn't make eye contact with any of the other volunteers. What would they think if she suddenly told them they might as well stop making these silly calls? None of it mattered. Jackson Garrett would be dead before the first primary.

The headache that had started out as only a nagging annoyance crept to the front of her brain and seized at her temples. She had aspirin in her shoulder bag but was afraid to stop what she was doing and find them. What if the gun fell out when she was looking for aspirin?

The man in charge was looking at her. She felt his gaze all the way across the room but didn't look up when he walked toward her. Was he going to tell her to leave? She wasn't doing it right. She wasn't fast enough, or persuasive enough when talking to potential voters. Oh no, no, he couldn't tell her not to come back. Volunteering here was the best way to keep track of what Jackson Garrett was doing and where he went. She couldn't lose this opportunity. How would she manage, if she was sent away?

"Em?"

She started even though she'd been expecting him to speak to her. When he put a hand on her shoulder, it took all her energy to keep from flinching. Like a whipped dog, she thought, any time a hand reaches for you, it's going to inflict pain.

"Hey," he said. "You've been at it a long time. It's time to quit. Next shift coming in. You don't have to work day and night. Take off. Come back rested tomorrow."

When she looked around she saw that everybody who'd been working when she started was no longer there. The young man seated next to her was replaced by a middle-aged woman, the middle-aged woman across from her was replaced by a young woman, probably a college student. She nodded to the young man in charge, she thought his name was Scott, and put her hands in her lap. Dumb. Did she think if she wasn't careful, they'd leap up on their own and start dialing.

"You've done a really good job," he said.

Em held her breath. Now he was going to say it, *but don't bother to come back. You're not fast enough. You're too old. We have somebody better.*

". . . So, I'll see you tomorrow?"

A second or two passed before she processed his words, then she smiled. "Oh yes."

"You have a pretty smile, Em, you should use it more often." He gave her shoulder a little pat, then went off to snag a new person who had just wandered in.

It was nearly dark when she left the headquarters. She didn't much like being out after dark. Not that it was late, and not that she cared what happened to her, but she had to complete her work. After that, nothing mattered. She pulled a soft cloche hat from her shoulder bag and put it on. She couldn't even remember what color it was, she had several in different shades. Aware of the importance of not being noticed, she was in the habit of changing clothes often, sometimes wearing a hat, trying to keep changing her appearance so nobody would remember her as the woman who was always around.

She was tired. How nice it would be just to go home and lie down. No! She straightened her shoulders. Not yet, not until she finished the job.

At Eighth Street, instead of simply walking on by, she stopped and looked up at St. Elizabeth's Cathedral. A big, imposing building, it looked exactly like a church should. Important, like God could perform miracles in this place. So many of the new churches looked like office buildings. How could you fear God and repent your sins in an office building? Before she could talk herself out of it, she was inside. Dim and hushed. Deep feeling of being in the presence of God. She lit two candles, one for herself and one for Alice Ann.

Moving slowly, in a dreamlike way, she sat in a pew and stared at the altar of God. She wanted a miracle, but the miracle she wanted was a sin against that God. For thirty minutes, she prayed. Then, still in her half-wake state she took confession. "Bless me, Father, for I have sinned." *And I intend to sin more.* She told the Father she had something in mind and it was a bad thing what this would lead to. She didn't tell him what these plans were and he didn't push her. She wasn't looking for forgiveness or absolution, but just being here and speaking vaguely of her plans made her feel eased, like a great weight had been lifted from her shoulders. The Father told her to say fifty Hail Marys and read a passage in St. Matthew. This is what a life is worth? Fifty Hail Marys and a bible reading?

As she was leaving the church, she saw a young woman across the street who looked like Alice Ann. A burst of grief gripped Em with such pain, she thought she couldn't breathe. Alice Ann, her daughter, the love of her life, dead now for almost twelve years. Nothing would bring her back. Em's pain was burned away by anger. Such hot anger that it owned her, possessed her, was the only thing that kept her warm, the only thing that kept her going.

She dug out her key and let herself into the motel. It was close to campus and because it was inexpensive many parents stayed here when they came to see their sons or daughters at Emerson.

"I'm home," she said.

Sitting on the end of the bed, she untied her shoelaces and slipped off her shoes, wiggled her toes at the relief. An eight-by-ten photo in a silver frame sat on the lamp table by the bed. She kissed two finger-tips and placed them gently on the face of her dead daughter in the eight by ten photo in the silver frame. The picture was taken the year Alice Ann graduated from high school. Soft blond hair, slightly dis-arrayed, as if caught by a gentle breeze. Smooth forehead, quizzical blue eyes, lovely pointed chin. Beautiful, she was so beautiful. "Soon, my child."

The feeling of destiny swelled in her chest.

Em had been against the marriage from the very start. She never liked Kirby Vosse from the first time Alice Ann brought him home. Her husband had said she was just being clutchy, hanging on because she didn't want to let her baby go, but deep down where he wouldn't admit it, he understood. He didn't want to let go either, but there was nothing they could do. Alice Ann was all grown up and ready to make her own life. She had chosen this young man. It didn't matter how they felt about him. Because Alice Ann loved him, they must find a place in their hearts for him.

"This is really the hardest part, you know? Waiting for the right time." Em took off her blouse and pants, hung them in the small closet and pulled on a nightgown. In the bathroom, she brushed her teeth and when she noticed herself in the mirror, she was startled at the lines and sags in her face. When had the frown appeared between her eyes?

My daughter is dead because of Jackson Garrett, she told her image.

Alice Ann had a sweetness with a desire to please. At first there had been a bruise, once a black eye, and another time a broken arm, but she only said she fell, she was clumsy, she just seemed to bump into things. That happened over and over and then . . .

Em got angry still, remembering her daughter in the hospital, so battered she was barely recognizable. Em had flat out asked her if her husband had done this.

"It was my own fault," Alice Ann had whispered. "I knew he was tired. I shouldn't have said what I did."

Dear God in heaven, Em thought, picking up her daughter's hand. "Tell me what happened." She spoke sharply, but it took more than that, it took repeated urging and pushing before Alice Ann would say anything. As near as Em could piece it all together from Alice Ann's stumbling words her daughter had been home alone, waiting for Kirby. He hadn't come home for dinner, it was late, she started getting concerned. She waited up for him and fell asleep on the couch with the television on so she didn't hear him unlock the door and come in. The first she knew, he was standing over her.

"Where have you been?" She wasn't prying, just concerned and glad he was back.

"You telling me I can't do what I want?" He'd been drinking.

"No, I—"

"Why do you always do this to me?" His voice was soft, almost a whisper and very sad.

Numb with fear, she didn't answer.

He shook her. "Why?" His eyes glittered and his breath was foul. Frozen, she didn't respond. He hit her low in her stomach and she felt the warm trickle of urine.

"Christ, look at you. Pissing all over yourself like a baby." By one arm, he hauled her to the bathroom and flung her at the toilet.

She sprawled across it and banged her head on the tile floor. A gray fog crowded her mind. He kicked her breast and stomach and throat. She gagged and knew she was going to be sick.

When she vomited, he yelled, "You're disgusting," and rubbed her face in it. Grabbing the back of her neck, he squeezed it hard and smashed her face against the side of the tub. Whimpering, tears and snot mixing with the vomit, she begged him to stop. He tossed her in the tub and her head hit a faucet.

When she regained consciousness, he was gone. She could barely move, the pain was so bad. It was a long time before she managed to get to the phone and call help.

Alice Ann was hospitalized for several days. Em told her she had to have Kirby arrested and somewhere she had to find the courage to testify against him. If she didn't, he would kill her next time.

Maybe, Em thought, she shouldn't have done it, shouldn't have pushed Alice Ann so hard, shouldn't have insisted she have him arrested. Maybe if Em hadn't been so angry, so intent on revenge, if she had snatched up her daughter and run far away maybe Alice Ann would still be alive.

Alice Ann's husband got a lawyer and the lawyer got him off. The husband bought a gun and killed Alice Ann. The lawyer was Jackson Garrett.

With everything set, Em felt restless. Waiting was something she'd never done well. She felt nauseated all the time and food didn't taste good. It was almost like her system was getting ready for the end. Anticipation left her feeling giddy.

When you lose a child, some part of you dies. You can't explain it to anybody who hasn't been there. You never get over it. You wake up with it, you carry it with you all day wherever you go, you take it to your grave.

It's almost over. Her world was at the verge of ending as she put herself on the path toward the final confrontation.

She turned on the television, pulled off her shoes and lay back.

When Cass turned on her television set, she discovered she was all over the news. The shot of her leaving the faculty dining room with her head down was played over and over on every channel. Hadley Cane put her press secretary spin on it and explained that Ms. Storm had only recently joined the team and didn't realize that all walls had ears, even those of the ladies room.

Free advertising for Jack, the seed planted in the voters' minds that Halderbreck was stupid, and payback for Halderbreck's suggestion that Jack would be second on his ticket.

Democracy in action.

29

———

"*If* you'd stop yelling, maybe I could figure out what you're going on about." Sean, with two large grocery bags, trotted up the steps, brushed past Susan in the doorway and plopped the bags on her kitchen table.

"Where the hell have you been?" She'd left messages all over the place and he hadn't called back.

"Jesus, you sound like my wife."

"You didn't answer the question." The media had been clamoring at her all day and she wasn't in the best of moods to begin with. Having to fight them everywhere she went didn't help any.

"Just like my wife." He turned to face her, leaned back against a cabinet and crossed his arms.

"Are you trying to make me lose my temper?" It wouldn't take much.

"No, darlin', though 'tis a delightful sight altogether." He started removing tomatoes, garlic, onions from a bag. "You want to tell me what you're going on about before I lose mine?"

"What are you doing?"

"I'm in the mood for a home-cooked meal, and since you can't cook, I'm the one who has to do it. Always been that way. You get into something and can't handle it. I have to step in."

Susan put her hands on her hips. "You only step in when you have a guilty conscience. What have you done?"

Bell peppers, baby squash, salad greens. Her kitchen table was beginning to look like the produce department at Erle's Market.

"Is there a place called Weir, Kansas?" He squatted, rummaged in the cabinet and came up with a large pot.

"I doubt it. Why?"

"I think I was there." With a woefully weary sigh, he crossed his eyes in a mad, blitzed-out-of-his mind dippy look. "I've been places today where no man has set foot since the beginning of the last century. They dig them out of the ice for the tourists."

"All right," she said. "You've charmed me out of being mad. Now—"

"No, really. That's where I was. Learned fascinating and highly suspect information from the natives."

She eyed him suspiciously, wondering what the hell he was going on about. He smiled benignly. Alarms went off. "My father sent you, didn't he? He bribed you and sent you out here to get me fired. That way I'd have to come back home."

"I can't understand why you wouldn't, *aghra*. Have you looked around at where you are?"

"I have an officer who wants to throw your ass in jail. I'm having a little difficulty understanding why I don't just let him."

"You'd just stand by and let me be arrested?"

She sighed and rubbed the tips of her fingers up and down her forehead. "I'd appreciate it if you'd stop behaving like a jerk and recall that someone hit a woman over the head and stuffed her into the trunk of her car to die. Someone also—maybe a different someone, but most likely that same someone—stuck a gun in the mouth of a paralyzed man and pulled the trigger."

"Sorry, Susan. What am I about to be arrested for?"

"Your fingerprints were found in her house."

"Yeah."

She thought he sighed, but since he'd banged the pot in the sink and turned on the water, she couldn't be sure. "Sean—"

He transferred pot to stove and turned burner on beneath it. "That's what I came to see you about."

"You were in Gayle's house."

He slapped a package of pasta on the countertop, set a bottle of olive oil beside it, brought out a bottle of wine from the other bag and took glasses from the shelf. "Where do you keep your knives?"

"Why the hell didn't you tell me? Top drawer on your left."

"I'm a reporter, Susan. I'm not in the habit of giving information to cops." He uncorked the wine, poured two glasses and handed her one.

"You want to explain?" She took the glass, held it up to the light, and admired its ruby color. She sipped.

"Friday." With the tip of a knife, he chopped onions with a precise rhythm. Chop chop chop. Shoved minced bits out of the way. Chop chop chop. "I ran into the hotel and Wakely, listing in his wheelchair, was waiting in the lobby. Half-looped, as usual, and mad as a viper. He kept saying, loudly, that he had to be somewhere and his keeper wasn't there."

"Keeper?"

"Murray, the physical therapy guy, who takes care of him. Being the sort of crafty investigative reporter that I am, I thought, aha, a gift horse. Far from looking him in the mouth, I'll put him in my rental car, and extract hitherto unknown secrets about Jackson Garrett." Sean put a dollop of oil in a skillet and turned the burner on under it.

"Where'd you take him?"

"I followed his directions. Turn here, turn there, that's the house, stop here. I got him inside, wheelchair and all. And that wasn't easy. For my troubles, I got nothing. He wouldn't even introduce me to the woman who opened the door."

"You took Wakely Fromm to see Gayle Egelhoff." It never hurt to state the obvious if you were arranging clarity in your mind.

"Yes." He scraped onions and garlic in the skillet and stirred them around. The resulting aroma made her mouth water.

"Don't try to tell me you didn't find out her name."

"When I got Wakely settled in the living room, I noticed a magazine on the coffee table just before I left. It was addressed to Vincent Egelhoff. I assumed she was Mrs. Egelhoff."

"Why?" she said with exasperation. "Why did he go to see Gayle and why didn't you tell me?"

"He wouldn't tell me who he was going to see, he wouldn't tell me why."

She eyed him suspiciously. "What did he say?"

Sean added chopped bell peppers to the sizzling onions. "He kept muttering to himself, 'No point now. And better left alone.' "

"What did that mean?"

"I couldn't get anything more out of him."

"Really?"

He held up a hand. "Honest to God's truth."

"Sure," she said flatly.

He dropped pasta into boiling water. "Wakely always talked about his good friend Jack. Best smoke jumper that ever was. Hero. Wouldn't be alive if Jack hadn't dragged him out of hell's fire. It was like a litany, repeating the same phrases over and over. That's all he ever said."

"You think there's something fishy there."

"It piqued my interest. Enough that I did a little research at the Hampstead paper on that twenty-year-old disaster."

"And you found out—?"

"Jack Garrett was a hero and saved the life of Wakely Fromm."

She took a sip of wine. "How was Fromm getting back to the hotel?"

"He said he'd call someone."

With a fork, Sean lifted a strand of pasta and tasted it for doneness. "I have no idea why Fromm went there. I took him because I wanted to pump him, get something the rest of the media didn't have."

"Why?"

"By the time *NewsWorld* comes out, that's all old news."

Susan picked up the bottle and topped off both their glasses.

"The whole situation with Garrett taking Fromm in, making himself responsible for the man, Fromm living with Garrett even after Garrett got married. It's just—" Sean shrugged. "The whole situation is unusual. I wanted to find out—" He broke off, thought a second, then added, "What I could find out, I guess. What does this say about Garrett? Would it continue forever? If Garrett were to be nominated, and an even bigger *if*, if he were to be elected, would Fromm go to the White House?"

Sean turned off the burner and dumped boiling water and pasta into a colander to drain. "Fromm and Garrett have known each other since—hell, I don't know, since they were born maybe. I'm interested in Garrett. Like I said. I'm a reporter."

"Are you looking for scandal? Dirty little secrets hidden away in dark holes until they grow mold and smell like defeat, that can be brought out in the light and spread before a salivating public."

"Good Lord, have you been reading Edgar Allan Poe?" He shook the colander and dumped the pasta on a platter, poured sauce over it and put the whole thing on the table.

"Dinner." He held out a chair for her.

She decided maybe she was hungry after all. "This is really tangled, Sean. I can't just let you waltz in here and do what you want. You may think it's funny, but I am the law enforcement in this town. And, if you laugh, so help me God, I will bash you over the head with that wine bottle."

He looked at her with horror. "And spill the merlot? I want you to know I paid—"

"Sean—"

"Sorry." He twirled linguini around his fork. "When you get all official, I get nervous."

"Any reason?"

"See?" Pasta securely wrapped around the fork, he took a mouthful, chewed and swallowed. "There you go again. What do you think I did? Killed the woman and poor old Wakely?"

She looked at him. "No." But Parkhurst didn't feel that strongly. Cops were always suspicious of the individual who found a homicide victim.

"Then why all this third degree, this where were you when the dog barked in the night?"

Eyebrows raised, she held her look.

"Oh, right. Just doing your job."

"So why were you at Gayle Egelhoff's house the night she was killed?"

More pasta twirling, more chewing, more swallowing. "To pump Wakely, like I said. No reason. Simple reporter's curiosity."

"What time was that?"

He took a sip of wine. "Nine o'clock, maybe."

"She died sometime between nine and two A.M. You and Wakely were the last people to see her alive."

"Except for the killer."

Susan ignored that. "Tell me about her."

"I didn't have a chance to find out anything. Mid-forties. A little nervous. As I was pushing in the chair, she said to Fromm, 'You have to tell the truth now.' "

"Go on."

"Fromm said, 'The truth is different for everybody.' "

"What did she say?"

"That was it."

"What else did he say?"

" 'Vince didn't.' "

"Didn't what?"

"I don't know. Wakely remembered I was there and closed his mouth."

"What else?"

"Nothing," he said.

"Nothing else? They didn't say anything else to each other? To you?"

"Nothing. That was it. The whole entire stock of words that were said in my presence."

"What about after you left and stood with your ear to the door?"

Sean drew himself up. "I'd never do such a thing. Besides, the door was solid wood."

30

$\mathcal{A}$s soon as his shift ended, Demarco picked up his laptop, headed for the hospital and tracked down the doc at the nurses' station writing on a chart. "How's she doing?"

"She lost a lot of blood." Dr. Sheffield, stocky, muscular, black curly hair, stood with his feet planted wide, arms crossed over his chest, like he was prepared to protect the castle from roving hordes.

"I need to question her."

"No." Sheffield went back to scribbling notes.

"I need to find out what happened."

The doc shifted his stance, gave Demarco a hard stare. "It was very dicey there for a while. She's not out of the woods yet. You can't bother her."

There were times when Demarco missed the Marine Corps. You didn't put up with shit like this. If you wanted something, you asked, and you got an answer.

Demarco shifted to civilian cop mode. Arrogant people only got more stubborn when pushed and if he wanted this guy on his side, he needed to back off. "Any permanent damage?"

"Physical? With a whole lot of luck, probably not. She's got a deep cut on her shoulder. Cuts on her hands. Lacerations and abrasions on her feet, minor stuff. A serious cut across her throat. It's been stitched. That's all that can be done for now. Later, she'll need plastic surgery. She has a fractured mandible. Upper teeth wired and lower teeth connected by tie wires for immobility."

"She can't talk?"

Sheffield continued with his chart and his notes. "With her jaws wired together, not very well." Stating the obvious.

"How long will it take to heal?"

"The jaw has an excellent blood supply. Six to eight weeks for the physical injuries. Psychological scarring is something else. Tremendous, I'd guess. That isn't my field."

"She has a computer at home."

"Good." Sheffield snapped shut the chart he was writing on and slid it in a slot, impatient, busy. Demarco was bothering him.

Demarco held up the case he was carrying. "Laptop. I'll ask, she'll type."

Sheffield wasn't happy, but Demarco kept chipping away and the doc did finally allow Demarco ten minutes, no more. Demarco, mindful of having said to Her Ladyship the Chief he'd be tactful, said thank you. He didn't know how the chief had made her bones on the job, but figured it was through some political shit about having more females to look good to the powers that be.

She was asleep when he walked in, looking young and vulnerable and bruised. Fluids dripping into her left arm, monitors on the wall behind her, wire cutters on the bedside table, handy for quick use in case of vomiting. He wanted the asshole who did this, wanted to grab him by the throat and smash his face. Snatching a chair, he silently lowered it beside the bed and sat. Three of his ten minutes went by before she stirred. Her eyes blinked open, she looked around wildly, face frozen in terror. She struggled to sit. He laid his fingers on her arm. "It's okay."

She stared at him, the glazed look left and recognition came into her eyes. She settled back into the pillow.

"Don't try to talk, it'll hurt."

Her hand went to the bandage on her throat and she trailed her fingers lightly across it and back. She swallowed, obviously painfully.

"You know how to use a computer?"

She shot him a look of such scorn, his mood lifted considerably. If she still had an attitude, she'd be okay.

"Right." He pushed a button to raise the head of the bed and placed the laptop on her thighs. "I'm going to ask questions, you type answers."

Her fingers tapped keys. *Cool.*

"How did you get hurt?" He stood at her shoulder to see the computer monitor.

Her face went blank. After a second or two, one by one black letters appeared on the white background. *Don't know.*

"Don't worry about it," he said. "Happens a lot. After an injury, you get amnesia. Docs even have a fancy name for it."

Suddenly, she tried to speak, winced, then typed *Gayle?*

"You asking if your sister was killed?"

She nodded.

"Yeah," he said. "Sorry."

Bad dreams. Thought maybe nightmare.

"What do you last remember?"

Furious typing. *You!!! Tearing up house!!!!*

He hadn't torn up anything, but he ignored that.

She looked uncertain. *What's today?*

"Tuesday."

She puzzled something out in her head. *Told me about Gayle?*

"Yes. You ran away."

A smug expression flickered in her eyes.

"Where did you go?"

Keys clicked softly. *Friend.*

"You stayed with this friend?"

Few hours.

"Then what?"

Walked around. Thought what to do. She shot him a look like it was all his fault. *Went home.*

"Why?"

I LIVE THERE!!!

"So? What? You thought you could just go back and we'd forget about you?"

Tired. Needed shower. Wanted bed.

"Okay. So what happened when you got there?"

Nothing at first. Food. Shower. Clean clothes.

"Then what?"

Somebody in house. Searching.

"Who?

She shrugged. *Man.*

"What man?"

Don't know. Getting a mite irritated, her fingers pounded the keys.

"What'd he look like?"

She hunched her shoulders and scrunched down lower on the pillow. *Heard him coming. Hid.*

"Then what?"

It was slow going, but typing out what she remembered seemed to help bring it back. When the intruder opened the closet door where she was hiding, he aimed the flashlight beam right at her eyes and she couldn't see. The only thing he'd said had been damn and shit a time or two when thrown objects connected.

"What makes you think he was searching for something?"

Another look of scorn. This kid had a good line of them and if he'd been the smiling sort he'd have smiled.

You see house? Mess!!!

"What was he searching for?"

Don't know.

"What did your sister have that was valuable?"

Get real!!!

"Money? Diamonds? Valuable stamps? Your Barbie collection?"

She didn't bother to type anything, she just adjusted the edge of her scorn number.

"Tell me about your sister, tell me about Gayle."

She looked at him, suspicion crawling over her face. *Why?*

"You're beginning to irritate me, kid. Because someone killed her and I want to know why."

Nothing valuable!!!!!

"Okay, then why was she killed?"

The kid did that thing again where she looked small and fragile and had Demarco worried about overtiring her. He didn't have much time left. Any minute either the doc would come in and throw him out or send someone to do it.

Black letters took off across the screen. *Father and mother squashed flat by tornado. Gayle married Vince. I lived with them. She took care of me. Always.*

She sniffed and like a little kid, rubbed her eyes with the back of one hand. He pretended not to notice. "Did Gayle seem any different lately? Worried about something? Scared about something? Special interest in something?"

Yeah. Don't know what. She and Vince argued a lot. He went off to see cousin. Had accident. Died.

A nurse stuck her head in the door and told Demarco he had to go, Miss Egelhoff needed to rest. He nodded. The nurse stood waiting for him to get the hell out. He asked the kid, "You want to keep the laptop?"

She shrugged. Pride wouldn't let her ask even for that much. He put it on the bedside table where she could reach it. She looked so fatigued her face was the blue-white color of nonfat milk and the dark bruises stood out like face paint.

"Keep the laptop till they release you, then we'll negotiate." He took a business card from his wallet and held it up. "Phone numbers. Also got my e-mail address if you need me for anything."

She typed something and he stepped back to read it. *They were fighting.*

"Who?

Gayle and Vince. Night before he left to go skiing.

"What were they fighting about?"

Don't know. Vince yelled. Said time to speak up.

"About what?"

She shrugged. *He laughed.*

"Officer," the nurse said in that warning tone nurses and teachers have down so perfect.

"I think if I don't go," he told the kid, "that woman is going to round up twenty-five strong men and try to throw me out."

She snorted.

He started for the door and she tugged at his jacket and typed. *She kept saying he was using a lie.*

"What lie?"

She shrugged.

"All right," he said. "I'll be back later. You sleep. No sneaking off anywhere."

She grabbed the business card and held it up to stop him from leaving. Her fingers clicked *How call? Can't talk. How e-mail? No Internet.*

He punched her gently on the shoulder. "Smart-aleck. Ask a nurse."

Susan gave another press conference, standing in front of the police department with reporters, cameramen, and television stand-ups behind a barricade of saw horses. A barrage of questions were thrown at her. She answered three. Yes, Wakely Fromm, Governor Garrett's friend, had apparently shot himself. No, at this time, they weren't treating it as a homicide. No, the governor wasn't a suspect in the death of Wakely Fromm, be it homicide or suicide.

They clamored about Vince Egelhoff and Gayle Egelhoff, both dead. Arlene Egelhoff, seriously injured. What about that? Was the Governor involved? Susan talked for two minutes without answering anything, then stepped back inside the department. Parkhurst gave her a thumb's up and followed her to her office where he leaned against the wall and crossed his arms like the ghost of Christmas yet to come.

"Even if it's a homicide," she said for what seemed like the thousandth time, "there's nothing to tie in Jack Garrett."

"Except the fact that they've been together for the last twenty years."

"That's evidence of caring, not homicide."

"We haven't even started to look for evidence," he said.

"I keep telling you, there's no reason to look."

"Sure, there is. We just haven't found it yet."

Demarco appeared in the doorway and Susan suppressed the sigh he always provoked. She didn't tell him to sit down. It would end up with her having to give him an order and that was a place she didn't want to go yet. Excluding his dislike of her, he seemed to be a good cop. As long as she could tolerate the iron rod up his ass and his manner that bordered on subordination, she'd let it ride.

"You get anything from the girl?" Parkhurst asked him.

"Not really." Demarco told them about the laptop and the question and answer bit.

"You got nothing," Susan said. "Not even a hint of who attacked her."

Demarco said through clenched teeth, "So far."

"You think if you keep questioning her, you'll get something more?"

"Maybe. The house was definitely tossed."

"By the same individual who attacked the girl?"

"It would seem so."

"Man?" Parkhurst asked.

"Yeah."

"Was the suspect looking for something in the house or looking for the girl?" Susan picked up a pen and tapped it silently on the desktop.

"My judgment, searching for something and the kid got in the way. Now he needs to get rid of her because she's seen him."

"You said she didn't get a good enough look to describe him," Parkhurst said.

"The intruder doesn't know that."

"Could the girl herself have taken the house apart?"

"She didn't cut her own throat. Tear the place apart?" Demarco shrugged. "Yeah, she could have. She's the type of kid who might do something like that, because she's angry, but I don't think she did."

"The intruder was looking for what?" Susan said.

"I don't know. Nor does she. She claims there's nothing valuable in the house. I'm inclined to believe her. I didn't find anything when I searched after the sister's body was found."

"Did he find what he was looking for?"

"No way to be sure."

Susan nodded. A person who searches for something, searches until he finds it, then stops and the remainder of the premises aren't tossed. In this case the entire house was torn up. "What is this girl angry about?"

Demarco looked at her like she was a half-wit. "The shitty way life has treated her." He waited a beat. "Ma'am."

Todd was the fuel that propelled this whole train, Bernie thought, as Todd came into the living room and started pacing from the fireplace, around the couch, to the foyer, from the foyer, around the couch, to the fireplace. "Politics," he'd told Bernie when Bernie got hired, "is show business and running for president is the greatest show on earth, not the circus with the elephants."

Jack Garrett couldn't get anywhere without Todd. Even though Todd was consumed with a nervous energy, he settled squabbles like a house mother, coaxed work from distracted troops like a general and survived hours of boredom like a Buddhist. Now, with the first primary on the horizon, the speed would roll and build until they were all racing as fast as a snowball barreling downhill, running on hysteria and adrenaline. After x number of days with no sleep, nerves get stretched so tight, the ends get frayed and tempers flash. All these people who'd worked together and played together and gotten closer than families would eye each other with the blinding insight that every other member of the team was a cretin, and just like with families there would be idiotic feuds and unwarranted jealousies and outright hatred.

The core group was all here. Leon Massy, media consultant, Hadley Cane, press secretary, Molly Garrett—the Governor was flying in from Topeka later—her assistant, Nora Tallace, Carter Mercado, the pollster, and Casilda Storm, though neither Mrs. Garrett nor Nora was happy about her. While Bernie liked Cass just fine, he was nervous about her being there since Mrs. Garrett had told him to get rid of her.

Todd was the boss, the trusted leader. His was the highest authority and his word was law. When Todd spoke, everybody listened. He was the one who asked questions, made decisions, kept his eye on the goal, and never lost faith. He requested, commanded, and raised his voice to a thin edge when he didn't get a quick enough response.

When Jack Garrett flew from one city to the next, Todd kept track of the polls, gave final okay on which ads to run, studied the opposition research and romanced the backers for more money. He was the one who told Garrett the unvarnished truth, fired troublemakers, demanded more work, figured the best angle on day-to-day events and worked out what Hadley should feed the press. From the constant advice given by each of them, he selected the useful and ignored the rest. If Garrett got the nomination and if he got elected—two very big ifs—Todd was a shoo-in for chief-of-staff.

Even though the D.C. primary was coming up fast, they were pretty cocky about winning there and were discussing a tougher nut. California. It was so big and had such a large population that Garrett couldn't do there what he did best. Meet people. Shake hands. That meant ads on television and radio, sound bites on local news programs, and column inches above the fold.

Leon was hammering the importance of dynamite ads in San Francisco and the Bay Area, Sacramento and the Central Valley, Los Angeles, Orange County and San Diego. "You get those, you get ninety percent of the vote."

He looked around the table to make sure they were all listening. "Battered women, education, and abortion are top of the list for ten percent of the white females most likely to vote."

"Whites are a minority in California," Hadley said. "We need to target the Hispanics and African-Americans."

"They don't vote in primaries. Seventy-five percent of them stayed home at the last primary. Do your math, ladies and gentlemen, that means only twenty-five percent went to the polls. We need to focus on the white folks to decide if the Governor'll be the party's candidate. White suburban vote is a big block."

"All those Black and Latino voters are going to wonder what's in it for them," Hadley said. "To win, you need the nonwhites."

"We also need the whites, we can't alienate them." Nora said.

Todd clenched his teeth. Nora pushed herself into these meetings and nobody, not even Todd, dared push her out. The problem was, she was disruptive and got everybody focused on being irritated at her instead of on the topic at hand. She was always throwing out something irrelevant or downright stupid. Or really scary-ass, like the governor should go to the funeral of a black kid. Todd tried to ignore that, but she kept on with it. Todd blew up and said, "Fine, we'll put that on the back burner."

"Now, Todd, I know what that means. You'll just ignore it."

"Nora, we can't just wait around for some kid to be shot."

"Well, just hire someone."

Bernie looked at her. A joke? Or was she actually suggesting they get a hired gun to blow away some innocent kid? Leon whistled softly under his breath. *We shall overcome.*

Bernie wasn't a hundred percent sure Nora was joking. A lot of her was invested in this campaign. If the Governor won, she'd be in a catbird seat, ready to snatch and press to her bosom whatever goodies came her way. She'd do a lot in her commitment to the campaign. Nothing about her was likeable, as far as Bernie could see. He'd wondered more than once why she was such a good friend of Mrs. Garrett and why Mrs. Garrett insisted Nora be included in their planning sessions. A stray thought ran through his mind that Nora had some hold on Molly Garrett.

Nora had thought Wakely Fromm was a handicap and had repeatedly said, "That old drunk costs you votes wherever we go."

For the most part, the governor ignored her, but on one occasion when she'd griped too much about Wakely, he'd told her, "Wakely stays. He's family. You're Molly's friend and are here by invitation."

Bernie wondered where Nora had been the night Wakely died.

It was late when the meeting was over. Bernie drove Cass home around two-thirty. She yawned and leaned her head against the seatback. "I don't think I'm cut out for politics. You people never seem to sleep."

"If you think we don't sleep now, just wait."

When Bernie pulled up in her driveway, she said, "You think Wakely shot himself?" Preoccupied as she was with her own inner demons she didn't have much head space for the hellhounds chasing anyone else. If she hadn't been so self-absorbed, would she have picked up on how unhappy he was?

Bernie looked at her, his face mostly in shadows, but the porch light lit up one side and the effect was to make him look like a tired harlequin. "I forgot you knew him."

"We were friends a long time ago. I never saw him after the fire where he was injured. It must have been hard. He was such a strong giant of a man."

"Hard to imagine Wakely a giant."

"You didn't answer my question," she said.

"Cops aren't letting it go. Makes me feel they have a reason to think maybe somebody else pulled the trigger."

She tried to remember what Wakely had said at Eva's party, something muddled about, "They killed her. They used her. They dumped her."

"This whole mess could sink the governor."

"Right," she said. "Keep your eye on the main point."

A half-shrug followed by a half-smile. "In politics, nothing else matters."

* * *

213

Sean waited until the guard went off to take a leak, then walked into the girl's room. She was asleep, but as soon as he planted himself in a chair, she opened one eye. Terror washed over her face. She started to speak, or maybe scream, winced and put her hand over the bandage at her throat.

"It's okay, Arlene," he said. "My name's Sean. I'm a magazine writer. I just came to see how you were. I brought you something to read." He put *Dreadful Sorry*, *Edge*, and *The Book of the Lion* on the bedside table.

She fumbled for the laptop on the bedside table. Sean helped her get it open and ready on her knees. She tapped in, *Storm trooper?*

"The guard?"

Quick nod.

"Urgent call of nature. He'll be right back. And undoubtedly, he'll throw me out."

Got ID?

"Smart girl." Sean took out his wallet, removed his driver's license and placed it against the monitor, put his press pass beside it, then his passport and a picture of Hannah. "My daughter. She's six. If she were here, she'd tell you I'm a really good guy, if a little slow sometimes."

Name's not Arlene.

"No? What is it?"

Moonbeam Melody.

"Ah. A pleasure to meet you, Ms. Melody."

What you want?

He put the four items back in his wallet. "What happened to you?"

Throat cut by psycho killer.

"Why?"

Don't you want to know who?

"Yes, but since I only have about thirty seconds, I thought I'd cut to the chase. Do you know who?"

No. *Don't know why either. Looking for something.*

"What?"

Don't know.

"What did you hear?"

214

Stuff being torn apart.

"Aside from that. Hear anything else?"

Suddenly she looked startled. *News.*

"News? Like a radio?

She thought a moment. *TV. Heard CNN.*

"The television set was on?"

Little. She turned a hand palm up, as though holding something the size of a deck of cards.

"Hold it right there! Know a good attorney, *Acushla*?" Sean said.

Her minder had returned and had his gun pointed dead center at Sean's chest. "Hands on your head!"

Sean winked at the girl as the guard marched him out. In the hallway, he was shoved against the wall, told to spread 'em, patted down and cuffed. Sean got the feeling the guy didn't get the chance to do this sort of thing very much and was thoroughly enjoying it.

Susan had just gotten to sleep when the phone rang.

"I get one phone call," Sean said. "I figured it should go to you."

In her sleep-befuddled state, it took her a second or two to figure out where he was and even longer to figure out what was going on. Sean was in jail and wanted her to get him out.

"What happened?"

"I was arrested for talking with the Egelhoff girl."

"God damn it, Sean, what the hell did you think you were doing?"

"Visiting a sick child, darlin'."

"I ought to let your ass sit in jail overnight."

"But since you love me—"

"I'll be right down."

"This is pretty embarrassing," Susan said.

"Thanks for the rescue." Sean gave the pickup fender a pat and climbed in on the passenger side. She fired it up and pointed its nose home.

He leaned his head back and sighed. "How'd I get here, Susan? Old and cynical and sad."

"Cynicism is underrated."

"What about sad?"

"You have too much Irish in your blood not to be sad. How did you get in that hospital room?" She was tired and cranky and sick to the bone of reporters, even if the one in question was Sean.

"Fatalists is what we are. All the Irish. Full of dark and captivating superstition. And at the same time sentimentally optimistic." He dropped the accent. "Did Fromm kill himself?"

She pulled the pickup into the garage and they went into the house. In the living room, she turned on a lamp beside the couch and another by the chair. Sean sat in the chair and switched off that lamp. He removed his shoes, put his feet up on the hassock, leaned back and closed his eyes. "Your underling left his post unguarded while he went to take a piss."

She tried to remember who was slated to watch the girl tonight. She'd have his head on a platter.

"Don't land on him with both feet. The poor guy thought he was safe enough. He asked the nurse to watch the girl while he was gone, but a crisis came up with another patient."

"Why did you want to see the girl? I thought you were here with the Garrett campaign. Does she have any connection to Garrett or the campaign?"

"Not that I know of."

Susan sat down on the hassock. "Give me the truth for once in your life."

"It's the truth she wants, is it? Now isn't that a matter of whose reality it is that it's filtered through? Not to mention degrees and viewpoints. All in all, isn't it better to have a well-told tale crafted with colorful exaggerations?"

"Sean."

216

"Right." With thumb and index finger he made circles on his eyelids.

"If you don't start talking sense, I'm going to take the poker and smack you with it." Susan grasped a foot and shook it. "Why had you been trying to talk with Wakely Fromm?"

"Nothing sinister in it. I already told you he interested me. Jack Garrett interests me. I thought I could get another slant on the man. From a guy who wasn't in the narrow mind-set, hell-bent on creating a successful presidential candidate."

"What did you find out?"

Sean shrugged. "Even in his cups, Fromm didn't dish out dirt."

"Is that what you were looking for, dirt?"

"Not necessarily. Just looking for what I could find."

"And—?"

"Jack was the greatest smoke jumper and the greatest hero that ever existed on the face of this earth. Fromm would lie down and die for him. Is that what he did?"

"What did you find out from the girl, Arlene?"

"She prefers to be called Moonbeam."

"Whatever. What'd you get?"

Sean looked all innocence. "You think if I had any pertinent information, I wouldn't hotfoot it down to your place of business and spread it on your desk?"

"Can pigs fly?" She shook his foot again. "Come on. Give."

"Anyone who calls herself Moonbeam Melody has God knows what going on in her psyche."

"So the kid is a romantic. What did you chisel out?"

"I don't know, Susan, I'm getting too old for this. She said her attacker, psycho killer, as she calls him, was listening to the news."

Susan frowned. "The intruder turned on the radio?"

"CNN. He wanted the latest in the political arena before he decided to slash the throat of a fourteen-year-old girl. By the way, what was he looking for in that house?"

"You don't know?"

"Do you?"

"He turned on the television set?"

Sean shook his head. "He had one of those little ones, the kind you hold in your hand."

She punched him in the shoulder.

"Ouch! What was that for?" He rubbed his arm.

"What kind of burglar carries a television set with him?"

"And listens to news," Sean said.

"Only political types," Susan said.

"They have to do it. They have to keep glued to what's going on. They can't help it."

"Ah, damn." She stood up, walked over to the couch and lay on her back. She stared at the circle of light the lamp made on the ceiling. "It was someone with the Garrett campaign."

"Most likely. Politics is the bloodiest sport in existence. No holds barred. Distort the facts, create rumors. Accuracy and authenticity get erased by illusion and innuendo. Voters' needs get tossed on the bonfire that feeds the ego of the candidate." Sean sat up and rested his elbows on his knees. "I'd hate to see Jack Garrett go down the tubes. I think he's a good guy."

"This isn't looking good."

31

Casilda wondered what the hell she was doing here, alone in the dark, standing on the tarmac, looking at a dinky little plane that didn't seem all that safe. Low clouds drifted across the moon and she shivered a little in wind that held an edge of coming winter. The terminal lights made dim smeary haloes in the mist, moths dived frantic death swoops around them. No matter how often she said she was of no use to them, she wouldn't be here long, Bernie kept giving instructions. And the odd thing was she kept following them. Must be a politician trick. That's how they got people to vote for them, nudging subliminally.

Bernie dashed up carrying a backpack and a briefcase. "Sorry, I'm late. You okay?" Transferring the briefcase to the hand with the backpack, he took her arm as though knowing she was thinking of defecting.

A limo drove up with Jack, Molly, and Nora, followed by the highway patrol and then a town car with Todd and Leon and Hadley. They all trooped up the stairs and into the plane.

Cass sat next to Bernie. "Tell me again why we're going to Florida."

"Campaigning."

"Why am I going?"

"Keep you involved."

The engine sputtered, the plane shuddered and started bumping along the runway. It took off and angled low to the southwest, nosed up through dark space and leveled off. It was a noisy little jet that made conversation difficult. She closed her eyes and must have slept, because the next thing she knew, there was sunshine and they were in Florida.

Later Wednesday morning, Cass and Bernie, heads together, were watching his handheld television on the patio by the hotel swimming pool. Todd and Leon were crowding behind them trying to see.

"Turn it up a little." Todd took off his glasses, held them up to squint at the lenses and put them back on.

"I am proud to announce," Senator Halderbreck said, with a politician's smile, "that former Governor Church Harnes has agreed to endorse my candidacy. Not only endorse, ladies and gentlemen, but he will chair my efforts here in Florida. The citizens of this great state know full well that Governor Harnes has no tolerance for games. He is a man who steps up when he sees a need."

"Isn't he dead?" Leon unpeeled the wrapper from a stick of gum and popped it in his mouth.

Cass squinted at the tiny television as Harnes stepped up to the microphone. Tall, with dark piercing eyes, hawk nose, heavy eyebrows, dark suit. He looked like a religious fanatic or a guru seeing visions after twelve days of fasting.

"Governor," a cookie stuck a microphone in his face, "what brought you back to politics after all this time?"

"There is a serious need here. Electing a president. President, ladies and gentlemen. We are in the business of choosing the most powerful man in the world. What this country needs is a serious candidate, one that can step right into that position and take charge. Some of you may remember a few years back when Florida was notable, some might say notorious, in electing the president. This time, we need to get involved ahead of time."

A ripple of laughter.

"Governor, what do you think of Jackson Garrett? You think he can step in and take charge, if he's elected?"

"The only place he's going to step is down. You think we can get the authorities to charge him with that?"

When the laughter cooled, he said, "Seriously, I know that Governor Garrett is a good man but, friends, good just isn't good enough and we have an outstanding man right here." His hand groped around a bit in search of the outstanding man he was hawking to the crowd and clamped on Halderbreck's sleeve. He dragged Halderbreck forward and threw an arm around his shoulder. Halderbreck looked rather anemic next to Harnes's flamboyance.

"This man. He's willing to tell it like it is, straight, no political double-talk."

"Senator, are you considering Governor Harnes as a running mate?"

"Too soon, folks, too soon," Halderbreck said. "I only got him to agree to this much last night, but, I gotta tell ya, this is the caliber of man the Halderbreck administration wants."

"Hey, hey, hold on there. You only paid me for today." Governor Harnes cuffed Halderbreck playfully on the chin, then turned serious. "But I'm going to be out there telling the American people this is the man we want in the White House."

Todd's cell phone rang and he pulled it from his pocket. "Yeah, Governor, we just saw it. Same old bullshit . . . no . . . no . . . yeah . . . later."

"Why isn't Harnes running?" Cass said.

"Well, sweetie, that's politics," Todd said.

"Do you think it'll make any difference down here?" Bernie turned off the tiny television and stuck it in his backpack.

"When did an endorsement make a difference?"

"What did the governor think?" Leon asked.

"He didn't see it, he was off listening to bible thumpers. Now, if Harnes is going to be telling the American public who to vote for, how come he's just now getting into camp?" Bernie said.

"Who knows," Todd said.

"Does it matter?" Cass asked.

"Fuck, yeah, it matters. Anything these assholes do gets my attention."

"Been to Disney World yet?" Bernie grinned.

"I'm saving it for my afternoon off. Speaking of days off, you ever gonna return my jacket?"

"I keep forgetting. As soon as we get back to Hampstead."

"Right. Don't forget." Todd yelled at the waiter across the patio to bring more coffee. "What else have Halderbreck's people got? What's their strategy? I can't figure out what they're doing."

"That's probably the idea. Let's hope they can't figure out what we're doing either."

"Neither can I," Todd said. "Listen, we gotta go. The governor is about to go on."

The all piled into the car and drove to a senior center somewhere in Florida. Cass thought even Bernie probably couldn't come up with the name of the town right offhand.

The room was large, walls a depressing prison-shade green, light struggled through narrow crank-opened windows that probably hadn't been cleaned since the Eisenhower administration. Long rows of metal tables filled the center of the room and stacks of folding chairs leaned in one corner. Apparently, everyone had to get his own chair. The only decorations were the American flag and a bulletin board with photos of a bus trip to the race track and announcements for coming events. Bingo, relaxation methods, singles night, weight-lifting for everyone, dance instruction.

The place was depressed and so was Bernie. "This is not going to be our finest hour," he whispered to Cass. She and Bernie had declined the boxed lunches and stood just outside the wide doorway with the press.

Jack was sitting at a folding table, box lunch in front of him. People at his table and the tables surrounding him were poking into boxes of their own. Cass wondered how long those boxes had been sitting out

222

and hoped they had nothing potentially lethal inside like tuna salad. Jack was nodding and listening respectfully.

The whole scene seemed absurd in some surreal way and she wondered why she wasn't home getting rid of unneeded belongings instead of here watching Jack Garrett eat a sandwich with a roomful of people who all had white or gray hair or a color so improbable genetics had never heard of it. She wondered how Monty the cat and Carmen the dog were getting along without her. Why was Jack here? This was his response to Senator Halderbreck and a forgotten former governor? The more she saw of politics, the more she didn't understand and she was beginning to wonder if Bernie, or even Todd, the wizard of campaign managers, understood anything.

A scrawny man with a buzz cut so short his pink scalp showed through thin white hair got up to introduce Jack. "Anybody remember Jack Kennedy?" Claps and cheers. "Well, we got us somebody a lot like him right here in this room. Charm. Charisma." He smiled with a lot of very white teeth. "You all didn't think I knew that word, did you?"

Bigger burst of claps and cheers, more for the introducer than for Jack, Cass thought. Jack got up. He mumbled, he rambled and seemed like he'd forgotten what he'd meant to say. Since Wakely died some of the fire and enthusiasm had gone. Jack had a dark look in his eyes and his zeal for speaking had lost its edge. Grieving for his lifelong friend, she thought. She knew about grieving. It never got finished. You think it's over and you pretend like you're living and then—maybe a scent, a sound, or a bit of music—and grief has its fangs in your throat again.

Then Jack started talking, just talking, not making a speech. "I want to say a few words about my opponent, Senator Halderbreck." Jack waited a beat. "He's a good man. A man of his word." Jack shook his head. "But there are some things we disagree on. I want to tell you about them, because they're important to you."

Back in stride, Cass thought, amazed as always at how he reached people and pulled them in. He mentioned cuts in cost of living adjustments for Social Security. A general grumble went through the room like a low hum. *Can't manage now. Prices keep going up.*

"... and we disagree about Medicare. Senator Halderbreck wants you to pay more ..."

Another hum, this one louder. "We always pay more and those bastards always pay less."

"... area where we disagree and that's the Middle East. We have got to give more attention to the consequences of our actions and by that I mean ..."

When Jack finished speaking, the crows started in on Bernie while Jack shook hands, hugged a frail woman, and talked informally with the crowd gathered around him. He was his old self, listening, touching, caring. A woman in a wheelchair smiled up at him and when he bent slightly toward her, she put her hand on the back of his neck and pulled him close enough to kiss his cheek. He kissed her cheek in return and she blushed like a girl.

Cass couldn't match up this man with Jackson Garrett, the man she had thought she'd marry. When she tried to superimpose this figure over the man she used to know, the man who was going to be her law partner and they were going to represent the poor and downtrodden, the edges blurred and she could only see the shadow of a stranger, an eerie reshaping of the man she thought she knew into a wraith who only resembled him slightly. The agony she'd felt when he didn't return to her after that forest fire in Montana seemed, looking back on it, pale compared to the pain she'd endured when Ted and Laura died. How things change, she mused.

Jack patted the elderly woman's shoulder and straightened. For an instant, she caught a look of—? Remorse? Did the wheelchair remind him of his old friend? Why remorse? Did he feel he hadn't done enough when Wakely was alive? Maybe she imagined it. Or maybe he had a pain in his back and regretted bending over.

32

The Coffee Cup, packed with media people, was doing a brisk lunch business when Parkhurst came in. Phyllis sent him a smile and nodded at the doorway to her left. He went into the empty banquet room and sat at one of the round tables.

It took her a minute or two to get to him. "I thought you'd like it better in here. It's quieter. I'll guard the door so they can't get in. I swear they're like a pack of hyenas. In your face, in your face, in your face. I don't know how you stand it. If I toted a gun, I'd probably shoot the bunch of them."

"Don't think I haven't thought of it." Without looking at the menu, he ordered a turkey sandwich, fries and coffee. She scribbled on her pad in that awkward-looking way of the left-handed. A minute or two later she came back with a thick white mug and filled it with coffee. He took a sip, it wasn't any better than what he'd been drinking all morning, and did nothing to get rid of the taste and smell of rot. When the food came, his appetite fluttered and dissipated.

Susan, ignoring questions and fighting off microphones stuck in her face, slipped through the door and sat across from him. "God, they never give up. I had to sneak out the back and then I run into them here." She rubbed her temples. "How was the autopsy?"

"Went well. You should have been there. Nothing like ripping open a body and lifting out parcels of insides to make you think of lunch. You want something?"

She snagged a fry from his plate before he could splatter catsup all over them and popped it in her mouth.

"That makes an even thirty thousand you owe me. Why don't you ever buy your own?"

She looked horrified. "All that fat and salt? It'll kill you." She lifted another.

When Phyllis came back, Susan asked for two eggs over easy, sausage links, and coffee.

"Fat and salt?" Parkhurst said.

"What can I say? An undeniable craving. I'm weak."

Phyllis set a mug in front of her, filled it with coffee and refilled Parkhurst's. Susan put both hands around the mug to warm them. "Has Demarco found the dog?"

"No sign of it." Parkhurst upended the catsup bottle and gave it a good smack, dumping red stuff all over the fries. "Some of the blood in her garage belongs to a dog, so it was injured."

"Maybe he killed it, too."

"If he did, where's the body?"

"He took it away?"

"Why?' Parkhurst bit into his sandwich and chewed.

"It tried to protect her. It was in the way, it could identify him?"

He laughed. "A talking dog maybe?"

"Hey, there are some bloodhounds that can now give evidence in court."

He gave her a sour look and bit off another hunk of his sandwich. "And the girl? Why was she hiding? Think she can identify him, too?"

"I don't know why you're in such a shitty mood, but it's beginning to annoy me."

"As opposed to my usual sunny self?"

She took a manila envelope from her shoulder bag and opened it. "Crime scene photos," she said. "Wakely Fromm. These are copies."

She snapped down a photo and another and another and another

226

until they formed a half-circle around his plate. Stark, harsh, ugly photos. What was left of Wakely Fromm, listing to one side in his wheelchair, mouth open, right arm hanging down. Gun on the floor. "You see anything there to suggest homicide not suicide?"

He pushed the remains of his sandwich and fries to one side. An autopsy just before lunch might be a good way to diet. He focused on the photos and wondered why she was so bitchy.

The nagging grain of sand scratching just out of reach wouldn't let him drop it and go along with suicide. He couldn't just do the paperwork and hand what was left of Fromm over to whoever was going to spring for burial. Probably his good buddy Governor Jackson Garrett. And it bothered him that Sean Donovan had found the body. Good way to account for fingerprints or fibers, any incriminating evidence at the scene.

He studied each picture. Been there, done that. What was it that bothered him about this? Was he missing something? Maybe the poor son of a bitch did check out. Tired of being a burden, when his buddy was trying a bid for candidacy as the first step toward the biggest job in town, Fromm moved himself out of the equation to make life easier for said buddy.

He studied the photos. Staged, the whole thing looked staged. By not looking at the pictures, but staring through them, they no longer had the same impact. Not pictures of a man, just so much garbage.

"What are you thinking?" she asked.

"Sean Donovan."

"Yes?" she said with a little edge of warning.

Parkhurst took in a long breath and let it out. He might not be much, but he was a good cop and he'd always gone after the answers, no matter what.

"I don't know, Susan." He took a sip of coffee. "Donovan's business card was found in the trunk of the car with the body of a homicide victim." Risky business, suggesting this clown she loved so much might be mixed up in a homicide. Good way to get his ass in a sling. "And when Donovan's confronted with prints, he confesses he met her."

"He explained that. He drove Fromm to Gayle Egelhoff's house

227

because whoever was supposed to do it didn't show."

"And then," Parkhurst went on as though she hadn't spoken, "he finds a second homicide victim. He didn't fall over or upchuck like any normal citizen. He looks at all that carnage, bone and brains smeared all over the walls, blood on the floor, and maybe makes some changes in the way it looks, whatever, he messes up the crime scene and then calmly calls the cops."

"He's been in lots of tight places and seen lots of carnage. He's been in countries you've never heard of, seeing wars so stupid you wouldn't believe it, with people slaughtering each other in creatively horrible ways."

He thought of Phyllis taking an order, writing it down with her left hand. "Left-handed," he said.

"What?"

"Wakely Fromm was left-handed."

Phyllis set a platter of eggs, sausage, and toast in front of Susan.

"If he was planning to off himself, he'd use his left hand." Parkhurst demonstrated, much to the interest of other diners. "Gun in his left hand, right hand under it for support, sticks the barrel in his mouth, pulls the trigger. Bang. The back of his head's gone. He's dead."

Parkhurst tapped one finger against a photo. "His left arm should have fallen over the arm of the chair and the gun should have dropped on this side." He tapped again. "Not the right side, the left. Using his left hand, there's no way that gun could get way over here. Even with a weird circumstance where the recoil might jerk his arm and the gun gets tossed, hits the floor and slides across the tile, it couldn't end up here."

"How do you know he was left-handed?"

"Haven't you been watching the news? That whole circus has been all over the tube every night."

"Yeah, so?"

"So watch some of those clips and he uses his left hand. To hold a fork, to pick up a glass—"

"That's barely suggestive," she said.

"He writes with his left hand. That do it?"

"You've seen him write something?"

"Saw him sign his name to a credit card receipt at The Blind Pig barbeque."

"You saw him." Susan took in a breath. "I was hoping for something a little more definite, like a suspect's fingerprints on the gun maybe, or signs of struggle."

"It's hard to find signs of struggle when half the victim's head is blown all over the wall." Parkhurst leaned back, picked up his mug and drank lukewarm coffee. He looked around for Phyllis and when he spotted her, held the mug in the air.

"Wakely's prints are on the gun," he said. "Smudged, like they would be if the gun was put in his hand by somebody else's."

"Or if he handled it a bit before putting it in his mouth."

Phyllis came over and topped off both coffee mugs. When she left, Susan said. "Why would anybody kill Wakely Fromm?"

"He was a drunk, and drunks can't keep their mouths shut."

"What could he say that was so important or damaging that someone would kill to keep him quiet?"

"He was probably also a pain in the ass. Where the governor goes, he goes. With the campaign just heating up that's a lot of places to take him."

Susan raised a skeptical eyebrow.

"It's not like he's just another person they have to make room for in the limo," Parkhurst said. "He has special needs. And somebody has to run around and take care of them."

"Isn't that why Garrett has Murray working for him? So everything Fromm had in the way of needs got taken care of? Throw in some wants and he gets those taken care of too."

"Come on, Susan, you know you have doubts about this."

"Yeah, I just don't want to have them." She sipped at her coffee and made a sour face. "How do you go about investigating a homicide with the governor right there in the middle of it. This is not a good thing to have, Parkhurst. This is a big problem. You are not going to have clear sailing."

"You're not making any sense."

"I seldom do these days. If Wakely Fromm was killed—*if*—and if he is left-handed, then that lets out the governor. Garrett would know Wakely was left-handed and wouldn't have made that mistake."

"They've more or less lived together for the last twenty years or so. Plenty enough time to build up anger and resentment. Maybe Mrs. Garrett got fed up. Can you imagine marrying the man of your dreams and he comes equipped with a crippled and belligerent friend who drinks too much? Think of the resentment that could build. The time and expense in taking care of Fromm for twenty years must have added up to a lot of dollars."

"Now you want me to beetle in on *Mrs.* Garrett," Susan said. "You are just a bundle of sunshine, aren't you?"

"She could be fed up with the situation, but wouldn't necessarily have paid attention enough to know Fromm was left-handed."

"After *twenty* years? With Wakely at her dinner table? What, is she blind and deaf?"

He shook his head. "Just angry and refusing to have him around for every meal and every party and not really looking at him when he was around."

"You have anything to back this up?"

"No."

She leaned over the table and gave him an intent look. "I'd be a whole lot happier if we had some concrete evidence. Like footprints in the blood. If somebody did kill him, there has to be something somewhere." She sent a watch-yourself look at Parkhurst. "And we can't just go trampling all over the Governor and his wife on some half-ass theory about left-handedness."

"That means we'll have to trample trying to find some."

"Yeah." She leaned back. "This isn't good, Parkhurst. You know what it'll turn into, don't you? It's just going to turn into a cluster fuck for the media, aim their cameras on Garrett, and speculate whether he was the shadowy figure stomping on the burning bag of shit."

He nodded. It was going to be a mess, anyway you looked at it. Shame, too. Near as he could tell, Garrett looked okay. Might even

230

make a pretty good president if he ever got that far, but this would be nearly impossible to handle under the usual damage control.

"There's a connection with the Egelhoff murder," he said.

"I know."

"Gayle Egelhoff talked with Fromm."

Susan nodded. "Yeah, so?"

"What did they talk about?"

"Old friend of dead husband. They talked about old times."

"She wanted to see Garrett."

"How do you know?"

"The kid who took care of Fromm. He gathered that from a conversation he overheard."

"Oh, great. He *gathered*. He could have made it up?"

"Why would he do that?"

Susan nibbled at a piece of toast. "What are you suggesting? The governor offed Gayle Egelhoff and then his old buddy—his old buddy who had nothing but praise for him and called him a hero. Loudly. That old buddy?"

"Yeah, that's what I'm saying."

"Why kill them? What about resentments on the part of Murray? It must get tiresome dealing with a man who drank too much and got loud and abusive. Maybe there was some pent-up stuff building there over the years."

"He only worked with him for three years. And I never heard that Fromm was abusive, just belligerent."

"So what? At least Murray's not the governor, or the governor's wife."

"Right."

"Sucks."

"Yeah."

"Damn it." She sighed and touched fingertips to forehead like she had a headache. "Talk to somebody with the Garrett campaign and see if anybody knows whether Fromm was left-handed."

When Phyllis came by to see if they needed anything else, Susan said, "Only to sneak out the back way."

Parkhurst said he'd see what he could find out. Susan nodded, not happy. He knew she was just as uncertain about Fromm's death as he was, but didn't want to open that can of worms and stick her hand in it.

"Try not to make anybody mad," she said.

"I'll be the soul of tact."

33

*D*emarco knew he was spending too much time with the girl. If he wasn't careful, Her Ladyship the Chief would say something, order him to step back, or even hand the case over. The hell with it, the kid did better when he was there, she wasn't as restless, so he stayed. Sitting by the side of the bed, legs stretched out, he waited till she drifted off in a restless morning nap before he lit out.

The day was warm, the air soft and the wind easy; over to the west sat a bank of huge cottony clouds. At the shop he turned in the squad, signed out, changed into civvies and picked up his Jeep. To clear his head, he rolled through the countryside with the sun riding over the shallow hills. He drove past a sprawling farm with outbuildings, tractor shed, hay bales being loaded into the barn. A man striding through a field gave him a wave. What would it be like to be a farmer? Hard life, always at the mercy of the elements.

Owning land, being responsible to it. Tilling and planting, coaxing things to grow, watching the sky for rain because there'd been too much, or not enough. Sniffing the air for change, which might mean hail that would wipe out a year's work and a year's profit. No, not for him. There was a certain pride in the man's walk, a strut that said, *all this is mine*, but owning something meant being tied to it, and Demarco didn't want to be tied to anything. That way led to heartbreak.

Getting time to move on? Nobody'd miss him, that was sure. After this thing with the kid was cleared, maybe he should take off. He didn't fit in here. Nothing new, he didn't fit in anywhere.

He got along all right with his partner Yancy. Christ, he nearly shit carpet tacks that time when Yancy got stabbed. The boy was bright and he was eager, but a couple of things rubbed against Demarco's skin a little. Yancy was kind. Kind was okay as long as you could be hard when you needed to, but the worrisome thing about Yancy was, he was developing some hero-worship. Demarco didn't want to be anybody's hero. And for Christ's sake, he sure didn't want to be anybody's mentor. He just wanted to be left alone to do his job. He'd told Her Ladyship the Chief he worked best alone and she went and hooked him up with a green kid who was so sweet bees followed him around. Yancy was a good kid, but Demarco was a lone ranger.

Even with Yancy soft as a kitten and Demarco a horny toad, they got along okay. The kid was honest and trustworthy—made him sound like a boy scout. What he should be, actually. It was an okay department for a small town. There was one old cop, nice guy, knew all the folks in town since they were pups. Parkhurst, lots of experience and a pretty good cop as far as Demarco could see. The problem with Parkhurst was, he had his own ideas about how things should go. They didn't always fit with Demarco's and that was laced with potential trouble. And there was Her Ladyship the Chief. The less said about her, the better. And Parkhurst wanted to jump her bones. He'd probably shoot anybody who said spit to her.

Demarco's neighbor was into Halloween in a big and irritating way. When he got home he found the place next door done up like a witch's den. Pumpkins scattered all over the lawn, black cats with arched backs and red flashing eyes stacked against tied bundles of cornstalks, owls nailed to trees, flying witch wrapped around the telephone pole.

He unlocked his door and let himself in. Home sweet home, bare of seasonal decorations, bare of people, bare of spirit and as empty as when he'd left last night. In the refrigerator, he found a bottle of seltzer and took a slug. He poked around at the spare offerings of food. Left-over pizza, half a ham and cheese sandwich, jar of pickles, block of cheese, something green.

He threw that in the trash and retrieved the sandwich, absently took a bite while he picked up the remote and clicked on the TV to catch the news coming up. Ad showing Governor Garrett at a play-ground talking with children. He took another swig of seltzer and leaned back with his feet on the footrest. Gayle Egelhoff, innocuous widow of a man who fought fires twenty years ago, was killed.

Laugh track on TV, idiot stumbling into table laden with food. Demarco clicked the remote. Ad showing Governor Garrett in a park talking about preserving our heritage. Demarco hit mute. Wakely Fromm, good friend of Governor Garrett, who also fought fires, died of gunshot wound, maybe self-inflicted, maybe inflicted by another.

He clicked the remote. Watched the weather forecast, then an ad showing the vice president earnestly talking about fighting the war on terrorism. At least, that's what Demarco thought he was talking about. "Who can fight terrorism better?" the ad demanded. The man had been there. The ad didn't say where it was he'd been.

Garrett, too, was a firefighter twenty years ago. Egelhoff, Fromm, and Garrett battled a forest fire where—five? six?—some number of firefighters died. Now Egelhoff and Fromm were dead and only Garrett was alive.

A woman named Cass Storm had just moved back to town, she had lived here twenty years ago and knew all three men. What connections besides proximity did she have with them? Nothing to do with smoke jumping as far as he knew. He'd check. Old angers and resentments that could lead to revenge? Nothing like a woman scorned to think of serious revenge. Was Storm a woman scorned? And if so, which one had scorned her?

What was big-deal political writer, Pulitzer prize winner, Sean Donovan, cousin of Her Ladyship the Chief, doing with the Garrett campaign? His business card had turned up in the trunk of the car with Gayle Egelhoff's body, his fingerprints were in her house.

Why was the kid attacked? Did she know more than she was telling? That was a given. Everybody knew more than he was telling. Right now the girl wasn't able to say much. What could she know? How did her assault fit in with the murders?

Maybe the bastard broke in thinking the house was empty and got a big surprise. Why break in? Looking for something? What? If it was the unknown suspect who killed the Egelhoff broad, had he left something in the house? Or worried that he had?

If so, it was nothing that leaped up in Demarco's face. He'd have to talk with the kid, walk her through the place, maybe she'd spot something missing. If the son of a bitch had any brains—which they often didn't—he'd just let it go. Nothing in the house—at least that Demarco had found so far—pointed a finger at anybody.

Rewrapping the sandwich, he tossed it back in the refrigerator and was eyeing the leftover pizza when Yancy called to say a reporter had gotten to the Egelhoff girl.

Demarco was livid that Her Ladyship's hot shit reporter cousin had been able to get to the kid. He felt like tearing the head off the uniformed officer guarding her door. Just the thing to get rid of the tension along the back of his shoulders.

"You manage to let anybody else in while I was on my way?" he demanded.

Officer Cooper, a lanky kid with red hair and pale skin that tended to flush under stress—like now—clenched his jaw. "Nobody but the doctor."

"How the fuck could you be so stupid?"

"Sorry, sir, I thought I had it covered. I was only gone a minute."

"A minute during which a suspect got to the witness. How long you think it takes to slip a knife under a girl's ribs? She could be dead because of you."

"Sorry, sir, it won't happen again."

"Damn right, it won't, or I will personally see to it that you'll be eating nothing that requires teeth. You need to take a piss, tie a knot in it."

The girl, scrunched down in bed, had the television on but wasn't watching it. She looked like she was fighting sleep in that dead tired way of little kids. She jumped when he came in.

Rummaging around on the bed, she found the laptop under the blankets. *Creeping up! Scared me!*

"Sorry. I thought you might be bored here so I brought you something."

She eyed him with deep suspicion. *What?*

"A game called Kill The Invaders. Ought to be just your style. Hey, might even get rid of some of that aggression you carry around.

Don't.

"You need anything from home?"

No.

"Just plain no? You don't want to throw in a few four-letter words and about ninety exclamation points?"

Ha. Funny.

He leaned back and stretched his legs out. "You sure you don't want anything? Don't girls always like to primp and need tubes and pots and stuff?"

Have never primped!!!!

"There you go with the exclamation points. Tell me what you want and I'll bring it."

She glared at him, then typed out carefully. *He touched my things!*

"The intruder?" Demarco nodded. "Not much I can do about that. Except maybe get a shovel and dump everything in the trash."

She scrunched her eyes tight as though afraid she might cry.

"You all right?"

She made that slight dip of her head that passed for a nod, avoiding too much movement that would arouse pain. She didn't look all right. She looked tense and frightened. *Where you been?*

"Why? You miss me?"

She started to scowl, then winced and wiped her face blank. *No way.*

She was trying so damn hard to be tough, he felt like ruffling her

237

hair. Instead, he grabbed her wrist and squeezed gently. "Did he scare you? The man who was in here last night?"

She gave him one of her looks of scorn. That's my girl, he thought, keep your spirits up. *Nice. Unlike you.*

"Nice? You just haven't seen my nice side yet. When I turn on the charm, all the women in a twenty-mile vicinity swoon and throw themselves at me."

You wish.

"What did he want?" Demarco pulled the armchair closer and slid down so he could see the computer screen easier.

She shrugged. *Called me Acushla.*

"Better than Moonshine. Why you want to call yourself that?"

Moonbeam!

"Moonshine, moonbeam, you got a perfectly good name, why don't you use it?" He knew why. She wanted a name that said, Look at me, I'm different, I'm important, I'm special.

Arlene dork name!!!!!!

"I've heard worse."

Name one.

"Eglantine."

She dealt him another look of scorn. *You made that up.*

"What, you never heard of the famous actress Eglantine Fontelle?"

She eyed him suspiciously, as if not quite believing there actually was such a person, but afraid she'd sound stupid if she admitted she didn't know.

Where's Rosie?

"Who's Rosie?"

Gayle's dog.

Ah, so there was a dog. "What kind of dog?"

Belgian Shepherd.

"You miss your dog?"

Not mine! Gayle's!

"I see. You don't like the dog."

A heavy sigh of frustration at his idiot brain started in her chest, but stopped halfway up when it hit the pain threshold. *Rosie only likes*

Gayle. My dog died. Her eyes glistened and she blinked furiously.

"When?" A thought passed through his mind that there might be a connection with Gayle Egelhoff's murder.

Long time ago. Years.

"Why didn't you get another?"

She shrugged. The kid had about as many varieties of shrugs as she had looks of scorn. *Too expensive.*

"Somewhere a dog is waiting."

She raised her eyebrows.

"I'll help you find him when you get out of here. What does a Belgian Shepherd look like?"

Big. Black.

"Like a German Shepherd?"

She did that nod thing. *Only Blacker.*

"Would it have run away?"

Never.

"You weren't home the night your sister was attacked."

Told you. Music Festival.

"Would the dog, Rosie, have protected Gayle? Gone after whoever was threatening her?"

Sure.

So, why hadn't it? He didn't know anything about Belgian Shepherds, but German Shepherds were aggressive. They wouldn't stand by while an owner was attacked. And if the bastard killed the dog, why hadn't they found its body?

Want my backpack.

"Where is it?"

Not sure.

"Did you have it when you snuck back into the house?"

Yes.

"Why do you want it?"

Has my stuff in it.

"What stuff?"

Backpack! Just bring it!

"Okay. Calm down. Where is it?"

A number five on the Richter scale of scorn came his way. *Bed*, she started to type, then stopped.

"In your bed?"

A limited scowl because of the possibilities of pain given a real one. *Bedroom I think!*

"I'll find it. What does it look like?"

Backpack. Black.

"Okay. Anything else?"

Hunched in on herself, she typed. *Only Gayle.*

"Sorry, kid. I wish I could."

She typed. *You found me?*

"When you were hurt? Yeah."

How know?

"A neighbor saw lights and heard noise."

The kid typed, *Mrs. Hadwent!*

"No. A Mrs. Cleary."

The kid nodded. *Always yammering about how she had went to the doctor's and had went to the drug store and had went to church. Gayle and I called her Mrs. Hadwent. Nosey old bitch!*

"Watch your language. Be nice about her. Wasn't for her, you'd be dead."

He squeezed the kid's shoulder and left. He liked her. She was a mess. She had nobody to take care of her. All that idiocy with the clothes and the foul language was part adolescent trying to figure out who she was and part aching heart crying out for somebody to look at her, pay attention, love her. He hoped a good foster parent could be found, one who genuinely liked kids and tried to do right by them, not one only interested in the monthly check. This girl was like a frightened kitten trying to survive in a hostile world. Somebody needed to take her in and teach her things. How to be independent without dressing like a hooker, how to take care of herself. Somebody who would let her feel safe, so she didn't have to hiss and spit all the time.

* * *

240

Demarco let himself into the Egelhoff place and stood just inside the doorway, sensing whatever the house chose to tell him. It was quiet, only the creaks and groans of an old house talking to itself. He pulled on a pair of latex gloves and covered his shoes with paper slippers.

In the living room, CDs had been tumbled from the shelf holding the player. Cushions uprooted or thrown to the floor. Dining room. China cabinet doors open, dishes and glasses shoved around, two wine glasses fallen and broken. Kitchen. Drawers open, dumped, cabinet contents shoved out. Master bedroom. Clothes spilling from dresser drawers, closet doors open. Kid's bedroom. Real mess. Maybe a little worse than when he'd searched the first time, but not much.

Whatever the asshole had been looking for had to be small enough to fit under a couch cushion, and fairly flat. Or he was just angry and took it out by making a mess. Unless he was smart. Then he'd have created just such a mess to suggest the item was small when it was actually as big as a VCR.

Demarco had no way of knowing if anything was missing. He'd need the kid with him to know that. Since she wasn't available, he'd see what he could find. Going under the principle that an individual brought something with him to the scene and took something with him when he left, Demarco searched. He was disciplined and method-ical, why he'd been so suited to the military, and went through the house inch by inch. He checked windowsills, crawled on floors, ex-amined corners and baseboards, looked with differing angles and dif-fering heights for scuff marks, footprints, palm prints discernable to the naked eye.

The kitchen was a bitch because of the enormity of the mess, food from the refrigerator dumped in the sink. Presumably to check the containers for the item in question. He opened the refrigerator door to see what was left inside. The dickhead hadn't dumped everything. He'd left five small containers, about six inches by four inches. So whatever he was looking for was bigger than roughly six by four and not over four inches in height.

Didn't exactly zero it down. Could be anything. Only thing De-marco knew for sure, it wasn't an elephant.

He searched both bedrooms. Down on his knees, poking under the beds, checking the closets, corners, and shelves and the only thing he got for his pains was a moldering apple core in the kid's room. And the backpack. He stood up, looked around, took in a breath and blew it out. Waste of time. That didn't irritate him. In the military time was often wasted.

Closet where the kid had hidden and pelted the intruder with such potentially lethal items as pillowcases and blankets. The floor was littered with them. Also candles and candleholders, broken glass flower vase, old Easter baskets, and a flashlight without batteries. He wondered if the vase had been a hit. It would help if the asshole had a broken nose or a facial cut that needed stitching.

The kid had said she jumped straight toward him from the top shelf. She'd landed on him and clutched at his jacket. She thought she'd heard it rip, but she was yelling so loud she couldn't be sure. If she was right, there might be threads somewhere. With his nose almost on the floorboards, he crawled along the length of the closet. He was about to give it up when he saw a little ball of crumpled paper caught in the door hinge.

Gently, with tweezers, he picked up the ball of paper and dropped it in a plasticine envelope. He could see it had some writing on it. He wrote the date and his initials on the envelope.

In the bathroom with the little girl's blood, now a dark rusty color, all over the floor, he was mindful of where he put his feet. Medicine cabinet had a bottle of aspirin, cotton balls, Q-tips, and nail polish.

After another run through to make sure he hadn't missed anything, he headed out. Anything more would have to wait until the kid was up to coming with him. One crumpled ball of paper wasn't much to show for the time and energy exerted in finding it. He drove to the shop, went in to his desk and examined the backpack. Earrings dangled all up the edges of the shoulder straps.

He put on a pair of latex gloves and unzipped the front pocket. A piece of notepaper folded in half. He unfolded it and read *As soon as they'll let me I'll come and see you. I've got lots to tell you. Stuff I can't put*

*in words if you know what I mean. Bart asked about you in school yesterday.
I think he likes you.* He refolded it and stuck it back.

The main section was packed full. Textbooks—geometry, English,
history. Clean socks—orange with black witches—sunglasses, a journal, bottle of water, granola bar, small package of tampax, pack of gum,
pens, pencils, erasers, and her journal.

The first page had Moonbeam, calligraphy letters in black, deco-
rated with green vines and purple thorns. He turned the page.

> *Damn damn.*
> *Very da-damn.*
> *This time cold.*
> *Shivering.*
> *Teeth ta-chattering.*
> *Heart hammering.*
> *Can't sit still.*
> *Worms crawling under skin.*

He assumed this was either very bad poetry or adolescent angst.
He flipped pages.

> *March 5*
> *Sherry made an A on the English test. I made a B+. Not fair. Mine
> was better. Just because I misspelled a few words and left out a few stupid
> commas.*

Nothing for the next three months.

> *July 4*
> *Fireworks. Big Deal. I don't know why I couldn't go off with the rest
> of them, but No, I'm too young.*
> *September 4*
> *Gayle's mad about something I don't think it's anything I did. I didn't
> do anything lately that would set her off.*

September 8

Figured out what's sending Gayle into bitching-mad. I think she's cross-eyed hopping because Vince is off to go skiing. Early snow storm, blah blah blah. He's going. Unless he's off to meet a girlfriend.

I didn't really mean it. He's okay. Tells stories about smoke jumping. Sounds pretty exciting. Maybe I'll be a smoke jumper. Jump down into raging fires though. Maybe I'll be somebody else.

He skimmed pages, not easy to do because her handwriting was small and cramped in some places, messy and sprawling in others.

October 6

I think Gayle has a boyfriend. How could she! At her age!! Vince has only been dead three weeks.

October 8

Haven't been able to see him. He always comes when I'm over at Sherry's or somewhere.

October 9

I finally saw him. Her boyfriend. Old guy in a wheelchair. Asked her about him. She said he was a friend of Vince's.

Demarco turned to get a better angle. He was already getting a headache from trying to decipher the kid's writing. Her handwriting was starting to bleed together. He squinted and rubbed his eyes. He was tired from being up all night with the girl and it looked like he'd be up all night again deciphering her scribbles. He hoped the dickhead guarding her room got the message. Any more instances of reporters wandering in and he'd have somebody's nuts in a vise.

He handed the plastic envelope with the crumpled ball of paper over to Osey Pickett who held it up and peered at it from both sides.

Osey resembled the scarecrow in *The Wizard of Oz*, the one who had no brain. Effective camouflage. He did have a brain and it worked lightning fast. Osey had no problem with Demarco. Didn't say much, Osey never had problems with anybody. Similar to Will Rogers that way, he never met a man he didn't like.

244

"If you'd get on with it, we could find out what it says."

"Right." Osey cleared an area in the center of his desk, got a clean sheet of paper, opened the baggie, and dumped out the paper ball. With two pairs of tweezers, he carefully pulled the ball open and straightened it. Scrap of paper torn from a larger sheet. Demarco leaned closer to read what it said.

take care of it
enough problems
Bernie

"You think the intruder dropped this?" Osey yanked open a drawer, got a magnifying glass and examined the scrap.

"Yeah."

"And Bernie is the Bernie Quaid who is with the dog-and-pony show trying to get Governor Garrett on the ballot as presidential candidate?"

"Yeah."

"You think somebody is saying he's going to take care of it, or something needs taking care of?"

"Yeah."

With tweezers Osey turned the paper over. Nothing on the reverse side. "What is it he's supposed to take care of?"

"Be nice to know, wouldn't it?" Demarco said.

"Is Bernie part of the note, or is it written by him?"

"Something else it would be nice to know."

"Yeah. Especially if he's supposed to tie up the problem by axing Gayle Egelhoff and getting rid of the girl. She know anything?"

"She says not."

"You believe her?"

"Hard to say. The kid's a first class liar. Rather lie than eat chocolate. On the other hand why wouldn't she give it up if she knows anything."

Osey leaned so far back the chair creaked. "Maybe she's thinking she'll try a little blackmail."

"That'd be right up her alley." Demarco ran a hand over his buzz cut. "I'd like to have a little talk with these political assholes."

"Uh—" Osey looked nervous. "You might want to run that by the chief before you go tromping around on powerful political egos."

Demarco nodded. "Just see what kind of fingerprints you can find."

Moonbeam was awake when Demarco got to the hospital, the head of the bed up, listlessly watching a talk show on television with irritating theme music. She zeroed in on the journal he held and grabbed at it. He held it high, but when she lunged again, he let go and she hugged it against her chest as though he might try to snatch it back. Scowling, she clicked off the television and got the laptop. *You read it?*

"Yes."

Effing weasel!!!!

"Watch your mouth, kiddo. Tell me about the man who came to see your sister."

What about him?

"Who is he?"

She shrugged.

Demarco didn't like shrugs. They'd have to talk about shrugs. "What did he look like?"

She rolled over so her back was toward him.

"Hey, talk to me."

She moved her head in a limited negative motion.

Putting a hand on her shoulder, he eased her onto her back. "I need to know," he said.

She squeezed her eyes shut.

"You want to know who killed your sister?"

Her eyes opened to slits glittery with anger and frustration. What she'd like to do was punch him.

"You want the bastard to get away with it? Is that what you want? Just let him walk away, like you don't care?"

Sullenly, she took the laptop and typed. *No.*

"Then you need to help me."

She rubbed a forefinger back and forth under her nose and typed *What?*

"Who was the man who came to see your sister?"

"*Wheelchair.*"

"On October nine," he said. "The man in the wheelchair was at your house. His name was Wakely. There was someone there on the nineteenth. Was it the same man?"

No.

With great restraint, he managed not to grab her by the neck and yell in her face, "Who was this other man?"

Don't know.

"Try to be a little more specific. What did he look like? Tall, short, hair color, eye color. That kind of stuff."

She closed her eyes, either to think or to shut him out. He could see how frail and tired she looked, dark bruises on her face turning purple, white bandage on her throat.

Old. Like you. Not dishy like Sean.

"Dishy?" he said with disgust. Almost got him a smile until she remembered it would hurt if she did that.

Don't know how tall. Sitting down. Light hair maybe.

The kid had a feverish look about her that worried Demarco. Cheeks flushed, eyes too bright. "Had you ever seen him before?"

No.

"What was he wearing?"

She flicked a fingernail on the lid of the laptop, then typed, *Brown pants, brown sweater.*

"Did you see a car?"

She nodded.

"What kind?"

She shrugged.

A boy her age would know the make, the model, the cost, and the gas mileage. "What color?"

Black. Big.

"You saw a man of undetermined height, wearing brown pants and brown sweater with light hair, driving a black car. Was anybody with him?"

Don't know. Maybe.

"How can you not know if there was one person or two?"

Friend's mom came to pick me up. Got in car. Drove away. Black car drove up. Two people in car. One driving.

"Anything else you can tell me?"

She nodded that short dip possible before pain kicked in, but didn't type anything.

"Okay, what?"

Woman!!

Gotcha! The little brat had led him along by the nose. He raised his arm like he was going to backhand her across the jaw.

She looked so pleased with herself, she probably would have giggled if her teeth hadn't been wired shut.

"You saw a woman on October nineteenth. Not a man. What did she look like?"

Maybe like Governor's wife.

"Molly Garrett? How do you know what she looks like?"

Saw her on TV. With friend.

Two people had come to see Gayle Egelhoff. At least one, the passenger, was a woman, the driver may or may not have been female. The passenger had the usual female characteristics. Moonbeam had seen news clip of Molly Garrett and her friend Nora on television. She didn't know which was Mrs. Garrett and which was the friend. Demarco couldn't get anything beyond that.

34

———

The time was edging toward nine o'clock before Susan felt she could pack it in and go home. Periodically throughout the day, she'd tried to get hold of Sean, but had no luck. She'd left messages that hadn't been returned. That morning when she'd set out for work, the sun had been shining and the weather warm. As she was crossing the parking lot to get into the pickup, it was dark and the wind swirled around her with sharp edges. She should have worn a coat.

Why were two people dead, one a definite homicide, the other a questionable suicide? How was Governor Garrett involved? Did he kill his old friend? Why? Because he was tired of being responsible for him? Did Molly Garrett kill Wakely Fromm? Why? Tired of him being part of her marriage? Would the governor answer hard questions? In a rat's ass. He'd just trot out a lawyer and stand behind him. Did Susan have any lever to make him answer? With the campaign gearing up for the primary in D.C., how much would the taint of homicide affect his chances?

"Oh, shit," she muttered as she started up the pickup. She didn't want to be investigating Governor Garrett. In fact, she didn't even want to be anywhere near him. She wanted him gone, suspects found that had nothing to do with him, and everybody connected with him out of her town.

Why kill Fromm even if he was a problem? Why not just ship him off somewhere with his keeper? Putting him in hiding was maybe something the campaign could work with, but the murder of his good friend and constant companion Wakely Fromm was a whole other loaf of bread.

She turned on the heater. The streets were quiet, nearly deserted and shadowy, a pale quarter-moon setting, a feeling of frost in the air.

What kind of connection was there between Gayle Egelhoff and Wakely Fromm? Why had he come to see her, what did they talk about, did Gayle want to see the Governor? If she did, it was probably not to get his autograph.

Susan drove into the garage, grabbed her shoulder bag and the stack of folders on the seat beside her, work she didn't get finished at the shop and intended to take care of tonight. The garage door rattled down. The wind snatched at the folders. She hugged them close under crossed arms and, head down against the wind, trotted to the kitchen door and went in the house.

Just as she dropped everything on the kitchen table, the doorbell rang. Now what? Turning on lights along the way, she looked through the fanlight, then yanked open the door. "Sean."

He came in carrying paper bags that smelled of food. "Hello, darlin'." He walked past her and into the kitchen where he put the bags on the table.

"What's this?"

"Enough work for today." He picked up the folders, went to the dining room and plopped them on the table. He gave her a tight hug and kissed her forehead. "How's everything going in the crime marches on department?"

"Where have you been all day? I've been trying to track you down."

"And here I am, at your service."

"What's this?" She gestured at the bags on her kitchen table.

He opened the bags and took out white boxes. "They came from

250

that little place on Main. Chicken with orange sauce, salad, bread, wine."

Susan set out plates, utensils and glasses. "It's kind of late to be eating, isn't it?"

"Not when you haven't done it all day." He scooped half the contents of the boxes on each plate and uncorked the wine.

Susan forked up a cherry tomato. "Sean, how well did you know Wakely Fromm?"

"I assumed that was the reason you wanted to see me. I didn't know him at all. He was just always there, in the background."

"Why?"

"Why what?"

"Why was he always there, why does the governor take Fromm everywhere with him?"

"That question could be better answered by Jack Garrett."

"I know that. You also know that the governor isn't going to answer my questions if he doesn't want to. What's the standard reply when anybody asked about Fromm?"

"That he and Garrett were old friends and had been together a long time."

When they finished eating, she cleared away the food containers and stacked the dishes in the dishwasher. Wineglass in hand, he wandered into the living room, set the glass on top of the old upright piano, and slid onto the bench.

"Was Fromm left-handed?" She switched on a lamp, then sat on the floor with her back resting against the hearth, cradling the bowl of the wineglass in both hands.

Sean crossed his left hand over his right and played arpeggios up and down the keyboard. "I'm not sure. I guess he was. Let me think." He played scales with both hands. "Yeah, I guess so. He used his left to eat with and write with."

Sean rippled through a series of fast chords. "I can see by your face that's not the answer you want. What's this about left-handed?" He crossed his left over his right and played a fast, intricate bit of fingering.

She shook her head.

"Something about his suicide?" Sean changed key and played another set of chords, a look of deep sorrow settling on his face. "Susan, no wonder you are depressed. This piano is terminal."

"It hasn't been tuned in a while."

"Darlin', what this piano needs is a whole lot more than tuned. Donate it to any church who'll take it and put it in isolation in the basement." He played a polonaise and then romped through "The Entertainer" making exaggerated grimaces of pain at the flat notes and the dead keys. "You're thinking he didn't kill himself?"

"It's a possibility."

Sean jumped right into "Jesu, Joy of Man's Desiring." "His right hand was stronger. He had more strength in his right hand. He'd injured the left somehow."

"How do you know this?"

Sean shrugged. "The only way I know anything. By asking questions." He swung his legs around and sat with his back to the piano. "You should take this thing out and shoot it, put it out of its misery."

"Sean—"

He took a swallow of wine. "You wouldn't be asking questions about what hand the man used to write with if you didn't have some doubts about suicide."

She sighed.

Sean leaned foreward on the piano bench, bracing a hand on each side. "He used his right hand because he couldn't have lifted anything as heavy as a gun with his left."

"This is general knowledge? Everyone knows about his weak left hand?"

"I don't know, but I doubt it. I'm an observing type. Also I talked with the guy."

"Why?"

"Why did I talk with him? Because he knew Jackson Garrett and right now Jackson Garrett is my job. Come on, Susan, I feel like I'm a suspect here."

She waited a beat. "You *are* a suspect, Sean."

35

$\mathcal{T}$hree-hundred-foot-high wall of fire, thundering like a waterfall, swept up the mountain. Jack struggled to run. Two hundred fifty feet to the top. He couldn't feel his legs. Chain saw weighed him down. Feet stuck to the ground. Shouts from the radio clipped to his vest. "Run! Run!"

The last thing a smoke jumper did was leave his equipment. If he did, it meant the situation was dangerously serious. When Jack dropped the chain saw, he knew he'd never make it. Through the radio, he heard the agonized screams of the dying. His mouth opened. Intense heat scorched his throat.

Another breath and he'd be dead. Fluid would fill his lungs, his throat would close in response to the super hot air, carbon monoxide would replace the oxygen in his blood, death would be quick.

"Jack? Jack!"

Fear pumped adrenaline through his system and his heart beat wildly.

"Jack! Wake up!"

Aware of his arm being shaken, he struggled to bring himself back from the dead. When he managed to open his eyes, he squinted in the light.

"Jack?" Molly, sitting up beside him in bed, rubbed a hand down his arm. "You're dreaming again."

Lingering tentacles of the dream clung in his mind. Beneath the echoes of men screaming for help, he could hear the television in the other room. Farm, he told himself. Hampstead.

Picking up Molly's hand, he kissed the palm. "Sorry I woke you. Go back to sleep." He tossed back the blankets and got up.

"Jack—?" She struggled out from under sheets, blankets, and comforter.

"Don't get up." He pulled on sweatpants and sweatshirt and went to the hallway.

Molly ignored his order—nobody told her what to do—slipped on the green silk dressing gown and went out after him, along the hallway toward the living room.

Todd, looking rumpled and tired, slouched on the couch, watching television with press secretary Hadley Cane. Leon was on the floor, propped against the wall, legs straight in front of him.

These people, especially Todd, never seemed to sleep. They were always studying the opposition research, watching the polls, keeping up on the latest developments. Molly ignored them and went into the kitchen to make a cup of tea. The kettle was just starting to shriek when Nora came in, wrapped in a green dressing gown very similar to Molly's. Molly felt a flick of irritation. Nora could sometimes be tedious.

"Tea?" she asked.

Nora nodded and got down another cup. "Why are you up? Jack having nightmares again?"

Molly put a tea bag in her cup, one in Nora's, and poured boiling water in each cup.

"These nightmares." Nora dunked the tea bag up and down. "You know what they're about?"

Molly shook her head.

"Did you ever ask him?"

Molly transferred a dripping tea bag into a bowl. "He won't talk about them."

"Maybe he needs to see a therapist," Nora said.

Molly sighed. "If that's a joke, it's not funny; if it's serious, it's political suicide."

"Did you tell him about—you know." Nora added her tea bag to the bowl. "Going to see that woman?"

"Of course not," Molly said. "And you're not to tell him either. He's got an awful lot on his mind now, he doesn't need anything else. I just wish he would get rid of that Cass woman."

"You think the nightmares might have something to do with her?"

"Honest to God, Nora, I don't know. He won't hear of telling her she's not needed."

The two of them stood in the kitchen talking in low voices like conspirators.

"Maybe she *is* needed." Nora opened cabinet doors, found a package of cookies, and set them on the counter.

Molly shot Nora a look. "What's that supposed to mean?"

"I don't know. I just wonder if there's something going on there. They were real close at one time." Nora opened the cookies and offered Molly one.

Molly shook her head. "Yeah, well, that was a long time ago."

"Is that what he's telling you?"

"Nora, what are you saying?"

"I'm saying she's going to be trouble. We have to get rid of her."

"Anything noteworthy going on?" Jack sat on the end of the couch.

"CNN just backed down on their prediction of your victory in the D.C. primary. They think all this tragedy is going to hurt you."

"Duh," Hadley said.

A perky newswoman with short dark hair was telling two newsmen, ". . . it's been quite incredible. When Jack Garrett first started campaigning for the Democratic nomination, the heavy betting was that he couldn't win over the current vice president. The smart bettors then started scrambling to rearrange their stakes. Governor Garrett had the voters thinking the vice president was right up there with the president in responsibility for the loss of public confidence in the stock market and the huge drop in the Dow in recent weeks, the discovery of allegedly illegal campaign contributions, the billions being poured into the war on drugs with, not only no success, but obvious failure, and continued spending to fight a war on terrorism that also is beginning to seem impossible to win."

"What can we expect in the next ten weeks?" a newsman asked.

"Now with two deaths, one definitely murder and the other a possible suicide, the voters have definitely changed their minds and Garrett is losing—"

There was a tap on the door and a trooper let Bernie in. Bernie tossed Todd a jacket.

"Hey, my jacket," Todd said. "You finally gave it back. And about time, too."

Leon scooted his butt a bit closer to the wall so Bernie could get past his outstretched legs.

"Doesn't anybody around here ever sleep?" Jack said.

Bernie thought Jack looked moody, like he sometimes got. Jack had a tough competitiveness that kept him moving, from town to town, giving the same speech half a dozen times and making it sound just composed as he stood there, dropping into bed and getting up in the morning, going to another town and doing the same thing day after day. A mind-numbing existence. Fighting fatigue and any doubt that he wouldn't be the Democratic choice, seeing dozens of local politicians, shaking thousands of hands, until his own was swollen and painful. But sometimes it was more than that, sometimes he just drifted off somewhere and when he was in that state, he wasn't reaching people like he could when he was hot. Bernie didn't like it that Jack looked distracted.

"You worry too much, Bernie." Jack stood up, put an arm around Bernie's shoulder, and nudged him to the couch. "Don't look at me like you're afraid I'm coming down with a virus. It's the end of the day. You look like shit, too."

Yeah, Jack thought, he probably did look like shit. Remembering Pale Horse Mountain did that to him. Jack leaned his head back and closed his eyes. Months ago, not years, like it sometimes seemed, just before he started seriously trying for a shot at the nomination, he'd spoken with the president and thought the president looked like shit. The job aged a man like nothing else. Jack wondered why someone hadn't run pictures, side by side, the day a new president walked into the office and the day he walked out. With this war on terrorism taking its toll, the president had aged several years in as many months.

"So," the president had said. "You think you're the man for this job? Well, my friend, you might think you've struggled with a monumental decision by deciding to run, but that's nothing. A presidential campaign is moving into a fishbowl. You don't eat, sleep, or take a crap without it being noted and discussed on the six o'clock news. Strangers run your life, and you begin to suspect even your best friends of hanging around only because of what you might be able to give them. You start to worry maybe you're not suited or not smart enough. And it's true." The president looked at him like he found Jack wanting.

Jack felt a warm lick of anger.

"Hey, it's not you," the president said. "It's everybody who thinks he should take a shot at this job. You've got humiliation waiting while you go begging assholes for the financial means to keep going, assholes who think you should be happy groveling for their filthy money."

Beside him on the couch, Bernie shifted and Jack opened his eyes. A picture of Bob Sallas was being shown on television. "Does this man look like a president?" Jack asked Todd.

"He thinks he does. And he fucking *wants* it."

"Naw," Leon said in his soft drawl. "He'll never get it. Shifty eyes. Look at 'em. Nobody's gonna vote for a man with shifty eyes."

A clip came on of local news, a shot of Chief Wren hounded by the media surging toward her in a wave whenever she left the police department, microphones shoved in her face, questions thrown at her.

She was the picture of a female black Irish warrior, black hair and eyes as blue as the lake of Kilarney. Jack wondered whether she'd figure out the answer to the murders.

36

"We're here in the hospital room of Arlene Harlow," the blond female newscaster spoke into the mike with solemn quiet to emphasize the seriousness of the situation and the place, "the young sister-in-law of Governor Garrett's friend Vince Egelhoff who . . ." The cameraman moved in closer to get a shot of the governor bending over to speak with the girl in the hospital bed.

The lights were too bright and too hot, the room was too crowded with a bunch of media people. Sean Donovan, Her Ladyship's hot-shit cousin, was one, politicals Todd Haviland, Bernie Quaid, Hadley Cane, and Leon Massy from Governor's staff, the governor, the governor's wife, her friend Nora, and highway-patrol cops.

". . . and Arlene can't speak to us right now because her jaw was fractured by . . ."

Demarco stayed clear of the circus and kept his eye on the kid who was starting to go gray around the edges. Tired, face slack, lips blue. Because of all the blood she'd lost when she was attacked, she fatigued easily. He could see her hands clench at the Arlene bit. Moonbeam was what she wanted. She was going to be a singer and call herself Moonbeam Melody.

Molly Garrett stepped close, spoke to the kid, smiled and patted her hand, then stepped back and stood by her husband's side. The politicals, Todd and Bernie, gave the kid a word or two, Leon and Hadley moved up and did the same, then the three of them faded back so the camera could have an unobstructed view of the governor. The blond was still talking into her mike when suddenly the kid's hands curled tight around the sheets and her eyes went wild.

The governor put a hand over one of hers. "Something wrong?"

Demarco pushed through to her. "What?"

She was scared stiff, frozen and small in the damn hospital bed, camera and lights focused on her face.

"Are you in pain?" the blond asked.

Demarco turned and shifted so the camera got his back instead of her face. "She'd like to ask you all to leave, but she's not able to talk."

"I don't blame you," the governor said. "We'll get out of here and let you rest. Concentrate on getting well." He leaned over, spoke something in her ear, patted her shoulder, put his arm around his wife and went out. Todd, Bernie, Leon, Hadley, Nora, and cops trailed after him.

"Okay," Demarco said. "They're gone. What is it?"

She typed furiously. *He was here!*

"The governor? Don't let it go to your head. He only did it to get on TV. Good for votes. Visit a sick kid."

Psycho killer!!!

He looked at her, trying to judge true or false. He didn't think she was lying, she was too scared. "You sure?"

She nodded.

"When?"

She pounded the bed with her fist. *Just now!!*

"Who was it?"

If a furious scared fourteen-year-old could be said to look sheepish, then this one did.

"Well?"

She slid down in the bed. *Don't know.*

"You don't know. But you're sure he was here."

Yes!!!!

"How do you know he was here?"

She scrunched in on herself, making herself smaller and typed. *I don't know! Okay?*

If she was playing games, it wasn't funny. "You know he was here, but you don't know why you know and you don't know who he was."

She glared at him.

"Were you asleep when this whole circus started?"

She lifted her pointed little chin a slight bit and winced at the pain. Had she been dreaming? If that were the case, why wasn't she frightened right away? Why wait until the whole circus had been there for several minutes? Something had scared her silly. The wild eyes and gray skin weren't faked. What was the trigger?

"What scared you?" Demarco asked.

Already said. Don't know.

"When did you start feeling scared? I know it wasn't right away. The whole side show was in here for several minutes, before you felt frightened."

Tears brimmed in her eyes and she, angrily, rubbed at them with her fingertips. *Don't know!!!!!*

"Okay, take a breath, close your eyes. Relax. Think about when they first came in."

Dumb blond called me Arlene.

"Right. You can hit her when you're stronger. The governor said something to you. What was it?"

Don't remember.

"Come on, now, tell me what he said."

She made a fist and pounded the bed. *Wasn't listening. Thinking about psycho killer. He was in room!*

"I believe you." Demarco didn't know whether he believed her or not, but he could see she believed it. "What was it that made you think so?"

Her chest was heaving as though she were having trouble breathing, she still looked gray, and was struggling to keep humiliating tears from spilling over.

"Okay. We'll talk about it more later." He tapped her wrist with two fingers. "Get some sleep. I'll hang for a while. The guard will be at the door at all times. Nobody will be able to get in."

It took a good while before she settled down, but fatigue finally took over and she drifted off. He waited until he was sure she wouldn't rouse again before he went out, worry heavy on his shoulders.

The guard, one shoulder propped against the wall, was flirting with a nurse. When Demarco looked at him, he hustled back. "She okay?"

"Sleeping. Was anybody here before the governor came?"

"Not a soul."

"You were here the whole time? Nobody else went in the room?"

"Yes, sir. No, sir."

"You're sure. You were here the whole time?"

The guard got huffy. "Yes, sir. All the time."

Demarco nodded. "If she wakes up, call me."

The day was warm and Demarco shrugged off his suit coat and loosened his tie as he went to his car. Uneasiness hung over his mind like wet fog.

Sucking in a breath, he hit the ignition. Too close to this one. From the time she came home dressed in that ridiculous outfit and looking like a teenage hooker, he was snagged. He didn't know why she got to him so much. Gutsy little kid, managing to keep a sense of humor, even with all the shit thrown at her.

He ought to step down, stay away from this case, let Osey and Parkhurst handle it.

Cass saw the tape of Jack in the hospital visiting the little girl on the ten o'clock news. When it was over, the blond newscaster was shown standing in front of the hospital. "The family dog is missing. We're told it's a Belgian Shepherd, similar to a German Shepherd and its name is Rosie. And the police say it may have been injured."

Cass looked at the dog sleeping on the rug by the hearth. "Rosie?"

The dog scrambled to its feet, ears alert.

Cass called the police department and reported she'd picked up a stray dog that may have belonged to the Egelhoff family.

Twenty minutes later, the dog barked and sped to the door. Cass opened it, expecting a uniformed officer, but the chief of police stood on her porch.

"Ms. Storm? Chief Wren."

Cass had seen her on the news often enough lately to recognize her and asked her to come in.

The chief bent down to pet the dog. "It's been injured," she said examining the wound on its head.

Cass nodded. "The vet said it was probably hit with something." She invited the chief into the living room.

"How do you come to have the dog?" Chief Wren sat in the wing chair by the fireplace.

Cass, sitting on one end of the couch, explained about driving to Hampstead during the thunderstorm and finding the dog. "How is the little girl doing?"

"Doing very well. She has some recovery time coming, but she should be fine."

The police chief asked questions about Gayle Egelhoff, about Vince Egelhoff, then about Wakely, and Cass's connection with each one. It didn't occur to Cass that the police chief, with all her politeness, was viewing her as a murder suspect until the chief started probing into her relationship with Jack Garrett. How stupid can you get? Of course, she'd be a suspect.

Arrested for murder? How's that for crisis intervention? It would certainly throw a snag into her plans for Halloween.

The chief thanked her, got up to leave, and said, "Can you keep this dog for a short while until I can make other arrangements?"

"Uh—okay," Cass said.

37

$\mathscr{B}$ernie wondered what Jack said when he whispered in the girl's ear just before they left the hospital. Jack and Molly, Todd and Leon climbed in the limo. Bernie got in the town car with Cass, Hadley and, alas, Nora. Thank God it was a short ride. Busload of crows trundled along in the rear.

The living room in the old farm house had been made into a mock-up of a television studio to give Jack prep time and practice for the upcoming talk show. Everybody took their places.

Todd, Carter Mercado the pollster, and Leon threw out questions. Bernie did the moderating. Nora, sitting with Molly on a couch pushed back against the wall, was her usual disruptive self, irritating everybody with idiotic suggestions and sighing theatrically at some of Jack's responses. It didn't take long before Todd was ready to strangle her. Cass, who only came because Bernie went after her and herded her in the car before she could escape, was in a chair angled in the corner, looking remote and far away. He slid a glance her way, worried about her. The Wanderer, Leon called her. Bernie thought she was wandering now. Hadley was in the dining room keeping tabs on the polls.

"Always remember the basic rule," Todd said. "Never talk about complicated issues. Stay completely away from them." Todd slid his glasses down his nose and peered over the rims at Jack to make sure he understood. "Completely."

"Right. Never talk about anything important."

Todd ignored the sarcasm. "Never. Because your opponents can grab a piece and run with it, distort every last word you say. If they're clever, which these are not." He waved a hand at nonpresent opponents. "But some of their handlers are."

He tossed out questions, Leon tossed out questions and Carter tossed out questions. Jack fumbled and stuttered.

They were all wanting a sound bite that would be picked up by the crows and spread across the news community to blunt the media blitz of fallout from the deaths of three people close to Jack. They weren't getting it. This rehearsal wasn't working and everybody knew it. They were getting boring sincerity. If this were the real thing, Senator Halderbreck would have won hands down. Even with the guy hired to critique and coach and Jack reading prescribed lines, it was obvious he was working with half a mind.

"Don't forget the economy," Leon said.

"Yeah, yeah. Cutbacks in government spending, businesses downsizing. Prices going up."

"Same-sex marriages," Carter threw in to lighten the mood.

"An abomination unto the Lord," Todd said in his character as Halderbreck.

"Okay," Jack said, "but what's your stand on this issue? And what's your position on gay rights?"

"Jack," Leon said.

"And while we're at it, what's your position on teenage pregnancies? Now me, I'm all in favor of passing out condoms. How about you?"

Okay, Bernie thought, Jack was getting dingy, time for a break.

"Stay away from condoms," Leon said. "Parents think you're handing out permission when you hand their teenagers condoms."

Jack placed fingertips against his temples, like he did when he was reaching the end of his energy reserves. Bernie wondered if they should cancel this, since it was just shambles around their feet, and let everybody go take a nap. Probably more productive than trying to pretend anything useful was going on.

Todd clapped his arm around Jack's shoulders. "We know you can do it."

"Thanks for your support, Mom. Any other words of advice?"

"Yeah, if the opponent is winning, bite his nose."

"That'll help."

Before the situation deteriorated even more, Hadley rushed in. "You guys should see this." She clicked on the television set in the corner.

For days, Leon had been trying to get Jack to cut some new ads and ditch the one they'd been using lately. Leon didn't think it had enough killer flavor. Jack liked it:

Voice-over with the resonate tones of a radio announcer said, "Senator Halderbreck promises, if he's elected president, he will raise taxes, spend more for defense and the war on terrorism, cut Social Security, cut Medicare and cut money for education." While the announcer is talking, words appear on the screen.

    1. Raise taxes.

    2. Spend more.

    3. Cut Social Security.

    4. Cut Medicare.

    5. Cut education.

Then a picture of Halderbreck appears, not an awful picture, not looking like a crook or a deranged Nixon, just friendly and smiling, but clearly looking befuddled and half-witted. The announcer says, "Do we really want this man taking away our Social Security and our children's future?"

On the screen, a shot of the GARRETT FOR AMERICA banner.

The ad Hadley wanted them to see was Halderbreck's response.

Halderbreck sitting on couch in cozy living room, fire in the fire-place, leans forward to watch six-year-old grandson, adorably chewing on pencil, work a page of math problems on a coffee table. Television set in the background. "Garrett For America" slide flashes on the screen.

Boy: "Who's Garrett, Grandpa?"

Halderbreck: "Nobody you want to know." Picks up remote and clicks. Garrett For America disappears and in its place:

JACK GARRETT. FACTS

His live-in companion for twenty years was a man.

He was recently in a hospital for tests. AIDS?

He is involved in a murder investigation.

He lived in sin while in college.

MORALITY. WHAT IS IT GOVERNOR GARRETT DOESN'T UNDERSTAND?

Boy: "Would you help me, Grandpa?"

Halderbreck reaches for the boy's pencil and scribbles answer to math problem.

"Son of a bitch!" Todd pounded his fist against the wall.

"We can't let him get away with this." Jack stomped to the back of the room and snagged a half-sandwich with dried curling bread and sank his teeth into it.

Bernie hoped the platter got refilled quick, running out of food was all they'd need.

"We gotta respond to this asshole." Leon struggled up from his chair, plodded to the table and ripped a slice of cold pizza from where it had glued itself to the box.

Bernie thought it had a layer of cardboard adhered to it.

Hadley said, "I have a copy of the tape coming."

"Get more pizza while you're at it." Leon ripped off the crust and dropped it back in the box.

"We need to be careful here," Nora said. "Maybe we should try a little spicing up. If we'd put Molly—"

Everybody ignored her.

"We gotta come up with something quick." Todd ran a hand through his hair as he paced.

267

"I say we use something positive," Leon said. "Give people some reason to like us, something to cheer about."

"I'm not sure positive is the way to go at this point," Molly said.

"Bernie?" Todd stopped and looked at him.

"After this piece of shit, we need to come out swinging." Bernie said.

"I agree," Todd said. "Leon? Any ideas which way to swing?"

Cass, looking tired and wishing she were somewhere else, absently rubbed the scar on her left wrist with her right thumb. "I think it's wrong."

"Fuck yeah, it's wrong," Todd said. "The question is what are we going to do?"

"No, I mean the math problem," Cass said. "It wasn't clear enough to be sure, but I think the answer was wrong."

Todd gaped at her, then looked around the room. Nobody else had noticed. "Hadley!"

She rushed in.

"Get our techno nerd," Todd said. "Tell him to bring whatever he needs to look at that tape when it comes. Zero in, enhance, focus. Whatever." Todd waved her off.

Twenty minutes later, Eugene the techno nerd was set up in the dining room. He fiddled with the mouse, clicking and moving. "All set. What did you want?"

"The paper on the coffeetable," Todd said. "Can you close in on that?"

Eugene made a square around it and enlarged it. Nothing but fuzz. He did some clicking and moving and it came into focus.

Twenty-seven minus eight. Halderbreck had written in eighteen.

"Hot damn!" Todd and Leon did high fives. Todd grabbed Cass and smacked a huge kiss on the mouth. "I love you."

Way to go, Cass! That got everybody animated and brought meaning to an otherwise wasted afternoon. Bernie thought maybe he'd marry the woman.

"Smart Vote—" Todd started.

"Uh-uh." Leon pulled out another slice of congealed pizza. "Garrett's smart, everybody knows that. The problem is, he's too smart. An intellectual, an egghead. It intimidates people, makes them feel dumb. We got to come up with something else. Bernie?"

Bernie shrugged. "Blow it up, make it clear, show it. Big white letters. Red slash over the incorrect answer. Correct answer beside it. Underneath put, DO YOU WANT THIS MAN IN CHARGE OF YOUR CHILD'S EDUCATION?"

"Yeah, yeah," Leon said, thinking. "Along those lines. We'll refine it, but that'll do." He got out his cell phone and started punching numbers.

Hadley brought in a fresh pizza. Phone pressed to his ear with one hand, Leon grabbed a slice with the other, and chomped off the pointed end.

Bernie opened a Coke and asked Cass if she wanted one. When she nodded, he handed it to her and opened another for himself.

"The bad news is," Leon chewed, "if we're gonna cut a new ad, we gotta do it now. The good news is I found a place that'll do it."

"No," Molly said. "Jack's got to be in Denver early tomorrow. He needs to rest sometime, you know? Tomorrow night he's got to be back here for that—that—thing. The man isn't a machine, even if you do treat him like one. You've had him going for three days with nothing but about two hours sleep."

"Jack?" Todd looked at him.

"Oh, hell, why not? I can always sleep on the plane."

"If we're going to do this, we have to be there in an hour."

"Let's get going."

On the way out, Jack grabbed a slice of pizza.

Em worked really hard on her list of calls and she was limp with tiredness when her shift was up. When she'd first started working, she'd stayed away from the other volunteers, didn't talk to them, didn't make eye contact, put in her hours and left without mingling, but as she worked side by side with these people, she got to know them and got to like them. Not all of them, of course, but most of them—the young man who'd hired her and the young woman who sat next to her and lots and lots of the others. And it occurred to her that it didn't matter if they remembered her. She wasn't expecting to live beyond tomorrow night. She could talk with them, smile at them, ask about their lives and their families and their plans, as long as she stayed away from what was in her mind.

On the way back to the motel, she stopped at Erle's market, picked up hamburger and everything needed to go with it, potato chips and baked beans and ice cream bars. For herself she got ingredients for salad. She didn't know for sure if Tyrell would drop by, but he'd been there last night and now she was counting on him. Why he came, she wasn't sure. He apparently had no parents, no one to take care of him. She suspected he didn't even have a place to stay. She enjoyed his company and enjoyed feeding him. She just wished she had a better equipped kitchen so she could do more than throw together something simple.

She wasn't sure either, why he hadn't harmed her that first night when she'd found him in the motel with the gun. Or the following night when he came back for the three hundred dollars. She'd gotten a membership in a gym just so she could hide the gun in the locker in case he tried to take it away. He had violence in him, she knew that. Just by being around him, she could sense it, but he hadn't hurt her, and if she was honest with herself, she'd have to admit she was lonely and her life wasn't so bleak when he was around.

She was disappointed he wasn't there when she got to the motel. She stashed the perishables in the tiny refrigerator and stacked the rest on a shelf. Before she got her shoes off, there was a knock on the door.

Even though Tyrell grumbled, she had him frying hamburgers and fixing salad. Never in the world would he admit it, but he enjoyed it. She wanted to tell him that after tomorrow, she wouldn't be here anymore, but she didn't know how. He'd want to know why and where she'd be. She couldn't tell him the only place she'd be was in hell.

38

All of a sudden it seemed there wasn't enough oxygen in the room and Em nearly choked as she tried to draw a breath. Don't stare at him, she told herself, don't stare at him. Even while she was willing herself not to attract his attention, she couldn't help wondering if he was the officer who'd kill her. Would it cause him trouble? Psychological problems? She hated to think that she'd cause him pain.

His name was Phil Baker. He seemed a nice man, sandy hair, friendly smile, relaxed manner. Until you looked at his eyes. There was nothing relaxed about them. They were intense and alert, and moving, always moving, watching, watching. They brought fear into her heart. Would he stop her before she could accomplish her mission? Had he ever killed anyone before? She knew that didn't matter. He wouldn't hesitate.

He sat at the table of phone banks. Stewart, the enthusiastic young man who was in charge of the local campaign headquarters, two Hampstead police officers, two unkempt young men—advance sound men—and four volunteers including Em sat in folding chairs on both sides of the table. The corkboard attached to the wall held a diagram of the field where the rally was to take place and next to it was a schedule.

271

In big letters: NOON. CANDIDATE ARRIVES FROM DENVER.

"Right here." Stewart got up and tapped the diagram with a pencil. "This is where I want the volunteers with signs. The press will be here and with the signs here, they'll be visible for television."

Yes, Em thought, perfect. From there she'd be close enough. She'd only have a few seconds and it had always worried her that, never having fired a gun before, she might miss. And it wasn't something she could practice. But if she got that close, she'd be okay.

"Names," Baker said, looking at the diagram. "Addresses and social security numbers of every volunteer."

Em wondered how deep they'd check. Would her name set off any flags?

"Right," Stewart said. "Anything else you'll need?"

"Yeah. List of everyone who'll be near the governor, on the platform, backstage, carrying signs. All your people," Baker's glance rested on each person at the table, "will be given color-coded badges that'll show where you're allowed to go, how close you can get. We'll be setting up detectors. Bleachers going to be ready?"

"Yes. They'll be all set by eight."

"Sound?"

"Yes, ready by eight."

"All right," Baker said. "This is how this is going to go." He went through every step of the procedure. Platform set up, sound system working, barriers for each perimeter erected. At ten o'clock sweep area for guns and explosives, at eleven o'clock check buses and cars with the media, at 11:15 start letting people in.

Em's hands felt icy. She hadn't realized they'd be so thorough. How could she have been so naïve?

Phil Baker got up and went to the diagram. "All along here we'll have highway-patrol and local cops. The only people allowed in here will be volunteers with signs, the press pool, and the governor and his people. Everybody but the governor and his staff gets checked off. All clear?"

Stewart went to the diagram. "At twelve fifteen, Governor Garrett arrives from the airport. Senator Roushe will be with him. They'll walk along here, the governor shaking hands as he goes. He'll be surrounded by prominent local supporters, among them several women. Good visuals and makes him appear liked by both sexes." He looked around to see if everyone was with him. "They proceed to the platform, should be there at twelve fifty-five. If all goes well, at one, the senator will introduce Governor Garrett and the crowd goes wild with applause."

Em was appalled at how tight the security would be. How was she going to conceal the gun, let alone pull it out and fire?

To make sure everybody got it, Baker went through the whole thing again. When he was done, he asked Stewart, "You know all your volunteers?"

"Sure. They're great. All of them."

The officer nodded. "We'll check them through anyway."

Demarco was worried about the kid. Look how easy that dipshit reporter cousin of Her Ladyship's got in her room. Any asshole with murder on his brain could wait until the guard blinked and just walk in. Little as she was, and weak as a kitten, it wouldn't take much. He'd told all this to Parkhurst. Until the guard was doubled, Demarco planned to spend as much free time at the hospital as possible.

He stopped at the computer place and for twenty minutes looked at computer games trying to figure out which one she might like. He'd spent more on computer games for her then he'd spent on anybody in a long time. When his Visa bill came in, he'd probably be surprised. He picked out one that looked complicated enough to keep her entertained. She had a sharp brain, that one.

Thoughts had been coming to mind about maybe trying for foster parent, when she was well enough to be released. What would Children's Services say? No, probably. He was single, worked long unpredictable hours, thirteen years in the marines didn't qualify him for foster parent. The poor kid needed somebody in her corner. Hell, he didn't even know if she'd want to live with him. They hadn't exactly gotten off to a good start.

He nodded at the guard as he went into her room and noted how fatigued she looked. The performance for news spots with the governor had taken a lot out of her. When she saw him she started a smile, then pulled it down to a sulky bored look. Protecting her image. Wouldn't want him thinking she was glad to see him. Moonbeam Melody didn't smile at cops, even if she was bored out of her mind and this particular cop was bringing another computer game.

"How you doing, kiddo?"

She typed, *How would you be doing if you were flat on your back with nothing to do, not even talk?*

"That's my girl."

She scowled at him. *I am not your girl!!*

"Sorry, got carried away for a minute. You are your own girl."

She typed furiously, *Woman!!!!*

He raised an eyebrow.

Well, I am.

"Okay." He tossed her the plastic bag he was carrying and slouched down in the chair beside the bed.

She ignored him as she studied the new game. *This looks good. Not like those mindless things you got at first.*

"You're welcome."

Her mouth curved up slightly. *Thanks.*

"How you feeling?"

She shrugged. *I want to go home.*

She no longer had a home to go to and maybe remembering that, a tear trickled down her cheek. Snapping open the newspaper he'd grabbed on the way up, he pretended to read. She wouldn't want him catching sight of tears, not his tough Moonbeam. If she did come and stay with him, they'd have to negotiate about the name. Take her to the firing range and introduce as Moonbeam to his friends? Nah.

She sniffed, grabbed a tissue and gave a good hard blow, then typed. When he didn't immediately look at the computer screen, she yanked his sleeve. He glanced at the screen. *I been thinking.*

"Yeah? About what?"

Sand.

"Sand? What? Sand in your shoe?" His cell phone rang, he unclipped it. "Demarco."

274

"The chief wants you right away," Hazel said. "Problems."

"Wants me where?"

Hazel gave him an address.

He hung up. "Sorry, kid, I gotta go."

Where?

"Work."

When will you be back?

"No way to tell. The governor's doing some rally thing on campus. It's all hands on deck. I'll try to come back later, but it might be late. You going to be okay?"

She gave him one of her looks of scorn, a little anemic and a little brittle around the edges but a, by God, look of scorn. *Course.*

He didn't want to leave. He wasn't one for premonitions and psychic flashes, but he had a cold feeling and he hated like hell to trust her to the guard.

39

$\mathscr{T}$he gun felt heavy enough in her bag that surely it must be obvious she had it. Em was so nervous she felt like she was poised on the edge of shaking apart, or like a tuning fork, she'd start vibrating with sound, if anything were to tap her. Stewart, the volunteer coordinator, was standing just outside the barriers at Wheaton's Field. Usually it was just an empty field used for some athletic event, she assumed baseball or soccer. Now more bleachers had been put up, the platform and sound system were ready. Buses with the press pool and more buses with volunteers were parking at the far end. Highway-patrol officers were covering the field with dogs and metal detectors. She'd thought of hiding the gun somewhere here last night and now was glad she hadn't. That would have been disaster, for sure. How was she ever going to get the gun past them?

Em prayed, asking a God she felt was going to condemn her to hell for His help one last time. Jackson Garrett's actions had caused a death. He deserved to be punished.

"Hi, Em." Stewart was distracted, watching Phil Baker talking with another man. When Officer Baker started to walk away, Stewart called out and trotted after him. Was this it? Em wondered. Did Stewart realize what she had in her bag and was telling the officer about it?

Everybody's background was going to be checked. Maybe they'd looked way back into hers and found she had a connection to Jackson Garrett. Maybe they found out he defended her daughter's killer, defended him so well he won an acquittal. Maybe this was the end right here, maybe this was as far as she would get.

She thought her intentions must be plain to anyone who glanced at her. With all that hatred in her heart, surely it must show in her face. Stewart nodded to Phil Baker and jogged back. Her knees felt weak. This was it, he was going to tell her, they found out about her, they knew what she was going to do, they were coming to arrest her.

"Glad you're here, Em. I need you to do something for me. Ross is a no-show. I need to get over there and check off our people as they go through the detectors." He handed her a clipboard with a list of volunteers. "Can you check on this side?"

She opened her mouth, but nothing came out.

"There's nothing to it." He thought she was nervous and was reassuring her she could do it. "You know everybody, just check them off as they pass through the detector. And be sure and give everybody a sign." He indicated the GARRETT FOR AMERICA signs stacked up by the entrance before he loped off.

And just like that, Em was on the right side of the checkpoint. She managed a stiff smile as she put a check beside each volunteer's name and reminded them to pick up a sign. When the last volunteer had passed through, Em grabbed a sign and inserted herself in the middle of the group. Highway-patrol officers lined up in front on the platform, facing the crowd. The volunteers started cheering. Em raised her sign to hide her face.

When Governor Garrett appeared, Em saw him in clear detail, the rest of the world retreated into fuzzy shadow behind him. The cheering of the crowd was muffled and periodic like broken static. Highway patrol, the woman who stood proudly to introduce him, were nothing but props in a distant play, one that held no interest for her. With the GARRETT FOR AMERICA sign in front of her face, she took in a steadying breath and prepared her soul for her final moments.

When Jackson Garrett smiled at the crowd and started speaking, she lowered the sign. The time had come, all the planning and the prayers and the help God had given her, the luck of running into Tyrell, had all come down to this moment. Her death was near, she only had one last prayer, that she could fire the gun before she was killed. In her fantasies, he would turn and see her, he would recognize her, resignation would come over his face, and then a look of understanding and rightness when she fired and the bullets struck. A life for a life. Justice at last.

She felt young, like she hadn't felt in thirty years, a surge of joy soared through her and she wondered if this was the precursor of death. When the soul slipped away, would the joy dissipate as eternal peace flowed in to take its place?

A life for a life. When God didn't let Tyrell kill her that first night and she thought Tyrell probably didn't even know himself whether he would or not, she was confident that God would give her the courage to carry this through to the end. Jackson Garrett would die. Alice Ann would be avenged. The three of them would be tied together throughout eternity. Carefully, Em laid the sign on the floor.

Jack saw Molly, faithful wife that she was, sitting in the front row with a look of expectant adoration, he scanned the crowd and saw Cass in the row behind. In her face, he glimpsed a shadow of the young girl he'd loved twenty years ago. He permitted himself a small smile for those innocent days and wondered what might have been. A hand circling in the air caught his attention and he watched as Todd squeezed through the crowd, obviously wanting to tell him something. Todd climbed up on the platform and the three people already standing there shuffled aside so he could wedge himself in.

Todd looked tired, Jack thought, and probably so do I. They'd all been working hard, putting in too many hours and the strain was beginning to fray the edges. With the D.C. primary coming up, it was only going to get worse.

The woman on the other side of him stepped to the microphone.

For a second, he'd forgotten her name. He really must be tired. One thing a politician should never do is forget a name. Gloria something— Shaw, that was it.

". . . of our chapter of National Organization of Women . . ." The crowd roared and volunteers repeatedly lofted signs skyward.

"They managed to get quite a crowd here," Jack murmured in Todd's ear.

Todd nodded. Jack smiled at Molly, looked for Cass again, and saw a dowdy woman behind her lay down her campaign sign. Did he know that woman? Another face he couldn't remember. He must really be losing it. At this rate, he'd lose his bid for the nomination.

"Listen," Todd said.

Jack tipped his head closer to hear. The woman wasn't smiling like the rest of the crowd.

". . . maybe a nut . . . maybe a grudge . . ."

The woman moved toward the platform.

Em stood there, willing Jackson Garrett's glance to reach her and when it did, she still didn't move. He was looking blank, like he didn't know who she was. She wanted him to recognize her. She wanted him to know what was going to happen and she wanted him to know by whose hand he was going to die.

Her intense focus caught his attention and they locked glances.

The roaring in her head blotted out the screaming crowd. She stuck her hand in her purse.

Jack watched her, trying to figure out why she looked familiar. Any politician worth his salt remembered names and faces, it was one of the prerequisites, and he was an old hand, why couldn't he place her?

"Just to be on the safe side," Todd was saying, "no unexpected side trips. No plunging into crowds. Okay?"

The middle-aged woman, with short, scraggly gray hair brought a gun from her purse. Jack felt mesmerized, like a rabbit in the head-lights, unable to move. She raised the gun. Jerking himself awake, he shoved at Todd. "*Nooo . . .*"

The next thing he knew he was slumped back on the metal folding chair looking down at a red strain spreading across his white shirt. The woman's face seemed to stand out from the crowd, she looked appalled, and her expression sickened. Then he recognized her.

"Mary," he whispered.

Two highway-patrol officers covered his body.

Tyrell saw two more cops pushing toward Em. He saw her shove the gun up under her chin, but couldn't hear the shot over the screaming, jostling crowd. He faded back and slipped through the crowd. Stupid bitch. What did he care if she blew her head off. He didn't like her anyway.

Cass wanted to scream. All she could actually see was the top of Jack's head and all she could see in her mind was Ted's body, twisted in that awful way after the drunk smashed into the car. And Laura, covered in blood. Cass shook her head and watched Molly Garrett trying to get through the crowd to her husband.

Cries and yells and shouts, everybody trying to figure out what had happened. Fear and panic. Milling mass of bodies, uncertain what to do, wanting to be away from danger. Cops shouting at each other, reporters chattering fast into recorders, or scribbling notes, photog-raphers snapping pictures.

Cass found herself shoving toward Jack. Local cops were trying to keep the crowd under control and prevent anyone from leaving. She elbowed people in her way and was caught in a strong grip. She strug-gled before she realized it was Bernie.

"Oh my God, Bernie. Is he all right? I need to go . . ."

"There's nothing you can do." Bernie's face was sickly gray, but his voice was calm.

With urging words and blunt force, the cops cleared a path through the crowd. Two paramedics raced by with a gurney, cops close around them. In seconds, the paramedics had Jack on the gurney and were running for the street where an ambulance waited. Jack's face was white, his eyes closed. Cass didn't know whether he was dead or alive.

In the pool of reporters, Sean watched the madness, the fear and frenzy of the crowd, the controlled fury and speed of the cops doing what they were trained to do.

"Is he dead?" a young female reporter asked.

Sean took out his cell phone and called his boss at home. He told her what had happened and suggested she get someone to the hospital ASAP. He'd be held up here until everybody was questioned, that could take hours.

"Done," she said. "Stay with it. And get me anything—and I mean anything—fact, rumor, or reasonable fiction."

"Right." He phoned his office and dictated his report.

Demarco slipped into the ambulance right after the highway cops. Sirens blaring, ambulance going flat out, careening around corners, showed how perilous the situation was. Also showed Garrett was still alive. They wouldn't need this kind of speed for a dead man. Maybe not much alive. Face gray, eyes open, sightless. Lots of blood from the hole in his chest. Gasping sound, like he was fighting for breath, except the sound came from the wound. Paramedics crouched on either side of him. "Lung's collapsing," one said. The other nodded and said to the driver. "We need to really pound it."

The ambulance speed increased and Demarco braced himself for a crash. Moving this fast and not stopping for cross traffic was apt to prove fatal. Who was the woman who shot him and how the fuck had she gotten in with a gun? The gasping sound grew erratic and different in pitch, then stopped altogether. The governor had died. Demarco was now looking at a homicide victim.

With a dying wail, the ambulance pulled up to the emergency room. Demarco stayed out of the way, as the paramedics yanked the gurney from the back and raced to doors that opened as they approached. Highway cops followed, Demarco stuck to their heels.

Nurses and physicians swarmed around the gurney.

"GSW right chest. BP eighty over fifty and falling. Pupils responsive." The paramedic spoke so fast the words were all strung together.

Adam Sheffield, ER physician, said, "On three, gentlemen. One, two, three."

Garrett was half-lifted, half-thrown onto the examining table. Dr. Sheffield listened to Garrett's chest while Maggie Mason, ER nurse, cut open the bloody shirt. "Pneumothorax," the doctor murmured. Maggie handed him a metal tube and he jammed it into Garrett's chest and threaded thin plastic tubing through it. Garrett's chest convulsed and then tremored.

"We have a pulse," Maggie said.

Bernie and Cass sat with Molly in a waiting room with maroon couches and gray tweed chairs. The television mounted on the wall played and replayed a tape of the shooting. Jack looking puzzled, then alarmed and pushing Todd away, starting to speak just as the bullet hit, then falling back and a dark stain widening on his white shirt. Bernie got up to turn it off, but Molly stopped him.

"I have to watch it."

Bernie looked at Cass, she shrugged, then nodded. If Jack's wife had to see this over and over again, then she had to. Cass, of all people, understood how crazy a woman reacted when her husband got killed. She wished she were the praying kind, she'd send pleading prayers to the almighty, but she didn't think her prayers carried any weight.

A blond female on television was repeating what she had already said half a dozen times or more. "Governor Garrett was shot tonight at a fund-raiser in Hampstead, Kansas. He appeared to push Todd

Haviland, his campaign manager, out of harm's way, suggesting he might have seen the shooter. The woman who shot him turned the gun on herself and we were told she did not survive the self-inflicted . . ."

"He saved my life," Todd said, his voice clogged with emotion.

"Does anybody know who the woman was?" Cass asked.

Bernie shook his head.

They waited. Cass studied the large painting on one wall, trying to figure out what it was. It was at least eight feet square, browns and yellows. It appeared to have pieces of tree trunks and maybe pieces of broken urns.

The president appeared on the television screen, sitting behind the desk in the oval office. "It is with great sorrow that I must report to the American people that a terrible tragedy occurred this afternoon. Governor Jack Garrett, my good friend, has been shot. I want to express my sorrow and outrage to the family and the country. My prayers and those of my family are with him, as well as those of countless others around our land." His face faded away.

The blond came back. "That was the president expressing his horror at this awful tragedy and relaying hope and compassion to the governor's family. The governor is in critical condition, I'm told. He was still alive when he reached the hospital, although he had stopped breathing and had no pulse. In the emergency room, procedures were taken to get his breathing started again. We're waiting for word from the hospital to tell us more . . ."

Cass reached out and took Molly's cold hand.

When the cops finally released Sean, he hustled over to the hospital and after a thorough check by security was allowed to join the mob of press in a waiting area designated to keep them all under close watch. With the number of bodies packed into such a small area, the room was stifling. He edged along the wall and bumped into Ty Baldini, the local pencil.

"What's the latest?" Sean asked.

"The Governor's still in surgery. Hospital spokesman is supposed to be with us shortly." Ty looked at his watch. "That was forty-five minutes ago."

It was another twenty minutes before a man in a gray suit came in. A barrage of questions were thrown at him. He ignored them and read from the slip of paper in his hand. Sean noticed the hand wasn't steady and the suit didn't look at the crowd of reporters and newscasters. Very likely, he hadn't had to make many statements to the press.

"Governor Jackson Garrett was admitted to this hospital at one thirty-seven P.M. Emergency procedures were immediately undergone to restore his breathing and then he was taken to surgery."

Questions came fast and furious. Is he still alive? Will he survive? Who shot him? Why? Did he know his attacker? How long was he without oxygen? What about brain damage?

The gray suit continued to read. "He is still in surgery at this time, where the surgeon is repairing the damage to his chest. Medical personnel will be with you shortly to answer all your questions. Thank you." He left with questions hurled at his fleeing back.

Hadley Cane came in. The room went still with everyone focused on her face trying to decipher her news from her appearance. All Sean could read was that Hadley was pale and her eyes were slightly red and puffy as though she'd been crying, but she had herself under control now. As Garrett's press secretary, she'd faced this bunch, or one like it, many times, but never under these circumstances and she was nervous, but she pulled in a breath and held her chin up. *Atta girl*, Sean thought.

"Governor Garrett is still alive, still in surgery. I'm not a physician, but I'm told everything is going well. The woman who tried to kill him, as you all know, shot herself and was pronounced dead on arrival at this hospital. At this time we know nothing about her, who she is, or why she shot the Governor."

"When will you know anything?"

"I can't answer that question. And before anybody asks anything else, there's nothing more I can tell you about her."

"How much longer will he be in surgery?"

"Nobody seems able to answer that question with anything but an estimate. I'm told it'll be maybe another two hours."

"Is he expected to live?"

"The governor is young, in good health and good physical condition. His chances of surviving are very good."

"How long was he without oxygen?" Ty asked.

"Due to the immediate response of the highway patrol, the quick arrival of the paramedics and the expert medical skill of the emergency room staff, a relatively short time."

"What about brain damage?"

"Since the time he wasn't breathing was so brief, there is every possibility that the governor's mental functioning is every bit as good as always."

Sean could see that she was holding herself tight, straining to be professional in the onslaught of emotions trying to take over.

"If he survives, will he continue to run?"

She pressed her lips together, probably to prevent a sharp reply. "That's a question that hasn't yet been addressed. Priority here is to save his life. Whether he'll continue is up to the governor. That's it for now. There'll be another update on his condition in an hour. Thank you."

Questions were tossed at her as she walked out.

40

By the time he was free, it was so late, Demarco thought the kid would be sleeping the sleep of the just and sedated. He was tired enough, he ought to just go home and crash instead of hitting the hospital, but hell, he'd told her he'd be back. He always kept a promise, anyway he'd never rest easy until he'd seen her. A few minutes wouldn't hurt, make sure the guard was doing his job, see she was all right, maybe sit with her a bit. He wouldn't wake her.

The guard sent Demarco a look when he came in and Demarco had the uneasy feeling the jerk hadn't stayed at his post. Her room was dark except for the glow of the computer screen which gave off enough light to see her sleeping form.

"Hey, kid," he said softly in case she was pretending.

She didn't move. Her pillow was on the floor, the sheets were twisted. He picked up the pillow, dropped it on the foot of the bed and sat down, just to be with her a few minutes. She must have been exhausted, poor kid, she didn't even stir. Stretching his legs out, he put his head against the chair back and closed his eyes. This time of night the hospital was quiet, no daytime hustle and bustle; a nurse walked down the corridor to check on a patient, then spoke to another nurse in soft tones.

Almost immediately, he realized the lack of movement and sound from the bed. No rustling of sheets, no noises of breathing. Nothing but stillness. He touched her hand. Cool. He placed fingertips against her wrist, then just under her jaw, couldn't find a pulse. He yelled at the guard, "Get a doctor in here! Now!"

He started CPR. The room exploded with activity. The crash cart came careening through the door. Nurses and physicians crowded in. One tried to take over the CPR. Demarco shoved her away and kept pushing on the kid's chest. Finally, the nurse convinced him to step back. A physician said, "Clear," and applied paddles to the kid's thin chest. Her body jumped and flopped like a rag doll.

The team worked for minutes, then the physician looked at the clock and said angrily, "Death at twenty-three hundred hours."

"No! Keep working on her!"

A nurse put a hand on Demarco's arm. "I'm sorry. She's gone. There's nothing more we can do."

Hot rage started in the emptiness of his chest and burned so fast up to his throat that he choked on it. "Everybody out!"

"Sir—"

"Out! Don't touch anything! This is a crime scene!"

"Any idea what she meant by sand?" Susan had lost track of how much coffee she'd consumed in the last four hours, but gamely took a sip from the latest refill. There was enough passion tearing in her office to use up all the breathing space.

Demarco's jaw was so tight she wondered if he'd be able to wrench his teeth apart to answer. He stood rigid in the doorway, stiff, straight, shoulders back, ready to charge. Parkhurst, almost as mad, paced back and forth in front of him. Since her office was small, he only got six steps before he had to turn and go the other direction.

"No," Demarco snapped.

"Mean anything to you?" she asked Parkhurst.

"Beaches, sandboxes, sands of time, hourglasses, footprints on,

287

sandman—" Beard stubble rasped as he ran his hand down his jaw. "Give me a minute, maybe I can come up with more."

These two volcanoes of barely contained fury were giving her a headache. Maybe she should send them to the parking lot and let them use up all that testosterone in hand-to-hand combat. The adrenaline pumped in her system by the girl's murder and its pursuant investigations had long since dissipated, leaving her with a caffeine jag that fought with fatigue. All the hours they'd put in had gotten them zilch, much to everyone's frustration.

The unknown suspect had called the nurses' station claiming to be Parkhurst and asked the nurse who answered to have the guard call the department from a landline and talk with the chief. Not wanting to leave his post, the guard had asked to use the phone at the nurses' station. The nurse had said she was sorry, but she couldn't let him. He had to track down a phone and the closest one he could find was the pay phone in the lobby. Apparently, the suspect had stolen a lab coat and stethoscope from the doctor's lounge, walked boldly into the girl's room and held a pillow to her face. They'd know for sure in the morning when Dr. Fisher did the autopsy.

Susan felt sorry for the guard. Clark was his name and he hadn't been with them long. Demarco and Parkhurst had both had a go at him. When they were done the poor kid was left with about as much starch as a dish rag.

"Sand," she said, and looked at Demarco. "You think the girl meant something about her attacker?"

"I don't know. I jumped to the conclusion she'd been thinking about the attack. It bothered her she couldn't remember. She tried to pull memory back from the blankness. Then you called."

Another chip to add to the pile on his shoulder. If she hadn't called, the girl wouldn't have been killed. Susan wondered why he'd gotten so fond of this girl. "Was there any sand in the house?"

"No, ma'am."

"Sandbox in the back yard? Craft-type thing made with colored sand?"

"No."

"Cat?"

"No."

"Was she asleep when you came in, still caught in a dream when she spoke?"

"Maybe. She was asleep when I walked in, woke up when I sat down." Demarco's fists were straight down at his side in a white-knuckle clench. "One of them killed her. Held a pillow over the face of a fourteen-year-old girl who was so weak she could barely pick up a plastic cup."

"Them?"

Demarco kept his gaze fixed on a distant spot just over her right shoulder. "Garrett," he snapped. "Or the politicos with him."

"And you think this because—?"

"She said so!" Demarco was teetering on insubordination and Parkhurst was close to blowing up at him.

Susan nodded. "And when you called her on that, she backed down. She thought her attacker had been in the room, but couldn't say why she thought so. Is that correct?"

"Yes, ma'am."

Parkhurst stopped pacing, put his hands on his hips and glared at Demarco. Demarco stiffened an already stiff spine. Susan sighed. "Who was in her room?"

"Garrett," Demarco said, "His wife. Campaign manager named Todd Haviland, guy named Leon Massy, another guy named Bernie Quaid, woman named Hadley Cane, woman named Nora Tallace."

"And some media people." She looked at Parkhurst. "Find out who they were."

"Right," he said.

"And—"

"Yeah. Go through the house again, looking for sand." He started for the door, Demarco stepped aside. A short nod from Parkhurst had Demarco falling in behind.

* * *

289

Jack tried to open his eyes. They seemed glued shut. His throat hurt. He couldn't swallow. He couldn't breathe. Panicky struggle. Suspended in darkness, the only sound a rhythmic *hiss thunk*. He struggled to move. Paralyzed. Panic faded as he slipped deeper into the darkness.

41

Jack floated in the darkness, sometimes sensing paler pockets around the edges and above, working toward them like an underwater swimmer aiming for the surface, then sinking down to drift and dream and watch images form, melt and swirl away like multicolored fog. A young man exuberant at the not guilty verdict. A middle-aged woman angry. A gun.

Without a struggle, his eyes opened. He was lying on a narrow bed in a dim room, arms stretched out and strapped down, muted light to his right. Something in his throat. Tried to swallow, felt like he couldn't breathe.

A stocky man with dark curls, wearing green scrubs loomed over him. "About time you decided to come back."

Jack tried to speak.

"Hold on, I'll get the tube out, then you can talk." He removed tape from Jack's face. "Cough."

Jack coughed and choked as the tube slid from his throat, which was sore and swollen. When he tried to shift slightly, searing pain clawed at his chest.

"Adam Sheffield." The stocky man tugged at the bandages over Jack's chest.

"Doctor?" Jack whispered hoarsely.

"Yeah. Fixed a bloody great hole in your chest. It's looking real good."

A syrupy gratitude came over him. Weak as a new-born infant, if he tried to express thanks, he'd probably snivel. "What happened?"

"You don't remember?"

"Not much. Lots of screaming. People milling around. Sirens." Jack stirred through the slush in his mind. "Lights. I remember lights."

Dr. Sheffield leaned against the bed and crossed his arms. "You're one lucky man, governor. The bullet missed your heart by that much." He held thumb and forefinger an inch apart. "Went at an angle up and came out the back, missing your spinal cord by about that much too. Tore up a lung pretty good, but that will mend."

Sheer relief flooded over him, of such magnitude that Jack was swamped, left flat and gasping for air. "I can walk?"

"Not right now, you can't, but give it a few days."

Jack took in a breath and relished the pain that came with it, because it said he was alive. A second time, he should have died and he survived. He was humbled and grateful. He would live as he wanted, he would walk, he would not end up like Wakely in a wheelchair.

Friday morning there was a soft tap on the open door and Todd came in. "Happy Halloween, Governor." He nudged the chair closer, sat down, curved his spine and stretched out his legs. "Thanks for saving my life."

". . . what?"

"You're a hero, you pushed me out of the way of the speeding bullet. 'Course it would have been better if you'd gotten yourself out of the way, too, but at least you're not a dead hero." Todd slid a chair nearer the bed.

"Cut . . . hero crap . . . who shot me?"

Todd took off his glasses, held them out and peered through the lenses, pulled a handkerchief from his pocket and polished them. "She killed herself."

292

"Who?" Jack's throat was sore, it hurt to talk.

Todd checked the lenses, then put the glasses back on. "Mary Shoals. Daughter brought a suit against her husband, claimed he beat her up. You defended the husband."

"Alice Vosse," Jack said, remembering. "Got . . . bastard off." Guilt lay pressed on his chest heavy enough to make breathing difficult. "Should have . . . let rot . . . in prison."

"You were doing your job. Defending your client to the best of your ability."

". . . he killed her," Jack said.

"You are not responsible for her death, or for her mother's either. You aren't God, Jack. You're just a good lawyer. What you need to decide is what you want to do now."

"Sleep."

"Good. When you get that out of the way, we'll get back to work. This is good for votes. Hundreds of people out there are praying for your recovery. If the primary was today, you'd win by a landslide."

"Molly?"

"She's on her way. You came back to the land of the living just after she left to go back and take a shower." Todd stood and put a hand on Jack's shoulder. "I'm glad you survived, buddy. After this, nobody will blame you if you decide to drop out."

"Sleep . . . let you know."

"What are you doing in here! Out!" The nurse crossed her arms and glared.

"I'll get the troops together."

". . . don't forget . . . Cass," Jack mumbled.

"Not a chance."

42

<hr />

After a long, futile, frustrating straight twenty-four-hour shift, Susan had Osey go out front and keep the media focused while she slunk out the back. Huge black thunderheads were rolling in and at four in the afternoon, it was dark as night. Susan crawled into her house, put a Brandenburg concerto on the CD player, cranked the volume up to window-rattling and collapsed on the couch.

Parkhurst and Demarco had gone through the Egelhoff house inch by inch and had found no sand, nothing related to sand, nothing pretending to be sand, nothing remotely similar to sand. She and Parkhurst had questioned campaign manager Todd Haviland, media consultant Leon Massy, general assistant wherever needed Bernie Quaid, press secretary Hadley Cane, and Nora Tallace, personal assistant to Mrs. Garrett. They'd even spoken with Molly Garrett who was so distraught by her husband's condition she could barely focus on the questions. The cameraman, female interviewer, and all press who'd been present had been tracked down and questioned. Nothing came from any of it. The governor was still in intensive care, his condition still critical, and no one would hazard a guess as to his prognosis. Wait and see, was the physician's answer to any probing. Osey and Yancy were checking into Mary Shoals, the woman who'd shot the governor.

Susan was drifting along the stream toward sleep when the doorbell rang, the sound drilled right into her tired brain and brought her up fighting for air. It was Sean toting a large, white paper bag.

"You again!"

"And gratifying it is to see you so thrilled about it and all."

"What's in the bag?"

"Food. When did you last eat?"

"What is this? You're always popping up with food. Like some genie."

"The hotel kindly packed it for me." He plopped the bag on the coffeetable, turned down the volume on the CD player and started removing clear plastic containers. "Roast pork. Salad. What they called French bread around here that is nothing but disguised Wonder Bread. And—" Like a magician pulling a rabbit from a hat he brought out a huge wedge of chocolate cake.

"What is it you're trying to get from me?"

"Only bringing you dinner. Just sit. I'll take care of everything." He went off to the kitchen and returned with knives, forks, napkins and two plates. He handed her one of each and sat cross-legged on the floor in front of the coffeetable. "Bad day?" He scooped salad on the plates and handed her one.

"You could say that." She stabbed a cherry tomato and popped it in her mouth.

"I'm sorry about the little girl. I heard she was smothered with a pillow."

"Fourteen years old and some asshole smothered her. A kid. A funny, smart, silly kid who called herself Moonbeam because she thought Arlene was dorky." Susan smacked down her fork. "God damn that son of a bitch!"

Sean went in search of wineglasses, filled one, gave it to her, filled the second and took a sip.

"It's a good thing you aren't staying long." She tipped the glass and took a good swallow. "Otherwise, I'd be an alcoholic."

"Damn right. It's your heritage, darlin'." He forked pork medallions from the plastic container. "You think it was a man? The attacker?"

She shrugged. "Who knows. At this point, I don't think anything."

"Hey." He put down his fork and picked up her hand. "It wasn't your fault."

"Yes, Sean, it was. It was my fault. I should have protected her."

"Suse, you had someone standing at her door."

"Oh yeah, look how effective that was. You got by him." She clenched her teeth. "God damn it, so did the creep who killed her."

Sean topped off her glass, put it in her hand, and guided it to her mouth. She took a gulp. "Why the hell didn't I put two people on her?"

"Susan, I don't mean to make light of your officers, but I venture to say they don't have a lot of experience in big bad ways."

She shot him a look, got ready to hit a defensive stance, then sighed. "Still."

"If you'd had two people watching her, the killer would have figured a way to get by two of them. If he was determined, he would have found a way."

Susan jabbed a piece of lettuce.

"Why was she killed?" Sean asked.

"I don't know." She reminded herself Sean was press and she shouldn't get tipsy in front of the press. "I shouldn't be talking to you."

"Weekly magazine," he said. "I'm not the daily news rushing off to meet the deadline."

"We're assuming he was afraid she could identify him."

"By we, I assume you mean you and Tonto."

"You're not funny."

"You always used to think I was."

"That was before I knew better."

"Why wouldn't he smother her immediately? Why wait two days?"

"Assumption again. This was his first opportunity." She swirled the wine and watched it circle in the glass.

"There you are, you see. He waited and went in when he found an opening. You couldn't have done anything."

"I could have put armed guards with shotguns around her bed. Goddamn it."

"If he was determined, he'd have found a way."

"Fourteen, Sean. She was fourteen. I failed her. I failed the department, and the town and—"

"And who?"

"Nobody. I just feel like a failure all around."

"Daniel? Don't tell me you're comparing yourself with your husband. He died four years ago."

"He was a good guy, Sean."

"I don't doubt it."

She smiled shortly. "Okay. I don't know what he would have done. I don't even know what kind of cop he was. We weren't married long enough for me to learn much about him. It's just that I've been thinking so much about him lately."

"I know, darlin'. I can see that," he said gently. "You're looking back, Susan. You can't do that forever."

She sighed. "Sean, do you think I should go home?"

"Absolutely."

She threw a pillow at him and he ducked.

"Now that that's out of the way, what's on your mind?" Sean set the cake in front of her.

"Sand," she said.

"Sand?" He stuck her fork in her hand and guided it toward the cake. "Like the beaches of home?"

"What else comes to mind?"

"Mr. Sandman. Sands of Iwo Jima. Footprints in the sands of time."

"I get that one a lot."

"Is there a prize for the correct answer? You think sand has something to do with the man who attacked her?"

Susan shrugged.

"What does sand have to do with her attacker?"

"I don't know," Susan said. "I don't know anything."

"Aw, Suse, don't use this tragedy to beat yourself up. You're already in a—"

She shot a look at him. "Yes?" she said darkly.

"—fragile state. This has sent you skittering along toward the edge."

She snorted. "The edge of what?"

"Your funk, depression, melancholia. Whatever you want to call it. It makes me want to yell at you, or smack you." He divided the last of the wine between her glass and his. "Drink up. When you're really drunk, I'll sing Irish songs."

"If you sing 'Danny Boy,' I'll smack you."

He tipped his glass and drained it, started to set it on the coffeetable, then glanced up with a thoughtful frown.

"Dawn's early light?" she said.

"A thought. One year for Christmas Lynn gave me some fancy-ass cologne or aftershave or something called Sand. Came in an artsy bottle that actually had sand in the bottom. There was a card with poetic descriptions of the rainbow of colors in the stuff and that it came from some deep secret part of the sea or some shit like that. Hannah liked to tilt it back and forth, shake it and watch the sand settle."

After a second, when his words got to her brain, Susan got up and went through the French doors into the small room off the living room that she used as an office and punched in Parkhurst's number.

"Tell Demarco to meet us at the shop. You can pick me up on the way."

"What's up?"

"Tell you when you get here." She hung up and went to brush her teeth and gargle.

Somebody had made a fresh pot of coffee. Susan poured a mug and carried it to her office. Parkhurst started to pace.

"Sit!" She hoped the Excedrin she'd taken would kick in soon. He sat, slid down, and rested on his spine. Five minutes later, Demarco arrived and stood at attention in the doorway. She sighed. "Who was in the girl's room when governor Garrett went to see her?"

"The governor," Demarco said, "his press secretary Hadley Cane, Bernie Quaid, who's assistant to just about everyone, campaign manager Todd Haviland, media consultant Leon Massy, Mrs. Garrett, her assistant Nora Tallace, highway patrolmen Phil Baker and Art van Dever. And the media."

"Did you get their names?"

"Cameraman Rich Laslo, blond TV newscaster named Kathy Wendell, mag reporter Sean Donovan. Ty Baldini from the local paper."

Sean had been there? He hadn't mentioned it to her. She leaned forward to pick up a pen and tapped it on the desk. "Any thoughts on what the girl meant by sand?"

"No, ma'am."

"There's an aftershave called Sand. Maybe her attacker wore it and she smelled it when he slashed her. Later, in the hospital, her memory may have been triggered by smelling it again." She glanced at Parkhurst.

"Don't look at me," he said. "Never touch the stuff."

"We need to find out if anyone who was in that hospital room uses Sand aftershave. Leave the news people till last. It's possible there's a homicidal maniac among them, but barring that, it's unlikely one of them slashed the throat of a little girl and then smothered her to finish the job. We'll start with the governor's people."

She told Parkhurst to take Demarco, track down and question Todd Haviland, Bernie Quaid, Leon Massy, Mrs. Garrett—who better than a wife to know if a man wore aftershave—Nora Tallace, and Hadley Cane. Highly unlikely the governor, in disguise, skulked into the hospital, but just to be thorough.

"And don't forget the highway patrolmen." She retrieved her coat from the coat rack.

"What about Donovan?" Demarco asked.

"I'll take care of him." She wondered if wearing a man's aftershave was a good way to set someone up. Anybody could buy the stuff and splash it on. Who would know if it had never been used before?

Slipping out the back door to avoid reporters and leaving the pickup in the parking lot, she tugged her belt tighter and moved in a brisk walk the four blocks south to Behren's Department Store at Eleventh and Main. The cosmetic counter was given lots of attention by three teenagers choosing eye shadow and lipstick. Edgy with impatience and worried that the media might get wind of what they were doing, it was all she could do not to tap her foot. When the girls twittered away, Susan asked the saleswoman if they carried Sand aftershave.

Oh, indeed they did, and very lovely it was, too. Would she like to buy some?

She would. Since it was a little steeper than she anticipated and she didn't have enough cash with her, she handed over her credit card.

43
———

$\mathcal{I}$n the five minutes it took Bernie to splash water on his face, put on his shoes and get to the living room, Nora's nonstop blathering about Jack needing time to recover and Molly stepping into his position and taking over as governor had Todd ready to strangle her. Bernie went straight to the kitchen and poured himself a cup of coffee—it was going to be a long afternoon. Todd was standing with his back to them, staring out the window at the black clouds hanging low in the sky. Leon gave Bernie a thumb's up from the other side of the room where he was selecting a sandwich from the assortment on the platter.

Bernie took a sip of coffee and wedged himself against the arm of the couch. "What's going on?"

Todd turned from the window. "We need to make decisions on how to play this until Jack is well enough to get off his ass and back on the trail."

"Well, that's a nice way of putting it, I must say." Nora sniffed. She was offended by what she considered unnecessary vulgarity.

"Where's Hadley?" Bernie thought the media consultant needed to be in on any planning sessions.

"Out doing—" Todd waved a hand. "Whatever the hell it is women do when they go out."

"Shouldn't we wait for her?"

"Yeah. While we're waiting you can go and pick up Cass."

Leon started singing softly, *"I'm just a poor wayfaring stranger."*

"Where is she?" Bernie asked.

"Why should she be here?" Nora said. "Molly doesn't like her and right now Molly can use all the consideration you can give her. She—"

"How the fuck should I know," Todd said to Bernie. "Find out."

"Is it necessary to be quite so profane?" Nora said. "I mean, for goodness sake . . ."

"It's going to get worse if you don't shut the fuck up!"

Bernie called Cass on his cell phone. When she answered, he said, "I'll pick you up in a few minutes. We're having a planning session and Jack wants you in on it."

As he anticipated, she said she couldn't come. "I'm really sorry, Bernie. I have an appointment at seven that I have to keep. It's really important."

Before he could tell her he'd be there in ten minutes, a solid knock on the door startled them all. Since he was the closest, he answered the door.

Highway patrolman Phil Baker had Chief Wren with him, her trusty sidekick Parkhurst, and a third cop who looked like he chewed nails for relaxation.

"Jack—?" Todd's face went white.

"This isn't about Governor Garrett," the lady cop said. "I need to ask a few questions."

"What about?" Todd said.

With some posturing about no questions without their attorney present, Todd went off to the governor's office with the chief and her head shitkicker. The other cop, who looked like he bent railroad tracks with his bare hands, put his back to the door and planted his legs wide. After a few seconds of surprise and shocked silence, Nora started up with her usual chatter. One look from the cop shut her up. Bernie wondered if the cop could teach him that trick.

"I need to go pick up somebody," Bernie said.

"Just sit down, sir. It'll only be a few minutes."

It was more than a few. When Todd was released, he said, in the interests of saving time, he'd get Cass.

"Do it right away," Bernie said. "She has some appointment at seven. Get her before she has a chance to leave."

Leon got questioned next and then Nora. Bernie was last. He'd assumed they were digging once again into who did what, where, and when at the time the governor was shot. And he was right, but to his surprise there were additional questions about the governor's visit to the girl in the hospital: where was everybody standing in the room, who spoke to the girl, who was closest to the bed, what had the Governor said to her, what had everybody else said to her, what was the order of their leaving, did anyone go back into the room after the Governor left?

Bernie was getting a little tired of answering questions in the dark. "What's this all about?"

"Just answer the questions," Parkhurst said.

"Another minute or two, Mr. Quaid," she said. "Who was wearing perfume?"

"Perfume?" he repeated. "I don't understand. What does perfume have to do with anything?"

"Did you notice any?"

"I probably wouldn't have paid any attention if I had."

"Does Nora wear perfume?"

Bernie grinned. "So much it makes your eyes water. Especially if you're in a car with her."

"And the press secretary, Hadley Cane?"

"Maybe, but I couldn't tell you what kind."

"What about you? Aftershave or cologne?"

Bernie was completely bewildered. What the hell did perfume have to do with the attempt to kill the governor? "No."

"Who does, Mr. Quaid? The men on the governor's staff, who wears aftershave?"

"I don't have any idea. Is there a law here that we don't know about? No aftershave allowed?"

"No, Mr. Quaid, no law."

When Bernie got back to the living room, Hadley had arrived and was perched on one couch tapping a shoe with impatience. She looked a question at him. He shrugged.

Susan went through a whole fistful of questions with the press secretary before getting to questions dealing with aftershave.

"Aftershave?" Hadley wrinkled her nose. "Why are you asking? I guess some do."

From the paper bag at her feet, Susan took out the bottle of Sand she'd bought, removed the top and handed it to Hadley. "Do you know who uses this?"

Hadley put the bottle under her nose and sniffed. She looked up. "The governor, I think," she said. "Sometimes." She gave the bottle back. "Molly buys it, but he doesn't like to wear anything like that in case, you know, it's off-putting to a voter."

44

Halloween. Almost six o'clock and this black night was tortured by a coming storm. Cass felt hollow inside and cold, but the closer it got to seven, the calmer she became. A year ago today at seven o'clock she had turned to say something to Laura in the back seat and a drunk smashed into their car. What Cass had said was lost in the mists. She should have died, too, along with Ted and Laura. Today she would make that right. In one hour she would end her pain.

She pulled her down jacket from a hanger in the closet, went to the dining room and hung it over a chair. While she sat at the Victorian desk, sleet chattered against the window as though tapping fingers beckoned. With a fluid leap, Monty lit on the corner, crouched and wrapped his tail around his front paws. She stroked the cat, feeling the silkiness of its fur. Rosie the dog crowded against her knee, laid her head in Cass's lap and looked up with anxious eyes.

Cass raised the dog's muzzle, slid a hand over her ears, and said, "It's okay." She looked at Monty. "Everything's going to be all right."

From the middle drawer, she took out a sheet of her aunt's stationery, white with a border of blue irises.

Dear Bernie
 Please take care of Monty and Rosie. There isn't anyone else.
                                                                    Cass

She hadn't known Bernie long, but when she'd said she couldn't join the campaign because it meant she might be away for long periods of time and she had these animals to look after, he'd promised he would take care of them if anything happened to her. Of course, he hadn't meant what she had in mind. He'd meant an accident, or something preventing her from getting home at the expected time, but he had made a promise and he would keep it. She knew he would.

From the bottom right-hand drawer, she took out the revolver, opened the cylinder and slotted in one bullet, hesitated, then put in the other five. Why not? She slipped the gun in the jacket pocket.

Roaring with fury, Rosie raced to the door. Seconds later the doorbell rang. Hackles raised, snarling, the dog threw herself at the door. Damn it, Cass had told Bernie she couldn't come to this meeting. As usual he just flattened her like a steamroller and kept right on coming. She'd intended to be gone when he got here, to leave the door unlocked so he'd have no trouble getting in and he could find the note.

She'd have to get rid of him somehow. Tell him she was expecting an important phone call and she'd come out to the farm right after the call came. Taking Rosie's collar, she tried to pull her away. "It's Bernie, silly dog. You love Bernie." The dog resisted with every pound, dug in her claws and strained toward the door.

Cass opened it, hanging on to Rosie. "Todd?" She had to yell over the dog's barking. "What are you doing here? Where's Bernie?"

"Tied up with cops." Todd stepped inside. Rosie twisted loose and leaped for his throat. He yelled and fell. They rolled on the floor.

"Rosie!" Cass grabbed the dog's tail and pulled. Rosie whipped her head around to sink wicked teeth in Cass's arm, realized at the last second who Cass was and let Cass drag her off Todd. With her claws scraping on the wood floor, Cass pulled her to the bedroom and shut her in. Barking, Rosie threw herself at the door.

"Fucking dog!" Todd muttered, examining the ripped collar of his expensive jacket. "You ought to have it put down. It's vicious."

"Actually she's very sweet. I don't know what got into her."

"Get your coat," he said. "Let's go." He gestured at her down jacket hanging on the back of the chair.

"You packing up to move?" Following her through the archway with her, he looked at the boxes stacked against the wall and picked up the roll of tape sitting on the top one.

"Getting rid of stuff." She never did get them to the church rummage sale. Somebody else would have to deal with them. "Todd, I really—"

"Come on, we don't have all day."

"I told Bernie, I couldn't do this."

Placing his hands on his hips, he looked at her. "You have to come."

"I don't."

"The governor wants you there, and I need you to drive."

"You need me to drive," she repeated flatly.

Todd held out the keys. "I'm fighting off a migraine and headlights can trigger it."

She took the keys and shrugged on her coat. "I'll take you out there, then I'm coming right back."

"Fine. Let's get moving."

"What do the police want with Bernie?" she said as she slid in the driver's seat.

"Questions." Todd snapped the seat belt in place. "Jesus, you'd think they'd get tired of their fucking questions, the same ones over and over."

"About the little girl who was killed?"

"About everything. Wakely, the girl, the Egelhoff woman, Jack getting shot. Who was where, who said what. It's never going to die down until they stop harassing us. Every time they come around, they bring the whole media circus with them."

Icy needles of sleet *pit-pitted* against the windshield and she turned on the wipers. At Eleventh Street, she turned left, the quickest way to get to Harper and then pick up Highway 10 to get to Jack's farm.

Hampstead was built on small hills and with the streets icing up, she had to concentrate on her driving.

As they passed the fast-food places and used-car lots at the edge of town, the dark seemed to thicken and press like a barrier the car had to push at to get through. The road climbed gently, but even though the rise wasn't steep, the car didn't have four-wheel drive and it wanted to slide back.

"Surely, the police don't think Bernie's guilty of anything." Like smothering a little girl. Cass didn't know Gayle Egelhoff and after twenty years she didn't really know Wakely anymore either, and while she was sorry about their deaths, it was the little girl that haunted her. How could anyone hold a pillow against the face of a little girl, feel that desperate struggle for air, and keep pressing until the fight stopped.

"Who the hell knows," Todd said.

Saturday night, Cass thought, when Bernie came to pick her up for Eva's party, the dog had wanted to tear him apart. He'd been wearing a jacket he'd borrowed from Todd. The next time Bernie had come, Rosie greeted him with ecstatic whimpers and slobbery kisses.

Could the jacket have set her off? If Rosie was injured trying to protect her owner, she'd might remember the attacker's scent. Was it Todd who Rosie wanted to tear apart? Todd hit the dog? Todd killed Gayle?

45

Just as Susan was thinking maybe she'd call it a day and leave for home, her phone buzzed. Now what? "Yes, Hazel."

"Call from a Bernie Quaid," the dispatcher said. "Says he's found a suicide note from Cass Storm."

"Where is she?"

"He can't find her and he's worried."

"Tell him I'm on the way. Parkhurst still here?"

"Yep."

"Reporters still around?"

"Does a hen lay eggs?"

"Tell Parkhurst to pick me up at Tenth and Main."

"Take a coat. Big storm moving in."

Susan slipped on her trench coat and kept a wary eye out for the media as she hiked the block and a half to the downtown area where Parkhurst was waiting.

"What's up?" he said as she climbed in.

She told him as he drove to Casilda Storm's house. Bernie, one hand on the dog's collar, had the door open as soon as the Bronco pulled up in the driveway.

"What's going on?" Susan asked. The dog obviously didn't like them coming in; it stood stiff, growled low in its throat.

"Cass. I'm afraid—"

"Do something with the dog, Mr. Quaid."

"She won't bite."

Right. How many times had she heard that?

"She's not mean, she's frightened. And confused. When I got here, I found her shut up in the bedroom. And Cass isn't here. Then I found the note. I don't know what's going on."

"Do something with the dog."

"Right, yes, okay." He trotted the dog to a bedroom and closed the door on it.

"Where's the note?"

"Dining room. On the desk." He started to show them.

"Why don't you sit down, Mr. Quaid. Did you touch the note?"

He nodded, backed up and lowered his rear to the Victorian sofa. "Picked it up without thinking."

Susan went around the stacked boxes into the dining room. "Is it Ms. Storm's handwriting?"

"Yes," he said, then "I'm not sure."

"Which?"

"You've got to find her!"

"Yes, Mr. Quaid. We will do that."

Bernie ran a hand through his hair. "I'm not all that familiar with her handwriting. I think it's hers."

"Okay. Just sit tight while we look around."

After she and Parkhurst made a pass through the house, she let out a breath of relief when they didn't find a body. Nor did they find any signs of struggle.

Susan bagged the note and sat in the wingback chair by the sofa. Parkhurst prowled.

"Cass is not in the house," she said.

"I looked in the bathroom," Bernie admitted. "I was afraid she'd be sitting in a bathtub full of bloody water."

"What makes you think she's suicidal?"

"Because she's sad, she's had this awful tragedy happen." He told

310

her that Cass's husband and daughter had been killed by a drunk driver. "She's struggling with depression."

"Where would she go? If she wanted to hurt herself. Since she isn't here, where would she go?"

"I don't know! Why aren't you looking for her!" In the bedroom, the dog started barking.

"Calm down, Mr. Quaid, you're upsetting the dog."

"Just find her."

"Why are you here?" she asked.

"We were waiting—"

"Who do you mean by we?"

"Everybody. Molly, Leon, Hadley, Carter. And Nora. We were waiting for Todd to come back with Cass." He took a breath, maybe to gather his thoughts. "I was going to pick her up but you were asking me questions." Little hint of accusation.

"Go on."

"So Todd went." Bernie ran his hand through his hair, scrubbing at the top of his head. "He never got back. He doesn't answer his cell phone. Cass didn't answer her phone. I don't know where he is. I don't know where Cass is. I don't know what's going on." The last was said on a rising note of anger.

Susan looked at her watch. Nearly seven-thirty. Todd must have left the farm around six. "Was there anyplace else Todd needed to go, anything he needed to do? Pick up pizza? Buy potato chips?"

"No. We were all waiting to get this strategy meeting underway, figure out what to do while the governor recuperates. He obviously can't keep up the same hectic schedule he's been doing."

"We'll find her, Mr. Quaid." Susan knew, and Bernie knew, those were just words. If Cass was intent on suicide and without knowing where to look, they would likely only find a body. If that.

"Go back to your meeting. We'll call when we find them."

"But maybe I can help. Maybe—"

"There's really nothing you can do," Susan said gently. "Go back to the Garrett farm and let us do our job."

Reluctantly, he nodded. He put a leash on the dog, took her to

the car and put her in the backseat. He started to get in and stopped.
"I just thought."

"Yes?"

"I've remembered a place she might go," Bernie said.

46

Sleet pelted the windshield and the wipers kept up a continuous *thunk* as they swept a clear arc. Cass hunched over the wheel to see the road. Todd watched her. Even in the dark, she could feel his eyes assessing. No anger was coming from his still body, no hatred or malevolence, only irritation. She was in the way and she had to go. The obvious, or what should have been obvious, if she hadn't been so stupid, so blindly focused on herself, was a cold awareness that seeped in through her hands and feet and spread throughout her body. He was going to kill her.

Mad laughter bounced through her head. He was going to kill a suicidal woman! Don't ever say God didn't have a sense of humor.

She clamped down on her back teeth to keep from howling, and pulled what senses she had together. If she just went along like a lamb to the slaughter, he'd get away with it. For killing Gayle and taking away Wakely's life, poor Wakely who had already lost so much, and the little girl. Fourteen. That was the most unforgivable. What would Laura have been like at fourteen?

Slowly, like recovering from a flu, she brought her mind back to the icy road. Only a few seconds had passed and Todd was still sitting silently in the passenger seat. She couldn't let him get away with it.

She had to survive and she had a big plus. The gun in her pocket. How fast could she get it?

Options clicked in her mind. She was the one in control of the car. She could speed up and drive headlong into a tree or a concrete abutment. That might kill them both, but as least Todd wouldn't get away with killing three people. She could let the car slide off the road into the steep ditch alongside. That would render the car useless until a tow truck came and hauled it out. Todd might just smash her head with something and say she was hurt in the crash. He'd walk away whistling.

If she did anything, he'd realize she knew. As long as he thought she was still in the dark, mentally as well as physically, she'd be all right. At least until they came to wherever they were going and her world came to an end.

"Make a right here," he said.

She nodded and made the turn onto the dark road. The world was pitch black, only her headlights glinting silver sparks from the slanting sleet. He took a roll of tape from his pocket—tape from her dining room—and tore off a strip. What was he going to do with it? Tape her mouth? He stuck one end on the dash.

Getting in the car with him had been stupid. Self-defense classes taught never get in the villain's car. And never go where he wants you to go, no matter what he promises. She'd left it too long. Now she was out here on Strahmeyer's Road getting farther and farther away from the possibility of help. Should she keep going or try to get out the revolver and hope she could shoot before he realized what she was doing?

He looked over at her and in the phosphorescent green of the dash light, his eyes seemed to glitter. For a moment, they stared at each other; then he shifted slightly, but that instant was enough. Knowledge had passed between them. She no longer needed to pretend, he was aware of what she knew.

From the glove box, he got a flashlight that he put in his lap, then he took out a gun and pressed it against her temple. Not an old revolver like the one in her pocket, but a modern, slim, far more deadly semi-automatic.

A lightning-fast thought zigzagged through her mind. Hit the door handle and bail. She didn't follow through with action because she believed with every fiber of her being that he wouldn't hesitate to pull the trigger. Slight squeezing of his finger and she would be very messily dead, brains all over the window and the seat.

It didn't matter if she was killed, but the little girl had mattered. Cass hadn't done anything to set right Laura's death, but she could do something for this girl's.

"Why kill me?" she said.

"Cops won't stop sniffing around until they have the killer."

"You're going to pin it on me? If you think that's going to work, you're crazier than I am."

Gun hard at her temple, Todd clamped his right hand around one of hers on the steering wheel and squeezed so hard she could feel blood pulse in her fingertips. "Do exactly what I tell you."

Part of her wanted him to pull the trigger. It would finally be over. Another part talked to her and called her a coward and yelled at her to do something and not let this bastard get away with killing a little girl. These two parts seemed to be talking to each other. Disassociation. Her shrink had talked about it.

"You think you can scare me? You think I care if you kill me? You are nothing but a piece of shit." *Way to go, Cass. That ought to calm him long enough so you can figure out how to get away. Yes, indeed, when the ship's going down, bash a big hole in the bow, I always say.* She darted a glance at him and saw sweat beads on his forehead.

"Shut up." The dangerous edge in his voice told her she'd pushed him past some point of no return.

"Make a right."

She turned onto another deserted road and passed a house with lights in the windows. "Nobody's going to believe it," she said.

"I'll make them believe. You confessed. You told me what you'd done."

"Why would I kill a woman I didn't know and poor Wakely and

the little girl?" If anyone happened to be looking out, all he'd see was a car driving in sleet that kept turning to rain and back to sleet. It was a night only a fool would be out.

"They were blackmailing Jack. You did it for him. Still in love with him. Thought he'd be grateful. Planned to get rid of Molly so he'd marry you."

She drove on until there was nothing but empty fields on both sides of the road. "That's just stupid."

"Yeah, well, to tell the truth you were babbling incoherently and I couldn't really understand half of what you were saying."

"How'd I get way out here? Hike through a thunderstorm?"

"You forced me to bring you. Held this gun on me."

"Why didn't I just shoot myself?"

"You're a whack job, who knows why? Kept saying you couldn't live with yourself. Pull up over here."

Cass eased the car to the edge of the road, hit the headlights, and turned off the ignition. A blacker dense area to the right she thought was a grove of trees.

"Both hands on the wheel."

She did as she was told. Several seconds. When he got out of the car, she'd have several seconds while he ran around to the driver's side to get to her. She'd get the revolver from her pocket.

A hand slapped down over both wrists and in an instant he had tape whipped around them. A panic attack threatened. She couldn't breathe. Clammy sweat broke out.

The gun was on the seat while he'd taped her wrists together and now he snatched it and jabbed the barrel into her temple. Would she hear the shot before she died?

"Release the seat belt." His voice sliced through her panic, the terrible calm of destiny set her free. Awkwardly, she fumbled for the release. He clicked his own seat belt loose, stuck the flashlight in his pocket and reached behind for the door handle. Not for an instant did he relax his focus on her.

He pushed open his door, slid out and yanked her across the middle console. The emergency brake gouged her stomach and a knee banged the steering column as he wrenched her from the car. He dumped her on the ground and backed a step. Her hands landed in mud. Cold water seeped into her jeans. Sleet was coming down so hard she could barely see. She struggled to her feet.

"Don't try anything or I'll kill you where you stand."

"Oh, right. As opposed to later? You going to try for another suicide? It really won't fly."

He flicked on a flashlight. "Move."

She started in the direction he gestured. In the distance was the darker blackness of trees, beyond that she couldn't see anything.

"I didn't want to kill him." Todd's voice, slightly higher than normal, had an odd quality of regret. "I had to."

"Oh yeah? Why is that?" She stumbled along the rocky uneven ground, shoes squishing in the mud, cheeks stinging with cold.

"He knew."

"And Gayle? She knew, too? What the hell did they know that was so important?"

"She wouldn't drop it, kept talking to Wakely, trying to convince him Vince was telling the truth." The flashlight beam wavered as he stumbled.

If she rammed herself into him, would he fall? Would that give her time to run? Hide herself in the dark? "And the little girl? She knew something, too?" Cass let contempt drip through.

With a forearm, Todd brushed drops of melted sleet from his forehead. "Sunglasses," he said. "Must have dropped them. Only wanted to find them. She was there."

"Sunglasses? You're too cheap to buy another pair?" She lurched against him in a trial, to see what he'd do.

He stepped aside and let her fall. "Prescription," he said.

She struggled upright with more mud on her clothes to show for her effort. "You meant it when you said you did whatever the governor needed."

"He'll win the nomination, and have a good shot at the presidency."

"Yeah? And what do you get?" Jack Garrett had this man kill three

317

people? The Jack she'd loved all those years ago would never have done that. What had changed him so drastically? Ambition? "Jack told you to kill me?" The words no longer had the ability to hurt, she was long past hurt.

"He doesn't know."

"Doesn't know," she repeated. She was getting tired, the flashlight beam wobbling through the dark was making her dizzy.

Her brain, cold and numb, couldn't assimilate quickly. "You're going to kill me and he doesn't know? That's really showing initiative. What do you get out of all this?"

"Chief of staff. When he's elected president."

"What did Wakely know?" Whenever she stopped, he prodded her with the gun.

"Vince. Made up a story. Threatened to talk to the press. Wanted money to keep quiet."

"You killed Vince Egelhoff, too?"

"He lost a ski pole. Terrible accident. Smashed headfirst into a tree."

Cass's ankle twisted as her foot slithered over a rock and she fell to her knees. Todd jerked her up. "He'd have ruined everything. I've worked too hard for this. It's here, right here within reach. Its goddamn *happening*. He would have taken it away. For what? A mistake twenty years ago. Something beyond change. I couldn't let that happen."

"How'd it go with Wakely?" she said. "He talked too much when he was drunk? Said something? You repeated it to Jack, saw it made Jack nervous?" The sleet turned to rain. Cass was soaked and cold to the bone. Loathing in her voice, she said, "He was a cripple. Couldn't run, couldn't fight. He couldn't even walk."

"I didn't want to kill him."

There was some mixture in his voice that Cass couldn't quite identify. Regret and that hard sense of entitlement that made his agenda more important even than another's life.

"I'm not a killer," Todd said.

"Yeah, you are. Did you make it easy for yourself? Give him a bottle of booze with a sedative in it? When he was so far out he couldn't even struggle, you shot him and staged the whole suicide scene."

"I didn't want to."

"I'll bet you stood there in the bathroom doorway and looked at his brains splattered over the walls and his blood dripping on the floor and went over it all in your mind to make sure you'd thought of everything." Rain fell harder. She shook water from her eyes.

"I was sorry."

Cass snorted. "And the little girl? Sorry about her, too?" Cass's voice was thick with scorn. "You cut her throat and left her to die. When she didn't, you held a pillow over her face. How hard is it to kill a little girl?"

"Shut up!"

"Jack has to know what you've done. At least, suspect. You really believe he'll keep you around if he knows? He's an elected official. He can't afford you. He'll throw you to the dogs." She finally realized where he was taking her. The Hanging Barn. It loomed in the distance, a blacker presence against the black horizon.

"Keep moving."

He'd string her up and make her look like another suicide, tell the world she'd killed a little girl. "You're a killer. He can't—"

"So is he!" Todd prodded her shoulder with the gun. "Keep moving!"

Rain turned to sleet again. With her hands taped, her balance was poor. She staggered and fell facedown in cold mud, so cold and tired she didn't care any longer.

"Get up!" He yanked on the sleeve of her jacket.

When she didn't move, he fired two shots, one right after the other. The bright flash of gunpowder so close blinded her and the sound was deafening. Dazed from the shock of two rounds fired in front of her face, she couldn't move. Clutching her jacket at the neck, he lifted her like a half-drowned kitten and hauled her to her feet. She could see his mouth moving, but could only hear the ringing in her ears and the muted roar of static. The muzzle flash left sparks of light etched on her retinas like leftover fireworks.

The roar in her ears crashed and softened like a wave rolling back to sea and then the noise splintered into sound that made words. "Move," he yelled.

Why? If he wanted to hang her in that old barn, let him carry her. He was going to kill her anyway. Why make it easy? Digging her own grave doing what he wanted. If she goaded him to the point where he shot her, he'd have a hard time making it look like suicide.

"Move!" He shook her until her teeth rattled.

Okay, maybe she was ready to go quietly, maybe she should do what he said. If she didn't go along, he might simply drag her. She didn't like the idea of what would happen to her legs and knees if he dragged her over the rocky ground. She'd wait for a chance. The gun was in her pocket, she could feel it banging against her waist.

She slipped and fell, tried to stand. A second try got her feet under her and she rose. Her knees felt weak, unable to support her. For a moment, she thought she would fall again.

The bright muzzle flash in her eyes was fading, and there was only blackness. At first she thought she was blind from powder burn or gases because the gun had been fired so close, then the dark outline of the barn appeared like a ship drifting into view and she realized she wasn't blind. There were no lights—moon and stars were hidden behind the clouds dumping all this cold sleet down on her. She'd never realized how dark night was without the glow of light from somewhere. It was oppressive, claustrophobic.

"Stand up." He shook her again.

Pain sizzled through her brain like lightning and he nearly upset her precarious balance. "This is standing," she snapped. "Stop shaking me."

Anger and resignation were fighting it out as she shuffled forward, sniffling and rubbing mud and snot from her face with bound wrists. She had to remind herself she couldn't let him get away with it. She had to make sure he paid for killing a little girl who called herself

Moonbeam because she didn't like her name. "Look, Todd. Just let me go. I'll never tell anybody. I promise."

"Shut up."

If she were to yank her arm away, could she stay upright and run? With her wrists taped together, her balance wasn't terrific.

Left hand clamped around her arm, he gave a hard jerk and spun her around until she was facing him. He stuck the gun in her face. "One wrong move, one little wiggle and you're dead."

She believed him. Her movements were awkward as she staggered over rocks and uneven ground toward the barn where she'd die. Mice and rats and other scavengers would feed on her dead flesh.

He held her jacket so tight he was nearly choking her and he jerked her arm around so he had wrists and jacket collar in the same hand. Her left arm was yanked against her face and she struggled to pull air through wet nylon. The sense of suffocation had her breath coming in short gasps as she fought panic.

Her jacket was soaked, her shoes were soaked, she was shaking with cold. Stumbling over the muddy, rocky ground, she edged toward the black hulking shape of the barn. Now that they were close to his destination, Todd relaxed his hold slightly.

She drew in a welcome chestful of air. When they'd been in the car, she'd sensed he'd been near the edge. Any little nudge and he'd have shot her right then to get it over with. Now that he was totally in control, he seemed to have stepped back from that edge.

"If Vince had just backed off," he said.

None of it was Todd's fault, it was all the victim's fault. The slight hill they were struggling up was slippery with icy mud. She went down on one knee. He nearly strangled her as he jerked her upright.

Breath coming in little grunts from the climb uphill, he slipped and yanked her off balance as he recovered. She remembered a recurring dream. She and Ted were skiing. He, the faster and better skier, tore down the mountain. She tried to catch up. Her skis kept falling off. She hurriedly put them back on so she could follow the tracks he'd left in the snow, but falling snow slowly filled the tracks. Seeing Ted

321

so clearly in her mind brought out a muffled whimper. Todd must have thought she was crying and loosened his hold slightly.

Ashes to ashes. Dust to dust. The meek shall inherit the earth. And unless she stopped being meek, she'd inherit her share of earth in the big barn just ahead. And the bastard would get away with making her out a killer. A killer of a little girl! Black night, black rain, black barn, she couldn't even distinguish earth from sky. She was acutely aware of the slight sucking sound as she pulled her shoes from wet earth, patter of sleet against her jacket, slither of wet jeans across her thighs. Was she hypersensitive because she would die soon and never again see or feel or hope?

Plead with him? Todd wasn't about to be swayed by a pleading female, especially one who got in his way. No, unless the gods decided to give themselves some quirky entertainment, she would die in a very few minutes. And he would tell the world she was a homicidal lunatic who hanged herself. Maybe she should jerk her arm away and scratch him. Get some skin under her nails for DNA evidence when whatever was left of her after mice, rats, and creepy crawlies were through with her was found.

He yanked her onto the gravel path that led to the two-story-high sliding doors on the old barn. Above the doors was the hayloft. Grunting, cursing, he pulled on a door and finally coaxed it open. He dragged her inside where the blackness was total.

"Colder than a witch's tit in here." Todd swept the flashlight beam around.

Shuffling, shivering, she moved at his prodding toward the wooden ladder leading to the hayloft. The third rung was slippery with ice where water had found its way through the leaky roof. Getting impatient, he shoved the barrel into her back.

She screeched like the madwoman she was. The sound echoed round the barn, rousing the voices of long dead horses in the wind whistling through the cracks.

Hurling herself backward, she twisted and raked his cheek with her fingernails. She smashed her head into his face and heard him cry out. He toppled back, instinctively throwing his arms out to regain his balance. A shot rattled the rafters as his finger reflexively tightened on the trigger. Roosting pigeons took off in a frantic flutter of wings.

He fell and she fell with him. As he hit the floor, he howled with pain and outrage and cushioned her fall. She landed on his chest and belly and heard the air leave his lungs with a loud oomph. Through it all, he managed to hang on to the hood of her jacket and it cut into her throat choking her, but he dropped the flashlight. It rolled and fell from the loft to the floor below where it put out a muted glow.

Gripped with a fierce desire to inflict as much damage as possible, she jammed her left elbow back into his face and with luck caught his nose. Screaming and spitting, she twisted away and felt her coat pull free. Shrieking all the while, she hit, she scratched, she bit, she kicked.

He pushed at her to fend her off. On elbows and knees, she crawled off into darkness until she hit the barn wall. Turning, she sat with her back braced against the rough wood and tried to listen. The banging of her heart and her own fast panting rushed through her ears. Forcing herself to breathe slow and deep, she listened past her body's joyous reveling at being alive to the constant patter of rain. A grunt. The scrape of a boot.

Todd getting to his feet.

She had no way of releasing her bound hands except to find the end of the tape and unwind it. In the dark, with cold numb fingers and her mind jangled with adrenaline, that was impossible. She wondered in all her rolling and tumbling whether the gun had fallen out. She patted her pocket. The hard lump reassured her. Hysterical laughter fizzled up in her throat. The gun she'd meant to kill herself with was going to save her life. Was that irony, or what?

Awkwardly, she forced her taped hands in her pocket. Searching fingertips scraped against the grip. She pushed, reached, pushed harder, until she could hook a finger around the barrel and work the gun free. She heard scraping sounds and sensed rather than saw Todd coming toward her.

"Stop!" she yelled. "It's over."

A shot and muzzle flash. She dropped and rolled. Another shot. Not moving, hardly breathing for fear he'd hear her, she waited.

"Make this easy," he said.

"I have a gun, Todd."

He laughed and she imagined his gun swinging toward the sound of her voice. Aiming way off toward the leaky roof, she squeezed the trigger.

"You bitch!" Enraged that she hadn't revealed she toted a gun in her pocket.

Keeping a secret from him during her kidnapping and prior to her murder apparently wasn't playing fair. Laughter bubbled up in her throat. "If you only knew!"

The black bulk of his outline moved. "Go ahead," he taunted. "Shoot me. Ever shot anybody before? It's not so easy to pull the trigger. The mess it makes afterward is beyond belief. You won't be able to do it."

She thought of Moonbeam. She thought of Laura.

When he reached the open doorway, she could just make out his silhouette against the rain.

Gun clutched in her right hand, she stretched out prone, rested her left elbow on the floor and aimed at chest height. She couldn't avenge the death of her own child, but she could damn sure wreak vengeance on the death of someone else's.

She pulled the trigger.

In the distance, she heard sirens.

47

The highway patrolmen clustered outside Governor Garrett's hospital room all but laughed in her face when Susan said she needed to speak with the governor. They wanted to hustle her right back into the elevator and she wanted to get in his room. No telling how long they'd have maintained their positions, squared off facing each other, if Bernie hadn't come along. He told her to wait a minute while he asked if the governor felt like seeing her. A moment or two later Bernie told the troopers Governor Garrett wanted to talk with her and she zipped in before anyone could change his mind. This was her last chance. Later today he was due to be transported by ambulance to the governor's mansion.

Propped up in a hospital bed, wearing one of those shorty gowns with one string untied, Jack Garrett was reduced to ordinary mortal. Face pale, bristle of beard with glints of gray, IV attached to one arm, bandaged chest, monitors above the bed recording the inner workings of his body.

"Good morning, sir. I'm sorry to bother you."

He smiled and it was all there—charisma, attraction, charm— whatever made him a man who could reach out and people would reach back. "Bother me and I can have twelve troopers in here in ten seconds."

She smiled back. "I'd like to ask you a few questions."

"I'm sure you would. Pull up a chair."

She tugged the armchair closer to the head of the bed and sat down.

"A wisp of smoke," he said, before she even got out her first question. "On a distant mountain in Montana. That's how it started and it ended with thousands of acres burned and six people dead. A series of mistakes compounded by bad luck, missed opportunities and misunderstandings. There were eleven of us. Dispatched to take on Pale Horse Mountain." So softly she could barely hear, he said, " 'And behold a pale horse: and his name that sat on him was Death, and Hell followed with him.' "

He shrugged off something. Memories? Regrets? "I'd been smoke jumping for five years. That summer was going to be my last. I was twenty-six years old, in my final year of law school. It looked like a routine fire and we thought we'd have it lined by morning."

"Lined?"

"Smoke jumpers don't beat out flames. They build a fire line around the beast using chain saws. They want to gouge a swath through the vegetation and remove the fuel. That way the fire burns itself out. Since we were such a small group and we just had limited equipment, we decided to start above the fire and build a fire line downhill, then hook up and around."

She nodded to show she was following.

"Firefighters try to stay away from a downhill fire line. Heat and flames rise. A crew wants to stay beneath the blaze at all times. Oh man, we were right there above that fire, not leaving any margin for error if something went wrong."

"Wakely was one of the crew?"

"He'd been fighting fires since he was a teenager and he didn't like the look of this one. *Fucking bad idea*, he said. *We shouldn't be here.* He was right. We were getting trapped with no escape routes. If the wind changed, the fire could move uphill faster than we could. That kind of fire makes you claustrophobic. It's so dark you can't see where you are, you can't see what the clouds are doing, you can't see what the fire is doing. You can hardly see the other crew members. To move quicker, we broke a hard and fast rule. We didn't prepare any good black."

"Good black," she repeated.

"Safety zones. Already burned areas where we'd have shelter if the fire should switch and chase us up the mountain. We screwed up bad." He shook his head. "We were really moving and thinking there'd be another place, another place, another place. Firefighters pride themselves on success no matter what the odds. Or the obstacles. We thought we could get the beast hooked. When we reached Horse's Teeth Ridge, we saw the fire was traveling uphill. Somehow we got scattered to hell and gone all over that ridge. Wakely and I made our way down to see how far it had spread and how much farther down the mountain we'd have to cut the fire line."

He closed his eyes. The monitor above his head started making erratic lines and she got concerned, wondered if she should leave. This was obviously affecting him, maybe causing harm.

Taking in a breath, he opened his eyes, not seeing her, but looking inward. "Increasingly heavy wind fanned the flames into an inferno so fierce even Wakely hadn't ever seen anything like it. Fire exploded all around us. Flames swept up the mountainside like the devil had let loose his evil. The smoke jumper in charge radioed. 'Get off the mountain! Now!' "

Beads of sweat glistened on the governor's forehead. "Stay away from the fire line, he told us. Go straight up Pale Horse Mountain. We'd find good black. We'd be safe."

He scrubbed a hand down his face. "Three men, including Vince Egelhoff, were on one end of the ridge, six were on the other end. We tried to radio, and got no response. We argued, Wakely and I. I wanted to start running. He said we had to find them. Tell them to go up instead of down the fire line. Going down is exactly what they'd try to do, if we didn't tell them. You never go up, because fire could just sweep right over you. You always go down. Because of the trust we had in our chief, we knew we had to go up."

He took a sip of water. "Wakely took off and so did I. Fire everywhere. Walls of flame. Black as night. Two-thousand-degree heat, over sixty-mile-an-hour wind. So strong it blew off my hardhat. Dead stuff on the ground kept tripping me. Airborne embers, spot fires everywhere. I didn't know where I was. Grass beneath my feet burst into flames. All thoughts of anybody else stopped. I started running to save myself. My legs ached. I was lugging a twenty-five-pound chainsaw, not really aware of it. You never abandon your tools. If you do, it means you're in a situation where you'll die. And that's when I knew I wasn't going to make it."

She could see he was in pain, but didn't know if the pain was here in this hospital room or back all those years on the mountain.

"A wall of flame was roaring up behind me, moving faster than I was, gaining with every step. I got five hundred feet from the top. Skin blistered, fire on all sides. Kept going. Fifty feet from the top, I was slapped to the ground by superheated gases. Like opening a blast furnace." He stopped and took another sip of water.

"I was on the ground and the beast was devouring me. Then Wakely appeared. He slung me over his shoulder and headed up. A burning tree fell on us. Somehow or other, I was underneath and he got the weight of a toppled oak. It crushed him. I thought he was dead. If I hadn't found the damn chainsaw, I couldn't have gotten him free. I barely managed to drag both of us over the top of that ridge."

"He came from where, the other end of the ridge?"

"Yeah. After telling three people to run up the mountain."

"Why did he come back?"

A sour smile. "I think to make sure I got out. He never was certain I wouldn't trip over my own two feet."

"He ran miles, through burning trees, thick smoke, to warn three men at one end of a ridge and somehow he managed to run all that way back to check on you?"

"Yes."

"How'd he do that?"

The governor placed his hands by his side and shifted his position.

"The man was a bear. Six foot four. Two hundred and forty pounds. Strength of ten. Tireless. A machine." Thin smile. "Came from sturdy pioneer stock."

She couldn't fit the image of the crippled Wakely slumped in a wheelchair into a six-foot-four frame with the strength of ten.

"He had all kinds of injuries and I don't suppose dragging him up the mountain helped any. Spinal cord smashed, third degree burns, concussion, broken leg, broken shoulder blade, cracked ribs. The man was a sack of broken pieces."

"And you were a hero."

"I was a coward," he said.

"Reporters and newscasters said you were a hero."

"Wakely was the hero."

"Why didn't you tell the world that?"

"Six people died in that fire because I didn't warn them. Three were saved because Wakely did."

"Could you have saved those six?"

"No," he said. "I would have been number seven."

"You let the world think you saved those three." Susan hadn't meant to sound accusatory.

The look of pain that crossed his face was so intense, she thought she'd better get a doctor in here.

"I came out with some third-degree burns. Plus minor scrapes and knocks, broken arm, broken bones in one foot, concussion. I sank into a hospital bed and there I stayed for some days. I didn't know what was being said. When I found out, I figured I'd let Wakely set the record straight. Give him some show time."

"Why didn't he?"

"He was two steps from death's door for weeks. When he finally rallied, he couldn't remember any of it."

"And so you let it go."

"I never meant that to happen. At first, the doctors said Wakely's memory would return. I wanted him to be the one. Stand up with all those reporters and newscasters and let the world know what a hero he was. But he didn't remember. Even after some months he didn't remember and time went by. A lot of time. So much I decided I'd hold a press conference and set the record straight. He said if I tried that, he'd tell them he'd suddenly remembered: He was the one who was supposed to tell the six guys on Horse's Teeth Ridge. They died. I went the other way and saved three people."

"Why would he do that?" That sounded like truth to Susan, but this man was a politician, he was used to making whatever he said sound like truth.

"I argued. He stayed firm. He was so adamant, I wondered if maybe he believed it happened that way." The governor scraped a thumb over a bristly jaw. "I should never have let him get away with it. I should have admitted to my cowardice."

"You took care of him."

"We were friends. He didn't have anybody. His parents were dead, he had no relatives."

"What happened that Wakely had to be killed?"

The head of the bed rose a bit as he pushed a button. "Shouldn't you ask Todd that question?"

"I have. He's not talking."

"Best thing in his position." Governor Garrett, slowly and wincing with pain, changed position again. "I can only guess at it."

"I'd like to hear your guesses."

"Vince," he said.

"Yes," she prompted when he didn't go on.

"He wanted money. He threatened to tell the world I could have saved those six smoke jumpers. If I'd gone to the tail of the ridge and warned them, they'd have made it out. He'd say he was there. He knows what happened, but I was only interested in saving my own skin."

"Did you pay him?"

"No. Todd wanted to. He was furious when I refused. I told him we'd just have to take what came if Vince went public with this story. Then Vince died, so it no longer was a problem."

330

"Cass Storm said Todd killed Vince."

"You believe her?"

"Todd is denying he said any such thing, but I do believe her, yes. Did he kill Vince's wife because she believed her husband, intended to go to the press with his story?"

The governor's face was gray and he was obviously in pain. "Probably."

"Why did Wakely go to see Gayle? Was he going to back Vince's story?"

"He could only have been trying to take her out of it."

"Then why was he killed?"

"Sometimes Wakely talked too much, if he had a little bit too much to drink."

The governor sighed, a sad weary sigh. "I don't know about the little girl, Gayle's sister."

"Sunglasses. He lost them when he killed Gayle. Prescription glasses he thought could identify him. When he came to look for them, she saw him. Even though she didn't get a clear look, he couldn't take the risk she'd remember something."

Susan's job was to protect that child and the failure would stay with her the rest of her life.

"All this just because I decided to make a try for presidential candidate. I didn't think I had a prayer. I just wanted to make a few speeches, get a few key issues out to the voters. Then it began looking like I had a shot. Nobody was more surprised than I was."

The governor rubbed a knuckle down his jaw. "Todd didn't ever hesitate. He was a man who took care of things and he meant to take me right into the White House. He couldn't let my cowardice get out. Who would vote for a coward? This is God's way of punishing me for twenty-year-old sins."

"Did Todd use the same aftershave as you?"

"Huh, actually it was mine that he used. Molly always insisted on buying the stuff for me and I passed it off to him, because he liked it and I didn't."

A nurse stuck her head in the door and said Susan would have to leave, she was upsetting the patient. Susan nodded and stood. "What did you say to the girl right before you left her hospital room?"

" 'May the sun shine down on you and bring you much happiness.' I guess that didn't come about, did it?"

"You were a hero," she said. "With a broken arm and a broken foot, you managed to get your friend out of a killing forest fire."

She thanked him for seeing her and wished him luck with his campaign. "I'm sorry we didn't do a better job of protecting you."

"When that woman shot me, I thought I was dead." With a soft trace of self-mockery, he said, "I reached up with outstretched hands and my fingertips touched the face of destiny."

48

Wind tore across the prairie and clouds fled like frightened souls. In its wake, tree limbs littered the streets, roofs were blown off, windows were broken, power lines were down. Around noon, irritated that she couldn't find Parkhurst, Susan asked Hazel to track him to his whereabouts and tell him to get his ass in here. Hazel told her he'd taken the afternoon off to tend to some personal business. Grumbling that cops shouldn't have a personal life, she plowed through work. A little after seven when she left the office, it was dark, daylight saving time had gone the way of dead leaves. Heavy sadness sat on the brain sludge in her mind. The governor shot, his close friend dead, his campaign manager arrested. Gayle Egelhoff dead. Fourteen-year-old girl dead. No relatives. Casilda Storm was arranging both funerals.

When she rounded the corner, she spotted Parkhurst's Bronco parked in front of her house and he was sitting on the porch steps, forearms resting on his knees. She drove into the garage, cut the ignition and slid from the pickup. Trudging around to the front of the house, she climbed the stairs and sat beside him. "What are you doing here?"

"A favor."

"For whom?

"Your cousin."

"Sean Patrick? What favor?"

"He left."

"Without saying good-bye?" Damn it. She'd been looking forward to a long evening of reminiscing, drinking, making snide comments about the rest of the relatives, maybe even getting pie-eyed. "Just like a man."

"He left a note." Parkhurst offered her a folded piece of paper held between first and second finger.

She eyed him suspiciously. "You read it?"

"Would I read someone else's personal note?"

She snorted. "Where'd he go?"

"The whole circus load of politicians and media left and he left with them."

She unfolded the note and a twenty-dollar bill fell out.

Soon as this campaign is over, I'm coming back and we're having a long talk. In the meantime, buy a pizza and share it with your Friend. Whatever else you want to do is up to you. Can't say I admire your choice, but then you never liked my choices either, so we're even.

Don't kick a gift horse in the teeth.

Love,
Sean

She flicked the note with a finger. "You never answered my question."

"What question?"

"What are you doing here?"

"He said I had a strong back."

"A strong back." She rubbed her forehead with her fingertips. She was trained to stay calm in the face of incipient lunacy. "I see. And do you?"

"Not anymore."

She wanted to ask him where he'd been all day, but instead she said, "What's this about a gift horse?"

"He said you have trouble accepting gifts and you kick and scream. Bite, too."

Waving the twenty-dollar bill, she said, "Want to share a pizza?"

"Sure."

As she almost never went in by the front door, she had to fumble for the right key. Once inside, she stopped dead. Where the old upright piano always sat was a shiny black baby grand. She turned to look at Parkhurst.

With a shrug of innocence, he held out empty hands. "I just helped the delivery guy bring it in."

"Who unlocked the door?"

"Right. I did that, too. Sean said no matter how much you beat me up I wasn't to tell you where it came from in case you feel a stupid obligation to return it."

"That means it was expensive."

"He also said the old one was taken out and humanely shot. Can you play this thing?"

With a half-laugh, she played a set of chords. "My mother was a musician. Children of musicians get piano lessons whether they want them or not. Order the pizza while I see if he left us anything to drink."

A bottle of claret sat in the refrigerator and a bottle of chardonnay sat on the kitchen countertop. Maybe she'd get pie-eyed with Parkhurst and think about choices, loneliness versus being alone and time to move on.

Maybe.

49

It was early morning when Cass went out to the garden. She stood under the maple trees with the sun just rising over the hills and rosy new light filtering through the red and gold leaves. Frost sparkled on the grass and a crisp bite hovered in the air. Winter was coming. The thought of the earth tucking in for a cold sleep tugged at forgotten dreams. Rosie the dog scouted the area, trotting around with her nose down.

It's been over a year, Cass thought, one year without Ted and Laura. There was a time when she didn't think she'd survive. "We've come home," she said. They didn't fill her mind as much now, there was room for other thoughts. Yesterday she'd taken the little leather pouch of mingled ashes from her purse and put it in a box with Ted's cuff links. The box sat on her dresser. She could eat, she could dress, she could talk with other people, but still unexpected times popped up when she'd feel what it was like to hold the warm weight of a three-year-old child. It wasn't a memory exactly, more an imprint that had been left in her body.

She no longer craved the earth around her bones, no longer wished to be dead. She couldn't actually say she was glad to be alive, but she no longer resented it. The stubborn fact was that she was alive.

"Monty the cat loves it here. He's found all the best hiding places." She smiled as Rosie ran up and nuzzled her hand. "And I have a dog now. Laura, you'd love Rosie. She's a great big black dog and Monty bullies her terribly."

A car pulled into the driveway, Bernie, bringing Murray, Wakely's physical therapist, to stay and take care of the animals while she was away.

The dog gave her a welcoming bark and tore off toward the house. "You'll never believe this, Ted. I'm working for a politician. And we're just about to take off."

Bernie and Murray got out of the car and went in the house. When she heard Bernie in the kitchen, she called, "Out here."

Bernie came out with two containers of coffee and handed her one. "Ready? Plane leaves in twenty minutes."

"Careful, you'll step on the worm!"

Startled, he looked down and with exaggerated care lifted his foot over the earthworm crawling across the stepping stone. "Sorry. Didn't know you cared so much."

"Hey, when I was a child, some of my best friends were worms." She took a sip of coffee. "Besides, they're good for the garden."

Bernie nodded, patted the dog's side, grabbed her muzzle and swung it from side to side. "I don't want to rush you or anything, but we need to get a move on."

"Give me one more second. And then I just need to get my bag."

Bernie nodded. "I'll wait in the car."

Holding the coffee with both hands, she stood in the center of the maple trees. If she listened very carefully, she could hear Laura's laughter under the whisper of the wind.